PR

Twilight Empress: A Novel of Imperial Rome

Theodosian Women #1

"An addictive read...Justice chooses her key moments wisely, weaving a decades-long narrative about Placidia's layered life as she rises to eventual leadership."
— *Kirkus Reviews*

"*Twilight Empress* is the kind of historical novel that dedicated fans of historical fiction will find satisfying and impressive...It is a rich tapestry of both historical research and vivid imagination." — *Midwest Book Reviews*

"A truly fascinating combination of recorded history and artistic literary license...is both compelling and addictive." — *Readers' Favorite* five-star review

"Solid historical fiction, with full marks for a little-used time period and setting. It totally gets extra points for giving us a female lead character who's not written about to death." — *Historical Novel Society Reviews*

Dawn Empress: A Novel of Imperial Rome

Theodosian Women #2

"Justice chronicles, with a skillful blend of historical rigor and dramatic action...a gripping tale of a royal sister's fraught political machinations. The prose is razor sharp, and the tale is as impressively unsentimental as it is genuinely moving."
— *Kirkus Reviews*

"A deftly written and impressively entertaining historical novel in which the author pays due attention to detail while ably crafting memorable characters and riveting plot twists and turns." — *Midwest Book Reviews*

"Justice has penned another outstanding novel...Highly recommended." — *Historical Novel Society Reviews, Critics' Choice*

"The prose is beautiful, sprinkled with vivid descriptions...fast paced and engaging, one of those novels that will keep fans of historical novels reading through the night." — *Readers' Favorite* five-star review

Books by Faith L. Justice

Novels

Selene of Alexandria
Sword of the Gladiatrix (Gladiatrix #1)
Becoming the Twilight Empress (A Theodosian Women Novella)
Twilight Empress: A Novel of Imperial Rome (Theodosian Women #1)
Dawn Empress: A Novel of Imperial Rome (Theodosian Women #2)
Rebel Empress: A Novel of Imperial Rome (Theodosian Women #3)

Short Story Collections

The Reluctant Groom and Other Historical Stories
Time Again and Other Fantastic Stories
Slow Death and Other Dark Tales

Middle-grade Fiction

Tokoyo, the Samurai's Daughter (Adventurous Girls #1)

Non-fiction

Hypatia, Her Life and Times

Rebel Empress

Faith L. Justice

Raggedy Moon Books

Rebel Empress: A Novel of Imperial Rome

Theodosian Women Book Three

2024
Raggedy Moon Books
raggedymoonbooks.com

Cover design by Jennifer Quinlan
historicaleditorial.com

Library of Congress Control Number: 2024900937

Hardback ISBN: 978-0917053337
Paperback ISBN: 978-0917053320
Epub ISBN: 978-0917053313
Audiobook ISBN: 978-0917053344

To all those hard-working public-school teachers and librarians who encouraged my reading and writing through the years.
Truly a national treasure.

"This was an act of open rebellion, made especially dangerous by the participation of the Augusta who had herself been a rebel since 443."

– Kenneth G. Holum,
Theodosian Empresses: Women and Imperial Dominion in Late Antiquity

Contents

Theodosian Genealogy

Emperors shown in Small Caps.

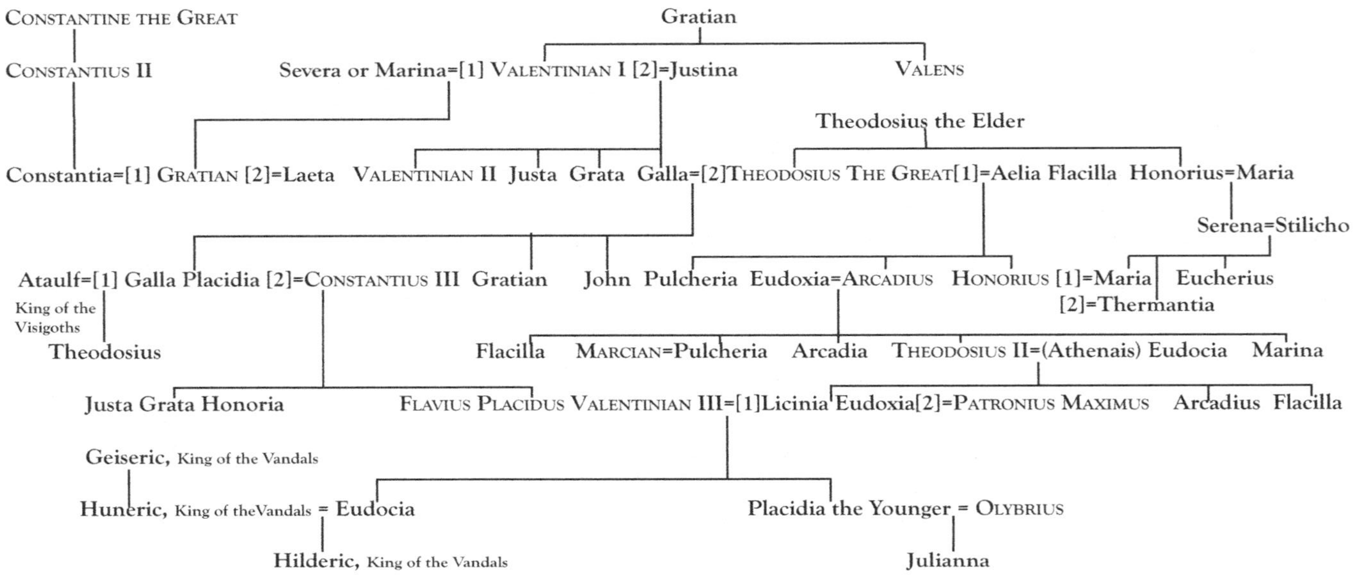

Note on Imperial Titles and Place Names

Imperial Roman titles evolved over time. The title AUGUSTUS (Latin for "majestic," "the increaser," or "venerable") is the equivalent of the modern "emperor," and was conferred on the first emperor, Octavian (great-nephew and adopted son of Julius Caesar), by the senate in 27 BC. Every emperor after held the title of Augustus, which always followed the family name. The first emperor conferred the title AUGUSTA on his wife, Livia, in his will. Other imperial wives (but not all) earned this supreme title. By the fifth century, sisters and daughters also could be elevated to this status, but only by a sitting Augustus. I use emperor/empress and Augustus/Augusta interchangeably throughout the text.

Octavian took his adoptive father's name, Gaius Julius Caesar, but later dropped the Gaius Julius. CAESAR became the imperial family name and was passed on by adoption. When the Julio-Claudian line died out, subsequent emperors took the name as a sign of status on their accession, adoption, or nomination as heir apparent. By the fifth century, it was the title given to any official heir to the Augustus. It's also the root of the modern titles Kaiser and Czar.

Children of imperial families were usually given the title NOBILISSIMUS/NOBILISSIMA ("Most Noble"—boy/girl). This is the closest equivalent to the modern prince/princess, though not an exact match. The title was usually conferred some years after birth, in anticipation that the child would take on higher office (Caesar or Augustus for a boy, Augusta for a girl). I generally use the modern term princess instead of *nobilissima* throughout the text, except in formal address and correspondence.

Aelia Flavia Flacilla, the wife of Theodosius I, inspired a new naming custom. Her seven-year reign set the pattern against which all Theodosian empresses were measured, particularly in the East. Flacilla brought four things to bolster her husband's rule: her family name AELIA (denoting her roots in Spain), fertility, charity, and piety. Aelia became a title of female distinction and was passed down as a symbol of dynastic inclusion among the Eastern empresses. The custom died out after over eighty years of Theodosian women rule and a new dynasty established its reign.

With one exception (Constantinople for modern Istanbul), I chose to use the modern names of cities and the anglicized rather than Latin names of provinces.

Characters

ruling Augusti in bold with dates ruled

fictional characters in italics

EASTERN ROME, CONSTANTINOPLE COURT

Flavius Theodosius Augustus II (408 – 450) m. **Aelia Eudocia (Athenais) Augusta**

Children:
Licinia Eudoxia Augusta m. Valentinian Augustus (of the Ravenna court)
Arcadius
Flacilla

Sisters of Theodosius Augustus:
Aelia Pulcheria Augusta m. **Marcian Augustus (450-457)**
Arcadia
Marina

Family of Aelia Eudocia (Athenais) Augusta:
Leontius of Antioch, father, chair of rhetoric at Athens Academy
Valerius, brother
Gesius, brother
Asclepiodotus of Constantinople, maternal uncle, head of *agents in rebus*
Doria (actual name is unknown), wife of Asclepiodotus

Later Emperor:
Leo Augustus I (457 – 474) m. **Verina Augusta**

WESTERN ROME, RAVENNA COURT

Flavius Honorius Augustus (395 – 423)
half-sister:
Galla Placidia Augusta m. **Flavius Constantius Augustus III** (421)
children:
Justa Grata Honoria Augusta
Flavius Placidius Valentinian Augustus III (425 – 455) m. **Licinia Eudoxia Augusta** (of the Constantinople court)
Their daughters:
Eudocia "The Younger"
Placidia "The Younger"

Friends, government and church officials, and servants in order of appearance:

Part I – Pagan Pawn
Paulinus, Theodosius' childhood companion, groomsman, and best friend
Olympiodorus of Thebes, pagan poet, diplomat, and historian
Nana/Elpida, head of the imperial nursery
Dorothea, servant to Athenais in Constantinople
Bishop Atticus, Head of Constantinople Church (406 – 425)
Melia, midwife to noble classes

Part II – Christian Consort
General Ardaburius, Master of Soldiers in the Emperor's Presence
Helion, Master of Offices
Sigisvult, Captain of Placidia's guards
Lucilla, Placida's servant and confidant
General Aspar, Master of the Cavalry, son of Ardaburius
Bishop Nestorius, Head of the Constantinople Church (428 – 431)
Antiochus Chuzon, Consul, leader of Theodosian Code project
Dalmatius, Archimandrite, holy man

Part III – Pious Pilgrim

Rufius Antonius Agrypnius Volusianus, envoy from Western court and Melania's uncle

Melania "The Younger" of Jerusalem, ascetic holy woman

Matthias, curator (money manager) for Athenais

Bassa, head of Melania's convent in Jerusalem

Bishop Cyril of Alexandria (412-444)

Barsauma, Archimandrite of Syria

Cyrus of Panopolis, Constantinople City Prefect

Chrysaphius Tzumas, Chief Eunuch and head of household for Theodosius II

Magdalene, servant to Athenais, spy for Chrysaphius

Father Severus, priest and religious advisor to Athenais

Deacon John, secretary and confidant to Athenais

Bishop Proclus, Head of the Constantinople Church (434-446)

Part IV – Rebel Empress

Yitzhak ben Levi, wine merchant, head of Jewish delegation

Martha, servant to Athenais in Bethlehem

Brother Cosmas, monk, religious advisor and confidant to Athenais

Father Gabriel, priest, secretary to Athenais

Rufus, Captain of the Jerusalem Garrison

Brother Julius of St. Stephen's Church

Basil, Prefect of Palestine

Theodosius, Archimandrite and Bishop of Jerusalem (451 – 453)

Count Dorotheus, military commander of Palestine

Rebel Empress

Part I

Pagan Pawn

May 418 - April 422

Chapter 1

Athens, early summer, AD 418

ATHENAIS SAT ON A STONE BENCH IN THE GARDEN, HER HEAD COVERED by a thick mourning veil that dulled the vivid flowers to a gray that matched her mood. Even through her grief, she heard the bees buzzing among the herbs. The scent of lavender refreshed her somewhat, but her limbs felt heavy from lack of sleep. What will become of this refuge after new owners take over? I must find positions for the servants. When did Creon say my brothers would arrive?

"Why can't I string two thoughts together," she mumbled to herself. "I should greet the other mourners."

But she didn't move from the bench. Her head felt full of wool.

The last three days of her father's illness she had rarely left his side. She read and talked to him when he was awake and constantly listened to his ragged breathing when he slept. Her heart filled with dread whenever his breath ceased for a moment. Now his body rested on a bier in the receiving room.

Athenais felt the incipient wave of sobs deep in her chest and longed for their release. She straightened her shoulders. *Not here. Not now.*

Creon, her father's colleague at the Academy, had proved a good friend in the end. Although Athenais had had doubts about her father leaving his final arrangements to such an absent-minded man, he arranged for the funeral feast and for the Academy fellows and students to visit the corpse. He even took up a collection so her father could be buried in the local cemetery with a small stone marker inscribed with his name and profession. *Leontius, Chair of Rhetoric. Father was so pleased with his appointment after so many years seeking such an important post. He held it for barely ten years.*

Seemingly from a distance, Athenais heard a drummer beat a solemn rhythm and a piper play a dirge. She stood as the sound grew nearer. Four men exited the receiving room with the bier slung on their shoulders, her father's body wrapped in a linen shroud. The mourners followed in a small, but solemn pack. The sight hit her in the gut and she gasped, trying to hold back her grief. It escaped in a thin keening sound, she hardly recognized as her own. Tears poured down her cheeks and she reached up under the veil to wipe her running nose with a linen kerchief.

Creon approached and placed warm hands on her shoulders as they shook with gasping sobs. "I'm sorry, my dear. Is there anything I can do?"

She looked up at his nearsighted face, contorted with concern. Athenais shook her head. "Thank you, Honored Teacher," she said in a husky voice, "for all you've done for me and Father."

She took a deep breath and stifled her grief. *Time for that when I'm alone. Now to see Father on his last journey.*

The small party wended its way through the narrow Athenian streets. The beautiful day, filled with mild summer sun and bird song, mocked the storm of grief that wracked Athenais' body and mind. *It should be raining—a howling wind with lightning and thunderclaps rolling over the hills.*

She clung to Creon's arm as they exited the east gate onto a rocky plain, dotted with a few twisted trees. The cemetery lay just outside the walls. The tombs of the rich lined the road, decorated with expensive stones and carved busts. The poorer plain tombs stood further back. On the edge, among unmarked graves, they approached a small pile of dirt next to an open pit.

She looked up at Creon. "The marker?"

He mumbled, "The stone will be installed later."

"I had hoped to bring his ashes to Antioch to bury with Mother's."

He patted her arm. "I tried, my dear, but traditional cremation is now outlawed as a pagan practice."

Such a forgettable place, she thought with bitter bile rising in her throat. *It should have been different: a rich marble tomb for a keen mind and loving father.*

The piper trilled a final dirge. The pall bearers lowered her father's body into the wound in the earth. Creon said a few words. It all passed as if in a dream.

Father is dead.

Does he tarry in the Elysian Fields, forgetful of his stay on earth, as our ancestors taught? Did his soul return to the Source to become something else in the universe, as the Platonists believe? Or is he simply gone—his existence extinguished, like other animals?

Athenais shuddered at this last thought and pushed it away. The idea that her beloved father didn't exist in any form she could touch or know other than his abandoned body, brought on fresh tears.

The Christians teach that if someone believes Christ was their savior on earth, their soul goes to a place called heaven, retaining their memories and personality, awaiting reunion with loved ones. That's comforting, but how do I know the truth? She wiped her tears. *For now, it matters little. I miss Father. My world is a bleak place without him, but I must persevere.*

He would want me to.

She stood for a moment by the open grave before tossing in a piece of rolled-up papyrus, bound by a green ribbon and decorated with a pink spring rose—the last poem she wrote before her father got sick.

"Good-bye, Father. I'm sorry you didn't get to see your sons once more."

She turned her back on the pit to see Creon passing coins to the gravediggers, pall bearers, and musicians. *Father was right to put Creon in charge. I've ably managed the household since I turned twelve, but I've been useless these last days.*

She heaved a deep sigh and took Creon's arm for the trip back into the city. "Thank you again, Honored Teacher for all you've done for us."

His weak eyes glistened with unshed tears. "Your father was a good friend to me, my dear. It was the least I could do." He patted her hand. "Your brothers should be here in a couple of months. Do you wish to stay in my quarters until they arrive? You shouldn't be alone during this time of mourning."

"Thank you." She was touched by the sentiment from this unsentimental man, but she wrinkled her nose at the thought of the smells wafting from the fuller's shop beneath his rooms. "That is a most generous offer, but I will be safe in our home until my brothers arrive. I have trusted servants to care for me and a little ready cash for food. The merchants know me and will give me credit, if need be."

Creon frowned and opened his mouth to speak.

She cut him off, "And you are welcome to stay at the house or visit as you like. I would welcome the company—especially around mealtime."

He nodded slowly. "That would do."

And so it begins: life without Father. An uncertain future for a dowerless overeducated girl of sixteen.

Chapter 2

Constantinople, Spring AD 419

"Gesius, it's so beautiful!" Athenais' gaze widened. She stood in the prow of a ship as it approached Constantinople. The fresh sea breeze, tinged with the smell of fish, flattened her heavy cloak to her body. She turned to her brother with a luminous smile. "And so big! It puts Athens to shame."

He pointed to the highest point in the city. "See that hill, with all the marble buildings sprawling down to the sea? That's the palace district where Theodosius Augustus lives with his sisters."

"So much space for four people?" She raised a skeptical eyebrow.

"It's also the seat of government. It houses the imperial guards, the treasury, and all the busy bureaucrats that run the empire, as well as the palace staff. Uncle Asclepiodotus serves there and some day I and Valerius hope to, as well."

"Father was proud of you boys, making your way in the capital city. He regretted having so little money to help you in your careers or leave me a dowry. Father—" Her throat closed with tears as a wave of grief crested in her chest. They came less frequently but with just as much force as the first shock of her father's death, nearly a year ago.

Gesius pulled her closer and tucked her under his arm. "Father did his best, but he was a better scholar than businessman." They stood, each immersed in their own thoughts as the shore grew closer.

Her brothers had been shocked at the state of their father's affairs when they arrived. Valerius, her elder by a decade, sold the property to satisfy creditors, leaving only a small legacy for each son and nothing for her. He left to return to Constantinople on an imperial packet ship, leaving Gesius to follow with Athenais on a slower—and cheaper—coastal merchant vessel. She found herself traveling with only meager possessions: a trunk containing her personal clothes and another with her favorite books. She wore a few jewels inherited from her mother: pearl earrings, a lapis lazuli ring set in silver, and a plain gold chain.

Father, I loved you so, but how could you have left me in such dire straits? She clutched at her favorite piece, a garnet-eyed phoenix-shaped fibula that held her cloak closed against the wind. *What awaits a poor scholar's daughter in a great foreign city?*

The captain approached and bowed. "Time to go back to your cabin. We approach the harbor, and the seamen need to move quickly on the deck."

"Of course, Captain." Gesius escorted her back to their rude cabin—little more than a shack that kept their sleeping pallets dry from the sea spray. A couple of other passengers slept on the open deck with the seamen. Space below was reserved for cargo on this merchant vessel.

Athenais sighed. "I hate being in the cabin when all the fun is outside." They had spent the nearly month-long journey mostly on deck during the day as the ship sailed from city to city along the west coast of the Asian province, spending the nights in safe harbors. Once docked, Athenais delighted in watching the constant stream of people and goods: wine and olive oil in large amphorae from Greece exchanged for bales of wool and baskets of grain in Ephesus. The wool and grain exchanged for pottery and luxury goods in the next port. They always left the ship for a hot meal and occasional bath in the towns because fire—even for cooking—was prohibited on the wooden ship.

"We'll be docked soon, then off to Uncle Asclepiodotus' house." Gesius lowered himself onto one of their traveling trunks. She sat next to him and leaned onto his shoulder with a sigh and a shiver of excitement.

"I suppose I should feel lucky that Uncle Asclepiodotus offered to take me into his household, considering we're his sister's children and he's under no obligation, but I feel—" she hesitated, searching for the word, "—reluctant? Unsettled?" She wiped an errant tear from her face with the back of her hand. "I miss Father." She straightened with a sudden thought. "What if Uncle forbids me to study or Aunt expects me to cook and clean? I can't make a living with my poetry. No parent would allow me to tutor their boys. With no dowry, marriage to a suitable man is out of the question."

"I'm sorry. I didn't mean to upset you." Gesius put his arms around her. "Uncle is an enlightened man and his wife has plenty of servants. No need for you to cook or clean." He hugged her and whispered in her hair. "Father always said your face would provide for you. You don't see your own beauty, but I do and so does every man between the ages of sixteen and sixty."

She tilted her head up so she could look into his eyes and smiled. "Then you must have a similar problem, because we have the same face." Both her brothers were handsome men, tall with regular features. Gesius, the younger brother by two years, had the same golden curls and blue eyes as she. Valerius favored his father with dark hair and striking hazel eyes.

"Ha!" His laugh came out as a sharp bark. "Pretty as I am, no maiden would have me until I can show her father I'm a man of substance." His arm tightened around her shoulders. "And that will happen. Valerius and I will soon advance our careers and we will take care of you, if our uncle is too strict."

"What of the prohibition against pagans and Jews in the government?"

"That's what the baptismal font is for, little sister!" Gesius grinned. "Valerius and I converted and are eligible for all positions. We've studied law and rhetoric. Uncle is well positioned in the government and saw to our initial placement. We should both be eligible for prefectures in a few years. You might even take a dip yourself."

Athenais frowned. *Become a Christian? I will have to study it first. I'm not impressed with their triple-god and pantheon of demi-gods they call saints. Too much like the superstitions of the ancients and their ridiculous squabbling family of gods and goddesses.*

She pushed out of his hug. "I'll think on that later, Brother. For now, I have enough to worry about meeting my aunt and uncle."

Chapter 3

HER ELDEST BROTHER MET THEM AT THE DOCKS, ACCOMPANIED BY a stocky older man with a hooked nose and bushy eyebrows. After she navigated the shaky gangplank, Valerius swept her into a ferocious hug and swung her around, making her giggle.

"Brother! Put me down! You're making a spectacle of us."

He dropped her gently onto the pier and she staggered, trying to regain her land legs. Valerius grabbed her elbow for support. "Easy. It sometimes takes a few moments to get used to solid ground."

He turned her to the older man. "Uncle. This is my sister Athenais."

"Uncle Asclepiodotus." Athenais dropped her eyes and gave the man a brief curtsy. When she glanced at his face, his eyebrows had ascended toward his gray-shot brown hair and a bright, but calculating, smile lit up his face.

"You didn't lie, Val. She's quite a beauty."

Athenais felt blood heat her cheeks. She wasn't sure if it was pleasure at the compliment or irritation at being discussed like a prize horse. *Uncle is not the spymaster for the government for nothing. He must be a complicated, intelligent man. I only hope he is also loving and considerate.*

"Uncle, thank you for taking me in." She raised her eyes. "I'm exceedingly grateful."

He embraced her in a familial hug, then stood with her at arms' length. "My wife would hound me to hell, if I didn't offer my sister's orphan daughter succor." His mouth turned up at one side into a quirky smile. "But it is my wish, as well, that you stay with us, as your brothers become established. Family must look out for one another." He linked arms with her. "Come my dear, your brothers will see to your chests. I have transport waiting."

He led her to a wagon, pulled by two mules. The driver stood at the animals' heads giving them each a handful of grain. Her uncle installed her next to himself on one of the padded seats that lined the sides of the wagon. He chatted of inconsequential things—the sea voyage, the food, the weather—as the imperial port slaves piled the chests in a second smaller cart. She replied cheerfully, if distractedly. After a few moments, her brothers joined them in the wagon, and she relaxed.

Valerius gave her a huge grin. "You'll love Constantinople, Sister. This is where everyone who is anyone lives or visits. You can almost feel the power pulsing in the city."

"So, you've become a poet in the last few years?"

His face pinked and he laughed. "Not as good as you, but something about this city inspires people. Athens feels like a sleepy backwater compared to Constantinople."

She bristled at the disparaging tone he used toward her adopted city but saw what he meant as the three men vied for her attention in pointing out various sites along their route. The docks bustled with men hauling goods from around the known world. The smell of dead fish overpowered the more delicate aromas of exotic spices and died wool. They joined a stream of wagons towering with vegetables and cages of live animals from the farms in the hinterlands making their way to the city markets. Each plaza had a statue, column, or fountain dedicated to an emperor or rich patron. The buildings got larger and more ornate as they traveled uphill from the poorer dock area.

"Let's take a detour through the Augusteum, Uncle." Gesius suggested. "Athenais was most impressed with the imperial precinct from the sea. Let her see it up close."

They entered a large plaza fronting the walled palace and surrounded with imposing buildings. "That's the Great Church, the seat of the Bishop of Constantinople." Gesius pointed to a large church where men rebuilt the steps and painters gilded the façade. "And that's the Senate House."

This more modest building sat directly across from the palace gate and included a stoa where men clustered, some gesturing angrily. *Some things are always the same in a polis. Men will always gather to complain, argue and harangue each other,* Athenais thought.

Her gaze traveled to the center of the plaza and she pointed to a large marble statue of an older woman dominating the plaza. "Who is the woman on the plinth?"

"Saint Helena, Emperor Constantine's mother. She was made Augusta and this plaza was dedicated to her after she retrieved parts of the True Cross during her journeys in the Holy Land."

"I've never seen a monumental statue of an actual woman before. Ancient goddesses, yes, and small ceremonial statues of an Augusta paraded around cities for an elevation, but nothing on this scale."

"If you knew your imperial history, you'd know that women have been quite influential with the emperors," Asclepiodotus said with a calculating look. "Pulcheria Augusta had a bust of herself installed in the Senate House, next to her brother's while she was regent. It still stands even though he has reached his majority."

Stung by his comment on her lack of education, Athenais said with flashing eyes. "I would welcome any histories you would care to recommend, Uncle. I do not wish to be ignorant in such an important area."

"Excellent!" He gave her an approving look. "I'll make sure to provide you with some. Your father's colleague Olympiodorus is working on a history of the current regime. I'll see if he would like to tutor you."

"Dorrie is here!" she squealed in delight, lapsing into her childhood nickname for the genial poet. She recovered her decorum at her uncle's frown. "My apologies, Uncle. Olympiodorus is my favorite of all Father's colleagues. He always treated me as a student when visiting, including me in discussions."

"Understood. I've had some professional dealings with the man. He's most unconventional and… uh… useful."

So, Father was right in his suspicion that Dorrie spied for the government when he went on diplomatic missions. It never made sense that a poet and historian would be tasked with such journeys and *Dorrie often hinted as much.*

"I look forward to meeting my old friend. Thank you, Uncle." Athenais nodded as they left the plaza. *Fascinating. I'm sure Dorrie will have much to tell me. I'm beginning to suspect that Uncle taking me in was not* all *for my own benefit.*

Chapter 4

At last, they pulled up to a sprawling villa across from the hill crowned with the imperial precinct. *Uncle is indeed doing well for himself. My brothers will surely benefit from his patronage.* The house was surrounded by a blank wall of white-washed brick with a large bronze-bound wooden gate set in the front and guarded by a heavily muscled servant armed with a substantial knife in his belt.

"Is this a dangerous neighborhood, Uncle?"

"No, my dear. He's only for show. The city garrison keeps the peace, and our servants patrol the neighboring streets. The criminals prey on the poor and vulnerable."

Athenais shivered. *Poor and vulnerable. Like me. Whatever Uncle's plan is, it must be a better fate than what awaits most dowerless friendless girls.*

The servant opened the gate, and her uncle escorted her through. The familiar Roman household layout immediately put her at ease. They passed through a dim, but beautifully appointed, public hall to a modest atrium complete with a small pool to catch the rainwater. *Uncle must conduct most of his business at the palace. This is not the elaborate waiting room of a noble patron.* They passed by a complex of private rooms—her uncle's work and reception rooms to the right and a large triclinium for formal dining to the left—to emerge into a riot of natural color and scents. All the public rooms ringed a lush garden in the center of the compound.

"Uncle it's magnificent!" Athenais closed her eyes and breathed in. "Do I smell apple blossoms? We had such a small garden in Athens and devoted most of it to kitchen herbs."

"Yes, my dear. We keep a small patch of herbs in the rear near the servants' quarters, but the formal garden is a particular project of my wife's." Pride tinged his voice. "She likes to collect and display exotic plants, among the more traditional specimens. Your friend Olympiodorus has been particularly good about bringing her finds from his various travels." He gestured toward the right. "Speaking of my wife…"

A small plump woman with graying red hair ran up the steps from the garden and threw herself at Athenais with a delighted cry. "Oh, my sweet child! I'm so happy you're here! And so sad it took your father's death to bring you to our shores." Her eyes glistened with tears. "I had my husband write to him many times asking if you could visit or live with us, but your father refused, saying you were his last treasure, and he wouldn't give you up."

Now Athenais' eyes overflowed. "Aunt Doria, I'm…" Her throat closed with tears, and she snuffled.

Her aunt patted her back and cooed. "It's alright, my dear. You're safe now. We'll care for you as if you were our own. My daughter is grown and has a family of her own, but they are in Pannonia far from here and I rarely get to see my darlings."

"Thank you, Aunt." Athenais hugged her and realized how much she had missed her own mother's warm soft presence over the past ten years. *I was only seven when Father moved us from Antioch to flee his own grief and now I repeat the pattern.*

"You've had a long journey and must be tired. Let's get you settled in your room, and you can rest before dinner." She linked her arm in Athenais' and pointed a chin at one of the servants. "Bring Lady Athenais' things to her room. You—" she waved at her husband and nephews "—will join us for dinner. Now go about your business."

They ascended the stairs to the second floor ringing the garden. Doria installed her in a pleasant airy room with windows opening onto the courtyard, much larger than her dark room in Athens. The walls were whitewashed and painted with a garden scene. A carpet woven in rich blues and greens adorned the tiled floor.

"It's delightful!" Athenais sat on a narrow bed, painted blue and piled with a feather mattress and pillows covered in rainbow-hued cotton.

The servant with her chests entered and Aunt Doria immediately started unpacking. She pulled out Athenais' small collection of rather drab clothes and held them up to the light. "This is all you have, my dear?"

Athenais pinked with embarrassment and wrapped her arms across her chest, as if to hide her gray travel stola. "I didn't need much in Athens. It was just me and Father. I think my favorite blue is on the bottom."

"We'll remedy that first. I know the best purveyors of fabrics in the city and employ an excellent seamstress. You'll need several more undertunics and stolae." Doria sorted her meager possessions between a carved wooden chest crouched at the foot of the bed and a lovely painted cupboard standing on one wall. "Your uncle is a distinguished administrator and you must not embarrass him when you go out in society."

When her aunt opened the chest of books, Athenais jumped from the bed. "I'll take care of those." Her eyes were drawn immediately to the mahogany table and chair just inside the door. It had a shelf over the table for her books and lined at the back against the wall were all the tools of a scribe: wax for seals, ink pots, quills, sand, waxed tablets, a knife for scraping off mistakes, and stacks of paper from coarse papyrus for drafts to nearly transparent vellum for final copies.

"For me?" Athenais passed her hands over the smooth wood and elegant paper taking in the fine texture. She uncorked a pot of ink and inhaled the sharp scent evoking the wonderful feeling of a finished poem. She turned, beaming at her aunt. "It's perfect!" She gave the older woman a hug.

"Oomph!" Her aunt laughed. "This was my daughter's room. She used the table for cosmetics. I've hidden a few things of that nature in the drawers." She opened the left-hand drawer and pulled out a polished silver mirror and comb set. "Lady scholars still need to apply makeup and tend their hair."

Athenais peeked inside and saw an assortment of pots and instruments for applying cosmetics. Her eyes began to water again.

Her aunt's welled with tears, as well. "I'll leave you to get settled and take a nap. I'll come by later and take you to the baths before dinner." With a final smile and sniff, her aunt left.

Athenais sat dazed on her bed, hugging herself tightly. A new life and the guidance of an older woman. For the first time since her father's death, she felt happy, safe, and… loved. Warmth spread throughout her body as a burden she hadn't realized she carried lifted from her heart.

Chapter 5

August 420

PAULINUS SIPPED RARE WHITE FALERIAN WINE FROM AN EXPENSIVE BLUE glass goblet and cast a critical eye over his host's villa. For a relatively obscure government functionary, Asclepiodotus had done very well for himself. The expansive dwelling rivaled many of the palaces owned by the oldest and most noble families in the city. As he savored a flaky berry tart with shaved sharp cheese on the top, Paulinus thought, *the spymaster clearly enjoys the good things of life. Does our friend engage in blackmail or financial speculation?* Paulinus shrugged. *If so, it is not my mission on this visit to investigate his business affairs.*

He turned his attention back to the conversation between his friend Olympiodorus and the brothers of the young woman he was here to meet. *I hope this girl is more suitable than the others.* From shy horse-faced spinsters to ambitious young wantons, the women paraded before him as candidates for imperial marriage were all singularly lacking in the presence needed for an empress.

"I have to admit the young Augusta has proved an astute politician and able administrator." Olympiodorus stated as he picked over the olives and chose one he found satisfactory.

"What?" Valerius sputtered, nearly spitting his wine. "Pulcheria's laws allowing the destruction of Jewish synagogues was a total disaster."

The historian sipped his wine and smacked his lips appreciatively. "But those actions were more moderate than you state. She forbade construction of *new* synagogues and allowed destruction of old ones only 'in desert places, if it can be accomplished without riots' if I remember the wording properly. It's not her fault that greedy zealous bishops overplayed their hands. She remedied the situation quickly when it came to her attention."

"And what about her ban on pagans and Jews in the government and the army?" Valerius glared.

"She's more pragmatic than you make her out to be. The Augusta just appointed Plinta and his son-in-law Ardaburius, two of the most able generals in the army, to new and important posts. Plinta is even named Consul. They're both Arians."

"Arians are Christians," Valerius countered.

"Heretical Christians, but Pulcheria has raised them to high honors. My point is that the Augusta is whole-heartedly committed to two goals: keeping her younger brother on the throne and expanding Orthodox Christianity. However, she is flexible if the second threatens the first. She knows that she needs a strong army, and she cannot waste good generals, if they are nominally Christian. Are you more enraged on behalf of the Jews or that you—like many of the young Hellene faction—had to be baptized before taking a prefecture?"

Valerius scowled into his drink.

Gesius laughed. "Don't fall for his tricks, Brother. You know Olympiodorus likes to stir the pot. To him, conversation isn't interesting unless men are arguing." He nodded at Paulinus. "As the emperor's friend and confidant, you practically live at the palace. What's your opinion of his sister?"

She's a controlling, conniving, power-hungry harpy, but I don't know these young men well enough to be that honest. Paulinus looked over the rim of his wine glass and said, mildly, "I agree with Olympiodorus. The Augusta is shrewd and able. How else could she take over the empire at age fifteen and hold it together during her brother's minority?"

"And almost totally exclude the former nobles that supported Anthemius during *his* regency. You"—Olympiodorus nodded at Valerius and Gesius— "are lucky your uncle was able to help in your careers, but most of the Hellenes have been out of power for five years and want it back. That's why we invited Paulinus to join us. We need to introduce a moderate voice into the palace and the best way is to find our young emperor a suitable wife. Paulinus, you know the emperor best, what are we looking for?"

"I love Theodosius like a brother, but he's an innocent. Pulcheria surrounds him with elderly eunuch servants and only tolerates plain, pious Christian women in her own retinue. He hasn't had much, if any, contact with girls of his own age except his sisters and they've been pledged virgins for six years."

"He's what? Nineteen?" Valerius scoffed. "We could put any pretty face and warm body in front of our emperor, and he'd fall in love."

"No!" Paulinus said with some alarm. "Any flirting or aggressive feminine wiles will only scare Theo off. He's not like his dimwitted father."

"The former emperor was a dimwit?" Valerius gave Paulinus a puzzled look.

"You're too young to know the story." Olympiodorus said. "Our previous emperor was accounted somewhat lacking in mental capabilities. His father was almost constantly in the field putting down barbarians and usurpers. When he died, he left two sons: seventeen-year-old Arcadius Augustus in the East and ten-year-old Honorius Augustus in the West. Honorius had an able man to raise him and his half-sister Placidia, in the same way our late regent Anthemius raised Theodosius and his sisters.

"Arcadius wasn't as lucky. He was of age to rule, but under the influence of court eunuchs and power-hungry nobles. A scheming eunuch put the pretty Eudoxia in his bed when he was only seventeen. She married Arcadius and ran the empire through her husband. It was a mercy when she died of a miscarriage and Arcadius followed four years later."

Paulinus took up the tale. "Fortunately, our great friend Anthemius came to power as regent for the underage Theodosius. He ran the empire justly and well until his death. He's the one responsible for the magnificent walls that surround our city. Unfortunately, the clever Princess Pulcheria outwitted all the court worthies and took over as regent. She still rules the East despite the fact the emperor has long reached his majority.

"I've been the emperor's friend since Anthemius installed me in the nursery to provide male companionship. Theodosius deserves to rule in his own right, but Pulcheria is a formidable woman, and he cares for her deeply. We cannot attack her directly or we will fail. Theo will always choose family over anyone else."

"Even the emperor's best friend?" Valerius asked.

"Yes." Paulinus shrugged. "But we Hellenes have had enough of Pulcheria's rule. She carries a grudge against us. Evidently Anthemius plotted to marry her to his grandson and the princess objected. She colluded with Bishop Atticus to have herself and her sisters declared virgins and escaped the trap, but held it against our whole class. We want a young woman who will counter the Augusta's influence with her brother and bring us back into his government.

We need a pliant candidate with no ambition to govern like Pulcheria or her mother before her."

"And that's where I enter the story," Olympiodorus chimed in. "When I learned of the scheme, I immediately thought of my old friend Leontius' daughter. A beauty with a good head on her shoulders, but outside the court orbit. When I got the sad news of my friend's passing, I contacted his sons and suggested they bring her here."

"Thank you, Olympiodorus." Asclepiodotus turned to Paulinus. "We believe we have a superb candidate for the emperor's wife. My niece Athenais came to us over a year ago and I've had ample time to know her. She is a beauty, well-educated, and malleable. She's also an innocent. Having grown up in a male household, she's not been taught the more manipulative wiles of her sex. She's gentle, loving, and has expressed only a desire to marry well and have a family of her own."

"And write poetry," Gesius added.

"Poetry?" Paulinus raised his eyebrows.

"She's actually quite good." Valerius admitted. "Our father indulged her and educated her in all the branches of literature. She even studied some philosophy and rhetoric."

"Does this paragon have any flaws? Does her education make her head-strong?"

Asclepiodotus glanced quickly at the brothers and cleared his throat. "She's not a Christian."

"That will be a major impediment. Theo is as religious as his sister. He would not marry a pagan and Pulcheria would categorically forbid it." Paulinus frowned. "Would she consent to baptism?"

Olympiodorus smiled. "She's a sensible girl. I'm sure between us, we could convince her that becoming a Christian would be the right thing to do for her family."

"So, when do I get to meet this marvelous young lady?" Paulinus grinned. "I have a number of other daughters and sisters to call on."

"Is now convenient?" Asclepiodotus waved his hand to the door. "My good wife and my niece are reading in the solar and would welcome meeting you."

"We'll be off, Uncle, and will call on you tomorrow." Valerius motioned for Gesius to join him. "We don't want to overwhelm our sister."

Paulinus smiled to himself. *We'll see if this paragon lives up to her family's praises. I hope so, for Theo's sake.*

Chapter 6

"AUNT, PLEASE! YOUR FLUTTERING MAKES ME NERVOUS." ATHENAIS PATTED the yellow silk cushion beside her on the bench. "Come sit before I faint."

Doria looked up in alarm from wiping an invisible speck of dust from an immaculate marble bust of a past emperor. She relaxed at her niece's smile. "You jest, my dear, but Paulinus is an important man. He's best friends with the emperor and very influential. Your uncle is anxious that everything be perfect."

"I understand it's important for Uncle and my brothers' careers to impress this man." Her mischievous smile softened into a sad one. "Father wasn't much for getting ahead. We entertained mostly colleagues; no one who could help further his career once he had his chair in rhetoric except Olympiodorus."

"Did I hear my name taken in vain?"

"Dorrie!" Athenais jumped to her feet, ran across the room, and threw her arms around his sturdy torso in a vigorous hug. "I'm so glad to see you. Why haven't you visited lately? Did you bring your parrot? I have some poems I'd like your opinion on…"

"Athenais, my sweet, slow down." He untangled himself and held her at arm's length. "First: I've been on a diplomatic mission. Second: no parrot today. And third: I'd love to read you new poetry, but I have a friend I'd like you to meet." He stepped into the solar and waved at a figure she hadn't seen lurking behind him. "Come in, Paulinus. This is Athenais."

Paulinus came out of the shadows into the light of the overhead oil-lamp chandelier followed by a frowning Asclepiodotus. The young man was quite good-looking: taller than average with dark curly hair and intelligent brown eyes that currently danced with amusement. A slightly crooked nose saved him from being too pretty. A smile flitted across his face, as if he tried to stifle a laugh.

Blood flushed her face. *Oh! I've embarrassed my uncle, but the great man Paulinus seems more amused than insulted.* She took a step back, lowered her lashes, and gave the men a slight curtsy. "My apologies, Sir. I'm not normally so indecorous, but Dorrie is an old friend that I haven't seen in years, and I was surprised by his presence. Please forgive my enthusiasm and don't blame my uncle or aunt for my unseemly behavior."

"Dorrie?" Paulinus turned to Olympiodorus and chuckled.

Olympiodorus smiled broadly. "I've known Athenais since she was a babe. As a child she had trouble saying my name and I've been 'Dorrie' to her ever since." He put an arm around her shoulders and wagged a warning finger at the rest of the room. "And she's the only one I allow to call me that."

The frown eased from her uncle's face, but he remained stiff-backed.

"Please gentlemen sit down, and I'll have the servants bring refreshments." Aunt Doria bustled into the group, settling guests, and ordering servants.

Athenais found herself next to Paulinus on the padded bench and took a sip of wine to settle her stomach. *Why would Aunt do such a thing? I know nothing of the court. Paulinus should be seated with Uncle.* She shot an anxious glance at the three older people chatting across the room, took a deep breath, and turned to Paulinus, who had just asked her a question. "What did you say?" *Zeus' balls, he must think I'm a lack-wit.*

"What are you reading?" He pointed to the slim codex tucked into the cushions.

She plucked it from its hiding place and clutched it, running her thumb over the words stamped on the brown leather cover. "I'm re-reading *The Iliad* and studying the Homeric style. I've been trying to compose my own epic poem based on the tale of Jason and the Argonauts but am having some difficulty."

"I'd love to read it when you're ready to share with an audience." He glanced at the book. "I prefer *The Odyssey*, myself. I find the wily Odysseus much more interesting than the heroes who had more brawn than brains."

"So do I!" She relaxed and smiled, back on familiar territory. By the time they finished their second glass of wine, they agreed on the importance of Apuleius' novel *The Golden Ass*, the unbelievability of the fantastical elements of Herodotus' *Histories,* and the brilliance of Cicero's treatises on politics, but disagreed on which was the better playwright: the Greek Euripides or the Roman Seneca. Athenais felt more animated than she had for months. *What a wonderful afternoon! I didn't know women and men could have such a lively discussion outside of their family.* She glanced at her companion over the rim of her glass as she took the last sip. *Paulinus is a remarkable man.*

He took her hand and rose. "I'm afraid I have to leave for another engagement, but I want to say, Athenais, I've had a lovely time and hope I can return to continue our discussions." He kissed the back of her hand and released it.

"Of course, Paulinus." She felt a warm blush color her cheeks and an even warmer spot on her hand where he kissed it. "You are welcome anytime."

Olympiodorus bounded across the room. "I must leave as well, my sweet."

"No, Dorrie, we haven't had a chance to catch up!" Disappointment stole the smile from her face.

"Soon, my dear, soon."

"I'll see you to the door, gentlemen." Her uncle ushered the two guests from the room.

Her aunt collapsed next to her on the padded bench. "Well, that went better than expected, given the start!" She fanned herself with her hands.

"I am so sorry about that, Aunt." Guilt at her initial unbecoming behavior flooded out her feelings of satisfaction. "Dorrie is a favorite of mine, and I haven't seen him in ever so long."

"I know, dear." She patted Athenais' knee. "It came up well in the end. You and Paulinus seem quite engrossed. What do you think of him?"

"Aunt! Is he a suitor? I thought this afternoon was about advancing the men in our family."

"It was, but that can be done in many ways." Doria pursed her lips and paused, thinking. "Your uncle and your brothers have gone as far as they can without a patron at the court even though they became Christians. Olympiodorus is a bit of an oddity at court being an unrepentant pagan, but his histories and poetry are well-received. The Master of Offices finds him useful as a diplomat and spy, but a pagan cannot be that patron. Paulinus could be and a marriage would strengthen that bond. My husband hasn't fully confided his plans to me. When I know, you will as well."

"Paulinus seems a good match, but I can't say I know the man's inner self after only an hour's conversation."

Doria hugged her and sighed. "My dear, it is rare to know a man's mind and heart before marriage. Sometimes it takes years. If a husband treats you kindly, consider yourself fortunate."

"Has Uncle been kind to you?"

"For the most part." Doria's gaze turned inward as if remembering harder times. "He's an ambitious man and made a good life for us here. His greatest regret is not having a son. That's why he is so attentive to your brothers." She turned to Athenais and raised her chin. "And you are like a second daughter to me. I will make sure any marriage proposal is to your advantage and with a suitable man. No old merchant looking for a third wife to care for him in his dotage for you!"

Athenais snuggled into Doria's ample arms. "Thank you, Aunt."

Paulinus paced through the garden, trailing his host and friend, deep in thought. *What a remarkable girl! I've never met a young woman like her. Not only beautiful, but fresh, genuine, warm, and smart; confident in her opinions. Her bookish ways will appeal to Theo.* An unexpected wave of regret washed over him. *Theo! Does he deserve such a woman? Wouldn't he be happier with a meek little mouse?* Paulinus shook his head. *But that's the point. We need a strong woman to counter Pulcheria…* his heart lurched, and he stopped in his tracks, forcing Olympiodorus to come back for him.

"Anything wrong?"

"No." Paulus wistfully looked back toward the solar. "She's perfect. Maybe too perfect."

The older man put an arm around his shoulders. "I recognize that look. Athenais affects most men that way. All are attracted to her beauty, but most stay for her kindness and her keenness. If I were younger…" He sighed and glanced at Asclepiodotus. "Keep your feelings to yourself, my friend. Remember your mission. Also, you don't want to get on the wrong side of the spymaster."

"Of course." *I can always hope Theo doesn't want such a treasure for a wife.*

Chapter 7

"Sister, I heard that the meeting with Paulinus went well yesterday."

Athenais looked up from *The Iliad* to see Valerius entering the solar followed by her aunt carrying a tray of figs and melon and a sweating ewer. "Quite well. Paulinus is a most charming man. Did you recommend him to our uncle as a possible suitor?"

Valerius' grin changed to consternation, and he quickly glanced at Doria. *What are those two up to?*

"It seems we misread the situation, my dear." Doria put the tray down and offered her a goblet of watered wine.

"How so?" She sipped at the drink, watching the two through lowered lashes.

"Paulinus was an emissary for a much more important client." Doria's face almost split in two with a wide smile. "It's not the emperor's best friend seeking a wife. It's the emperor himself!" She put her hands to her mouth to unsuccessfully suppress a cascade of giggles.

"What?" Athenais choked on her drink. "That can't be right. I'm a poor girl with no dowry, the daughter of a scholar. Paulinus might make an exception to marry me, but the emperor?" She turned to her brother. "Val, this can't be true."

"It is, Athenais." Valerius nodded. "The emperor is of age and needs a wife to continue the dynasty. His sister dithers in the task. Pulcheria is consumed with preparing for a possible war with Persia, giving us Hellenes an opening while she is distracted. Theodosius commissioned his best friend to help him find a suitable mate. Paulinus believes you might be the right one, but there are a few impediments."

"Beyond my poverty and lack of social status?"

"Your beauty and intelligence count for much more. Besides the people of Constantinople will be thrilled if the emperor's consort is a woman of humble origins."

"But..." Athenais sputtered, tried to take in this stunning change of fortune and... failed.

Doria cut in. "They won't be so thrilled if that woman is a pagan. Pulcheria would likely forbid the marriage, if her religious brother didn't turn away from the match."

"I won't do it. I won't worship that ridiculous triple god of the Christians." Athenais crossed her arms as the familiar pain of loss and dread spread from her stomach. *And I won't go into a loveless marriage just to be a broodmare for the emperor! I know nothing of the court and their ways. I'll have no friends or family close. Why should I leave this warm loving home to go to such an uncertain fate?*

"You don't need to actually worship Christ, just get baptized." Valerius cajoled.

"You mean, lie and pretend?" she snapped, trying to find a way out of what felt like a tightening trap.

"Of course not, but you've studied philosophy. Surely you can reconcile your beliefs with those of the Christians. They've absorbed several of the ancients' ideas already."

"And if I refuse?" Athenais glowered at her insistent brother.

"Father spoiled you for anything useful, Athenais. He indulged you and you think the world revolves around your wants and needs." Valerius fumed. "What about your brothers? Your aunt and uncle? You could do more for this family than anyone and you refuse?"

"So now it's all about you? I should sacrifice my happiness for your ambition?" Athenais shouted, vibrating with anger.

"Enough! Both of you!" Doria stood and pointed to the door. "Valerius, leave this to me."

Shocked by her aunt's authoritative tone, Athenais shrank back onto her bench. Valerius left, muttering about ungrateful females and shooting her venomous glances.

"Now drink your wine, Athenais, and cool your temper with a slice of melon." They sat in silence for a few moments until the heat left her face. "Good." Doria took her goblet, set it aside, and enveloped Athenais in a warm hug. "Now, my dear, tell me what you really fear. I'm sure that with your intellect, you can find what you need to be yourself while also professing this new religion."

Athenais snuggled in the warmth of the older woman's arms. "Thank you, Aunt." She sniffed, stifling a sob. "I don't want to give up my life here with you. Val is right about one thing; I need love in my life. Even in the difficult times, I knew Father loved me. We cared for each other. My brothers and uncle look at me and see a pretty face they can use to further their careers. They care nothing about my welfare, but you took me in and treated me like a daughter this past year—a loved and valued daughter. I feel safe here."

"Oh, my sweet thing." Doria tightened her hug. "I do love you. I promised that I would look to your welfare and not allow an unsuitable marriage. What could be more suitable than wedding the most powerful man in the world? But I don't want you to be miserable in a suitable marriage. If offered—and that is still in the future, if it happens at all—you *can* refuse."

"I can refuse the Emperor of Rome?" Athenais muttered.

"From all reports, the Augustus is a kind, fair man. He surely would not want a reluctant wife. That would be humiliating." Doria sighed. "I believe you're upset at the suddenness of this and have yet to consider the good that can come of it—for you as well as your brothers. Let's take this one step at a time. We'll host a salon and have Paulinus bring the emperor to meet you. That way you two can see if there is any attraction."

"That sounds reasonable." Athenais sat quietly thinking. *Aunt makes sense. I do have some choice, and nothing is certain. It* was *childish of me to take so violently against the idea when I know nothing about the alternatives.* "I want to talk to Olympiodorus. He's writing a history of the court and can help me understand what would be required of me, as well as counsel me regarding conversion—if I so chose."

"Excellent! I'm sure Dorrie can answer all your questions." She chuckled. "But don't tell him that I call him that behind his back!"

"I won't." Athenais smiled. *If nothing else comes of this, at least I'll get to see more of my old friend.*

*****

"Look who came to visit." Doria beamed at Athenais as she escorted Olympiodorus into the autumnal garden. The sun still provided warmth, but the evening required a shawl if she wanted to stroll among the final blooms of the year.

"Now what's this I hear about you having doubts about being baptized, my sweet." He wagged his bushy eyebrows at her. "Afraid of a little water?"

"Dorrie!" Athenais smiled at him, but didn't rush in for her normal hug. "I'm so glad you could come. I have need of your *honest* advice. You never lied to me as a child or made up fables to gloss over unpleasant truths."

"And I never will, now or in the future." A worried frown marred his rugged face.

"Both of you sit and I'll have a servant bring you something. Wine, Olympiodorus?" Doria, as usual, took charge of the social niceties.

"Of course! This seems like thirsty work."

"Athenais?"

She shook her head. "Lemon water for me, Aunt."

The older woman bustled off and Athenais indicated a bench in the shade of a grape arbor. "Please Dorrie, I really do need your help. My heart is torn and my mind awhirl. I need a friend experienced in the ways of the world to help guide me."

"Of course, my dear. Anything I can do, I will."

They sat on the stone bench while a girl served their drinks and Doria chose another bench a discreet distance away—within the socially required eyesight, but not within ear shot if they kept their voices low.

"A fine vintage. Your uncle knows his wines." Olympiodorus eyed Athenais over his goblet. "Now how can I help you, child."

"Are you involved in this plot to marry me to the emperor?"

His bushy eyebrows shot up. "It's not a 'plot,' my dear. This is how marriage among the elite works. Parents and guardians look for the most advantage in a match for their children, whether it's money, prestigious alliance, or influence and power. And yes, I brought you to the attention of a certain faction of powerful men: Isidorus, the son of the previous regent and Paulinus among them. They seek to place a woman of their own values in the court to counter the religious regime of the young Augusta."

"For what purpose?"

"The advantages for each are numerous. Isidorus wants the power his father Anthemius wielded as prefect—to the city's great advantage—while he lived. Even if you marry, I hope he doesn't get his wishes. The man is not his father and seeks power for corrupt purposes. You know your uncle and brothers' motivations. They are more narrow and socially acceptable."

"And Paulinus, how does he fit into this scheme?"

"Young Paulinus is of the Hellene faction placed in the palace by Anthemius as a companion to the emperor when they were boys. Anthemius was a shrewd man. He knew the young princess Pulcheria had an outsized influence on her younger brother and wanted a male counterweight. Paulinus has performed brilliantly."

"So, he lies and pretends?"

"No! Paulinus genuinely loves Theodosius and has only his best interests at heart. His motivations, unlike the others, are purer. He wants to find a young woman who could be a loving companion to his friend, while also providing an alternative to the strict religious regime the young Augusta imposes on the court and her people. Someone kind, clever, and strong enough to stand up to Pulcheria and provide some lightness to the court."

"And what do you get out of this, Dorrie? Money, land, titles?"

"Do you really think so little of me after all this time?" He took her hands in his and looked her in the eyes. "I help the daughter of my friend make of her life what she wishes with a marriage that provides wealth, security, and the power to influence the world for the better. I get to help a brilliant young woman shine on the world stage."

"At what cost to me?" Tears welled in her eyes. "I lose my family, my freedom, and face a lifetime of strife in a hostile home."

"Ah my child, it is the fate of all women: to leave their parents' home, enter their husband's and be subject to his rules." He put a gentle finger under her chin and raised her head to look into her eyes. "That is the fear talking. Not everything has to be bleak. What do you want in a marriage?"

Athenais sat quietly for a moment. "I haven't thought about the specifics. I always had vague dreams of a loving husband, a large family, and a comfortable home."

"Laudable goals, but pedestrian." His eyes sparkled. "You are a strong and clever woman, Athenais. Do you not want something more challenging? Do you not harbor some higher ambitions?"

"Well, I'd like freedom to pursue my studies and some recognition for my scholarship and poetry."

"That's better. Anything more? If you had the resources of the empire at your fingertips, what would you do with them?"

"I'd expand the university here in Constantinople. I've been here over a year and have come to believe it's a shadow of the Academy in Athens. It's not worthy of the imperial capital." She tapped her chin as she thought. "I'd also hold salons for scholars and poets to best show their work and provide an appreciative audience. I'd be a patroness of the arts and literature, providing money for struggling writers and sponsoring public art and sculpture. I would…" Her face fell. "How could I do such things on my own?"

"Imperial woman traditionally have their own funds and carve out their own spheres of influence. Pulcheria and her sisters build churches and give money to charities. There's no reason you couldn't build classrooms, endow chairs, and provide public art for the good of the city—if you were the emperor's consort."

"Really? You think I could accomplish so much?"

"You underestimate your abilities. Your beauty enthralls men, but your kindness wins their hearts and gives you power. You are a good match for Theodosius in temperament and interests. As his consort, I promise you, Athenais, you will be happy in this marriage and do much good for yourself, your family, and the people of Constantinople."

"Thank you Dorrie. I have much to think on." A brief smile lit up her face. "It looks like my next step is studying Christianity. If I can find a way to convert without betraying my beliefs, I'll consider it—but no guarantees! Can you recommend any good texts for me to study?"

Chapter 8

Two weeks later, Athenais and Doria entered a side door of the Church of the Apostles where Bishop Atticus had temporary quarters while the Great Church was still undergoing reconstruction. She looked around in amazement. "Even the back rooms are sumptuous, Aunt. I had expected spare corridors and humble spaces, not gilded wood, mosaic floors, and silk hangings

"The leadership of the church is akin to the nobles of our secular society, my dear. You shouldn't expect them to live like the monks and the desert fathers."

"Why not? They worship the same god. Should they not live the same lives of poverty and holiness?"

Doria sighed. "Add that question to your list for the good bishop. I don't know why; I only know what is. You should be honored that the bishop is meeting with you to answer your questions."

"I'm sorry I'm such a disappointment, Aunt, but I struggle with the basis of Christianity. I've read the scriptures and many commentators both Christian and pagan. There is much to admire, but also much that seems fantastical. I know that the church teaches that the canon is the Word of God, but it seems more likely the words of men. After the first century, the history of this new religion smacks of politics and power rather than true belief."

"And you would let that stand in the way of marrying the most powerful man in the empire? Can you not set aside your qualms and embrace the admirable qualities?"

A quiver entered her voice. "You promised, Aunt. You promised I would have a choice."

Doria gave her a sad smile. "I did and I will keep my word. But my counsel is the same. Talk with the bishop. See if he can answer the questions that your catechism tutors cannot. But take all the factors into consideration, not just the religion. Your uncle and I do quite well, attending services on holy days and tithing to the church for charitable works."

She tried and failed to keep the accusatory tone from her voice. "Maybe if I could attend the occasional service and give money to the church, I wouldn't mind, but I will have to live the life of a true believer. I will be most unhappy, as will be the Augustus, if I only have the shallow commitment of a convenient Christian."

"Athenais!"

"I'm sorry, Aunt." At the stricken look on her aunt's face, she softened her voice. "I cannot keep up a pretense. The emperor needs a wife who can support him in all his endeavors including his religious beliefs."

"I understand, my dear." Doria patted Athenais' hand. "I just ask that you do your best for your brothers as well as yourself."

They entered an antechamber to the bishop's quarters where a brown-robed monk with ink-stained fingers, looked up from his labors making fair copies of correspondence.

He smiled. "You must be Lady Athenais and her aunt Lady Doria. Paulinus said to expect you at this hour. Let me see if the bishop is ready to receive you." He scurried to a heavy oak door and pulled it slightly open to announce, "Your Excellency, your visitors have arrived."

"Send them in."

"This way." The monk opened the door wider and ushered the pair into the room, announcing, "The Ladies Athenais and Doria, niece and wife to Asclepiodotus of the Augustus' Master of Offices service."

Bishop Atticus, head of the Church of Constantinople, sat behind a massive mahogany table, covered with neat piles of reports and letters. He wore severe black robes, embroidered with silver crosses at hem and sleeve and belted with silver links. His only jewelry, a heavy gold signet ring on his left index finger.

He's smaller than I thought he'd be. Athenais thought, *but he has kind eyes and laugh wrinkles. Maybe he won't dismiss my concern out of hand.*

Athenais and Doria bowed to the bishop.

"Thank you, Brother Antony. You may leave us." The bishop nodded to his assistant.

The monk bowed out the door.

Bishop Atticus waved toward a comfortable-looking couch facing a low table and cushioned chairs. "Ladies, please sit."

They took the padded couch and Atticus settled himself in a chair opposite. He smiled. "I'm afraid I'm a bad host. Would you like refreshments? I can recall Brother Antony."

Doria fluttered her hands. "No, no, Your Excellency. We will take up little of your time. My niece has been studying in preparation for baptism but has some questions of theology that her tutors couldn't answer to her satisfaction. Has the noble Paulinus informed you of our, uh, delicate situation?"

The bishop's eyes sparkled with amusement, and he seemed to be trying to suppress a smile. "Yes, Paulinus has spoken to me of the possibility of marriage between your niece and the Augustus. He's right in that the Augustus would not marry a pagan. The Augusta would surely oppose the match, as well, and Theodosius does not make an important decision without his sister's advice. Paulinus also informed me that Athenais is quite learned and studied philosophy. For my own part, I welcome Athenais to our community whether or not she marries the Augustus. How may I help you, young lady?"

Athenais looked directly into his eyes. "I have trouble believing in the resurrection, which is a core belief in your religion. The story seems borrowed from other traditions. Osiris of Egypt, Dionysius of Greece, Mithras of Parthia—all sons of gods, all resurrected after death and elevated to godhood. There is historical evidence of Jesus as a man and preacher, but his resurrection seems improbable. If I cannot believe in that tenet, then I cannot be baptized a Christian."

"I see." The bishop rubbed his bearded jaw. "What have you been taught that contradicts the Christian teaching?"

"Philosophers for centuries have rejected the large pantheon of local gods. They teach there is a beginning, an unknowable ineffable creative force that only a few can catch a glimpse of with years of mathematical study and meditation."

"Ah! You've read Hypatia, the Lady Philosopher of Alexandria's work."

"Some." Athenais shrugged. "Many of her students fled to Athens after the great lady was murdered in Alexandria by a Christian mob. My father hosted them occasionally and I listened in on their discussions." She gave a wry smile.

"I must admit when I tried to read her mathematical treatises, I struggled mightily. Pythagoras and his theorems were too much for me."

"Did you know that many of Hypatia's students serve in high positions in the Christian Church? Bishop Synesius of Ptolemais was the best known. They all reconciled their philosophical beliefs with the requirements of baptism to lead their flocks." Atticus chuckled. "You are not the first, nor will be the last to question the resurrection. Bishop Synesius once said, 'As for the resurrection such as common belief admits it, I see here *an ineffable mystery*, and I am far from sharing the views of the vulgar crowd on the subject.' Why do you think these tales of resurrection are popular among several religions?"

A slow smile bloomed across her face. "I once had a similar discussion with my friend Olympiodorus many years ago. I think that people who have no time for education or philosophy—those who work hard just to survive—need something to believe in. Tales of resurrection give them hope for a better or different life. Participation in community rituals and beliefs gives them security, whether those are prayers, feasts, or fasts. There are always keepers of the mysteries that people can go to for advice, inspiration and intervention with the divine. They cannot take the time out of their daily lives to study the divine or engage in elaborate daily rituals as do the monks of today or priestesses of old."

"Excellent!" Atticus clapped his hands, startling Doria. "We're getting close. Jesus' teachings are radical and unique. 'Turn the other cheek', 'love they neighbor as thyself', 'give away your riches to care for the poor' are among the most disruptive to a society based on power and using violence to maintain that power. There were many 'messiahs' over the centuries doing miracles and preaching to the masses. Some even claimed to raise the dead. Jesus' message of love and peace sparked a fire among the downtrodden, which spread to many classes. That probably wouldn't have happened without the resurrection story. It was the gateway to spread his radical message and create a better world here on earth."

"But was Jesus the son of God *and* God himself? And what of this Holy Spirit? I was raised to believe in a single Divine, not this triumvirate. Most philosophers gave up the worship of the old gods even before Jesus made his appearance, believing the gaggle of various gods to be creations of humans rather than humans being creations of the gods."

The bishop shrugged his shoulders. "I have come to believe that all gods are God, pale reflections that allow all men and women to somehow see the divine in themselves. The more human the god's behavior, the more comfortable the worshiper." He grinned. "And the more mysterious the god, the happier the philosopher. What are you taking away from this discussion, Mistress Philosopher?"

Athenais sat, head bowed, for several moments thinking about the bishops' remarkable statement. *All gods are God? I can see that as a workable belief. Worship varies from culture to culture, but it's the behavior of individuals that is important. Can I live by the Christian tenants of kindness, charity, and love? I hope I already do.*

Her aunt fussed with her stola, alternately clutching then smoothing the fabric. Atticus sat quietly, his face settled into a contemplative half-smile, seemingly unfazed by her silence.

She raised her face and smiled. "I believe I'm happy, Bishop. Gregory of Nazianzus said, 'It is difficult to conceive God, but to define him in words is an impossibility.' Jesus' godhood and resurrection is an ineffable mystery. His teachings are not. They are practical, demanding the best behavior of us. I will try to live up to them in my life as a Christian…and philosopher."

"Then my job is well done." Atticus chuckled. "If you are successful in your marriage quest, please come tell me of your conversations with Pulcheria Augusta on these subjects. She is a fervent believer, not out of ignorance, but out of a certain rigidity of character. The canon and rituals gave her comfort in a time where little was available to her. But she is a true daughter of Christ and lives his teachings to the best of her ability."

"Thank you for your time and guidance, Your Excellency." Athenais rose taking her aunt's hand. "I hope we will be great friends in the future."

"As do I, Mistress Philosopher." He led them to the door and saw them out.

"Well, Aunt? What did you think?" Athenais linked arms with her.

"You lost me at 'ineffable creative force' my dear. I'll leave philosophy and the finer points of religion to you and the good bishop." Doria patted her hand. "But I do have plans for your meeting with the Augustus."

Athenais smiled to herself as her aunt plotted. *I never felt so light. I didn't realize how much this weighed on me. Now I can greet the emperor with honesty and affection.*

Chapter 9

Home of Asclepiodotus, September 420

Lady, Domina Doria asks that you join her in the garden. The guests have started arriving."

"Tell her I will be down shortly." Athenais sent the young servant on her way and took a moment to pass final judgment on her looks in the polished silver mirror: only the lightest make-up, no kohl and only a touch of carmine on the lips. Since she was in her own home, she wore her golden hair uncovered, intertwined with false braids to create a complicated confection on top with her own curls cascading down her back.

She stood up from her desk and smoothed the blue silk stola—embroidered with white roses at neck, sleeve, and hem—over her hips. Her aunt's lapis lazuli earrings, necklace, and bracelet completed her look. *Aunt's right, blue does bring out my eyes.* Her heart started to beat faster as if she faced a great danger, not an amusing salon. She took a deep breath. *I can do this. I need to forget that the emperor is coming and treat him I as would any guest of my uncle's. I need to get to know the man not the ruler. And Dorrie will be there to help.*

Athenais left her room, head held high. She went down the steps and passed into the formal part of the garden. Small groups already congregated wherever there was seating. Trampled rosemary and mint lightly scented the air. A young man strolled by, strumming his seven-stringed kithara and singing popular love songs. Servants glided among the guests, carrying trays of tempting delicacies and flagons of wine. She was startled to realize that there were several older matrons—friends of her aunt's?—as guests. Her father had never had women at his entertainments, except for her, and she had to sit behind a curtain unless needed to serve food or drink.

"There you are my dear!" Her aunt approached absent-mindedly patting at a curl of her formal red wig. "Olympiodorus is already here and wants to talk to you."

"Wonderful. Where is he?"

Doria guided her to a nearby group of men where her friend held forth. As he saw Athenais approaching, he clapped one young man on the back and declared, "I'll be happy to read your treatise on the Huns. They are a fascinating race. Send it to me and I'll give you notes. Excuse me gentlemen while I attend to more beautiful company than yourselves."

Following his gaze, three young men stared at Athenais with various reactions. One looked stunned, another appreciative, and the third disapproving. *He probably doesn't think women should read either, much less make a presence at a salon.* Athenais smiled at the trio. *His loss.*

"Doria, thank you for delivering her to me." Olympiodorus put a hand on Athenais' back as if to usher her away. "I'll chaperone while you attend your guests."

Doria nodded and moved in closer to ask in a low voice. "Do we know if our *special* guest is coming?"

Olympiodorus gave a sly smile and dropped his head to whisper, "Paulinus tells me the emperor is scheduled to inspect his troops outside the city this morning in preparation for the Persian War. He will attempt to persuade his friend to attend. Evidently, Theodosius has been more amendable to breaking the rules lately. According to Paulinus, he is feeling restless under his sister's rule, but nothing is certain."

"Well, whether he comes to this salon or not, it is good for Athenais to be known beyond our family." Doria turned to her niece. "Enjoy the salon my dear. Dor—er—Olympiodorus will introduce you to his circle of writers and poets."

"So, I'm Dorrie to all and sundry now, my little Squirrel?" He turned to Athenais. "Should I tell everyone of my pet name for you and how as a child you stuffed your mouth so full of sweets your cheeks bulged?"

Athenais laughed and took his arm to walk toward a more secluded spot. "Oh Dorrie, do what you will. Having a pet name doesn't diminish your standing, it just means that someone cares enough to give you one, whether it's out of love or hate."

"Well said, my dear, and have I mentioned yet that you are as beautiful as your namesake."

"The city or the goddess?"

"The city." His gaze drifted beyond the walls. "Constantinople is gaudy in its newness. It feels raw with constant construction and restless population. It doesn't have the beauty or grace, the sense of history, of Athens."

Tears threatened to spill from her eyes as her heart suddenly yearned for her peaceful predictable home in Athens forever entwined with her father's love. She sniffed and wiped her eyes. *That peace and contentment is gone with my childhood. I'm a woman now and need to see to my future and that of my family.*

"Oh, Athenais, I'm a clumsy fool to talk about your home and bring on sad memories. Let's talk of something fun. Why does your aunt insist on wearing that improbably red wig?"

Athenais giggled. "The color of her hair has faded, but she doesn't want to dye it. A friend of hers attempted to make her dark tresses red using madder and it all fell out. Aunt Doria has been frightened of going bald ever since and wears a wig when she wants to look her best."

"Not such a bad idea." Olympiodorus swept a hand through his own thinning hair. "Come, there's a fellow poet you should know."

He shepherded her toward an older man with a graying beard and sparkling dark eyes. They spent a pleasant hour conversing with the guests until someone called on Olympiodorus for an accounting of his most recent adventures at the Hunnish court. As he launched into his story, a crowd gathered round and Athenais listened avidly.

"The court was in an uproar. I barely arrived and King Donatus dead! Of course, his successor, King Charaton, accused me of spying and murder. Only quick talking and the magnificence of the emperor's gifts kept me from the Huns' wrath."

Dorrie is such a great storyteller! I wish I could travel and have such adventures. I never seem to get beyond the walls of my home.

When he finished his tale, she grabbed his arm and demanded, "Tell us of your sea adventures. I never tire of hearing those stories."

Olympiodorus looked past her, and his eyes widened.

She glanced over her shoulder to see Paulinus with a slight young man in riding clothes approach their group. *The emperor? He looks like an ordinary young man.* She turned away blushing. She listened as her friend continued his tales of wandering and perils at sea, but had trouble concentrating. *Good gods, I can feel their eyes on me. Maybe I should leave? No, I can't embarrass Uncle Asclepiodotus that way. The emperor's only a year older than I. He's probably just as scared of meeting me as I am of meeting him.* The thought settled her, and she relaxed.

Olympiodorus finished his tale and Paulinus approached arm-in-arm with the emperor. "Well met, Olympiodorus." He dropped the young man's arm, bowing slightly to her. "Athenais, may I present my good friend Theo?"

"My pleasure." Eyes wide, she bowed, but otherwise did not acknowledge his rank. *The emperor has a pleasant face, if a bit thin.* Her stomach roiled as she searched for something to say. She settled on, "Theo, do you like poetry?"

"Yes! Very much," he mumbled and blushed, seeming a little dazed.

I was right! He is as awkward at this as I am. A wave of sympathy for the young emperor washed across her and brightened her smile. "Then you've come to the right place. My friend," she nodded to Olympiodorus, "will be reciting some of his work later. It's quite good."

Theo's face broke into a wide grin, and he stood silent until Paulinus nudged him in the ribs. "I… uh… I understand you write verse as well."

"I only dabble." She lowered her lashes and shrugged. *Great! Now he thinks I'm a stupid girl and falsely humble.*

"I'd love to hear some." Theodosius stood clutching his hands and shuffling his feet.

Paulinus stepped forward, taking both by the elbow. "Perhaps this is too public a place." He led them to an alcove shaded by a fig tree. "Sit here and get acquainted. I'll send a servant."

They sat quietly for a few moments while the emperor looked around at everything but her. *Why is he so nervous? I thought he lived with a bevy of sisters.* Athenais finally asked, "Where did you ride this morning?"

"Uh, what did you say?" Theodosius looked embarrassed.

"I asked where you had been earlier. You're dressed for riding." Athenais asked more confidently.

"Inspecting the troops. It's my responsibility, you know." He responded in a pompous tone, then glanced at her with despair. His shoulders slumped and Athenais wanted to put her arms around him and tell him all was well, but her uncle's servant brought them goblets of wine. Theo grabbed one and took a gulp. He set the goblet aside, taking a deep breath.

Athenais smiled and said in the soothing tones she would use to calm a scared puppy, "I've always admired people who learned to ride. I'm afraid my exercise is confined to walking and wielding a pen."

"I enjoy riding, but I find wielding a pen to be more satisfying. Some of my friends call me 'the calligrapher.'" Theodosius seemed to relax a little and a small smile lit his serious face.

"How delightful! What do you copy?"

"Mostly ancient texts. Some Holy Fathers, some historians." His breathing slowed as he talked about his favorite hobby.

"I'd love to see your work sometime."

"I'd love to show you." He gazed at her, then a shadow crossed his face and he asked with some alarm, "Are you visiting your uncle? For how long?"

His question recalled her sadness, which she still struggled to control. "My father died two years ago. Uncle Asclepiodotus and Aunt Doria were kind enough to take me in."

"I'm so sorry to have invoked painful memories."

"I miss him very much." Tears glistened in her eyes. "My mother died when I was quite young, and he was both father and mother to me." *Now's not the time to cry before the emperor. Get a hold of yourself girl!*

She heard a raucous squawk and looked behind her, startled, and smiled. "Olympiodorus has brought out his pet parrot. He is most amusing and can sing in several languages. I like when he dances." *Thank my namesake goddess, Plato is here and will get me out of this awkward situation.*

"Then, by all means, let us go watch this wondrous bird." Theodosius stood, held out his hand, and accompanied Athenais back to the grape arbor.

Plato the parrot put on quite a show, but Athenais only remembered the emperor's readiness to leave her company at the first opportunity. She left the salon shortly after he did with a sense of failure. *Why do I feel this way when I didn't even want this match?*

Chapter 10

November 420

"THE BEST OF NEWS!" DORIA BURST INTO THE BEDROOM WHERE ATHENAIS worked on her newest poem.

"What?" She looked up startled.

"Paulinus is bringing the Augustus for a visit this afternoon. You must be made ready." Doria went to her clothes trunk and started rifling through her gowns. "Go to the baths immediately and I'll find something suitable for you to wear."

"But," Athenais frowned, "we've heard nothing for two months after the salon. I thought the emperor dissatisfied with me."

"It seems just the opposite. Young Theodosius is quite smitten and could not work up the courage to visit you, feeling he had made a fool of himself the last time."

"That poor boy. He is more sheltered than I am. No wonder we both faltered in the meeting." A wave of anticipation submerged her lingering regret over the salon outcome. *So, all is not lost and my struggles for philosophical insight into the Christian religion are not for naught.*

"Yes, yes, poor boy and all that… now get to the baths while I arrange everything." Doria shooed her out of the room.

Later, Athenais peeked into the receiving room to see how the arrangements fared. She nodded at the transformation done so quickly: fresh flowers in vases; wine on a sideboard; a table set with an array of fruits, nuts, olives, cheeses, sliced meats and delicate pastries; and two servants ready in fresh livery. The sharp fishy scent of garum warred with the aroma of ripe apples and the yeasty smell of warm bread.

Doria saw her lurking in the doorway. "Out! They've arrived in the courtyard. I'll bring you in when it is time to make an entrance. You should not be lingering."

Athenais, amused, sat in the anteroom waiting for her aunt to summon her. This time without a large audience, she felt calmer and more in control of her fate. *Theodosius seems a nice young man. I just need to get to know him. With time we can have affection as well as companionship,* she reassured herself. *But is that all I want? Dorrie and I spoke of so much more.* She gave a mental shrug. *First things first.*

Her aunt waved to her from the door and Athenais entered the receiving room dressed more simply this time in white silk with blue birds embroidered on her gown and a blue silk wrap pinned at her shoulder with her mother's gold phoenix fibula. The emperor stood with his back to her, talking to Paulinus. Both wore more formal tunics than last time, but their boots indicated they rode rather than taking a litter. Theodosius didn't wear the imperial diadem which would indicate his rank. *How often does the emperor go about the city as a noble so as not to attract the attention of the populace?*

Paulinus looked over Theo's shoulder. His smile widened as he whispered something to his friend.

Theo whipped around, tangling his feet, making a clumsy turn. Blood rose to his cheeks. *Oh, no! I must make him feel welcome or he might bolt again.*

"Augustus." She gave him her best smile and dropped into a deep curtsy.

"Please, in your uncle's home, call me Theo."

"As you wish."

"Domina, have you heard the latest story about our Master of Offices?" Paulinus took Doria by the arm and led her to a bench in the furthest corner of the room, giving Theo and Athenais some small measure of privacy.

Theo shot his friend a grateful look.

"Our servants have set out refreshments. Will you allow me to serve you, Aug—uh—Theo?"

He nodded, and they made their way to the sideboard where he picked up a handful of almonds and nibbled them as she poured him a goblet of wine.

"Is that all you care for?" She proffered the goblet.

"I'm afraid my appetite deserts me in your presence. I care only for your company." His large brown eyes—his most attractive feature—shone with eagerness.

He really is smitten! I don't think he could lie to me that smoothly. She felt the heat rise in her cheeks, but before she could reply he said, "Oh! I have a present for you."

"What is it?"

He led her to a cushioned rosewood divan, retrieved a package, and handed it to Athenais. A nervous grin flitted across his face.

She sat and inspected the gift. It felt like a book and was wrapped in a white silk veil with gold-thread leaf designs.

She undid the silk cord, letting the fabric drift aside to reveal a small, leather-bound codex. The title stamped in gold on the binding declared it the play *Helen* by the ancient playwright Euripides.

"It's exquisite!" Athenais brought the book to her nose to sniff appreciatively. "I love the smell of new books—leather and fresh ink!" She opened the codex to inspect the lovely script and thick parchment pages. She turned to him with shining eyes. "Have you read it?"

"I did the copy work myself."

"It's fine work. Some of the best I've seen." She ran her hand over the stiff leather cover.

"I chose the story because your beauty outshines Helen's," Theo said softly.

"I like the play because Euripides shows Helen to be a faithful wife to Menelaus, wrongly used by the gods." Athenais clutched the book to her breasts. "I'll treasure this always. How did you know I value books over jewels? Or that Euripides is my favorite?"

"Paulinus told me."

She laughed, patting the seat on the bench beside her. "Of course he did. Paulinus is a good friend to us both. He's been by to visit a couple times since the salon."

A slight frown marred Theo's face. "What did you talk about?"

"Mostly he sang your praises and made excuses that you were busy with the war in Persia." She bowed her head slightly. "I thought you disliked me after our first meeting, and he was being kind."

"Never! I just… uh… wanted to bring you the gift first." Theo sat by her side and picked up her hand. He turned it over, running his thumb gently down the lifeline of her palm. A warmth spread from her womb and tingled in her breasts. She breathed faster and gave a brief shiver. She was more used to living in her mind than her body. Her body's reaction confused and startled her.

Theo's face blushed then paled. He dropped her hand. "I'm sorry. I did not mean to be so forward."

"I do not think you forward, Theo. I find you most considerate." She sat in awkward silence regaining her composure for a moment before tapping the codex. "Do you like the classical writers?"

"I haven't read as widely as I suspect you have. We tended to study the writings of the church fathers."

"I've read Clement, Origen, and more recently Synesius. They were Christians *and* philosophers." She put the codex aside and clasped her hands together. "There seems much to be learned from both schools of thought."

"Are you studying with anyone?"

"Bishop Atticus is tutoring me in the Christian faith. I'm to be baptized soon."

"That's wonderful!" His smile blazed. "Would you do me the great honor of taking my mother's name at the baptism? She was called Eudoxia."

"'She of good reputation and judgment.' What a lovely name! Maybe I could use the Greek version Eudocia so as not to confuse people with your sainted mother. But—" she hesitated. "Theo, the great honor would be mine and I'm not sure it would be appropriate. I wouldn't want people to believe I have pretensions or unwarranted ambitions."

"No one would accuse you of pretensions and you could never have unwarranted ambitions. You're the sweetest, most honest girl I've met."

"Am I the only girl you've met?" she teased.

"Over the past two months, Paulinus has dragged me all over the city to meet the most available flowers of femininity that our noble families could produce. None compared to you in beauty, intelligence, or temperament. I knew from the moment I set eyes on you at the salon, I wanted no other woman but you at my side. Once you're baptized, of course."

He took her hand again and clasped it between sweating palms. His lips smiled, but worry lines appeared on his brow.

Athenais' heart leapt and she trembled as she tried to take in the meaning of his words. *This is happening. The Emperor of Rome wants to marry the dowerless daughter of a scholar. Dorrie was right that I don't know my own power.*

"Uncle Asclepiodotus will have to give his permission," she said in a low voice.

Theo laughed and brought her hand to his lips. "I think that will not be a problem."

"And the Augusta, your sister?" Athenais knew *she* would be the real impediment to the marriage.

"Leave Pulcheria to me. It might take some time, but she will come around and love you as I do."

Love and security for me and my family. How can I ask anything more?

Chapter 11

April 421

PAULINUS APPROACHED THE NOW-FAMILIAR BRASS-BOUND DOOR OF Asclepiodotus' compound with a sense of despair. He had been Theo's go-between for several months as a series of crises roiled the government. His friend had only been able to leave the palace a handful of times to visit Athenais. *I introduced Theo to every eligible girl in this city, but he has eyes only for Athenais. I had hoped, in his innocence, he would be attracted to another, but that was not to be. Of course, I could always sabotage this match by giving poor advice to Athenais about how to handle Pulcheria.* He shook his head and straightened his shoulders. He and others had carefully prepared Theo to outmaneuver Pulcheria. *I won't dash my best friend's chance at happiness and freedom from his domineering sister even for my own heart. I love Theo and Athenais both too much.*

When he approached Athenais and her aunt in the receiving room, his resolve strengthened. Athenais sat with a glow on her face and animation in her speech. She exuded happiness and contentment. *I have a duty to perform and will do my best to bring this match to a happy conclusion for my friend and my love. It's best that I put all thoughts of Athenais away.* But when she turned her brilliant blue eyes on him and sprang to her feet with a cry of, "Paulinus, my friend. Welcome!" a knife twisted in his gut, and he had trouble breathing for a moment.

"Athenais. Doria." He gave the women a brief bow to allow him a moment for composure. He produced a smile and a joke. "Ready to learn the care and feeding of an Augusta? She's a fearsome beast and will need a good deal of training."

"Do I look like a beast master?" Athenais struck a dramatic pose and cracked an invisible whip. "Ha! Back, beast!"

Doria gave her a sad smile. "Comedy is all well at the theater, my child, but this is serious business. Both of you take a seat. Paulinus," she turned to him, "what does Athenais need to know before she meets with the Augusta?"

He helped himself to a goblet of well-watered wine before sitting on a green silk padded chair. "That's a complicated question, Domina." He swirled the contents of his goblet, thinking, while both women watched him. He took a drink, set it aside, and leaned forward, elbows on his knees and hands clasped before him. "The Augusta is a brilliant politician and has been since she was young. I've never met a woman—or man—with her abilities. Under normal circumstances, I don't believe we could make this match happen, but Pulcheria is distracted. The war in Persia is not going well and she has resorted to appealing to the dead saint of victory to save them."

"We attended the *adventus* of Saint Stephen's bones." Athenais nodded. "That was quite a spectacle. Theo looked magnificent carrying the cross before the bishop's wagon. I did feel sorry for the older men who carried those large candles following the saint's remains. It was a long trek from the gates to the palace on foot. The people were quite impressed."

"Pulcheria planned that, down to the last detail. She's a master of religious theater."

"I thought the Augusta was a true believer." Doria frowned. "Are you saying it's all for show?"

"No, Pulcheria is deeply committed to her religion. She lives the gospel and considers it her duty to care for the poor and destitute while inspiring the masses with magnificent churches. But she's not above using the drama of religious ceremony to control the ordinary people of Constantinople and use them as a counterweight to the nobles." He took another sip of wine. "That's important, Athenais. You must initially conform to the religious practices of the palace. Theo and his sisters pray several times a day and you must join them, if you wish to gain their trust and love."

"Sounds tedious," Doria muttered.

"It is!" Paulinus grinned. "I must attend Theo when I'm in the palace, but it's necessary to maintain their regard. They look askance at those less committed than themselves."

"You said 'initially.' Does that mean, I can stop going when I please?" Athenais asked.

"No. You must establish yourself as a loving and loyal wife. Until Theo raises you to the rank of Augusta, you will be his wife and consort, but Pulcheria will outrank you. You will have little influence beyond your personal relationships—which could be considerable given Theo's love for you. You mustn't do anything to jeopardize that regard."

"That shouldn't be difficult. I love Theo. He is a most considerate man and I want to please him. I believe we can build a loving life together that satisfies both of us."

Athenais' face took on a dreamy look that tugged at Paulinus' heart. *If only she could feel that way about me!* He pushed that thought to the deepest recesses of his soul and returned to the task at hand. *This is the match I worked for, but Athenais needs a bit more spine if she is to fulfill the Helene faction's expectations.*

"When you give birth to an heir, Athenais, Theo will most likely name you Augusta. That rank will give you more autonomy and standing in the court. What you do with it will be up to you, but I counsel keeping as close to the family practices as you can. You'll know when the time comes that you can start loosening the ties that bind and introduce some of your own will to the larger court."

Athenais blushed prettily at the mention of a child. She had often expressed her desire for a large family and Paulinus hoped she got her wish, not only for her own happiness, but because having children conferred considerable power on an imperial spouse. Theo's mother and grandmother were both fecund women and used that to great advantage for themselves and their husbands.

"So that's all? Love my husband and do my duty to him and the church? I think I can manage that."

"Don't be naïve, child." Doria shook her head. "You've read your histories. The imperial court is a snake pit. Your husband is your first defense, but you will need more than that to survive and be happy. You must build allies at court among those you trust. It's important that you help promote your brothers and uncle to positions of power so they can protect you from jealous courtiers."

"Of course, Aunt." Athenais said with some heat. "I'm not that naïve. I understand my role in promoting my family, but I want something out of this marriage for myself, as well."

Good, she is willing to speak up for herself! Paulinus distracted Doria with one of his favorite ploys to give Athenais a chance to cool down. "Speaking of snake pits, have you heard the latest news from the palace?"

"No! What's happening?" Doria leaned forward. The woman was an insatiable gossip.

"Honorius, Emperor in the West, just raised his half-sister Placidia to the rank of Augusta and her consort General Constantius to Augustus and co-emperor. To compound things, Honorius named their infant son Valentinian Caesar and heir to the West. All without consulting the Eastern court. Both Theo and Pulcheria are furious at this move and are rejecting the elevations. They sent the ambassadors from the West packing and refuse to put up the traditional commemorative statues."

"Isn't Placidia the princess that the Goths took as hostage when they laid siege to Rome?" Athenais' eyes gleamed. "She married their king for love if I remember right."

"Yes, it was a tragic story but probably over romanticized." Doria gave Paulinus a sly smile. "My husband has spies in the Western court and claims Placidia is as devious or more so than Pulcheria. She probably nagged and bullied her brother into naming her and her husband Augusti." She turned to her niece. "In any case, my sweet, you must take Theo's part in any controversy with the Western court. Any son of yours should take precedence over the son of a half-sister in ruling the West. Honorius has married twice and has no issue, nor is he likely to have any. Your children would have a stronger claim."

"I believe we're getting a bit ahead of ourselves, ladies. Athenais must earn Pulcheria's blessing before she can even think of a son who could rule in the West." *And if she is successful, my fate is sealed.*

Chapter 12

Imperial Palace, April 421

"Are you ready?" Paulinus asked as they approached the door to Pulcheria's receiving room.

Athenais took a few deep breaths to settle the fluttering in her chest. "I think so."

He smiled at her, "Remember, she isn't really a beast, but a concerned sister. Appeal to her love for her brother, his need for an heir, and assure her of your true Christian beliefs. Theo has staunchly defended you. He has made his wishes clear, and you have only to be yourself to charm his sister."

Athenais gave him a nervous smile and wished heartily that he could accompany her. He left her at the door in the care of a palace servant. She straightened her spine. *I can do this. I must.*

"The Lady Athenais." The servant announced after escorting her into Pulcheria's quarters.

Given Pulcheria's reputation, Athenais wasn't surprised by the barren nature of the Augusta's room compared to the lavish decorations of the public rooms in the palace. No tapestries adorned the walls for warmth or pleasure. No carpets cushioned her feet on the stone floor. Niches stood empty of art or flowers. Another servant stood at the back wall by a side table with ewers and plain silver goblets. Pulcheria sat on an unpadded wooden chair, angled across from a similar one flanked by a small stone table. *How sad that she thinks she must deprive herself of every comfort or source of beauty. No wonder the nobles of the*

Helene faction are fearful of her influence on Theo. It must be a drab court.

"Augusta." Athenais gave a deep bow. Paulinus had advised that in a private setting it wasn't necessary to give a full obeisance.

"Come here child and let me look at you." The Augusta waved her to the chair.

Athenais bristled at the 'child' appellation. Pulcheria had only three years on her but looked many years older in her gray woolen stola and dark hair covering. The Augusta seemed tall for a woman, but that might just be her erect posture or lean look. *Too much fasting*, she thought. Athenais was glad for her modest appearance. She wore no cosmetics with only plain gold bracelets and pearls in her ears for adornment; her hair tucked under a thin veil.

"Would you like some refreshment." Pulcheria indicated the waiting servant. "Wine? Lemon water? Pomegranate juice?"

"Lemon water, please."

Pulcheria nodded to the servant. "Pomegranate juice for me."

Athenais sat quietly as they both sipped their drinks. The fluttering returned to her chest. *What is the Augusta up to? Is this silence a ploy of some kind to make me uncomfortable? I can't speak until she speaks to me.*

Pulcheria put down her plain silver goblet and finally asked, "I understand you are an orphan?"

Athenais took a breath before answering. "Yes. My mother died when I was quite young. My father, almost three years ago."

"We share that affliction. It's a trial to lose one's parents in youth, but adversity can also give one strength. I understand you have two older brothers who care for you."

Is she looking for common ground? She sounds almost sympathetic. "They are both in Theo's… the emperor's, service, stationed away from Constantinople. When Father died, he left the bulk of his small fortune to my brothers. For me, there was just enough money to travel here to my aunt and uncle."

"That's particularly harsh, not to provide for a daughter."

"My father loved me, but always said fortune would favor me," Athenais tried to keep the defensiveness out of her voice. *I was lucky to have a loving father. From all accounts, the Augusta had a lonely and harrowing childhood.*

"Impoverished sons can go into the civil service or the army. They have the means to make their way in the world. Leaving a daughter without a dowry for a good marriage condemns her to the charity of others. Have your brothers been generous?"

"Enough to provide for my upkeep. Little more." Athenais said. "They have new families of their own to provide for and give what they can. My mother's brother is a most generous man and treats me like a daughter. His wife has been a comfort to me."

Pulcheria's eyes narrowed. "Have you considered holy orders? Many women find it a satisfactory alternative to marriage—even want and poverty."

So that's her game! Athenais felt the angry heat flood her cheeks. "I've only recently embraced Christ as my savior. The idea of becoming a holy woman did not occur to me." She took a sip of her water as if thinking, then said. "The whole city knows of your devotion, Augusta. Have *you* considered taking holy orders?"

Pulcheria nearly choked on her juice. "I have had more secular concerns to occupy my talents. If I took holy orders, I would be under the command of the bishop. That's not appropriate for Regent or Augusta."

"I see." Athenais nodded. "You are Regent no longer, but still Augusta. Please forgive me. I am new to these ways." Tired of the verbal jousting, she put her goblet down to look Pulcheria in the eyes. "Augusta, I know this match is not of your choosing. I met Theo… the emperor…"

"You may call him Theo in my presence."

"I met Theo purely by accident. Paulinus brought him to a salon at my uncle's. We talked and laughed. He treated me with great kindness. When I told him my story, he said he would rectify my father's error. I thought he intended to provide more money to my uncle for my upkeep. I had no idea he intended marriage."

"If you find the match offensive or not suitable, you can refuse." Pulcheria's voice held a hint of satisfaction.

Does she believe I am being coerced? Does she think I'll withdraw so readily? Athenais laughed. "Maybe if he had proposed a sinful alliance, but Theo would never do that. He is honorable and kind. I have grown to love him and wish this match to be successful." She dropped her smile and remembering Paulinus' advice said, "But I know it will not be if we do not have your blessing. Theo loves you so much and respects your opinion. He would be terribly unhappy in a home where his two great loves warred."

"I would not let that happen." Pulcheria's voice sharpened "Theo and the empire are my first concerns. My key objection is with your newness to the Christian faith."

As Paulinus warned, I must tread carefully here. "Bishop Atticus himself has tutored and baptized me. If you have doubts, please consult him about the profoundness of my devotion to the Christian teachings. He said you two had a most cordial and trusting relationship."

"Yes, he helped me when I was most in need—in that case to thwart a marriage, not to facilitate one." Something in Pulcheria's face shifted and her eyes sparkled at the memory of her triumph.

"Theo told me that story! You and your sisters pledged your virginity to Christ and your brother's reign, preventing the regent from marrying you off and gaining the enormous favor of the church and the people of Constantinople in the bargain. A brilliant move."

"I am fully committed to the church. That wasn't a gambit." Pulcheria's voice hardened. "Nor was it a ploy to preserve our independence. I needed to protect Theo. There had already been one attempt on his life. I refused to bring another man into our home who might have challenged Theo for the diadem or arranged for a convenient 'accident.' We can trust no one fully except family."

Athenais answered softly. "Forgive me, I did not mean to make light of your sacrifice for your brother and your people. Bishop Atticus speaks most highly of you and your Christian acts of charity. I hope to gain an equally high regard from you and the good bishop."

"An admirable goal, my dear." She put a hand on Athenais' arm.

"Thank you, Augusta." Athenais bowed in her chair. "You do me too much honor."

"Until such time as I give you permission to address me as 'Sister' you may call me Pulcheria in private."

"I have never had a sister." Athenais said with honest wistfulness. "It's a bit overwhelming, but I look forward to having three. I'm sure we'll be close. Aren't we all near in age? Arcadia is but a year or two older and Marina a year younger, I believe."

"They are pledged virgins, as am I. I doubt we'll have much in common."

Athenais ignored the coldness in her prospective sister-in-law's attitude and said in a mild voice, "I am new to your faith, but look forward to learning from you and your sisters. If you give the marriage your blessing, I will be joining in your daily observances and hope to emulate your charitable works."

"As any wife should." Pulcheria nodded.

Athenais stifled a sigh and continued with her final argument, "I realize you consider me a disruption to your family, but I am a needful one if the dynasty is to continue. I assure you, Pulcheria, that I love your brother and want to protect him as much as you do. An heir will help bolster his position and my love will give him comfort and surcease from his daily responsibilities. I know you want that for Theo."

"Of course." Pulcheria's eyes softened." Now, tell me what you have studied in your catechism, so I may correct any errors in your understanding."

After nearly an hour of grilling on scripture, Pulcheria gave her a chilly smile. "Bishop Atticus was an apt tutor and you a good student. I have no important objections, my dear. If Theo is happy with you, I am content."

"Thank you, Pulcheria. I look forward to the day I can address you as 'Sister.'"

"Yes. I will consult with Theo on an appropriate wedding date and make all the arrangements." She gave a weary glance at a waiting pile of papers on her work desk and sighed. "You may go."

"As you will, Pulcheria." Athenais rose and gave her prospective sister a brief bow before exiting the room. A sense of rising elation pushed out the twittering anxiety. *I passed the test! Theo and I will be wed! Thank you dear Paulinus for all your support and advice. I must arrange a suitable gift for my friend. New riding boots or a book?*

Chapter 13

Imperial Palace, Constantinople, June 421

M*Y WEDDING NIGHT... AND I LOOK SO TIRED!* ATHENAIS OBSERVED herself in the full-length silver mirror while a gaggle of giggling servant girls prepared her bed. *Not surprising after the day I've had. At least the private religious ceremony was brief and the signing of the marriage contracts took only moments after weeks of negotiations between the palace and Uncle. But the afternoon at the hippodrome and evening banquet! I have never met so many people. How am I to keep them all in mind? I'm exhausted.*

Tomorrow. I'll think about that tomorrow.

She turned to inspect her personal bedroom decorated in her favorite colors: blues and greens. An overhead oil lamp chandelier shed soft light on the spacious room. Lavender-scented incense provided a much-needed calming note to the air. *Exhausted, but nervous still.* Her eyes moved to the huge bed that dominated the space with embroidered silk covers and feather pillows and she blushed. A cosmetics table with a smaller silver mirror sat on one wall opposite a tall wardrobe containing more robes than she could possibly wear in a month. An elaborate trunk, inlaid with exotic woods in a geometric pattern, contained a wealth of silk and linen tunics, veils and other sundries for her wardrobe.

She had passed through her workroom before entering this room and noticed a desk, complete with all writing necessities. *I see Theo's hand in this. As a fellow scribbler, he would know just what I need. Speaking of my husband...* a full body blush spread warmth from her face to her toes. Anticipation mitigated her fatigue.

She turned to the servants. "Attend me. I must be ready for my husband."

The girls shot each other sly glances. Two came forward to take off her jewelry: imperial purple amethysts adorning her neck, wrists, and ears. She had already shed her gold embroidered purple cloak closed with a huge amethyst set in a gold starburst fibula. The servants wrapped each piece in silk and stored them in a casket of chased silver decorated with a scene of Diana hunting in the forest. *How did this pagan scene get past Pulcheria's eyes?*

Two more servants removed her white silk stola embroidered all over with stiff gold thread. *I'm glad to get out of that. It's beautiful, but I've never worn anything more uncomfortable.* A third servant stripped her of her sweaty undertunic, sponged her down with rosewater and dressed her in a plain blue silk robe that was almost transparent.

"Domina?" the final servant indicated a chair at the cosmetics table. Athenais sat, eyes closed as the woman unwound the strings of pearls and amethysts from her hair and removed the false braids and curls. "You have beautiful hair," the young woman murmured, gently combing out her tresses to lay in waves down her back. "It will be a pleasure caring for it."

"Do you tend the Augusta and the princesses, as well?" Athenais opened her eyes to look at the young woman in the mirror.

"No, Domina. The Augusta and her sisters wear their hair short under their holy women's veils. I have nothing to do but tend their wigs for formal occasions."

A secession of female chatter and movement in the mirror caught Athenais' attention. Theo stood in the doorway. He hesitated and turned slightly, as if to leave.

"Theo?" Athenais turned to him and put all her love into her voice. "Beloved, I've been waiting for you." She waved to her servants. "You are dismissed." They streamed out leaving her alone with her husband. *Husband. Am I ready for this? Is he?*

They had had little time together these past months. Thankfully, Doria had provided graphic descriptions of what happened between a man and woman and counseled her on how to pleasure a man and herself. She only hoped Theo had some prior experience or that Paulinus had provided him with a similar education. *He must lead. I don't want my husband to think I'm a wanton.*

Theo held out his hand to his wife. "Pray with me?"

She felt her eyebrows go up and ducked her head. "Of course, Husband."

They knelt at the private altar nestled in a niche appropriately decorated with a painted image the Virgin Mary and her babe and recited the Lord's prayer. Theo lapsed into silence, eyes closed, lips moving. Athenais peeked at him with a side glance. He was a handsome man if slight of stature. He smelled musky. Her breasts tingled and groin throbbed. *Is this the feeling Doria described?* He rose, took her hand, and led her to the bed.

"Do you wish me to undress you, Husband?"

"No! I... uh... I'll do it myself." He snuffed all lights but one candle, doffed his loincloth and outer robes, leaving only a short linen tunic to cover his nakedness. Athenais slipped into bed wearing only her silk shift.

Theo pulled back the covers and crawled into the bed beside her. He lay still, breathing shallowly.

Is he tired? Scared? Better to postpone than have a disaster. Athenais put a hand on his arm. "We do not have to do our duty tonight, my love, if you don't wish it. We can hold each other and sleep. It's been a long and wearing day for us both."

He rolled over, his face in darkness and said in a low, trembling voice, "I dreamed of this night and dreaded it both. I come to this marriage as virginal as you."

"That is a great gift to offer God and each other." Athenais stroked his shoulder. "Take me into your arms and hold me close."

Theo pulled her to his chest and sniffed her hair. He suddenly spasmed, crying out, "Oh, God!" as he released his seed.

Athenais lay still against him. She felt a sticky wetness soaking through her tunic. He pushed her away, mumbling, "I'm sorry," and fled to a washstand.

Athenais, shocked, lay quietly in the bed. The damp spot on her shift cooled and stiffened. *What am I to do? How can I help him?*

Stifled sobs from the dark corner tugged at her heart. *Poor Theo!* He was more lost than she.

"Theo, Beloved? Come back to the bed." She heard nothing for several moments. "Please, Husband, I need you."

Athenais heard a rustling sound as he pulled his soiled tunic over his head and came back to her. He crawled under the covers, huddling naked on the edge of the bed.

She stroked his back. "Dearest. There is nothing to be ashamed of. I've heard this sometimes happens to men. You will grow again, and we can do our duty."

He shuddered under her touch. She took her hand away.

Eventually his breathing evened and deepened. Athenais sought her side of the bed. *What did I do? What did I not do? How can I fix this?* Eventually, she fell asleep, face scrunched in worry.

Athenais woke just before dawn to hear Theo praying at the altar. She peeked at his bowed form, dressed in a coarse woolen robe, which must have itched and abraded his skin. He left shortly after.

She went to her cosmetics table and sought a small knife used to pare her nails. With a sigh, Athenais cut her thumb and let several drops stain the linen sheets. Doria had warned her that she needed to bleed on her wedding night. If she didn't, gossips would say she wasn't a virgin, casting doubt on any children she had.

"Aunt Doria, I need you," she muttered to herself, half sobbing.

"Domina?" The young hairdresser from last night peeked in from the doorway. "Do you require assistance? It's almost time for matins and the Augusta asks for your attendance at prayers."

"Yes. Please assist me." Athenais wiped her eyes and stood. The young woman entered with eyes downcast. "What's your name?"

"I am called Dorothea, Domina." The servant gave her a brief curtsy.

"Will you be my personal servant?"

"Me and a few others, Domina. The Augusta assigned us to you, but you can dismiss us, if we do not satisfy you." The girl gave her a tentative smile.

"I have no intention of doing that, Dorothea." She sighed. "I forgot about the family praying so many times a day." *I don't even get a bath after my wedding night. Maybe I can sneak one in between matins and prime.*

After a quick wash and change into a modest robe and veil, Dorothea led her to the family chapel in the Daphne, the oldest part of the palace. Theo, flanked by his sisters, knelt before a lovely altar, holding a magnificent gold cross studded with gems and gold candlesticks. Scenes from the lives of the Virgin Mary adorned the walls. Athenais slipped in beside Marina as they recited the Lord's Prayer before finishing with a final three psalms.

As they rose, her stomach gave an audible rumble, which prompted a sharp look from Pulcheria and a quickly suppressed grin from Marina. When Pulcheria's back was turned, Marina slipped her a date rolled in crushed almonds and indicated silence with a finger to her lips. *Tomorrow I'll have Dorothea bring me a slice of bread before matins!*

They exited the chapel in silence led by Theo and Pulcheria. Outside, her sister-in-law turned to her. "I expect your prompt attendance to all our prayers, Eudocia."

"Athenais."

"What?" Pulcheria seemed surprised at the correction. "Your baptismal name is Eudocia."

"Yes, and I will use that on formal occasions. But my family and friends call me Athenais, don't they, Husband?" She turned to Theo with a shy smile and pleading eyes. *Please Theo, stand up for me in this small thing.*

"Yes, my love." He looked at his younger sisters, avoiding Pulcheria's sulphureous gaze. "It is my wish that you call my wife Athenais in private."

"Theo, come we have business to attend to." Pulcheria linked arms with her brother. "Sisters, accompany *Athenais* to our work room and see that she makes it to prayers on time."

So, this is how it is to be. Pulcheria wishes me to disappear into her flock of chaste women while she dominates Theo. I will have my work cut out for me if my husband is to stand on his own.

Chapter 14

"SO, HOW GOES MARRIED LIFE, MY FRIEND?" PAULINUS HOPED HIS VOICE SOUNDED hearty and not despairing. He slapped Theo on the back as they walked from the exercise yard to the baths. For five days after the wedding, he had stayed at his estate outside the city, finding it too painful to haunt the palace with Athenais in it. Theo had ordered him back saying he missed his company.

"I don't want to talk about it." Theo turned apple red.

"What? Is there a problem?" Paulinus stopped with a hand on Theo's arm. "You can tell me. We've shared everything since we were boys." He grinned. "Pulcheria still doesn't know the true story about that scar on your knee, does she?"

"No." Theo turned a pained face to him. "But this is different."

"How so?"

When Theo refused to answer and glanced significantly at their entourage of servants, Paulinus nodded. "Let's get you to the baths. A massage and hot steam will make you feel better."

An hour later, alone in the steam room, Paulinus tried again. "No ears to hear but mine, Theo. What's going wrong? Is there a problem with Athenais?" His heart skipped a beat at the thought that she might be suffering in some way.

"No, my wife is perfect." Theo turned his face away. "It's me. I'm consumed with evil lust whenever I'm around her and I—" Theo hung his head, hands drooping over his knees. "—I spill my seed too soon."

"You haven't consummated the marriage?" Alarm added urgency to his voice. *I should have anticipated this. I knew Theo was devout, but thought he would be more natural with such a beauty as Athenais.*

"Once, two nights ago, but she shuddered in agony and bit her lips so as not to cry out." Theo looked up at him with a haggard face. "I will not cause her such pain again. I cannot even look at her without shame for my actions."

"The sentiment is laudable, Theo but, living around a gaggle of chaste women, you are somewhat ignorant of the female body. It is not unusual for a virgin to feel some discomfort the first time she couples." He paused for thought. "Remember the first time you rode a horse?"

"What does that have to do with it?"

"You were sore afterwards, weren't you? You had aches and pains in strange places. When we engage in a new physical activity, whether it's riding, swordplay, or coupling, we feel discomfort which goes away with repeated action." Paulinus reached out to his friend. "I guarantee you that Athenais' pain will pass swiftly and—with gentleness—you two can do your duty and enjoy pleasure."

"But that's the other problem. I shouldn't feel pleasure. Lust is a sin." Theo's face set in a stubborn look.

"I don't agree, but maybe you should talk to a priest."

"Father Marcus taught me that spilling my seed and experiencing lust is a sin. There's no need to consult anyone else. I'm a sinner in God's eyes and doomed to hell."

"I'm sure we can find a solution, Theo. Let's clean up. You stink from our workout. You have petitioners this afternoon and Pulcheria will make you even more miserable than you are now, if you're late." *And I need to see Athenais. We must fix this fast.*

PAULINUS ACCOMPANIED THEO TO SUNSET PRAYERS THAT EVENING LOOKING FOR a quiet word with Athenais—something nearly impossible in the palace. Even the hallways of the private family areas were lined with guards and servants that moved to the walls and looked down as the imperial family passed.

As they left the chapel, Theo gave his wife a guilty look and turned to him, "Dinner in my quarters, Paulinus?"

"I have a message for Athenais from her aunt and will be with your shortly, if you give me permission to speak to your wife."

"Of course, I'll see you soon." Theo fled down the hall toward his suite of rooms.

Pulcheria's gaze followed her brother, small frown lines appearing between her brows.

Paulinus shook his head. *Does she know the agony Theo is in? Does she care?*

Pulcheria shooed her sisters ahead of her and turned back to snap, "Don't dawdle, Athenais. We eat with or without you."

Athenais linked arms with Paulinus and said in a low voice, "Thank the Good Lord. I haven't seen a friendly face in days. Well, except for the first day when Marina gave me a sweet to tide me over to noon meal. I'm sure Pulcheria put an end to any sisterly feelings she might have had for me, because that hasn't been repeated."

Paulinus was appalled at Athenais' appearance. She was thinner and dark shadows ringed her eyes. Even her golden curls looked limp and lifeless. He patted her hand. "Theo has told me something of his troubles."

A deep blush stained her cheeks and when she looked up tears welled in her eyes. "I'm so miserable, Paulinus! I rarely see Theo and then he barely looks at me. Pulcheria orders my life from dawn prayers to midnight prayers. I barely get any sleep and not enough to eat. I've resorted to having the servants smuggle me apples and bread—which I'm sure Pulcheria will put a stop to when she hears of it. And she will. She knows everything that goes on in the palace."

Pulcheria's voice echoed down the hall, "Eudocia Athenais, attend me!"

Athenais dropped his arm and pleaded, "Help me, Paulinus. Talk to Theo. Have Aunt Doria call on me. I don't know how much more of this I can take before I leave Theo and cause a scandal."

"Stay the course, Athenais. We'll get this sorted out." As she turned to leave, he saw her swallow her tears and lift her head. *Good, she isn't completely broken. If she were, I don't know how I could live with myself.*

The next day, Paulinus waited, pacing outside the women's workroom, to escort Doria from the palace. Priests and monks were the only men allowed to mingle with Pulcheria' retinue of women. *This is torture being so close but not allowed to see for myself how my love is doing.*

When Doria emerged, he looked over her shoulder, but couldn't catch a glimpse of Athenais.

"Come Paulinus, show me the way out of this maze. I don't know how anyone finds their way around here."

She linked arms with him, and they strolled down the hall talking of inconsequential things until they were heading home in her litter.

She leaned back and sighed. "Things are as bad as you suspected, Paulinus. I thought I was sending my niece to a life of luxury and power; that her position would give her freedom. She is practically enslaved, answering the whims of the Augusta. Her husband can't—or won't stand up for her."

"I feel I'm to blame for this. I thought Theo would treat her like a goddess, but I forgot for him there is only one God. He is convinced his feelings of affection and desire are sinful. I've tried talking to him, but I don't think any secular person can shake his religious beliefs. What can we do?"

"I've been giving that some thought, my young friend." Doria reached over to pat his knee. "Athenais suggested that Bishop Atticus might be the key. She studied with him while preparing for her baptism and feels he could help. He's a confidant of both the Augustus and Augusta and they respect his religious views. Could you approach him and ask his help in setting our young emperor on the right path? Not only for Theo and Athenais' sake, but for the good of the empire. We can't have an heir within a chaste marriage."

"I'll make an appointment to see the good bishop tomorrow." He looked out the window to give himself a chance to order his feelings. "How do you feel Athenais is faring? Will she be able to hold out until we get Theo on the right path? I hate the idea of her suffering for one minute, much less days."

"Leave Athenais to me. I'll be visiting every day, even if I must knit socks for all the poor in Constantinople. Athenais is stronger than you think. Don't let her beauty fool you into thinking she is fragile. Even with some preparation, she was taken aback by Pulcheria's grip on Theo and the sisters. She won't settle for such a life for herself and already plans some improvements. But—" she wagged a finger at him. "—she can't do it alone. You whisper in Theo's ear about other ways he can make his new bride happy like promoting her uncle and giving her brothers' positions closer to home. If we can increase the family, we can dilute the control Pulcheria has over it."

"Thank you, Doria." He took her hand. "When you see Athenais, tell her I—" he hesitated to choose his words carefully. "—tell her I will make this right. That she will have her dreams."

Chapter 15

THEODOSIUS, SECOND OF THAT NAME, EMPEROR OF EASTERN ROME since he was seven years old, slumped in the Bishop of Constantinople's receiving room with lowered eyes and a nervously tapping foot. His sister's voice from their early years of comportment training echoed in his ears, '*Theo, straighten your shoulders, raise your head. You are Augustus. Act like it or no one will respect you.*' He tried to follow his absent sister's advice and looked up to see the good bishop's encouraging smile.

"Welcome, my son. I understand you have some concerns about the sins of the flesh to discuss with me."

"Yes, Father." He took a deep breath and launched into an embarrassed description of his marital congress with a growing sense of despair. Theo stuttered to a halt and slumped again in his seat. *Will the bishop find me a wanton sinner? Will he recoil from my evil?*

He felt Atticus put his hands on his bowed head. The bishop sighed. "My son, lying with your lawful wife for the purposes of conceiving a child is not a sin in the eyes of the Lord. On the contrary, he orders us to be fruitful and multiply."

"I understand that part, Father. It's the lust I feel for my wife that twists my soul. I look at her and my member swells and stiffens, my thoughts become disordered. I can't see her or touch her without that shameful feeling that I am sinning. I scourge myself by wearing a hair shirt, but that does no good."

"It is not for you to determine penance for sins, my son. God gave that power to his priests, and I see no need for atonement. You have done nothing wrong."

How can he say that? Theo raised his head and frowned. "Sometimes, I spill my seed before entering my wife. When that happened in my sleep, Father Marcus gave me verses to study and prayers to say as penance for the sin."

"Then you were a child. Now you are a married man. Do you do this with your wife to avoid conceiving a child? *That* would be a sin."

"No!" Theo felt the blood rise in his face. "I just… uh… lose control. I love her so much and want her so badly…" His voice trailed off as the thought of Athenais in her silk tunic resulted in an embarrassing engorgement. *Not here! Not in front of the holy bishop! More proof of my lack of control and sinful urges.* He dug his nails into his palms and gave thanks for his voluminous covering robes.

The bishop continued, "You are not a priest, Theodosius. God does not require you to live chastely."

"But chaste living is accounted a great gift to God. That is why the desert fathers and mothers, priests, and bishops choose celibacy. That is why my sisters remain virgins."

"The key word is 'choice,' my son. Not all priests or bishops choose that life. Synesius of Ptolemais was not alone in keeping his beloved wife as a condition of accepting his bishopric. And, yes, Melania the Younger and her husband lived in a chaste marriage, but it was agreed to by both parties after several years of marriage, not required by God. As to your sisters, there was more than a religious urgency to their choices."

Puzzled, Theo asked, "What other urgency?"

"That is for you and your sisters to discuss. But this is just as, if not more, important. Listen closely, Theodosius." Atticus leaned forward to take both his hands and looked directly into his eyes. "You are the Emperor of Rome. You have a duty to your people to cherish your wife, create a family, and raise an heir. You are a man with a lawful wife and *have the right to feel attracted to her*—but no other! Your soul is in no danger, and you need no absolution. As to the … uh… loss of control, that should moderate in time. If it doesn't, consult a physician, not a priest."

Theo retrieved his hands and sat back. "My feelings are sanctioned by God? I can desire my wife?" He raised his head smiling with hope. "I am not a sinner?"

"You have not committed fornication. If you need them, I can provide the gospel verses, but be at ease. Your attraction to your wife is natural, to be expected, and not in any way sinful." Atticus shook his head. "Go home to Athenais, son. May God bless you and your consort with many healthy children."

"Thank you, Father!" Theo sobbed, tears running down his face. "You have lightened my soul."

That night after evening prayers, for the first time, Theo linked arms with Athenais as he left the chapel with her instead of Pulcheria. At his sister's frown, he said. "I've arranged to dine with my wife this evening in her chambers. Good night sisters. We'll meet you for midnight prayers."

Obviously dismissed, Pulcheria gave them a stiff nod and headed down the corridor with Arcadia and Marina in tow. Marina looked over her shoulder as they left and gave him a sly smile. *Ever the one for a joke. I often wonder if Marina is happy in her chaste life. She seems more suited for the secular world. The bishop said my sisters made a choice to live as pledged virgins. I know Pulcheria chose, but did Arcadia and Marina? Or did Pulcheria choose for them?* He shook his head. *That's a discussion for another day. Tonight is a new start to our marriage.*

He smiled at his wife. "Shall we, my dear?"

She looked up at him with her brilliant blue eyes and an arched a brow. "Of course, my love."

When they entered her suite, he noticed she had already made some changes. The empty niches were filled with vases of flowers and statues. Several shelves filled with books stood over a large inlaid work desk, strewn with ink-covered pages. He dropped her arm, headed over to the desk, hand out to snatch a page. "What are you working on?"

She slipped ahead of him, shielding the pages with her body. "It's a surprise for you, my love. Please don't look. It's not ready." A becoming pink blush stained her cheeks.

He put his offending hand behind his back and leaned in to whisper. "Whatever you wish, Athenais. I can wait." He glanced again at the desk as they went through the door to her private dining room. "But try not to make me wait too long."

"Oh, Theo! Did you arrange all this?" Her eyes swept over an intimate table set for two with gold plate and crystal goblets. Flickering candles added an illusion of life to the garden scene frescoed on the walls. A male servant stood at attention next to a sideboard loaded with covered dishes exuding the enticing smell of roasted lamb with cardamom and the fresh scent of vinegared greens.

"Do you approve? Paulinus suggested you might like a more substantial evening meal, not being used to fasting on Wednesday and Friday." He grinned.

"It's lovely! I've so longed for a quiet meal where we could talk." She gave him a sad smile. "I feel we lost touch with one another in the preparation for the marriage and my settling in. I've hardly seen you alone for months. I worried that I had done something wrong."

"Never, my love." He gathered her to his chest in a tight hug and said into her hair, "I'm the one at fault, but that's past us now. I love you my darling and want you to be happy and fat. You've grown too slender lately."

"Pulcheria doesn't set the most elaborate table for our family gatherings."

He laughed. "No, she doesn't. I don't think she's had a spiced dish or goblet of wine for years." He guided her to her seat. "So, let's take advantage."

When seated, Theo turned to his beautiful bride with sparkling eyes. "I have news that I think will please you."

"What news?" Athenais leaned forward expectantly. When he didn't reply immediately, she admonished him, "Don't be a tease, Husband."

"Your brother Gesius will be leaving his post in Illyricum and returning to court. I promoted your uncle Asclepiodotus to *comes sacrarum largitionum*—head of the office that collects taxes. Gesius will assist him in supervising the mints and paying the civil servants and troops."

"What a wonderful surprise! Thank you, Husband." Athenais reached across the table to clasp his hand. "I love having my family close. It was hard when my brothers left Athens for Constantinople, then left the city for the provinces."

She let go and settled into her seat with a satisfied smile. The eunuch poured them wine and served the first course of eels pickled in garum sauce. "So, my love, how goes the war in Persia?"

"Not well, I'm afraid." He frowned. "But that is not proper talk for this dinner. Tell me what you are reading now."

They spent the rest of the meal talking of inconsequential things. As the last course was served, Athenais nibbled the honeyed pears.

"Not to your liking, my love? I can have something else brought in." Theo frowned in concern. She had eaten sparingly of the lavish meal, sampling each dish, but not finishing the plate.

"It's all delicious, Theo." She sipped her sweet wine. "I'm afraid my appetite has lessened over the past two weeks. Besides sleeping on a full stomach gives me nightmares."

"Oh, my sweet. What could possibly give you bad dreams?"

"I dream of loss. Losing my mother and father. Losing your love." The candles sparkled on the tears glistening in her eyes.

"Never, my love." He turned to the servant, "You may leave. You can clear the room tomorrow."

"Come, Athenais. Let's go to bed." That brought an eager smile to her face. *Paulinus was right. She doesn't fear the pain. Maybe it wasn't as bad as I thought.*

With Paulinus' advice in his ears and Bishop Atticus' blessing lightening his soul, Theo followed his wife to her bed with a sense of confidence and excitement he hadn't felt in weeks.

Athenais cuddled on Theo's shoulder stroking his nearly hairless chest as he half dozed. *At last. Thank you, Aunt!*

Doria had visited each afternoon and joined her in the women's work room to sew altar cloths and knit socks for the poor with the two younger princesses and Pulcheria's retinue, while the Augusta attended to court business. She and her aunt had become quite adept at murmuring to each other under the drone of the priest reading gospel verses. Her aunt's visits had become a moment of sunshine in an otherwise dull existence.

"I think Paulinus has taken care of our problem." Doria had glanced over her shoulder at Arcadia. "Bishop Atticus has given his blessing and Paulinus is advising your husband on the finer art of satisfying a woman."

"I want more than a physical relationship, Aunt." She sighed. "I need him to love me and trust me. I want him to stand up to Pulcheria and be the emperor I know he can be."

"You *have* his love. The emperor is besotted with you. As to Pulcheria?" Her aunt shrugged. "All in good time, my dear. Once you give birth to an heir, you can ask for the moon. For now, you might start by attending your husband's audiences. You shouldn't be hidden away from the court. You need to be seen and make allies among the nobles. Start with small requests to make your life more comfortable."

"If I ever see my husband outside the chapel, I will."

Doria gave her a brief smile. "Be ready for a surprise tonight."

"What is it?" Athenais leaned forward. "It's been so long since anything pleasant has happened."

"If I told you, it wouldn't be a surprise." Her aunt stifled a laugh. "Just remember a man is most generous after coupling."

You were right, Aunt.

A brief snore from her husband brought Athenais back to the moment. She wanted to wash, but Doria had advised that staying prone after the act increased the chance of pregnancy. Her aunt had had some trouble conceiving and passed on the lore her midwife had provided that resulted in her only child, a daughter.

"Are you alright?" Theo roused to ask. "I didn't hurt you, did I?"

"No, my love. I'm quite happy." She pulled his face around for a deep kiss and felt his member stiffen against her belly. "Would you like to go again?"

He gave her a brief hug, then sat up. "I would, but we must clean up and go to midnight prayers."

"Must we?" She sat up and leaned against his shoulder, stroking his arm. "Most households hold private prayers only three times during daylight hours. Only holy men and women interrupt their sleep to pray at night."

"I *am* a holy man. God chose me to be emperor and his representative on earth. Bishop Atticus anointed me in His name." He put his arm around her shoulders and kissed her hair. "We are not most households, my love. We are the imperial family and must set an example—even if it is one most others don't follow."

"I understand, Husband." She lay quietly for a moment. "May I ask a favor?"

"Anything, my love."

"I wish to attend the court and sit at your side."

He frowned. "The court is quite dull. Wouldn't you prefer the company of Pulcheria's ladies?"

She laughed. "Have you sat for hours with silent women sewing and knitting? They do good work, but I feel I could do so much more. If you let me attend court, I could listen to petitions, speak on your behalf to the nobles, advise you. I could be an extra set of eyes and ears for you, Husband. Besides, don't you want to show me off? How will the people ever get to know me, if I spend my days hidden away in the palace?"

"Pulcheria is my chief advisor, and I don't intend to replace her." He pursed his lips in thought. "But I take your point about being seen. It would be good for the people to see a harmonious imperial family, as well as an observant one."

"Thank you, Husband!" She gave him a swift kiss. "Now we should prepare for midnight prayers." *All in good time as Aunt Doria counseled. Uncle is promoted, Gesius is coming home to an important post, and I can attend court. Pulcheria can wait for another day.*

Chapter 16

September 421

Athenais covered a yawn as Dorothea combed out her hair. She had been feeling increasingly fatigued the last several weeks, but Aunt Doria told her that was natural, and she would get her energy back in a month or two. Athenais had been disappointed when she got her courses the first and second months after the wedding, but the third month proved more fruitful.

"Domina, do you wish anything else of me?" The girl put away the combs and tidied up the cosmetics table. "Will I sleep in your room tonight?"

"No, Dorothea, I expect the Augustus after his meal with his sisters." Athenais had continued to join the family meals in Pulcheria's quarters for a few weeks after reconciling with Theo, but finally rebelled at the monastic atmosphere and fare. She decided to take her meals in her own quarters and asked Theo to join her. Her husband decided to split his evening meals between his wife and his sisters, but always sought her bed afterward, negating the need for a servant to sleep at the foot of her bed—a practice she had found discomforting from the first, but was considered palace protocol and couldn't be avoided.

Athenais took to her bed and read until falling asleep.

"My love."

Athenais came out of a deep sleep and yawned. Theo gently shook her shoulder.

"Yes?" She looked up at him blinking and trying to clear her sleepy mind. A bone-deep fatigue gripped her.

"It's almost time for midnight prayers, my sweet. You should dress."

"I can't." She turned murmuring into her pillow.

"Are you ill? Should I call a physician?" Theo turned and shouted through the door, "Dorothea! Bring a physician, quick!"

"No!" The alarm in her husband's voice cut through her brain fog and she sat up, gripping his arm. "I'm not ill, my love. I'm with child." She saw her servant peeking through the doorway and shook her head. "No need for a physician, Dorothea. You may shut the door."

"You're with child?" A brilliant smile replaced the worry on his face. "This is great news." He wrapped her in a strong hug, then pushed her away at arm's length. "That didn't harm the baby, did it?"

"No, Theo." Athenais laughed. "Until it quickens, the baby is too small to be hurt by a hug. However, Aunt Doria did give me strict instructions to do as my body dictates in these early months. When I'm tired, I should rest. When I'm hungry I should eat for the sake of the growing child. Tonight, I am very tired and will not attend midnight prayers. Will you stay with me?"

"No, my love. I'll not disturb you, but will give the good news to my sisters at prayer."

Disappointed, Athenais looked up at him. "Will you keep this a secret for a few more weeks? Aunt Doria says this is a dangerous time for the baby and half don't make it past the first few months. She had several miscarriages early in pregnancy. I don't want anyone to know until we have a good chance of keeping this child."

"Of course, my love." His eyes went wide, and he pulled her to his chest with strong arms. "My mother died of a miscarriage. We will do all that is possible to safeguard your health and the baby's."

She pushed out of his suffocating hug. "I'm so sorry, Theo. I forgot about your mother's tragic death. How old were you?"

"Only three. Nana told us that she visited the nursery once a week, but I have no memories of my mother, except her scent. Her hair always smelled of lavender."

"My mother kept us close. I intend to do the same." Athenais smiled at the memories of her mother sitting on the floor, rolling a ball to her, telling her stories of animals and their foibles at bedtime, and combing her hair in the morning. *I lost you too soon, Mother, but I'll tell my baby of the grandmother he never got to meet.*

"The nursery was such a lively place with us four and later Paulinus and a few other boys Anthemius brought in to keep me company. Pulcheria always seemed exasperated with us. Even at such a young age, she took control." His eyes got a faraway look. "We've got to get the nursery ready. And Nana! I'm sure she will come out of retirement. When will our son arrive?"

"Next spring, April, if all goes well. But, Theo," she put a hand on his chest, "I don't want a nurse to care for our children. I want to do it myself." *And I certainly don't want Pulcheria or anyone she appoints raising my child!*

He chuckled and pulled her closer again. "I'm sure you and Nana will work everything out. We were a handful. If we have a large family, you'll probably be grateful to have someone care for them day to day while you deal with more important things."

"What more important things? All I do now is pray, sew, and look pretty by your side at the occasional audience."

"Patience, my love." He stroked her hair. "When we have an heir, I'll make you Augusta and you can have your own retinue of women and money to do with as you please. I'll make sure of it." He kissed her forehead. "Now rest. I'll make your excuses to our sisters."

She nodded, rolled over and was back asleep before her husband crept from the room.

Athenais woke late in the morning refreshed, but disappointed. Theo had not come back to her bed after prayers. She stretched and laughed aloud. *What a difference a solid night's sleep makes! I'm going to ask Theo to allow me to skip midnight and dawn prayers for now.*

She spied her servant, who after all, had slept on a mat at the foot of her bed. "I'm sorry, Dorothea, you didn't have to stay the night."

"But I do, Domina! You should never be left unattended." The girl's eyes twinkled, and a shy smile spread across her face. "Especially now."

"Dorothea, don't go gossiping. If I hear that the entire palace knows that I'm with child, I'll know who to dismiss."

The servant's eyes went wide. "Of course, Domina. Your secret is safe with me. But you should know that everyone in the palace watches you for signs that you bear the next emperor. If you gain or lose weight, eat too much or too little, are accounted ill, everyone counts on their fingers the date of the birth."

Athenais sighed. *The girl is right, and I won't be able to keep this secret much longer. I should attend the audience this afternoon and head off what gossip I can.*

"I'll take my breakfast in bed. Lay out my court clothes for this afternoon."

"As you wish, Domina." Dorothea scurried from the room.

That afternoon, Theo escorted Athenais to the receiving room. They proceeded down the long two-story, columned hall glinting with gilt and marble in a stately manner. *Intended to impress or intimidate the embassies to the Augusti? Possibly both.* The courtiers made low bows as they passed. He seated her on an ornate chair one step down from a dais that held two equally tall chairs for Theo and Pulcheria on his right. Today, they received petitions and rendered justice: Theo as magistrate, Pulcheria as his advisor, Athenais as observer only. She put a hand over her stomach. *But not for long. I will soon be equal in rank with my sister-in-law.*

Master of Offices Helion approached. "Augustus. Augusta. Lady Consort." He bowed. "An emissary just arrived from Honorius Augustus of the Western court. He craves an audience."

"Send him in," Theo said with a frown. He leaned toward Athenais, "The last time Uncle Honorius sent an envoy, it was an unmitigated disaster. Early in the year, Honorius elevated his sister Placidia to Augusta, her husband General Constantius to Augustus, and their son Valentinian to Caesar and heir to the West—without consulting me."

"How inconsiderate." Athenais murmured. She remembered Paulinus amusing Aunt Doria with gossip about that visit. In preparation for Athenais' marriage, Paulinus had regularly passed on information that touched on the relationships between the distant family members.

Pulcheria snapped, "It was more than 'inconsiderate.' Honorius had no right to elevate the General to co-Augustus without consulting Theo. And naming that infant his heir! We refused to recognize their elevations and sent back the commemorative statues. I understand Aunt Placidia and General Constantius were not pleased."

"Their elevations were unlawful?" Athenais knew the answer to her question, but it gave Pulcheria pleasure to school her in these things and—at this point—she wanted to keep her sister-in-law ignorant of the extent of her knowledge.

"Not unlawful—a sitting Augustus makes the laws—but Theo is the presumed heir. He should have the prerogative of naming his own colleague in the West or ruling the combined empire, if he wishes, upon our uncle's death. May the Good Lord give Honorius a long life."

Theo echoed, "May the Good Lord bless and keep our uncle."

"What of Placidia? Was he wrong in elevating his sister?" Athenais asked.

"No, my love. An Augustus can elevate a mother, sister, or wife on his own. Your time will come." Theo flashed her a secretive smile.

Private conversations echoing around the audience chamber quieted as word passed that something unusual was happening. The envoy entered and progressed down the length of the room. He was young for such an important post, dressed in an elegant dark blue tunic embroidered with silver thread at the neck and hem. His bright white senator's toga draped in perfect folds over his shoulder, his only jewelry a signet ring on his right index finger. *Smart man! He has obviously studied this court and its austere culture.*

At the foot of the dais, the herald announced, "Senator Bassus Herculanus, special envoy from the Most Noble Honorius Augustus of Ravenna brings his warmest greetings to Your Most Gracious Serenities."

"May God grant you long life and health." Herculanus bowed low and passed a scroll impressed with the western emperor's seal to the herald. The man handed it to Theo.

He broke the wax and read it with a slight frown marring his face. Theo sighed and handed the missive to Pulcheria. "It is not how I wished this to be resolved, but it takes care of one awkward situation."

She scanned the page briefly. "General Constantius is dead? Of what?" Her sister-in-law pointedly did not use the general's augustal title.

"Pleurisy, Augusta." The envoy looked sorrowfully at his boots.

"How fares our uncle, without the advice of his patrician?" Pulcheria asked.

"As best as one might expect, given this grievous loss. Placidia Augusta is providing solace." The man's eyes darted away.

Ah, did our good ambassador make a slip by calling Placidia "Augusta?" Athenais took a swift look at her husband and his sister out of the corner of her eyes. *If they are upset, they hide it well.*

"Master Helion, see that our imperial envoy has suitable quarters and hospitality," Theo ordered.

Athenais knew that not only Helion but the head of the *agents in rebus* would personally wine and dine the envoy, extracting as much information as they could about the complicated situation at the Ravenna court. *I wonder if Uncle is happy with his promotion. I should invite him to visit me soon and tell me what is happening in the empire.* She pursed her lips in thought. *No, Uncle is little better than Pulcheria, believing that I am here for breeding not ruling—which should be left to the men of the family. I feel so in the dark.* She shot an angry glance at Pulcheria. *Maybe Olympiodorus is at court. He would gladly share his thoughts on the state of the empire.*

After both men bowed and left, Pulcheria said to Theo, in a low voice, "I believe our aunt is making her move. I hope Helion can gain some knowledge of her motives."

Theo watched the two men's retreating backs. "Perhaps Placidia seeks power to expunge the stain of her infamous marriage to that barbarian king."

"More likely she seeks to protect her son and provide for his future." Athenais added silently, *as will I.*

Theo gave her a tender look; Pulcheria a speculative one.

Dorothea was right. I'll not be able to keep my secret much longer.

A week later after noon prayers, Pulcheria confronted her. "Theo told me you are frequently ill in the morning and that's why you don't attend midnight or dawn prayers. Have you consulted with the court physician?"

Athenais shot a look at her husband. He shook his head and shrugged. "There is no need, Sister."

"A midwife then?"

That didn't take long. "Just my aunt Doria. We will shortly engage a midwife."

Pulcheria surprised her with a genuine smile. "Good. I'll have the court physician make recommendations. We want only the best for you and the future heir." She turned to Arcadia and Marina. "Come sisters, we should plan a special dedication for the coming child."

All three gave her brief hugs before leaving the room. Marina's came with a light kiss on the cheek and a murmured, "Well done, Sister."

"Did you tell her?" Athenais hissed as her sisters-in-law continued down the corridor.

"No, my love. I swear!" He raised his right hand and crossed his heart with his left. "Pulcheria is astute and knows all that goes on in the palace. Your servants probably report your every move to her."

"I want that to stop! Give me sole control over my servants to keep or dismiss. I want none of Pulcheria's spies in my rooms." She crossed her arms over her chest and glared at her husband. "And I will hire my own midwife. This is *our* child, Theo, not Pulcheria's. *We* will make the decisions concerning his care and education."

"Pulcheria only wants what is best for us, Athenais. She loves us." Theo's eyes pleaded for understanding. "She has my utmost confidence."

"She is not your mother, nor mine." Athenais sighed and took his arm. "We are adults, Theo, capable of making our own decisions. Your sister has strong opinions, but they are only opinions. When she advises you on imperial policy, you decide whether to accept her advice or not. When it comes to my health, I will decide who to trust. When it comes to our child, we will make the final choice." Surprised at her own forthright ardor, she paused before asking more softly, "Are we agreed on this, my love?"

"Yes, Athenais, we are agreed. I will make it known to my sister, that you will make all decisions about your health and the birth." He patted her arm. "But she will probably recommend midwives anyway."

"That is fine, as long as she knows that I might reject them all in favor of someone who pleases me more."

"Of course, my sweet."

IT GALLED ATHENAIS THAT, IN THE END, SHE ACCEPTED A MIDWIFE FROM Pulcheria's list.

"What did you expect? That the Augusta would provide you with an ignorant healer from the slums?" Doria laughed at her when she grumbled about it. "Melia is the best in the city, Niece. She trained under a woman physician from Alexandria and attends all the noble ladies. You will be in good hands."

Chapter 17

Birthing Room, Imperial Palace, April 422

Shortly after midnight of the Ides of April, Athenais waddled around her bedroom with Doria holding one arm and Dorothea the other. Melia and two assistant midwives huddled in a corner conferring. A pain gripped her, moving from her back to the front. She gasped and stood still, panting.

"Midwife, we need you!" Doria yelled.

Melia approached and put a hand on Athenais' rippling belly. "You are doing well, Lady. The baby should be here by dawn. Keep walking, it eases the pain and helps the child descend."

"My back hurts." Athenais whispered.

"Come, Lady." Melia led Athenais to a chair. "Lean over and grab the arms while I massage your back."

Athenais sighed as Melia's skilled fingers rubbed and prodded at her back, easing the tightness. When another contraction gripped her, the pain stayed in her belly.

"I haven't felt the baby move for nearly two days." Athenais finally gave voice to a fear she had held to herself. "Is he alright?"

"Yes, Lady. Birthing is just as hard for the baby as the mother. It is not unusual for babies to go quiet for a day or two before their ordeal. I sometimes wonder if they know what is coming and conserve their strength for the birth." She shrugged. "Of course we will never know for sure."

After several hours, the pains came almost continually, and Melia moved Athenais to the birthing stool—a wide seat with a hole in the middle, through which Melia would deliver the baby. Doria went to the door and announced, "It's almost time." She returned to grip Athenais' hand and whisper, "Not long now, Sweetling."

Through a haze of pain, Athenais watched as her sisters-in-law entered and immediately kneeled at the altar niche to pray. The other ladies of Pulcheria's retinue crowded into the room to witness the birth and attest to the legitimacy of a child who would wear the imperial diadem. Their bodies produced an almost unbearable heat in the crowded room.

"I'm too hot," Athenais whimpered, sweat poring off her forehead.

Melia motioned to Dorothea. "Get a couple servants to cool your Domina."

She nodded and shortly Dorothea and two other servants provided some relief by fanning Athenais with palm fronds.

Another pain gripped her, and she screamed, startling the chaste women who had never witnessed a childbirth. Momentary laughter bubbled in her chest. *I'm sure after this, none will be tempted to stray. I might even ban Theo from my bed for a while.*

When the pain subsided, she loosened her crushing grip on her aunt's hand and turned her head to the midwife. "I'm so tired. When will this be over?"

Melia used gentle hands to explore her stomach. "The worst is over, and the baby is in a good position. Soon you will want to push. When that happens follow my voice and do as I say, as we talked about earlier."

The worst pain subsided. She took a few deep breaths and felt a renewed energy. Athenais nodded. "I'm ready." A deep need to push this child from her womb came over her. "Now!"

"PUSH!" Melia commanded.

One of the assistant midwives held the groaning Athenais from behind on the birthing stool, while the second prepared a warm bath for the baby. Athenais continued to labor for several minutes, growing weaker with each effort to push.

"Stop and breathe." Melia knelt to examine Athenais through the hole in the seat. "I see his head. Push again."

This time Athenais bore down with all her remaining strength and, with a long-sustained groan, felt the baby tear through her body.

"Well done, Lady." Melia held aloft a tiny body, smeared with blood and mucus, a pulsing blue cord still attached to its mother.

Athenais held her breath until the infant wriggled and let out a mewling howl.

"It's a girl!" Melia announced.

"A daughter!" Athenais eagerly reached for her child.

"In a moment, Lady." Melia tied off and cut the cord then handed the child to one of her assistants. "Let us clean her up. You have one more task."

Athenais watched as the woman carried her precious child to the bowl of warm water and began bathing her.

"Push again, Lady. We need to get the afterbirth."

Athenais strained and Melia caught the afterbirth in a bronze bowl. After a close examination, Melia smiled. "It's all here and there are no abnormalities. You should make a full recovery, Lady."

"Thank you, Melia." A sudden feeling of lethargy came over her. All Athenais wanted was to go to her bed and sleep. She slumped, heavy-lidded, on the birthing stool.

"You did well, child, now it's time to rest," Doria murmured in soothing tones as Athenais slumped in exhaustion. Melia's assistants helped her to stand, washed her tired body, and clothed her in a fresh shift with cloths tied between her legs to soak up the trickle of blood. Doria helped her to her bed.

"You will bleed for several more days, but no heavier than a normal month." Melia advised her. "Drink strong beef broth and eat liver to help strengthen your blood."

"My baby?" She looked toward the bath and was startled to see Pulcheria holding a swaddled bundle and looking at her child with a beatific smile. Athenais reached out her empty arms. *No, she mustn't take my daughter!*

Pulcheria saw her gesture and approached, putting the swaddled infant into her arms. "You did well, Sister. I'm sure Theo will be happy."

Tears flooded Athenais' eyes. "Thank you." She yawned.

"We'll let you rest now." Pulcheria gave a last pat to the baby's head and made shooing motions with her hands to the ladies in the room.

Athenais nodded, one hand protecting the small bundle at her side. "Tell Theo—" Her eyes had trouble staying open.

"I will." Pulcheria pulled the wool cover over Athenais as she fell into an exhausted sleep.

*****

THEO GROANED ON THE MASSAGE TABLE next TO PAULINUS' AS THE SLAVES KNEADED their shoulders. "Too much wine last night, my friend?" *Maybe I shouldn't have encouraged him to drink so much. He has always had a weak head for wine.*

Theo grimaced. "I do believe Pulcheria cursed me as she left my room last night, but I don't remember much."

"Pliny recommends two raw owl eggs for a sore head after a night of wine."

"Raw owl eggs?" Theo made a retching sound.

"I prefer cabbage leaves, myself." Paulinus grinned at his friend. "Cheer up, brother. You only get to celebrate your first-born once."

"But Pulcheria will be angry with me. She rarely partakes of wine and looks down upon those who overindulge."

"Your sister should be more understanding."

"Pulcheria is a bit rigid when it comes to comportment."

Paulinus chuckled. "She's a bit rigid when it comes to everything."

"Her actions come from a place of love. She has spent her life protecting me and the empire. Having Athenais in the palace was a big adjustment for her. One she has made willingly."

I doubt that! Paulinus thought. But Pulcheria was a sore subject with his friend, and he learned to avoid that thorny issue when he could. He turned to a safer topic. "The baptism is in two days. What will you name the child?"

"We've decided on Licinia Eudoxia."

"Licinia is a good old Roman name—'turns to the light'—and Eudoxia for your mother. Names carry meaning and sometimes influence fate."

"Athenais wanted to name her Helen Eudoxia for 'ray of sunshine' and the fact that my first gift to her was the Euripides play of that name copied in my own hand. I liked the name, but it is too Greek and would not be acceptable to the Roman nobles. We compromised on Licinia."

"What honors and gifts do you plan to bestow on the mother of your child? Athenais has proven her fertility. Isn't it time she be elevated to equal status with your sister?" *Thank God things had improved for Athenais after she became pregnant. I couldn't bear the idea of her suffering this past year as she did those first weeks.*

"All in good time my friend. Pulcheria has agreed that we should elevate Athenais after the first of the year."

"That far away?" Paulinus sighed. "Of course, my friend, that is your prerogative." *We need Athenais as an Augusta by her husband's side to signal that we're back in power, but we can work on some other fronts until that happens.* "She'll be disappointed, but perhaps you could promote her uncle. Asclepiodotus has performed well in his current position. With the Persian War winding down, we need good men to end it. Having a member of your family as prefect of the East wouldn't be a bad thing."

"I hadn't thought of that. I've been so used to having only sisters to care for, I sometimes forget that I have several male relatives now who can protect my interests at court and abroad." Theo sat up as the slave scraped the oil from his body. "I've been thinking about replacing General Anatolius in the peace talks. Do you have any recommendations?"

At last! It looks like we've softened Pulcheria's iron grip on his rule. "General Procopius would be an excellent negotiator."

"Anthemius' son-in-law? I've heard good things about him. I'll have the Master of Offices invite him to talk." Theo swung his legs down to the floor, stood, and stretched. "That's better, I feel almost human. Let's go to the cold pool for a plunge."

Paulinus shuddered. "The cold pool! Why not the steam room?"

Theo laughed, "And you call yourself a Roman?"

Paulinus slapped Theo on the shoulder. *But that's the issue, my friend. I think of myself as Hellene.*

Chapter 18

The night before her baby's baptism, Athenais lay in her bed, watching another woman suckle her child. Her full breasts throbbed, ached, and leaked through the binding cloths Melia had recommended. Noble women never suckled their own children, and it would be a scandal if she fed her baby. Pulcheria, Theo, even Doria had insisted this was the best way to raise her daughter. She didn't remember if her own mother fed her, but it didn't feel right. She clutched her chest and leaned over in pain, not only from her leaky breasts, but from her aching need to hold her baby.

"Domina, may I be of assistance?" Dorothea's soft voice broke through her misery.

"Yes. Prepare one of the hot poultices and the medicinal draught Melia recommended to dry up my milk." She lay back on her cushions, trying to stem the tears trickling from her closed eyes.

After applying the poultices and taking the draught, she drifted off to sleep vowing, *I can't win this battle, but I will win the war. No one will stop me from mothering my child.*

The next day, Theo came to visit after the service. "Athenais, my love, how are you feeling today?"

"Better. Melia says I should be able to leave my bed and walk around in a couple of days." She peeked over his shoulder. "Didn't you bring Eudoxia? I want to hold her."

"Nana took her to the nursery, where she is being fussed over by a bevy of nurses and servants."

"But not her mother!" Athenais sat up. "I want my child in my room where I can hold her when I wish."

"But my sweet, that isn't done."

"I don't care what is or isn't done. I want my baby and I want her now." She threw the covers off and swung her feet to the floor.

Startled, Theo grabbed her shoulders. "No Athenais. Don't endanger yourself. Melia said to stay in bed for a reason. What good for you to have your child but leave her motherless because you left your bed too early."

His logic struck a nerve and she lay back on her pillows. "I feel perfectly fine. Did Melia tell you something she didn't confide in me?"

"No, my love, but we should follow her advice."

Athenais felt pressure building in her chest as a wave of sadness crested into a cascade of gasping sobs.

Theo flung himself into the bed and held her while murmuring soothing nonsense into her hair.

The storm subsided into a few hiccuppy gasps. "I'm sorry Theo. I don't know what came over me." She wiped her streaming eyes and settled with a sigh into the crook of his arm. "You avoided my bed these last few months and I missed you terribly. Your sisters are always busy with the government or charity work. Now to have my baby taken from me… I feel so alone." A fresh spate of tears threatened.

"What of your Aunt Doria?" Theo hugged her close. "Doesn't she visit?"

"When she can, but her daughter and grandchildren just came in from Pannonia." Athenais said with a trace of bitterness, "I'm assuming none of my family were at the baptism since Pulcheria arranged it."

"Your brothers are on errands for me and your uncle conferring on the Persian peace talks." Theo's face colored a deep red. "I'm sorry I didn't think to invite your aunt, but it was a small gathering, just me, my sisters, Paulinus, and Bishop Atticus. I'll send for your aunt at once."

"Thank you." She put a hand on his. "But make sure she knows it is at her convenience. After all, I'm not going anywhere soon."

"Of course, my love." A sly smile crept across his face. "I have some wonderful news for you."

"What? Don't make me guess!"

"I'm promoting your brothers and Asclepiodotus. Your uncle will be consul next year."

She clapped her hands together. "That's wonderful. Aunt Doria will be so pleased."

"And this is for you." He took a silk bag tied to his belt and fished out a magnificent lapis lazuli ring set in gold and surrounded by sapphires.

"It's beautiful, Theo. I've never seen its equal." She slipped the ring on her index finger and admired it.

"That's just one part of the set. There are matching earrings, necklaces, bracelets and best of all—a diadem!" he said with a flourish and a grin.

"A diadem? I'm to be made an Augusta now? I thought Pulcheria wanted you to wait till next year."

"It is my choice and I want to elevate you now. The official papers are prepared, and an announcement will be made tomorrow. Our daughter is baptized, and you will receive the blessings of a new mother in the church in four weeks' time. You will do that as Augusta."

"Oh, Theo! I'm overwhelmed." Athenais asked shyly, "Can I have my own retinue?"

"You will have court ladies of your own as soon as you can select them, young matrons of the noble class to keep you company and reflect your status as my consort and Augusta."

She threw her arms around him. "You've made me so happy, Theo!"

Athenais lay quietly in his arms for a moment savoring these tokens of his affection, then sat up. "And I have a gift for you, Husband."

"You did all the work, my dear and I'm satisfied with your gift of a daughter. I'm sure our next child will be a boy."

"This is a gift of my mind, not my body." She gestured at her makeup table. "Look in the second drawer on the right."

Theo climbed out of bed and opened the drawer. "This?" He held up a slim package wrapped in a silk veil. "Do I recognize the covering and ribbon?"

Athenais nodded, pleased that he noticed she used the wrappings from his first gift to her.

Theo brought it back to the bed and carefully unwrapped a volume bound in brown leather with, "Heroes of the Persian War" stamped in gold on the cover. He opened and read, "To my husband, Flavius Theodosius Augustus II, from his most loving wife and consort Aelia Eudocia Athenais on his great victory in the war against the Persians." He glanced through the first couple of pages of the *encomium*.

"Lovely work, my dear. Very Homeric. I like this verse about General Procopius 'whose tactical genius proved that the Immortals could be slaughtered like any other Persian.'" A slight frown marred his plain face. "You do know that we barely fought to a draw. We will be lucky if after the peace talks we go back to our original borders."

"History is written by us, my love. The people will believe you led them to a glorious victory in a land far away from their everyday lives. I must admit Pulcheria's cunning use of victory images on coins and the adventus of St. Stephen's bones prepared them for a triumph, which you can declare once the peace talks are done. I and other literary lights will affirm their beliefs with these poems, which will be read aloud in theaters and public places."

She took the volume, paged through, and pointed. "This verse about your courage and wisdom could be put on the pedestal of the victory column that Pulcheria is planning. I understand it will go on the Field of Mars in Hebdomon where the troops muster and train?"

"Indeed, it is perfect." He folded her into his arms.

"And I can have Eudoxia in my room?" she murmured as she snuggled in his arms.

"Anything you want, my love."

"I am content with my daughter close, my words carved in stone, and your love."

Part II

Christian Consort

February 423 - August 431

Chapter 19

Imperial Palace, February 423

"Well told, my friend." Athenais laughed at Olympiodorus' story of his most recent adventures. She leaned back in her cushioned chair and smiled as her retinue of court women peppered the man with questions. *Dorrie always plays well with my women. I think I'll have that talented young kitharode to play for us tomorrow. Maybe I'll recite some of my poetry while he accompanies me.*

"Are you happy, Augusta?" Paulinus asked at her elbow.

"Oh, please! You know you can call me Athenais in private. I've known you longer than anyone at court except Dorrie." She paused and a thoughtful expression replaced her smile. "To answer your question, I am much happier." Her hand swept the room. "I've made so many changes since Eudoxia was born and Theo raised me to Augusta. It's a delight to have women—wives and mothers—of my own age for companions, but they can never be friends in the same way you and Dorrie are."

"Why's that? They seem learned and pleasant."

She raised an eyebrow—a habit she had observed Pulcheria use to devastating effect. "You of all people should know the politics of the court. You navigate it well. All these women are here to promote their families. And none would dare tell me if my poetry is poorly written. I don't want to be another Nero who everyone flatters to his face while laughing behind his back. You and Dorrie are honest with me."

"I'm sure Pulcheria would give her honest opinion. Why not seek her out?" He suggested with a teasing smile.

"Speaking of Pulcheria," she gave a heavy sigh. "She's the constant thorn in my side and the impediment to my complete happiness."

"How has she outraged you recently?"

"She stormed into my private room to accuse me of some ridiculous conspiracy to promote pagans and Jews."

"Your uncle's law declaring it illegal to harm peaceable citizens because of their religion? That went into effect two years ago. Why is it a problem now?"

She nodded. "The sticking point seems to be that the local governors are enforcing the penalties too strictly. Christians are paying large fines for their depredations and don't like it."

"We worked hard to get that law in place." Paulinus shook his head. "Years ago, Pulcheria passed a law that allowed local citizens to destroy synagogues in the desert. She was new to being regent and it was her first stumble."

"What happened?"

"Zealous Christians like Barsauma, the mad monk of Syria, took it too far and started burning synagogues in the cities and attacking Jews, pagans, and those Christians they considered heretics. Jerusalem, Antioch, Alexandria—all the great cities were in chaos for a year or more. This newer law penalizing such behavior was to protect all our Roman citizens."

"It sounds to me like the governors are at fault. Perhaps they are taking a cut of the fines and don't want to give up the extra revenue."

"That's very possible." Paulinus shrugged. "Even likely. That's one of the rewards of being a governor and has been from the time of the Republic."

"It's odd that Pulcheria ignored that possibility of controlling the situation. She could replace the corrupt men with more honest ones, but she seemed more concerned with how the Christians would judge Theo and his reign. At the time, we argued philosophy and the merits of different kinds of rulers. I suggested that an emperor should be emperor of all and respectful of their rights and religions to keep the peace."

"Let me guess." Paulinus grinned. "She argued Constantine's 'One Emperor. One Empire. One God.' That deep-seated belief has guided her since she was a child. You will never turn her from that path or stem her efforts to realize it in Theo's reign." He sat quietly for a few moments; his gaze turned inward. "I've been hearing disturbing rumors of unrest in the provinces lately, especially among the bishops. This happened within the past month?"

"Yes. I've seen little of her since and Theo hasn't mentioned any problems."

"Pulcheria is up to something. She probably feels threatened by the changes you've made and the increasing influence of your family." He looked at her with some alarm. "You need to be careful, Athenais. Pulcheria is loved among the people for her charitable work and respected by the church for her vow of chastity and her support of all things Christian in the government. She might be marshalling opposition to your uncle's law as a pretext for purging our faction from the government again. If there is a general uprising against it, all who side with Asclepiodotus might be tainted with his disgrace."

"But it's not my uncle's law, it's Theo's. He must sign all constitutions for them to be legal."

"That will be no matter, if he feels he was deceived." He gave her a sad smile. "We both know how easily your husband can be led."

"That's unfair, Paulinus. Theo is a kind-hearted man, but could be a strong leader if he can get out of Pulcheria's shadow. That's what I wish for his future."

"I hope you're right, my dear." He patted her hand out of sight of the court ladies. "Send Dorrie to me when he's done here. We have some planning to do. In the meantime, do nothing to draw Pulcheria's gaze."

"Since being elevated to Augusta, I've resumed regular prayer attendance. It pleases Theo and I find the routine meditative. I understand the religious community's devotion to it." She gave him a rueful smile. "I just wish we could skip the midnight prayers. Once Eudoxia was no longer an infant, it was restful to have her move to the nursery and give me a full night's sleep."

"Beloved?"

Athenais turned to spy Theo at the door, face drawn and eyes haunted.

Be careful! Paulinus mouthed as he rose and greeted his friend. "Theo, have you come to join the fun? Olympiodorus is most amusing today."

"No, I must speak with my wife. Now."

"Of course, my love." Athenais turned to the room of silent women and servants. "Thank you Olympiodorus for a most entertaining afternoon. Ladies, I'll see you all tomorrow."

The court trooped out murmuring greetings and bowing to Theo as they left. Paulinus drew Olympiodorus away on the other side of the door.

What gossip will spread through the palace and the city now? She hurriedly reflected on her behavior and could produce no overt reason her husband would be offended or suspicious. She and Paulinus always met in the company of others and maintained an appropriate physical distance. *What has so disturbed Theo?*

"Dorothea, get the Augustus some refreshment." The girl started toward the sideboard.

"No. I want nothing. You are all dismissed." The servants crept out a back door, shooting each other apprehensive glances. It was extremely rare for the imperial couple to be left with no servant in attendance.

When the last one left, Athenais rose to greet her husband. "Come sit, my love, and tell me what disturbs you so."

She took his hand and led him to her favorite blue silk divan. His hands shook and his breath came in ragged gasps, as if he had run a far distance. She took his face in her hands and turned it toward her. "Please, Theo, what is amiss?"

He blinked at her owlishly a couple of times, then turned away. He fumbled in the breast of his tunic, retrieved a ragged scrap of parchment, and handed it to her. "It's from Simeon the Stylite. He addresses me as Flavius Theodosius denying me the title of Augustus."

"He is an ignorant, if revered, holy man. Perhaps he doesn't know the proper address."

He pointed with a shaking hand. "Read it."

She read:

"Since your heart has grown arrogant and you have forgotten the Lord your God who gave you your diadem and the throne of empire, and since you have become friends, comrade and protector of the faithless Jew, know now that you will soon face the punishment of divine justice, you and all who share your view in this affair. You will raise your hands to heaven and woefully cry: "Truly because I have denied the Lord God has he brought this judgment upon me."

"I don't understand." She shook her head. "Is he cursing you? For what?"

"Yes, he's cursing me!" He turned haggard eyes that flared briefly with anger. "For that law protecting the Jews and punishing Christians. Your uncle misled me, he did not discuss the penalties with me and now all the bishops of the land are calling me to account. This curse is dangerous, not only in God's eyes, but the people's. I must go to church and publicly repent. Pulcheria is arranging the procession. I want you by my side, so all can see that you have nothing to do with your uncle's heresy."

"Of course, my love, we will leave as soon as we are dressed." She leaned in to give him a hug, but he pushed her away.

"I must approach The Lord with a pure and humble heart." He rose and stumbled toward the door.

"Theo," she put a hand to her own rapidly thumping heart. "What's to happen to my uncle?"

He looked back over his shoulder. "He'll be dismissed along with all who urged me to this unholy course. I'll revoke the law and send copies of the revocation to all the bishops and governors."

Poor Aunt Doria and Uncle Asclepiodotus, to be raised so high and to fall so far! There's little I can do for Uncle, but perhaps I can shield Doria from the worst of the fallout.

Paulinus is right, Pulcheria did this, stirring up the bishops and holy men. Did she understand what hell she was unleashing on her brother? The threat she posed to his sovereignty? Did she engineer this so she could swoop in and save Theo, binding him closer? She shook her head. *I will find a way to pry her malignant presence from my husband's side and restore my family's honor.*

After the evening meal, Theo lingered in her room. "Coming to bed, Husband?" She rose from her cosmetics table where she had abandoned her formal jewelry and nodded toward the welcoming bed. She had found, after their rocky start, that Theo was a gentle and generous lover. Everyone knew that a woman couldn't conceive unless she felt pleasure and her husband did his part to make sure she conceived again.

"Not tonight, my sweet."

She turned in surprise. "Why not? All's well. The people accepted your repentance with wild acclaims. Bishop Atticus praised your wisdom and promised to spread the word of your revocation among the bishops. Is it not a night to celebrate heading off a disaster?" She could feel the heat rising in her body and gave him a slow smile.

He shook his head. "No. I owe God penance for being led astray. I will not indulge in the pleasures of the flesh for a period."

"Does Bishop Atticus require this of you?" She put her hands on her hips, exasperation coloring her voice. "What is the penance and for how long?" She was eager to provide him with a son and disappointed that she hadn't already become pregnant during this year after her daughter's birth.

"The good bishop didn't make any demands of me." He looked down at his silk slippers and mumbled like a little boy caught in some ill deed. "I promised God to add another fast day to the week, drink only water, wear a hair shirt, and shun your bed for a full month if the people accepted me."

"Fine, no bed for a month." She said through stiff lips. "That doesn't mean we can't spend time together or show each other affection." She called through the open door, "Dorothea, bring me and the Augustus goblets of cucumber water," then took a seat on a reclining divan. "I'll join you in your penance. Sit with me and let me soothe your brow as your sacrifice soothes your soul."

"I love you, Athenais." He laid down on the divan, head in her lap. "No Augustus could have a more perfect mate. I knew you would understand and encourage me." His smile lit up his face and tugged at her heart.

Dorothea entered with their drinks, put them on a side table and quickly exited with a bow when Athenais darted her eyes toward the door. Over the past two years, the mistress and servant had become quite close with Dorothea anticipating Athenais' needs.

Athenais hummed a soothing children's song while smoothing her husband's hair back from his brow. He relaxed and the worry lines disappeared from his face. "Better, my love?"

"Much." A frown ruined all her work, and he sat up quickly. "I've made another decision that I fear you won't like."

She chuckled. "Tell me. It can't be as bad as depriving me of your love for a month."

He picked up her hands and looked away. "I'll not be using your verse on the base of my triumphal column."

"What?" She jerked her hands away. "Why not? You promised me my words would last a thousand years in the stone." A wave of disappointment choked her, and she gasped. *My immortality lost! Parchment lasts but a few generations, destroyed by age, bugs and fire, but stone lasts forever.* She tried to swallow her tears, but a few spilled out onto her cheeks.

"I'm so sorry, my love." Theo took her into a hug. "I know this is important to you, but I have to show the people that God gave us victory over the Persians, not me."

"What will it say instead?"

"I haven't worked out the entire inscription, but it will say something about my victory due to the vows of my sisters. They made a great sacrifice to God for my rule and should be acknowledged."

"But their words are already in stone. 'I dedicate my virginity to the church and my brother's rule. I will take no husband but Christ and have no children other than my people' is carved into the altar dedicated to Mary Theotokos in the Great Church for all to see. Pulcheria's words. Her vow. Carved in stone." The hurt transmuted to anger. "Did Pulcheria propose this?"

"No, my love. She knows nothing about it. It is my wish only to honor God and my sisters." He took her hands back and looked directly into her eyes. "I promise I will have a thousand copies of your poem made and distribute them throughout the empire. Many more people will read your words than can read an inscription on a stone plinth."

Partially mollified, Athenais dried her eyes and reached for a goblet of water. *A month of water and plain fare. I did promise, but I'm not wearing a hair shirt!*

Chapter 20

March 423

H*OW WILL THIS CHANGE THINGS?* PAULINUS THOUGHT AS HE HURRIED down THE hall toward Athenais' quarters. *I'm sure we can use this to our advantage.*

He approached her suite and confronted the herald, "I must talk with the Augusta. At once. There is news from the western court."

The man seemed to fill the doorway with his bulk, arms crossed over his chest. "The Augusta is not to be disturbed in the two hours after midday."

"I bear a message from the Augustus. Let me pass." *Which is only a small lie. I'm sure Theo would want Athenais to know this news.*

The man moved aside and Paulinus continued through the receiving room toward Athenais' workroom where her favorite servant stood guard.

"Dorothea, I must talk with your mistress now. Please ask if she will receive me."

The girl slipped through the door and returned within moments. "The Augusta says that she always is available to your honorable self." She opened the door wider and stepped aside.

Athenais sat at her work desk, a more sumptuous version of the one she had at her uncle's.

His heart lurched as he noted she was only now beginning to recover some weight and energy after her month of penance. By the third week, he had begged Theo to release her from the vow because her health was in danger. He refused and it was the first time he had been truly angry at his friend.

"Paulinus, my friend." She stood and met him halfway across the room. "You are one of only three people I would allow to interrupt my writing time." She took his arm, guided him to a chair, and took one opposite him across a low table. "Dorothea, bring us refreshments."

"Who are the other two?" he teased.

"Theo, of course, and unfortunately Pulcheria. Although she never asks, just barges in whenever she wants." Frown lines marred her white forehead. "But let's talk of more pleasant topics. Dorothea said you have important news."

"Dispatches have arrived from the western court. Emperor Honorius exiled his sister Placidia from Ravenna and remanded her to Theo's custody. She and her children will be arriving soon by sea."

"What did she do to deserve such a harsh punishment? She didn't murder anyone with her own hands, did she?" Athenais clasped her hands in excitement. "I heard she dispatched her first husband's assassin with a knife and fed his body to the dogs."

"Those are old stories, much exaggerated. I'm sure an imperial princess would never stoop to such actions."

"I wouldn't be so sure. Women are not fainting flowers. There is little I would not do to protect the ones I love."

"But would you act in anger? Kill in revenge?"

"Probably not." She shrugged. "But what crime sends our aunt to our shores? Will we have to keep her in close confinement?"

"General Castinus, Honorius' closest advisor since Placidia's husband died, accused her of treason. Supposedly, she colluded with the Goths to overthrow her brother and put her son on the throne."

"If true, that demands the death penalty!" Athenais frowned.

"Placidia claimed innocence and put up a good defense. Lacking evidence of her guilt, Honorius allowed Placidia to retire to Constantinople where Theo could keep an eye on her. She was born here and still has a palace in the city and estates in the East."

"I heard a rumor that she and her brother were more than close since her husband died. There was talk of incest."

"You haven't met the Western Augustus. Honorius married twice and both his wives died virgins." Paulinus chuckled. "More likely General Castinus is making a political move by spreading such lies. Her personal guards have been brawling in the streets to quell such scurrilous insults." He sat back. "No. Castinus' move feels more like politics than passion. With Placidia banished, he can control the emperor. But her arrival provides an opportunity for us."

"How so?"

"Placidia is a powerful woman, skilled in the ways of the world. You could learn much from her." He gazed at her expectant face. "I know you've been lonely with no female companion of your own rank. Especially since Doria retired with your uncle to their country estates in disgrace."

"I do miss her and her guidance." Athenais sighed. "Do you really think I could be friends with Placidia? Theo's sisters have resisted my so-called charms for two years."

"Only Pulcheria has resisted. I've heard both Arcadia and Marina speak up for you on more than one occasion and urge Pulcheria to more moderation and Christian charity toward you."

"Have I done anything that requires her charity or forgiveness?" Athenais snapped.

"No, my dear. Your very existence and Theo's love for you is enough to inspire her jealousy. It will probably be her downfall."

"Possibly." Athenais looked pensive. "I look forward to Placidia and her children's arrival. It will be nice to have more children in the nursery. Her Honoria is five and Valentinian four, I believe. My Eudoxia is too young for other companions, but imperial cousins would be perfect."

"It's not too soon to think of Eudoxia's future. Placidia had to flee, but her son is still a likely heir to the West. When Honorius dies, Theo could try to rule the entire empire as his grandfather did, but that is a mighty task and would require him to travel the breadth of the land."

"Not likely. My dear husband is a homebody. He leaves the palace for special services at the Great Church and the occasional horse ride with you, but little beyond Constantinople and our estates. I had hoped we might travel. I would love to visit Athens and Antioch, my adopted and natal cities. What most surprises me is that Theo has shown no interest in a pilgrimage to Jerusalem to visit the holy places."

"You could go on your own."

"I couldn't… could I?" She looked thoughtful. "I wouldn't need Theo's permission?"

"You are Eudocia Augusta, the first lady of this land. You have the right, the money, and power to travel to the Holy Land, if you wish. Look at the changes you've already brought to this court. You can do so much more, my dear. Learn from your aunt, when she comes, how a woman might rule."

"As usual, you've given me much to think about my friend."

Good. I've planted a seed. My love should have a life beyond children and poetry. She's destined for more.

Chapter 21

April 423

THE THREE AUGUSTI MADE A FORMIDABLE TRIO ON THE DAIS OF THE formal Daphne audience hall. Athenais sat on her husband's left hand with Pulcheria on his right to receive their western relatives. Athenais covered her excitement with a calm face. *At least I learned something from Pulcheria's early comportment training.*

A trumpet blast announced the arrival and a herald read out Placidia and her children's names and honors for the assembled court. *Placidia and her children look pale. Did they have a difficult sea voyage?*

Her aunt flushed when the title of Augusta was omitted from the various honors given to her, but she recovered quickly, raising her chin just a little more. *Paulinus was right. Placidia seems to know all the right moves. She doesn't act like a refugee, but has the sense to dress ambiguously, so as not to offend.* Placidia wore a dark blue silk gown embroidered with gold thread in swirling leaf patterns, topped with a plain imperial purple cape, faced with red silk and held in place with a gold fibula in the shape of a wolf's head. Strands of pearls threaded her aunt's dark curly hair in a way that suggested a diadem but didn't quite usurp that prerogative reserved for Augusti. Her small children were also appropriately dressed in imperial purple and followed in their mother's stately footsteps down the long room, heads up and eyes straight ahead.

"Welcome to our court, Aunt," Theodosius offered, as Placidia and her children assembled before the dais under the neutral smiles of the full court.

Pulcheria added, "I trust you had a felicitous journey?"

"We had one violent storm, but God saw us safely to your shore." Placidia returned her niece's gaze with an equally frank stare. "Thank you for your concern."

"I have found, when God is gracious, it is appropriate we honor him in some way." Pulcheria gave her a chilly smile.

"I vowed to build a church when I return to Ravenna," Placidia answered dryly. "And I intend never to tempt His good will with another sea voyage."

"A church is an appropriate recompense." Pulcheria nodded approval.

Athenais rose and greeted her aunt with a kiss. "I am so pleased you and the children landed safely. I'm looking forward to your company." She smiled and took Placidia's arm. "Why don't we retire to a less public place, and have some refreshment? I'm sure you are fatigued after your journey."

Athenais noticed Pulcheria's frown. *Upset already, Sister?*

"I'll join you when I've finished my audience." Theodosius nodded to Placidia, but did not rise. "My sister and wife will take good care of you and your children, Aunt."

Pulcheria's face twitched at being so obviously dismissed with the women and children. Athenais suppressed a laugh.

"Of course, Brother." Pulcheria recovered by taking charge. "This way." She led them to her favorite antechamber, used to impress visitors with her piety. Athenais thought of it as her sister-in-law's expanded monk cell. Its multi-colored marble walls bare of paintings; no statues adorned the corners or carpets the floors. Pulcheria positioned herself at the head of the room on a plain wooden chair. A couple of duplicates faced a cushioned divan across a low table. Athenais suspected Pulcheria used the visitor's choice between hard and soft seating as a character test.

Athenais deliberately sat on the cushioned divan and patted the seat beside her. "Join me, Aunt. You will allow me to call you that, won't you?"

Placidia removed her purple cape, which a servant immediately whisked away, and accepted Athenais' offer.

Pulcheria waved the children over. "Come, let me look at you."

They approached but did not bow. Valentinian shuffled his feet, stopping when his older sister Honoria pinched him. Both were good-looking children with their mother's dark curly hair and large brown eyes. The girl stared at Pulcheria with frank curiosity and a faint frown. *That one has some spunk. I hope Pulcheria doesn't squeeze it out of her.*

"Do you have tutors? How advanced are you in your subjects?" Pulcheria queried.

The girl's eyes grew moist. "We had to leave everyone behind." *Poor child! I know what that is like.* Honoria firmed her quivering chin and reported, "I know my Greek and Latin letters and can read some. I like history best. T-tutor was teaching me sums and differences."

Pulcheria raised her eyebrows. "And your brother?"

"Val—" she nodded at her brother, shifting his weight from foot to foot, as if needing to relieve himself "—is just starting to learn his letters. Mother is teaching me to ride. Val is too little."

"Am not! You've only one year on me." Valentinian muttered. He kicked his sister's ankle. "Ouch!" he cried as she pinched him again.

"Children!" Placidia jumped up, grabbing each by the arm. "Apologize to your cousin for your poor behavior."

Both children bowed, mumbling an apology.

"Very good." Pulcheria nodded. "You may go to the nursery."

A servant stepped forward to take their hands. The children looked to their mother. At her nod, they went quietly with the young woman.

Placidia's face transitioned from tight annoyance to affectionate worry as she watched them go. Then she turned back to Pulcheria. "My apologies, as well, Niece. They are fatigued from the journey."

"Understood. We will find them new tutors. Have they started religious instruction?"

"No. They attend private services in our apartments." Placidia frowned. "I think them too young for formal instruction."

"I began my studies when I was Valentinian's age. I will consult with Bishop Atticus for a suitable candidate."

Placidia's jaw tightened, but she didn't object.

Good. Given her position, she probably knows from her agents all she needs to get along with Pulcheria. "Sit, Aunt. Have some refreshment." Athenais drew Placidia back to the divan. "You must be fatigued as well."

Servants brought food and drink—hearty red wine, fruit, and honey cakes. Pulcheria indulged in her usual water. Placidia nibbled at a date stuffed with honey and nuts.

"Aunt, what brings you so precipitously to our shores?" Athenais asked, as trivial conversation about children and the weather wound down.

Pulcheria leaned forward as if eager to hear Placidia's side of the story.

Placidia looked up from her wine. Dark smudges under the older woman's eyes attested to her trials. "My brother is increasingly prey to suspicions inflamed by those ministers closest to him. Given his current state of mind, I felt it best to remove my children and myself to a safer residence."

Pulcheria's face puckered in a worried frown. "Is your brother's rule stable in the West? Do we need to send troops, or a trusted minister?"

"There is no need for intervention—at this time. My brother's vacillations are of a more personal nature. General Castinus manufactured a plot and lured my retainers into an unwise action to discredit me. He convinced Honorius I did not have his interests at heart."

"This breach between brother and sister disturbs me. You have no family but each other. It is not seemly to have this disharmony."

Athenais watched in fascination as Pulcheria seemed to have some empathy for her aunt's situation. *I shouldn't be so surprised. Her love for her brother is only second to her professed love for God.*

Placidia set aside her wine. "Our circumstances are somewhat different, Niece. You are older than your brother. You shared many experiences, guided him in his youth, built trust between you. Honorius is my elder by several years, and a half-brother. Except for a few years as young children, we lived apart. During these last years, we worked closely, but rumors and falsehoods easily lead him astray. It is my understanding my oldest brother—your father—had a similar temperament and was much influenced by your late mother."

Pulcheria gave her a pointed look. "Males of our line do seem to benefit from the gentle guidance of the females."

"Pulcheria is modest." Athenais set down a goblet she had barely touched. "She is Theodosius' wisest and closest advisor. Everyone knows, if they wish something done by the Augustus, they must come to Pulcheria." *Best to put Pulcheria off with a compliment than a criticism and I'm not wrong.*

Pulcheria shot Athenais a sharp glance.

"It is well known how ably Pulcheria ruled during her brother's minority." Placidia nodded toward her niece. "Your charity to the poor and devotion to God and your brother are admired throughout the empire."

Pulcheria looked towards the heavens—in this case, a ceiling painted dark blue with gold trim. "God put us on earth as His Viceroys. It is through His will that we rule, and we show our devotion through good works and fair governance."

"A most admirable mission, which I would like to duplicate in the West, but sadly must bide my time until my brother can be persuaded to the right course." Placidia suppressed a yawn. "I *am* fatigued after our journey. My residence is barely fit to live in, and I slept poorly last night."

"How thoughtless of me." Athenais put a hand to her mouth. "You must stay with us until your palace is properly furnished and staffed." She waved over a servant. "Tell my chamberlain to prepare the west suite." She turned back to Placidia. "The rooms will be ready shortly. Let's go to the nursery so you can reassure your children."

Placidia rose. "God's grace on you, Pulcheria."

"And you, Aunt." Pulcheria nodded.

"This way." Athenais linked arms with Placidia as they left the room. "I am looking forward to getting to know you and your children better. My daughter is only one but has no companions."

Placidia's shoulders relaxed, and her eyes softened at the talk of the children. "I, as well, Niece. I know how lonely it can be at court without females of your own rank to confide in. I hope I can rely on your guidance here." Her lips turned up in a rueful smile. "Pulcheria is almost as formidable as that storm at sea. I'm anxious to hear how you've navigated such choppy waters."

"I'll be happy to give you advice, Aunt, but let's get you settled and comfortable." Her voice took on a rueful tone. "Unlike many in the court, I don't believe Pulcheria is a bad sort. Just overly religious, and very protective of Theo. She will be watching closely, to see if you try to influence him unduly."

"I do not wish to become a power in this court." Placidia sighed. "I just want some rest, and safety for my children. I am most grateful for your warm welcome and any advice you can give me for succeeding in my quest."

"Perhaps we can be of benefit to one another. I have been at court only two years and yearn for a friend of equal rank." A shadow passed over Athenais' face. "Pulcheria's nature does not turn to friendship and, as you are probably aware, the women at court have considerably more than an Augusta's friendship at heart. I am constantly bombarded with requests for appointments and favors."

"I understand your loneliness. What of the younger sisters, Arcadia and Marina? Are they more welcoming?"

"Somewhat. They are out at a charity mission today representing Theo and Pulcheria. They rarely attend court. Pulcheria dominates their lives, but they seem content. Neither has spoken to me of any unhappiness."

"Is your husband affectionate?"

"Theo is my dearest friend and perfect love. If not for him, I would have wasted away. Theo and Pulcheria keep such a dull court. I am used to a livelier intellectual set. I studied literature and philosophy at the Athens University."

"I heard. Why do you not entertain on your own? You could have a salon and invite the leading thinkers and artists."

"I host small gatherings, but I must move slowly. Pulcheria and Theo still suffer much from the unsavory reputation of their mother. Pulcheria wants no hint of scandal. Here is the nursery." Athenais' face lit up as she entered. She moved to a small, but ornate bed guarded by an elderly heavyset woman. "Nana, how is my angel today?"

The woman continued knitting, showing a gap-toothed smile. "She's been as good a child as I've ever known." She winked at Placidia; a familiarity allowed by only the oldest of retainers. "I heard you were coming. Do you remember me, Princess? I used to give you sweets to fatten you up. Always such a little bird."

"Of course, Nana. I have children of my own now." Placidia's face softened, seeming with pleasant memories.

The nurse nodded. "I looked in on them. Your daughter reminds me of you at that age. You were five when your father died, and your cousin Serena took you away to Rome. A sad day for me." The knitting needles continued clicking as the old woman's voice subsided into a murmur.

Athenais picked up the sleeping baby and turned to Placidia. "My daughter, Licinia Eudoxia."

Placidia studied the infant. "She's precious, Athenais. She will rival Helen of Troy."

"She has already surpassed me. She barely cries and everyone in the nursery comes running to relieve her least discomfort. Theo is so entranced he named me Augusta upon her baptism." Athenais blushed. "Pulcheria was not pleased. She wanted to delay my elevation for months, but finally had to give in."

"I heard. She seemed even more adamant that my elevation be rescinded. It wasn't—in the West." Placidia said with a hint of bitterness in her voice. "Where are my children?"

"In the next room." Athenais put the sleeping baby back on her bed and escorted Placidia. *So, her status is still a touchy spot. I'll be careful of that in the future.*

"Mother, where were you?" Honoria leaped from a chair, where she had been perusing a codex, and came to hug her mother's knees.

Placidia disentangled the little girl and said sternly, "You know perfectly well I was with your cousins. We will stay here for a while. What do you think of that, Val?"

"I want to live on the boat!" The little boy gushed.

Placidia shuddered. "We will never set foot on a ship again."

He burst into tears. Placidia picked him up to soothe him.

The abandoned little girl looked forlorn watching her mother and brother.

"Honoria." Athenais held out her hand. "Would you like to meet your cousin?"

The child glared at her brother. "A boy or a girl? How old?"

"A girl, still a baby."

"Alright then."

Poor child! Maybe Honoria will take an interest in little Eudoxia. Both children could use some sibling affection.

"This way." Athenais took Honoria's hand and led her into the next room to see her baby cousin. She glanced over her shoulder to see a dewy-eyed Placidia crooning a lullaby to her son. *Yes, Placidia might be just what I need: a knowledgeable and experienced woman I can trust. We can help one another and, hopefully, I will find a friend.*

Chapter 22

Placidia's Palace, Constantinople, May 423

Athenais entered her aunt's residence with a heightened sense of curiosity. Since moving to Constantinople, she had only known two homes. Everyone always came to visit her, not the other way around and she relished this peek at another woman's life and tastes. The complex was larger than her uncle's villa, but not near as sprawling as the imperial palace. The outside presented the usual blank stone wall of a noble's city residence, but the inside swarmed with workers remodeling and refreshing the neglected palace.

"This way Augusta." The smell of fresh paint and plaster dust tickled her nose. She suppressed a sneeze as Placidia's chamberlain led her through renovated rooms. "Domina waits for you in the small triclinium."

She followed the servant to an intimate dining area—evidently not the formal triclinium used to serve a large party. This was a special dinner with Placidia at her residence because Athenais wanted to be away from Pulcheria's spies. *Although my sister-in-law probably already has people in Placidia's household, I'm sure my aunt has enough sense to use only trusted servants for a dinner with me.*

"Aelia Eudocia Augusta," he announced at the entrance.

Placidia, conferring with her personal attendant Lucilla in a corner, immediately turned at her entrance. "Niece, welcome to my home. Please be seated." She waved a hand at a small table set for two and gave a last-minute direction to the servants. All left except Lucilla, who stood by a sideboard laden with food and drink.

Placidia is as astute as I hoped. "It's lovely, Aunt." Athenais took her seat and admired the frescos, so real they looked like you could walk through the walls into a summer garden. "Excellent work. You will have to give me the artisan's name."

Placidia joined her at the table. "I would be happy to. I know that red paint is popular now, but it reminds me of blood." Placidia gave a slight shudder. "I've seen too much of that color. I find that the green of the forest or blue of the sea are more conducive to conversation and calm digestion."

"I'm sorry to have sparked dark thoughts, Placidia. I hoped our conversation would touch on more pleasant topics." Over the past month, Athenais had learned much about her intrepid aunt and her tragic story. *It's a wonder she's still sane after all her losses.*

"As do I." Her aunt signaled her servant, and the woman brought a first course of pickled quail eggs and vinegared greens.

Athenais watched with fascination as Lucilla served efficiently and silently. The woman shadowed her mistress nearly everywhere in the imperial palace and had spawned considerable speculation. Dorothea mentioned that the imperial servants thought Lucilla was mute and possibly even deaf, since she and her mistress seemed to communicate primarily with hand signals. Her horribly disfigured left cheek hinted at a violent past. *How long has this woman served Placidia? What secrets does she hold close?* Athenais mentally shrugged. *Another conversation for another day.*

After the main course dishes had been cleared, Lucilla served the final treats. As they sampled raspberry tarts, Lucilla poured a sweet plum wine. Only then did Athenais get to her point. "You've had a month to settle in here, Placidia. On the night we first met, you said your only wish was to find a quiet and safe refuge for you and your children. How goes your mission? Are you well cared for? Are you in any financial distress? I would be happy to help if you have any needs."

"My curator is helping me get my affairs in order. He managed to bring some cash and personal jewels of mine with him overland with my *bucellarii*—my private guards." Placidia hesitated, as if tallying her assets, before saying, "I still have the revenues from my mother's estates, but my brother has confiscated the revenues from my Italian and African holdings." A touch of bitterness puckered her mouth. "Those are my inheritance from my father. My friend Count Boniface of Africa has offered me a loan while my curator negotiates their return. In the meantime, I live frugally." She took a sip of her wine. "Something I've done more than once in my past."

"Theo told me your Gothic guards are billeted with the palace troops." And Dorothea told her that the company of tall blond barbarians caused quite a stir among the populace. The captain, a young man named Sigisvult, seemed prickly concerning the reputation of his mistress. It was rumored that he had led the brawling in the streets when accusations of incest arose at the Ravenna court.

"A temporary solution until I have the funds to house them elsewhere." Her aunt appraised her over the rim of her silver goblet. "Thanks for your concern, Niece, but all is in hand. I've grown close enough to you over the past month, to know when you are agitated. What's the real purpose of this visit? What has Pulcheria done recently to put you into such a state?"

"No more than the usual. I feel her eyes on me wherever I am in the palace. I never know which servant or guard is reporting back to her."

"Even the girl Dorothea? She seems to attend you well."

"As well as any other." Athenais shrugged. "She fills me in on the servant's gossip, but can give me no information on Pulcheria's thinking or movements."

"It's important to build loyalty among those closest to you." Placidia gave a proud glance at Lucilla. "Lucilla and I have saved each other's lives. The men in my *bucellarii* would die for me and I for them."

"Forgive me, Placidia, but you've led an... uh... adventurous life. I'll never lead an army or—I hope—take personal revenge on my enemies."

"And I would never wish that life on someone else. I don't regret them, but my past actions are a terrible burden." Placidia gave her a grim smile. "But there are other ways to build loyalty. Your husband and Pulcheria seem to have devoted followers without leading an army or wielding a knife. How do they manage?"

Has Placidia studied the great Socrates? She seems skilled in his teaching methods. Athenais spent a moment collecting her thoughts. "They have similar, but different paths. Theo creates loyalty through his kindness. He rewards his friends with wealth and positions."

"Anyone of means can buy loyalty for a time—until someone of greater means comes along and buys it for a higher price. I am near destitute, but my personal guard has not deserted me because we share ties of blood and oaths."

"But the fact that Theo is their benefactor creates some obligation."

"Depending on the nature of the man, the obligation can translate to loyalty or to resentment that he is dependent on another for his livelihood." Placidia shrugged. "It's sometimes difficult to predict which. I've found that true loyalty cannot be bought, it must be earned through mutual regard and trust over time."

"I believe Pulcheria has been more successful than Theo in that regard. He has but two true friends, Paulinus from his childhood and me."

Placidia raised an eyebrow. "You don't number his sister among his true friends."

Athenais shook her head. "Pulcheria loves Theo—almost as much as she loves God. But, if Theo strays from her conception of orthodoxy, she will break with him and try to take the empire with her. Pulcheria has spent the last ten years lavishing money on the church and living an exemplary Christian life. The church fathers are always open to her suggestions and she to theirs. But I believe she has been most successful in earning the respect of the people of Constantinople. I thought at first that her charity work was for show—required if she were to present herself as a holy woman. I learned differently. Pulcheria genuinely cares about the poor and needy. She doesn't send others to do her work; she personally feeds the hungry and cares for the sick. The people know that her devotion is true and love her for it."

"Having the love of the people is one of the most powerful weapons in a ruler's arsenal. The people of the city of Rome have been my staunch supporters since we all starved together during the Gothic sieges. I and my aunts spent our fortunes to feed the city and cared for the sick with our own hands during the famines and plagues that followed. I originally proposed my exile from the Ravenna court to Rome, but Castinus is clever and wanted me far away from anyone who might give me aid. The city of Rome will support my return and that is no small thing."

"You plan on your sojourn with us being a short one?"

"An interim, but I know not how long. That depends on what happens in Ravenna. If Castinus is the power behind my brother, I have little hope. Honorius is childless and my son is his acknowledged heir."

"But—"

Placidia cut off her protestation with a raised palm. "I know Theo and Pulcheria do not agree, but that is part of my mission here: to gain their trust and support for my son's future. This empire is too great for one man—or woman—to rule." She smiled. "I'm hoping we can be of mutual assistance in securing my son's succession and your more prominent role in your husband's government."

"I didn't say I wanted a more prominent role in his government. I just want to be on an equal footing with Pulcheria. To live my life without her interference."

Placidia raised one eyebrow. "She will never allow that. You must replace her or suffer her control over your life. I've known women like Pulcheria; we are alike in many ways. The fight for the emperor's ear is fierce and even more fierce for his love. You have an advantage, you can whisper in his ear in bed, but if Pulcheria has breath, she will fight you for his love."

"I think I've known that all along, but didn't want to admit it. I thought I could gain Pulcheria's affection and trust, that Theo's love could be shared, but she thinks what is given to me is taken from her."

"I admire my niece, but pity her as well." Placidia looked thoughtful. "I know no other Augusta who could outwit a court of talented accomplished men to rule an empire at age fifteen. Pulcheria is a remarkable woman. Hardship hones a person's skills or breaks them. I was your age when I was taken hostage by the Goths and set upon my current path. Pulcheria was but a child when her father died leaving a boy emperor on the throne. So many things could have gone wrong and ended in tragedy for her brother and sisters. She learned early how to survive and thrive, but I feel she had more loneliness and fear in her childhood than love and joy."

"But Theo is no longer a child, and she should defer to him, not overshadow."

"I agree and it will be a shock to Pulcheria when she learns that for herself. Her need to protect and guide Theo is all she's known since she was a child and she will fight to keep her place at his side, seeing all others who seek to influence him as her enemy."

"I'll remember that as I move forward. I'm still hoping I can gain my sister-in-law's trust. I don't want to rip Theo's heart apart in a direct contest of wills." Athenais looked at her aunt speculatively. "If what you believe is true, Pulcheria should welcome your return to Ravenna and assist you in your efforts. There will be one less female relative to challenge her supremacy."

"I'm counting on my niece seeing the advantages of my returning to the West." Placidia smiled. "In the meantime, I understand your husband likes to ride in the countryside for exercise. Do you think he would mind my company?

It would be an opportunity for us to get to know one another better—away from prying eyes—and riding is my favorite recreation."

"I'm sure that can be arranged." Athenais saluted her aunt with her cup. "I'm sorry for the circumstances that brought you to our court, but most pleased that we can be friends and allies while you are here."

Chapter 23

Imperial Palace, August 423

"ARE YOU SATISFIED WITH YOUR CHILDREN'S TUTORS?" ATHENAIS ASKED Placidia as they watched little Eudoxia run around the nursery. A young servant girl followed closely to pick her up or comfort her after a fall. Her daughter seemed to have gone from walking to running with no effort at all. Placidia's children studied in a separate room with a priest.

"They do well."

"What about their religious studies? Has Pulcheria's choice been too rigid?"

"Surprisingly not." Placidia shook her head. "I had expected to intervene if he was too strict or attempted to teach beyond the children's ability to understand, but Brother Marcus is kind. He instructs the children through parables and stories. Val has grown quite attached. Don't tell Pulcheria, but he also rewards the children with occasional sweets."

"So that's where Marina got her penchant for sweets! Brother Marcus taught the imperial children after Arcadius' death. How delightful that he came out of seclusion to take up his old duties. Theo has many pleasant memories of the man. I believe between him and Nana, they were the only source of adult affection in the orphaned children's lives."

"I've tried to adhere to Pulcheria's wishes with my own religious observances. Fast days are no problem, I've had to go without in the past." Placidia shrugged, seeming to leave much unsaid.

"But?" Athenais felt a mischievous grin tugging at her lips. "I notice you quit the palace for your own residence well before midnight prayers."

"Only so the children can get their rest." Placidia said with a studied innocence.

A delighted squeal from Athenais' daughter pulled her attention back to her child. "Come to Momma," Athenais coaxed. Eudoxia toddled over to her outstretched arms. Athenais pulled the little girl onto her lap with a grunt and a flood of love for the small soul she had created. "Do you want a little brother or little sister?" she whispered into her daughter's gold curls. She was only three months pregnant and not showing, but her absence at midnight and morning prayers had already fueled speculation throughout the palace that another imperial baby would join the nursery in the new year.

"She grows more beautiful every day." Placidia observed. "You have been so good to me and the children, Athenais. I want to propose a match to tie our families closer. Do you think Theo would consent to a betrothal between Valentinian and Eudoxia?"

"Oh, what a marvelous idea!" Athenais laid her cheek on the girl's silky hair. "Since she was born I've dreaded the day she would be sent off to some foreign land and a strange noble's bed. I pray this second child is a boy so I will not lose him." Athenais smiled. "And of course Eudoxia will have the best mother-in-law. I can count on you to love her as much as your own daughter."

Placidia winced, then covered it by reaching for the child. "Would you like to marry Val, my precious?" She cuddled Eudoxia and the child bared her baby teeth and laughed. "I think that means 'yes'." Placidia sobered. "We still have to convince Theo and Pulcheria."

"Leave them to me. Theo no more wishes to lose Eudoxia than I do. This is a perfect solution. Pulcheria vowed never to marry, not only because of her religious convictions, but to avoid the very entanglements we fear for my little one. She did not want to be bartered off to some stranger, Roman or not, as part of a political settlement."

Placidia nodded. "I leave you to argue the merits of the case, then."

"We will make this marriage happen." Athenais' voice resounded with resolve. She knew Placidia's political motives: marriage ties would make Valentinian a more favorable successor to Honorius in Theo's eyes, but she didn't care. Her daughter would stay in the family and be well cared for by Placidia.

"Speaking of my love..." Athenais rose to greet her husband with a robust kiss as he came through the nursery door.

"What brings you to the nursery at this time of day, Nephew?"

He lifted Eudoxia and chucked her under the chin before handing her to Athenais. "I'm afraid I bring distressing news." He raised Placidia to her feet and held her hands. "My dearest aunt. I'm sorry, but your brother Honorius is dead. We just received the dispatches."

"Oh! God rest his soul." Placidia pulled her hands away to cross over her heart. "What did he die of?"

"Dropsy."

"My poor brother." Placidia shook her head. "His health has been fragile for some time."

"Honorius knew he was dying and sent several documents. Among them is a strong recommendation that General Castinus administer the West in my name."

Placidia could not keep the anger from her voice, as she raised her chin and said, "I've known some with dropsy who were not quite right in their minds at the end. It would not surprise me if Castinus persuaded Honorius to this course, or even substituted his own wishes for those of my brother. By rights, Valentinian should be Augustus. Honorius confirmed my son as heir three years ago."

"Without my consent. It is my right to make that choice." Theo gave her a sharp look.

Behind her husband, but in view of Placidia, Athenais put a finger to her lips. Placidia lowered her head and moderated her tone. "Of course it is your decision, Nephew. You are now the sole Augustus of the Roman Empire, and will choose the colleague you feel best. Now is not the time to discuss this important matter; after the mourning period will be soon enough."

His hesitation to agree with his aunt said much to Athenais. *Could Theo want to rule singly, as his grandfather did? If this next child is a boy, will he want to name him to the Western throne? What if a frustrated Placidia fomented a civil war on her son's behalf? I must reassure her of my support. We should announce the betrothal as soon as possible—if I can convince Theo and Pulcheria this is the right thing to do.*

Placidia bowed. "I should tell the children. Honoria was fond of her uncle."

Chapter 24

October 423

"NOT BAD FOR AN EARLY DRAFT." ATHENAIS MUMBLED TO HERSELF AS SHE sanded a parchment to absorb the extra ink on her latest poem. *I'll have Olympiodorus look it over before I do more work.*

A slight fluttering in her womb brought a smile to her face, and her hand to her rounded stomach. The baby had recently quickened, and she felt more at ease about her pregnancy. Melia assured her all was going well, and she should have a healthy baby, but her dreams were disturbing. *No wonder with the last couple of months of upset. Why do Theo and Pulcheria keep negotiating with that odious General Castinus? Poor Placidia is at her wit's end practically haunting the palace trying to get them to affirm little Val as the heir. I thought having Eudoxia formally betrothed to the boy would be enough to tip the scales in his favor, but I was wrong.*

"Augusta, there is a message from the Augustus." An imperial page stood in the doorway of her workroom. "You are to join him at once in the consistory."

The formal council room? Pulcheria staked that out early as her personal domain and made it clear I was welcome in the general audience chamber, but not in the room where decisions are made. This must be an emergency!

"Any word on why?"

"Not from the Augustus, but a rumor spread from the audience chamber that a man named John has declared himself emperor in the West."

I didn't predict this! If anyone rebelled against Theo, I thought the general would be the best candidate.

She stood and rushed to the door before slowing to a more sedate pace suited to an Augusta. Maintaining that pace as she navigated the hallways to the consistory, took all her self-will. As she approached, she met men of the council going in the opposite direction. They all stopped talking, moved to the side of the hallway, and gave her a bow as she passed. She kept her eyes forward and ground her teeth. *Damn such protocols. I need to know what is happening before I get into that room. Has Theo decided? Where is Placidia?*

"Theo!" Athenais cried from the door, before noting the presence of General Ardaburius and Master of Offices Helion. She blushed at her lack of formality, then hurried inside. "I heard what happened in the audience room. Is it true?"

The guards shut the door and Theo pointed to the papers on the table. "It seems we have rebellion in the West. A civil servant called John has declared himself Augustus. Pulcheria believes our betrothal of Eudoxia to Valentinian panicked General Castinus. He believed we kept him at bay while preparing to replace him with the boy and his mother. Castinus knew Placidia would not tolerate him in her government after his machinations to banish her, so he raised another he could control."

"An astute assessment." Athenais admitted. "What are we to do?"

Theo's glance strayed to his wife's rounded stomach. "We have a decision to make. This usurper must be ousted, but who will take his place?"

"Would you rule the West as well as the East?" Athenais asked.

"Sister?" Theo turned to Pulcheria.

"You are a worthy Augustus, but the West would be a terrible burden both in terms of turmoil and treasure. Our grandfather named his sons co-rulers, because he knew neither could hold the empire together on his own." Pulcheria rose. "However, I will aid you in whatever you decide."

"Athenais?" Theo's gaze softened.

"I will accompany you wherever you travel. If you lead an army yourself, I will be in your tent."

"I won't lead an army, my sweet. That's why I have generals." He turned to Ardaburius. "General, what's the military situation in the West? Will the army stand with this upstart John? Will they be a threat to an invasion force?"

"The armies in the West are weak and disorganized after decades of fighting the barbarians. General Castinus had some slight success in Gaul, which slipped away when the Gothic auxiliaries left the field. I doubt he could put up much of a fight. Felix, who leads the Italian reserves, is barely competent. Their most able general, Boniface, is in Africa."

"Boniface is a good friend of our aunt's." Athenais said. "He sends funds to Placidia for her upkeep, since Honorius confiscated her western inheritance."

"So, Boniface would likely support Placidia if she led an invasion in Valentinian's name." Theo rubbed his smooth-shaven jaw. "We could send fewer troops if Boniface came from Africa. Guard!" Theo shouted. "Send in the scribe."

A rabbity older man scurried into the chamber with a satchel from which he pulled parchment, ink and pens. "Your Serenity has need of my services?"

"Yes, take down these words…" Theo continued to dictate his orders.

A short time later, Placidia raced into the council chamber, her haste reflected in her appearance: plain tunic, dusty cloak, and unadorned hair rather than her usual meticulous court apparel.

"Dearest Aunt, we have a serious development in the West." Pulcheria spoke before Theo could, perplexing Athenais. *Why didn't Theo speak first? He's the Augustus!*

Placidia whipped off her cloak and took a seat. "I heard. John declared himself emperor. He supervised clerks and has no military background or blood claim to the diadem."

"The upstart has the nerve to demand I acknowledge his claim over your son's." Theo's mouth twisted. "I imprisoned his envoy."

"You favor our claim?" Hope lightened her aunt's features.

Pulcheria waved a hand as if dismissing an insignificant problem. "Of course we favor your claim. The empire is too big to rule alone, and Theo and I have all we can handle here in the East, with Ruga and his Huns threatening in the north and the Persians restless on our eastern borders. We leave the rest of the barbarians to you."

The scribe brought Theo several parchment pages. Grinning, he signed each with a flourish, put his seal to the wax, and handed them to Placidia. A smile dawned over her face as she read the eastern imperial confirmation of her elevation to Augusta and Valentinian's to Caesar and heir to Honorius.

"You named me Regent." Placidia put down the decrees. "Thank you, Nephew."

Pulcheria gave a smile bordering on warmth. "You are the best person to rule in your son's name. You know the people, the barbarians, and the bureaucracy.

It is always better to have blood protect blood during a minority."

"This one," Theo waved the last sheet, "is an order to General Ardaburius to prepare an army to invade Italy and take back the imperium for Valentinian. I will accompany you myself and crown my young cousin in Rome."

Placidia rose and bowed. "My sincere thanks to you, my dearest nieces and nephew. God sent me to you for succor in my darkest hour, and you gave freely of your love and wisdom. I and my children have lived with you in amity. We will not forget to whom we owe our future good fortune."

Athenais left her chair and embraced Placidia. "I will miss you, Aunt, and so will little Eudoxia. You are my closest friend. I count the days until we are reunited. God keep you safe."

Theo joined them, putting his arm around his wife's waist. "Fear not, my love. It will take many months to complete our plans and gather the army. Placidia and the children will be with us through the winter. Leave us now. You need your rest." He kissed her cheek. "Placidia, please stay and help us plan the usurper's downfall."

Athenais left, a sense of satisfaction flooding her body. She put a hand on her stomach. *If anyone can prevail in the West, Placidia will do it. My son will rule in the East and my daughter in the West. Who would have predicted such heights for a poor scholar's daughter?* A niggling thought spoiled her happiness. *But to succeed, I must raise my children without Pulcheria's interference. Will Theo stand with me?*

Chapter 25

March 424

"Dorothea, send for Melia. It's time." Athenais sat up in bed with a groan. "And get me a clean shift. My water broke."

"At once, Augusta." Dorothea hurried to the door and sent a herald for the midwife, who inhabited an adjoining room during the last month of Athenais' pregnancy. Her servant came back with a clean linen tunic and helped her change. "Should I comb your hair?"

"Yes, I must look my best for the ladies of the court," Athenais said dryly. Her pains had started hours before, but she had delayed calling for the midwife, wanting a few more hours of privacy before her public ordeal.

Damn custom! It's so… so… embarrassing to give birth before the entire court. At least my ladies have had the experience and will be sympathetic. I thought those poor virgins of Pulcheria's would faint the last time.

Athenais' chuckle at the thought of fainting virgins turned into a low moan as another pain gripped her body. "I should get out of bed and walk." Dorothea took her hands and helped Athenais to her feet.

Before they finished a handful of circuits, Melia and her two assistants bustled into the room, followed by her sisters-in-law. Arcadia and Marina settled in front of the altar to pray. Pulcheria approached with a concerned smile. "Are you well, Sister?"

"As well as can be." Athenais doubled over with an intense pain. When it passed she asked, "Would you send for Placidia?"

"Certainly. I'll notify your court as well, so they can witness the birth." Pulcheria left to make arrangements.

"The pains are coming quickly, Augusta. On the bed, so I may examine you." Melia helped her lie back on the bed, knees up. She explored Athenais' rippling stomach with gentle hands. "The baby is in a good position, Augusta. I believe he will be born soon." She turned to her assistants. "The birthing stool, now!"

"That quickly?" Athenais gasped. *So much for tidying my hair.*

"Second babies are usually easier and quicker than first births, Augusta. Let's walk, until you feel the need to push."

With Melia on one side and Dorothea on the other, Athenais paced her bedroom while it gradually filled with ladies of the court. Pulcheria took her place with her sisters praying at the altar, but Placidia was absent. At last, the intense pains subsided and Athenais gave a great sigh.

Melia sat Athenais on the stool and examined her. "I see the head, Augusta. When you feel the need, push!"

With the confidence that she would soon have her son in her arms, Athenais pushed.

"Again!"

She felt the baby leave her body.

"It's a boy, Augusta."

Athenais leaned back into the arms of the assistant with a wave of euphoria. *I have a son. Thank God. Theo will be so pleased.*

Melia fussed over the baby and hurried to the washing bowl.

"Why isn't he crying?" Athenais sat up in alarm. "What's wrong, Melia?"

The midwife ignored her questions, desperately rubbing the baby's body with a warm towel. "The siphon, quick!" One of the assistants handed Melia a hollow tube, but Athenais couldn't see what was happening with her baby. Pulcheria joined the midwife, and they exchanged a few words. Her sister-in-law glanced at her with a pitying look. The ladies of the court averted their eyes.

"Tell me what's happening to my baby!" Athenais screamed. In her heart, she knew. *He's dead. My baby's dead.* A pain knifed through her from her stomach to her heart to lodge in the base of her throat. She had trouble breathing past the sobs.

"Push again, Augusta," the assistant directed in gentle tones. "We must deliver the afterbirth."

Athenais gave a weak groan and collapsed into the woman's arms, tears streaming down her cheeks.

Pulcheria turned to the court ladies. "All of you out. The Augusta needs rest and quiet. Go pray for her health and quick recovery." The ladies trickled out with low murmurs and teary-eyed glances.

While Pulcheria conferred with Melia, Arcadia and Marina approached. "We are so sorry, Sister." They took her arms and helped her to bed. In a daze, Athenais was aware they sponged and dried her bleeding body, combed and braided her hair, and settled her onto fresh bedding, all the while murmuring in soothing tones words that Athenais couldn't comprehend.

Once in bed, she grabbed Marina's hand in a crushing grip. "I want to see him."

"Of course." Arcadia walked over to Melia and returned with a small, wrapped bundle, which she placed in Athenais' arms.

He looked like he was sleeping, except for a bluish cast to his lips. Golden eyelashes feathered his white cheeks and wispy curls covered his head. She unwrapped the swaddling and counted his fingers and toes. "He's perfect," she mumbled. "No disfigurement." She looked up at her sisters-in-law and cried out with all her blooming grief, "Why?"

Pulcheria and Melia joined them at the bed's edge. Pulcheria took her hand. "I'm so sorry, Sister. This is a great loss to us all, but you are young and can have more children. God has called this little one to Him to be forever bathed in His grace."

Athenais yanked her hand away. "God did this? Then He has a lot to answer for."

Pulcheria gasped as if struck.

"Augusta," Melia cut in. "We don't know why some babies are born blue and not breathing, but it happens. It might be a defect of the body or blood that we cannot see. All goes well with the mother and the baby seems healthy, but at birth they don't survive. I did all in my power to save him."

"It wasn't enough!" Athenais glared at the midwife.

"Let us take the baby, Athenais." Pulcheria commanded.

"No." Athenais wrapped her arms around her son and turned her back on the quartet. "Go away."

"Leave her for the moment." Melia suggested. "She needs to hold the baby before she gives him up."

"I'll get my brother. He can talk some sense into her."

"No, I don't want to see Theo. Leave me, all of you."

Chapter 26

SOMETHING BAD HAPPENED.

Placidia felt the anxiety in the palace as she rushed through the halls. Small knots of people gathered in niches and cross ways, whispering and frowning. The occasional court lady showed signs of tears. They clogged the passages.

"Make way for Placidia Augusta." Sigisvult, the captain of her guards, cleared the way.

Thank the Good Lord for Sigisvult, my most loyal follower. He had been her man heart and soul since that bloody massacre in Barcelona. She still had nightmares about that day and the week following. She shook her head. *Leave the past in the past.*

The crowd thickened outside Athenais' quarters where two burly imperial guards blocked the door. They stood aside for Placidia with brief nods, but blocked Sigisvult from entering. "Augusta!" he cried.

"Stand down, Captain. I'm in no danger from my nieces and nephew. Stay here until I return or send word."

He nodded and, frowning, took a place next to the other guards.

She crossed the receiving room to Athenais' anteroom where she found Theo and his sisters huddled outside the closed bedroom door arguing. Melia and her assistants cowered in a corner.

"I came as soon as I got word." Her nephew's eyes were red. *Damn it! Of all days I was outside the walls. I should have been here.* "Athenais?" She held her breath, fearing the worst.

"No." Her nephew shook his head and said in a voice hoarse with tears. "The baby. My son."

"I'm so very sorry, Theo." She held out her arms and he came to her with a sob. "She won't see me, Aunt. She keeps the baby in her arms as if he is alive. She screams and threatens to kill herself if anyone comes close."

She patted him on the back until his sobs subsided. After a few moments, he collected himself and straightened. "Can you help us? We sent for her aunt Doria, but she's a day away. I fear for Athenais' sanity. You two have become close over this past year."

"I'll do what I can." She looked over his shoulder at the three sisters.

Arcadia and Marina wiped teary eyes and smiled in relief. Pulcheria's face set in a stern mask, she said, "We will do what we can, as well, Aunt. Come to the chapel, sisters. We'll pray that God gives Athenais the strength to weather this storm." She looked at Theo. "Will you join us, Brother?"

"Soon, Sister. If Placidia is successful, I want to comfort my wife. We both lost a child. We should be together."

"As you wish." Pulcheria nodded and left with her sisters in tow.

"Melia!" Placidia turned to the midwife, who approached with slumped shoulders and a downcast gaze. "Come woman, I'm not going to execute you—unless some dereliction of duty is uncovered. Has the court physician examined the baby?"

"No." Melia straightened and gave her a direct gaze. "The Augusta will let no one approach, much less take the baby. Neither I nor my assistants caused the baby's death. He was born with a blue cast to his skin and not breathing. I tried to revive him by clearing his nose and breathing into his mouth, but he was gone. This does happen. Not often, but it does."

"I understand. Life is short and uncertain, and we don't always know God's plan. The physician will determine if there is any evidence of wrongdoing."

"He'll find none." Melia turned away with her head held high.

"One more thing." The midwife turned back and Placidia asked, "Do you have any remedies that might calm the Augusta? Perhaps a five-petaled yellow flower with an acrid smell? It produces a red tea when crushed and brewed."

"A common remedy used for centuries. The herb is known as St. John's wort. How do you know of it?"

"I had need of its soothing properties many years ago."

The midwife nodded. "I have some with me. I'll brew up a cup. Should I add a drop of poppy juice?"

"Not now. I want to talk to Athenais if I can. Maybe later you can send the poppy if she is too distraught." Placidia turned to Theo and put a hand on his arm. "I'll do what I can to help her. When the tea is ready, send it in with Dorothea. Athenais trusts her."

Placidia took a deep breath, steeled herself for battle, then shook her head. *In my grief, I went to war. Athenais is a gentler soul. She will battle herself, not someone else.* Placidia opened the door and quietly entered the room. A couple of oil lamps failed to lighten the gloom. The coppery smell of blood roiled her stomach.

"Athenais? It's Placidia. May I come closer."

There was no response from Athenais. *Has she worn herself out? Was this just a temporary storm?*

"Placidia?" A lump shifted under the covers of the bed and Athenais sat up. "Where were you? I needed you," her niece moaned.

"I came as soon as I got word, my dear." She picked up the nearest oil lamp and approached the bed. "I was reviewing the invasion troops on the plains of Hebdomon with General Ardaburius."

Athenais nodded. "Of course. You were looking after the interests of your son, like a mother should." She cuddled the small still shape in her arms. "My son is dead. He will never feel the sun on his face, fall in love, have a child of his own. He'll never rule in his father's place."

Placidia let out a small sigh. *Thank the Lord, her thoughts are not disordered. She knows her baby is dead and grieves. I've known that pain and borne that loss.* She set the lamp on the side table. "May I join you in the bed?"

Athenais nodded dully.

Placidia kicked off her leather riding boots and settled on the edge of the bed. She opened her arms. "Come here, child. Cry as much as you need to."

Athenais snuggled into her arms, with quiet sobs. A few moments later she sniffled. "I thought I had cried myself out earlier, but the pain comes in waves."

Placidia hugged her close. "I know. I also lost a son. My first-born died of a fever only a couple of months after his birth. We named him Theodosius after my father."

"We were going to call him Arcadius after Theo's father."

"A good name. May I see him?"

Athenais moved the linen wrap from the baby's face with a gentle finger and handed him to Placidia.

Placidia gazed on the still face while quiet tears trickled down her cheeks. *He's fair like his mother. My Theo had a head of dark curls like mine.* The thought of the small silver coffin lying alone in the church in Barcelona brought echoes of the searing pain Placidia felt so many years ago. *When I rule the West, I'll bring my baby home so we may rest together.*

"A beautiful child, my dear." She handed the still body back to his mother. "I know you want to hold on to him forever, but this loss is not only yours, but your family's and your people's. They must be allowed to mourn as well. Shared loss helps us all heal."

"I know that in my head, but my heart wants us to stay in this safe bed for a while longer." Athenais covered the baby's face again and turned haggard eyes to Placidia. "It hurts so much!"

"I know it doesn't feel like it now, but the pain does lessen over time."

"Does it ever go away?"

"No, but it transforms. Mine is more like a memory of pain that I don't want to forget. That memory keeps my son alive in my heart. It took me a long while and the help of a good friend to recover from my loss."

"What friend?"

Curiosity about others is a good sign. Athenais doesn't seem to be in as dire straits as I was. "Gaatha, my sister-in-law. She cared for me day and night until I could care for myself. She reminded me that others loved me and needed me. I still had four stepchildren to care for and a husband, who was the love of my life."

"My sister-in-law reminded me that God took my child, and I could replace him soon enough," Athenais nearly spat.

"Pulcheria doesn't have a child and never will. How could she begin to understand? I'm sure she meant to comfort you." Placidia sighed. "Many told me the same thing, not knowing what distress it caused. We walk similar paths, but not the same one. All I can advise is to let those who love you help in any way that you need. Theo sits outside your door in tears. He not only mourns his son, but fears for your sanity and health. I pushed my husband away for months and still regret the time lost."

"Poor Theo!" Athenais cried. "I've been so selfish."

"Augusta?" Dorothea stood in the open door. "I have a restorative drink from Melia. May I come in?"

"I suggested the brew to Melia. It helped me in my darkest hour." Placidia said in a low voice.

"It's not poppy juice, is it? I don't want to sleep."

"No, this helps the sadness. The drink doesn't get rid of the pain, but helps you live with it."

"Bring it in, Dorothea." Athenais held out a welcoming hand.

Theo loomed in the doorway.

"If you're up to it, maybe you should let Theo in to see his son. It would help him with his grief as it helped you with yours." Placidia suggested.

Athenais clutched the small bundle to her breast and Placidia thought she might refuse, but she sighed and called out, "Theo, my love, I need you."

Her nephew fairly flew to his wife's bedside.

Placidia rose. "I'll leave you two to your sorrow. If I can be of any service, call on me day or night."

Theo clasped her hand to his breast. "I don't know how to thank you, Aunt."

"Take care of your wife, Theo. You need each other now." She looked down at the grieving mother. "Trials can make a marriage stronger or break it apart. It's an almost unbearable loss, but some good can come of it, if you wish it."

Dorothea hovered with the brew. Placidia took the cup and handed it to her nephew. "Give her this. It will help. Melia will give Dorothea instructions on its use. Athenais should be able to give up the baby soon for burial. Spend as much time with her as you can spare over the next few months. I'll take my leave and be back tomorrow—or sooner if needed."

"God's blessings on you, Aunt."

"And on you, Theo."

Placidia led the servant girl to the door and shut it behind them. "Don't go in again until called. They need this time together. Work with Melia. She knows what to do for the Augusta's recovery."

"Thank you, Augusta. I truly feared for my mistress." Dorothea gave her a deep bow then glanced up with teary eyes. "I'm so glad you are here in this trying time."

"As am I, child." *Everyone must walk their own path, but sometimes it helps to have an experienced guide.*

Chapter 27

March 425

"THANK YOU, AUNT, FOR ACCOMPANYING ME TO THE SERVICE. WITH YOUR leave-taking tomorrow, I know you are exceptionally busy." Athenais linked arms with Placidia as they left the private imperial chapel. "I can't believe it's been a year since we lost little Arcadius."

"It was a lovely memorial. Did you write the service?"

"Yes." Athenais blushed. "Writing about my lost child helped me through the worst months."

"We all deal with grief in our own way. I picked up a knife, you a pen, and Theo a cross."

Athenais patted her rounded stomach. "You were right about letting in those who loved me. Theo and I have been closer than ever, Aunt Doria and my brothers have returned to court, and even Pulcheria has been more circumspect in her criticism. But I've missed you, Placidia. It's been a long winter with you in Thessalonica."

"The extra year allowed General Ardaburius to hone his troops, but I was sorely vexed at the delay. The troops sail for Italy within the week." She shuddered. "I wish them well. The seas are stormy this time of year and I fear for them."

"I understand your dislike of sea voyages. You and the children had a greenish cast when you arrived at our court two years ago." Athenais chuckled. "Has Pulcheria planned your promised church in Ravenna?"

"No, she's been singularly busy with the Huns' incursions on your northern border." Athenais smiled. "But she has reminded me of my promise to God on more than one occasion. I'm looking forward to our overland trip with General Aspar. He is a most creative leader and cavalryman. I have a fondness for the cavalry." Placidia's chin firmed. "But it's well past time that I got rid of the usurper John and secured the diadem for my son."

"I'm sorry, Aunt!" Guilt softened Athenais' voice. "Between our sorrow and the Huns, we detained you far longer than planned, but we love and support you. I couldn't ask for a better friend and regret that Theo can't accompany you himself. He wanted to elevate young Val to Augustus in Rome. Neither of us travel much beyond our gates and he wanted to see the Mother City."

Placidia patted her arm. "I understand he's been in delicate health lately. Stomach troubles?"

"Yes. The physician has him on a bland diet."

"Take good care of him. Your Master of Offices Helion will be an adequate substitute. And perhaps it's a good thing. I didn't want to put Theo in peril during my campaign."

"Will there be much danger?" Athenais' gasped. "Shouldn't you stay safe here in Constantinople while the generals take to the field."

"I sometimes forget how sheltered you are, my dear." Placidia laughed. "Yes, there will be danger, but I do not go running onto the field with a sword in my hand. I have planned most carefully and hope to avoid fighting altogether. The people of the city of Rome back me and have since I didn't abandon them during the Gothic sieges. They minted coins showing me and Val as Augusti. My friend in Africa, General Boniface, has cut off the grain supply to Ravenna, so the hungry citizens there have no love for the usurper. Civil war brings nothing but destruction to the people. I pray God grants me the means to avoid it."

"How do you plan to cross those impenetrable swamps surrounding Ravenna?"

"I'm hoping an Angel will guide me."

Athenais laughed. "Are you taking pages from Pulcheria's gospel?"

Placidia's eyes twinkled, and a smile tugged at the corners of her mouth. "Years ago, a young boy helped me escape from my brother's court through the marshes. If I can find him grown, he might guide my army back. Angelus was quite a scamp. His sort are survivors. I'm hoping to renew our acquaintance."

"We all pray for your success in this venture, Placidia."

Her aunt nodded. "Which way is the nursery again? I swear a magician comes between my visits and moves the corridors."

Athenais laughed and guided her aunt to the left. "This way. I checked on the children this morning. Val is doing well with his lessons and Honoria seemed content to play with little Eudoxia. We will all miss them when they go."

"The nursery won't be empty for long, and Eudoxia has learned from Honoria to be a kind older sister."

Athenais put a protective hand over her stomach. "If God wills it."

"Are you in poor health?" Placidia turned anxious eyes to her.

"No. Melia says all is going well, but she said that the last time."

Placida squeezed her arm. "I know it is difficult, but try not to fret. Do what you can to keep yourself calm and healthy. If you wish, I can postpone my leave-taking until after the baby arrives."

"Oh, no!" Athenais cried. "We delayed you enough. I won't leave your people in distress because of my fears and fancies. They need you more than I."

Placidia nodded. "I'm proud of you, Athenais. A good ruler will always choose her people over her own personal comforts. You are a worthy consort to your husband."

"Thank you, Placidia. You've been a wonderful teacher. I hope we can continue our friendship through correspondence."

"Assuredly. My wish is that you can visit Ravenna and Rome someday."

"I would love to!" She patted her stomach. "When the children are older and the borders safe."

A cloud passed over Placidia's face. "Don't put off your wishes too long, my dear. For some things there are never the right times, and you must do what you can when you can."

Athenais leaned her head onto her aunt's shoulder. "Good advice, as always. I will miss you terribly."

Chapter 28

Imperial Palace, May 425

I*T'S SO GOOD HAVING MY FAMILY AROUND ME.* ATHENAIS SURVEYED THE DOMESTIC scene with a sigh of contentment from her seat on the floor. Eudoxia drooped in her arms, having worn herself out chasing a ball. Athenais' brother Valerius was winning another game of latrones from Paulinus based on the pile of white stones on his side of the board. Her aunt Doria sat nearby embroidering a blanket for the coming baby. This room always soothed her—filled with warm carpets, cushioned chairs, and children's toys. A soft spring breeze wafted the scent of orange blossoms from the garden beyond the open doors. The late afternoon sun faded from the sky. A servant lit oil lamps to chase away the shadows.

Almost time for Eudoxia to go to bed. She held her daughter a little tighter when a profound sense of sadness overcame her. *Someday she'll leave me to go to the West. I'm sorry, my child.* She rested her head on her daughter's golden curls. *If this next baby is a boy, I can keep him close. Please God, I need a son. Theo needs an heir.*

Theo put aside a pile of reports with a satisfied smile. "Good news from Ravenna," he beamed at the room.

"Don't keep us waiting, my love." Athenais looked up. "How goes the war?"

"Helion writes that Placidia took the city by stealth and quashed a rebellion led by a soldier named Aetius and a band of mercenary Huns. They travel soon to Rome to acclaim young Valentinian Augustus."

"I'm so pleased for our aunt. She hoped to avoid a civil war and all the destruction that causes. Placidia must have found her Angel to lead her across the swamps."

Athenais set Eudoxia down and struggled to stand up. Theo quickly crossed the room to give her a hand.

"Thank you, my love." Her heart quickened at the love showing on his face. "I shouldn't get down on the floor when I can't get up!"

"Do what you want, Dearest. I'll always be there to offer a helping hand."

"Nana?" Athenais turned to the watchful nurse in the corner. "It's time for Eudoxia to go to bed."

"No!" Eudoxia seemed to come awake with a burst of energy and clutched her father's leg. "Story first, Papa!"

He lifted her into his arms. "What do you want the story to be about?"

"Lions!" She gave a miniature roar.

"Lions? They're too scary for bedtime stories. You'll have nightmares."

"Won't!" Her little face screwed up in concentration. She roared again.

He pretended to be frightened. "See, lions are scary."

Her lower lip trembled; tears sparkled in her eyes. "All right, my little princess. Lions it is." He took her to a comfortable couch and settled her on his lap. Her head rested on his breast. "I'll tell you the story of Daniel in the lion's den and how the Lord saved him."

Athenais walked over to Paulinus and her brother, stretching her back. *Not long now.* "Who's winning?"

Paulinus looked up with a grin. "Your brother cheats!"

"Do not!" Valerius countered. "You owe me five solidi."

"He bleeds me dry, night after night." Paulinus faked a swoon.

"Then stop playing with him," Athenais scolded.

"How will I ever win my money back, if I stop playing?"

Athenais rolled her eyes, but said, "If that's what it takes to keep you at court, I approve." She had seen little of Theo's friend during the past year. He seemed to always be on some mission or checking on distant estates. She had missed his easy ways and sense of humor.

She turned as Theo carried Eudoxia to her nurse and kissed her sleeping face. He wiped his eyes before turning back to beam at Athenais. Her heart swelled. *I am so lucky to have such a loving husband and tender father for my children.*

Before she could say anything, Pulcheria, Arcadia, and Marina entered. The easy chatter and laughter stilled. Theo glanced at the gathering dusk, held out his hands, and smiled. "Sisters." Arcadia and Marina smiled back. Pulcheria kept that pinched sour look that marked her face more often of late.

If she's so unhappy here in the palace, why doesn't she go live in one of her own residences? The thought had crossed her mind more than once over the past years. *Maybe Theo can convince her to reside elsewhere.*

"Your wife and her family are not joining us for evening prayers?" Pulcheria glared at the gathering.

"You know I cannot kneel in this state, Sister. Will you not say extra prayers for my health and safe delivery?" Athenais asked sweetly.

"Come sisters," Theo all but shooed them out the door. He threw a frowning glance over his shoulder as he left.

"Really!" Aunt Doria snorted. "What is wrong with that woman? Does she not understand your need for rest?"

"She cannot help herself, Aunt." Athenais shrugged. "She has seen me as a rival since before I entered the palace. I pity her. Theo may listen to her, but a loving sister will never be able to replace a loving wife and family."

"You've done well, Athenais." Paulinus said with a sad smile. "Theo couldn't have a more perfect mate."

Then why are you so sad, my friend? She wondered.

"Sister, have you spoken with Theo about my appointment as *comes rerum privatarum?*" Valerius distracted her. "With me in charge of the emperor's private estates and revenues, I can best look out for your interests. Anyone other than family might be tempted to steal from you."

"Already done, Val." She yawned. "Theo should talk to you about it soon."

"Come, Sweetling, let's get you to bed." Doria took her arm and guided her from the room. *Yes, it's good to have family near—at least some of them!*

"May I join you, my love?" Theo stood in her bedroom doorway.

"Always, my heart." She set aside her codex and patted the bed covers. "I believe I can't sleep unless we've had our private chat before bed."

"I don't want to tire you." He slipped into her room to take his accustomed place at her side on top of the covers.

She snuggled under his arm, her head on his chest. "I've been giving some thought to your question."

"Which one?"

"What I want after the birth of our baby."

"Let me guess. Jewelry?"

"No."

"A country estate in your own name?"

"No."

"A marble bust of you for the Senate House?"

"No!" She lightly slapped his arm. "After all this time, you don't know me at all."

He chuckled. "I know you well, my love. You want books."

"In a way. I'd like to expand the Constantinople University. It is woefully inadequate for a capital city. I want to endow thirty chairs in grammar, rhetoric, philosophy, and law."

"You don't want to build a church?"

"Pulcheria builds churches all over the city. I leave that to her." She kissed him on the cheek and cuddled closer. "I grew up in the Academy in Athens. Our university here is a pale copy. Your government needs well-educated people to run your empire. Men who know their math and law and are well-schooled in ethics and philosophy."

"I don't know, my love." He frowned. "Pulcheria might not approve."

"Pulcheria has her place in your government. She will see the advantages if you present them to her. These teachers can train our civil servants and offer a path to prosperity for those endowed with intelligence and talent, but little wealth or connection. Why would she be set against that? Surely you can show her the advantages of this expansion and how it would make her life easier."

"Possibly."

"There is a boon for you as well. How many times have you complained about the chaotic state of the imperial laws? The magistrates' frustrations over contradictory constitutions and obsolete rules? With a class of well-educated men, you could bring order to the mess."

"A Theodosian Code?"

"It would be a legacy, my love. All yours, but you will need people to do it." She gazed into his doubting eyes. "Please let me help you in this."

He sighed. "I like the idea. Let me think on it."

She lay quietly on his chest listening to his breathing before bringing up the next topic. Talking to Theo about his sister was always tricky. Athenais learned early to approach the subject with some delicacy. "Did prayers sweeten Pulcheria's sour mood?"

"Not completely."

"Why has she been so upset lately?"

"You don't want to know the details." He laughed. "She seems at odds with most of the council lately and spreads more discord than amity."

"Do you agree with her positions?"

"Not always and when I take a different tack, she nags me constantly to change my mind."

"That's not right, Theo!" Athenais pulled away to look directly into his eyes. "You're the Augustus. Her role is to advise, not dictate. If you chose a different way, she should support you and applaud your wisdom, not undermine your confidence."

"I wish Pulcheria would stop seeing me as the little boy she had to protect." He chewed his lower lip in thought. "I love her, but I think she's unhappy here in the palace and it colors all she does."

"I'm so sorry, Theo. I know I'm a source of her unhappiness. She continually complains to me that I should have more priests and fewer poets reading to my ladies. I've tried to please her, but I believe nothing less than my pledge to marital chastity would satisfy her."

Her husband patted her rounded belly. "We certainly can't have that, my love."

She sighed. "If you asked me to, I'd give up my salons. That might go some way to smoothing her ruffled feathers. I don't want to cause disharmony in your life."

He hugged her closer. "No, my love, I won't ask you to give up anything. You don't ask Pulcheria to change and she shouldn't require it of you. I know you are a good Christian woman and loving wife and mother. Pulcheria needs to keep to her own sphere."

"Is there anything you can do to help her see your way? Perhaps a gift to Pulcheria after the birth would help soften her antagonism toward my expansion of the university."

"A bribe?" He laughed. "You've lived with my sister for four years. Nothing can bribe her."

"No, dearest, not a bribe. An acknowledgment of your love and esteem. You are showing the court that you value both of us equally and should assure your sister of your love. What would be a suitable gift? One that shows your generosity and can give Pulcheria the freedom to live her life as she wishes without the irritations of my salons?"

"She has some estates inherited from our father outside the walls. My sisters don't live there because it is inconvenient to travel to their charitable missions and the court." He mused. "I could give them residences inside the city."

"What a wonderful idea! Pulcheria can order her household as she wishes and still advise you. Arcadia and Marina can continue representing the imperial family through charitable works in the city. That is a perfect solution, my love."

"Yes, rather elegant." He held her close. "I'll have the papers drawn up tomorrow and give them to Pulcheria after the birth. I'm sure she'll be pleased."

Athenais yawned and settled in his arms with a satisfied smile. *Whether she is or not, my life will be considerably more pleasant with her gone from the palace.*

Chapter 29

June 425

"NOT THE BLUE AND GOLD. I PREFER THE GREEN TUNIC WITH THE SILVER trim." Paulinus directed his servant. "The Augustus frowns on ostentation at his audiences and the silver is more subtle."

"Yes, Master."

The man pulled the green tunic over his head and belted his waist with a matching green leather belt with silver studs and a buckle in the shape of a wolf's head. His green leather boots sat at the side of the bed.

The room was smallish compared to his personal quarters at home, but this guest suite in the palace afforded him ready access to the emperor. Access he had eschewed for nearly a year after the death of baby Arcadius. *My heart broke every time I saw Athenais looking so lost and sad. Thank the Good Lord, her most recent labor went well, and she delivered a healthy baby girl. A boy would have been better.* A crushing dread had lifted from his soul when he got word that mother and child were doing fine. *Three pregnancies in four years can wear a woman out. I'd hate for my goddess to lose her looks and vitality. I hope Athenais doesn't try again soon for an heir.*

He heard a disturbance in the receiving room before Theo burst through his door and shouted at the servant, "Out!" The man scurried from the room and his friend started pacing, a hurt scowl marring his features.

"Theo, what has you so agitated? Would you like some wine?" Paulinus moved toward the ever-present ewer on a sideboard.

"No wine, friend. I've found that wine seldom makes my mind sharper or moods more pleasant—especially the next day." Theo rubbed his temples as if trying to relieve a headache. He had remained steadfastly sober after the birth of his first daughter.

"Then what can I do to relieve your distress." He turned suddenly and cried. "Is anything wrong with the Augusta or the baby?"

"No Athenais and Flacilla are healthy and content. That's why I'm bringing my troubles to you. I don't want to disturb their peace."

"What troubles?"

"Pulcheria." Theo continued pacing. "I knew she would oppose my gift to Athenais of endowing chairs at the university, so I gave my sister a gift to show her my affection and esteem: two residences here in the city and the palace at Hebdomon, fully staffed, and a contingent of guards."

"A most generous gift, my friend." Paulinus crossed his arms over his chest and leaned back against the wall. "I take it she didn't appreciate your generosity?"

"She threw it back in my face." Theo stood dejected with his empty hands outstretched. "She suggested that it was a plan by Athenais and her brother to get rid of her so they could control me and the empire."

"What a ridiculous notion. You are a strong Augustus who makes decisions for yourself, not an ignorant boy tossed by every whim that comes his way."

"And I said as much to her. What I didn't say is how much her disdain hurts." Theo's eyes glistened, but no tears fell. "Why doesn't she trust me? Why doesn't she believe I can be the ruler she taught me to be? She believes me to be a weakling and a failure."

"Do you believe the same?"

"No!"

"What will you do to prove her wrong?"

"I've already dismissed her from her councilor duties and ordered her from the palace. I will rule on my own. It is long past time."

"Good! May your reign be long, and your name go down in history, Flavius Theodosius Augustus." Paulinus gave his friend a deep bow. *She did it! My goddess excised that grasping bitch from Theo's side. Now he will be the Augustus this empire deserves.*

Chapter 30

The Great Church, Constantinople, April 428

Athenais exited the imperial wagon on the arm of her husband, followed by six-year-old Eudoxia. Athenais felt three-year-old Flacilla too young for the long and—sometimes—arduous religious ceremonies of the Easter service at the Great Church.

It seems so silly to take a wagon across the plaza when we could walk from the palace, but, as I'm constantly reminded by the eunuchs, "That's not done!" Makes me almost nostalgic for my rows with Pulcheria. Resisting her sister-in-law's strict religious rules seemed an easy exercise compared to bucking the rigid protocols of the Master of the Household for formal processions.

All were dressed in imperial purple, from their leather slippers to the amethysts sparkling in their diadems. Athenais held her head high, out of pride and the need not to disturb the towering confection Dorothea had built out of her blond curls and seeming yards of fake braids, held together with sewing thread and strands of pearls. *I should have a wig made like Aunt Doria's for these occasions. It would be much simpler.*

She wanted to smile and wave at the assembled horde of people who cheered and chanted during their progress, but again, "that's not done." Both she and her daughter wore thick silk veils to hide their "sacred faces" from the crowd and preceded at a stately pace up the steep steps of the Great Church to the vaulted propylaeum—the monumental entrance hall decorated with two-story granite columns topped with capitals decorated with Greek crosses. *Theo did well when he rebuilt this church. It's a testament to his greatness.*

They continued through an atrium decorated with multi-colored floor tiles and reddish-purple porphyry columns to the basilica and central altar. Tall narrow windows near the ceiling let in a little natural light, but the gloom was mostly dispersed by hanging oil-light chandeliers and standing candle sticks. Inside the basilica, the earthy scent of frankincense dominated. Athenais breathed deep. *So like rosemary, one of my favorites.*

They continued up a short flight of stairs to an overhanging balcony reserved for the imperial family. Directly across from them, Pulcheria, Arcadia, Marina and a coterie of their virgins occupied a duplicate balcony. The new bishop, Nestorius, sat on his throne behind the pulpit in full Episcopal raiment—gold pectoral cross and ring, casula embroidered with gold and silver crosses, and crozier in the shape of a gold-headed shepherd's crook.

I miss Bishop Atticus. He was such a good friend to me and Theo, may he rest in grace with God. Theo struggled to fill the bishop's chair over the past two years. The church leaders fought over the coveted spot until they reached a compromise candidate, the elderly and harmless Bishop Sisinnius, who lasted but one year. Upon his death, Theo sought to avoid the rancor of the past election by choosing the bishop himself. He rejected Pulcheria's man Proclus and was rejected by his favorite candidate the holy man Dalmatius, who hadn't left his monk's cell for forty years. He settled on an outsider, Nestorius from Antioch, a renowned speaker and learned churchman. With Pulcheria's blessing, the new bishop took his post in time for this Easter sermon.

Athenais removed her veil and observed the women across the hall. Arcadia pointed at the altar and said something to Pulcheria, who frowned and shook her head. Athenais stared, trying to discern what upset her sisters-in-law, but couldn't see anything wrong. She only came to the Great Church for important holy days, much preferring the more casual services of the palace priest for regular Sundays, so was unfamiliar with the normal decorations.

"Is there something amiss at the altar, Theo? Your sisters seem upset."

He surveyed the scene and took a sharp indrawn breath. "Pulcheria's portrait is covered and the gift of her robe as an altar covering is missing."

"Maybe Bishop Nestorius has a different esthetic in mind for the sacred space around the altar. It is his church now and he should be able to choose the symbols that please him. I'm not sure I'd want a picture of Pulcheria glaring down at me from behind the altar."

"It wasn't a portrait of Pulcheria Augusta, it showed the Virgin Mary with Pulcheria's features. She gave it to the church at the Feast of Mary in December to great acclaim." Theo frowned. "I'll have a discussion with the bishop. Pulcheria won't be pleased."

Pulcheria Augusta or Pulcheria as the Virgin. Same thing in my mind and probably hers! Athenais had resigned herself to the fact that her husband and his sister were still bound by their religious devotion. Pulcheria and her virgins joined Theo and the bishop for communion and a meal after services. She, as a non-virgin, was denied entry to the sanctuary and was just as happy to avoid her sister-in-law. *At least she isn't interfering with the government now.*

A feeling of expectation rippled through the worshipers as their new bishop approached the pulpit, acknowledged the imperial presence, and launched into his sermon on the resurrection. They stood rapt as he quoted the gospels and expounded on their meanings. After the final prayer, the worshipers chanted "Hosannah! Peace to Bishop Nestorius! Glory and long life to the Augustus!"

Nestorius stood basking in the adulation for several minutes, before indicating with his hands that people should stop. "Go in peace, my friends, on this blessed day when Christ rose and saved us all." He left the pulpit, attended by a phalanx of priests and monks, to retreat to the sacred sanctuary behind the altar.

Athenais turned to her husband. "The new bishop is certainly a vibrant speaker, Husband. The people seem pleased."

"Nestorius did well for his inaugural, but he failed to call my sisters 'Brides of Christ' among our honors and titles and the people noticed."

"As did your sisters. I've never seen Pulcheria with such a stormy face. She may be regretting her approval of your choice."

"I'm sure this is just an omission on the good bishop's part. He is new to the city and our ways. I'll speak with him after communion and straighten all this out."

She patted his hand. "Without a doubt, my love, you will handle this." She glanced at the restive crowd as they waited below for the imperial family to leave the basilica. All had been on their feet for the lengthy sermon. "Come Eudoxia, it is time for us to return. Husband, we'll see you at evening prayers."

She covered her hair and face with her veil and inspected her daughter to make sure she was also covered. Theo nodded and offered his arm for the procession down the stairs, where he broke off with some of his guards, and she continued to the wagon for the short ride to the palace.

Inside she doffed her veil and sighed. "What did you think of the new bishop, Eudoxia?"

Her daughter pushed her veil aside and looked thoughtful. "He has a lovely voice and I liked his stories. I'll ask for a copy of his sermon to study, so I can discuss it with Father."

"That won't be necessary, dearest. You have enough work to do with your normal studies."

"But I want Father to be proud of me. He always instructs me to know my gospels and love God."

"You please your father in many ways, child. Say your prayers with love and grace in your heart. There is plenty of time to understand the gospels later."

Eudoxia leaned back with a frown. "As you wish, Mother."

I fear for the girl. It is right that she wishes to please her parents, but she is already showing signs she will follow her father's path of rigid religiosity. I must not let that happen. She will know love and freedom and power to make her own choices, not be dictated to by clerics and monks.

THEO ALWAYS LOOKED FORWARD TO THE EUCHARIST SERVICES AT THE GREAT Church. The litany of prayers and ritual reenactment of the Last Supper made him feel closer to God. Communing with the church elders in the most sacred part of the Great Church with the bishop officiating was an intimate ritual, out of sight of the common people.

If I were not born for the diadem, I believe I would have made a good bishop. The life of the church appeals to me more than signing laws, settling property lines, and moving troops around. He smiled as he inhaled the sweet smoky smell of myrrh burning in the censers. *Yes, I could be happy here.*

The faces of his wife and children laughing at some trifle flashed across his mind and he sighed. *But I have other obligations. I will serve God in my role as Augustus and His Viceroy on earth.*

He spied Bishop Nestorius talking with his archdeacon, Peter, and veered to join them. Nestorius bowed as he approached. "Your Sublimity, please forgive me. There is a commotion at the gate to the sanctuary and I must attend to it. Please continue to the altar and I will join you shortly."

Theo nodded and took the extra time to pray, kneeling at the altar. Nestorius returned and administered the Eucharist. It was only when he and the holy men trooped out to the Easter banquet that he realized his sisters were absent. *How strange. Pulcheria enjoys communion and suppers with the bishop as much or more than I. What could have delayed her?*

He turned to the bishop. "My sisters are not in attendance. Do you know the reason?"

Nestorius looked at him in surprise. "Women cannot be in the sanctuary. I turned them back at the gate. Their presence would befoul this sacred space."

"My sisters are pledged virgins and your previous brethren have welcomed them to the sanctuary for the Eucharist and following meal."

"Augustus, those bishops erred. I know some believe virgins through their sacrifice 'give birth to God,' but this is an error. Women are the daughters of Eve, through whom sin came into this world. I told the Augusta this and bid her leave us in peace."

"I thought through Mary Theotokos all women are blessed. Bishop Sisinnius preached that the female can no longer be held accursed, because the Mother of God surpasses even the angels in glory."

"That is a doctrinal error. Mary was not Mother of God. She was blessed to give birth to the Christ child and should be referred to as Christotokos. She did not redeem all women from the sin of Eve. Only Jesus Christ can redeem our sins. This spreading worship of the Virgin Mary as the Mother of God is dangerous. If we elevate Mary in this way, are we any better than the pagans?"

"I hadn't thought of it that way." Theo nodded. "My sister is a great follower of the Virgin Mary. She dedicated several churches and altars to Mary Theotokos across the city."

Nestorius grabbed the emperor's arm and his eyes blazed with passion. "You must correct your sister in this. Whoever claims—without qualification—that *God* was born of Mary prostitutes the reputation of the faith. Has God a mother like Zeus?" He shook his head with some violence. "No! And we must not let this belief lead us astray."

Have I been in error all these years? May God forgive me. I must learn more about this and correct my thoughts and beliefs. "I understand your basic premise, Bishop, but I and my people have been taught that the Virgin gave birth to God the Son. Instruct me in your thinking so that together we can lead my sisters and our people to the right path."

"It is a subtle difference and easily misunderstood. Because God is One but manifests as Three is confusing to many people and Mary as God-bearer elevates that confusion. People might now believe that Mary gave birth to God before time began, which John specifically contradicts in the Gospel, 'Mary did not give birth to God before time began; she gave birth to the human incarnation of God the Son.'"

"So, you are not contradicting the blessedness and grace of the Virgin Mary, but believe the literal interpretation of Mary Theotokos will lead people to heretical thinking?"

"Exactly! Elevating Mary Christ-bearer to Mary God-bearer leads the ignorant to place her in a pantheon equal to God. Instead of praying to God, they will pray to His 'mother' to intercede on their behalf, because what son would deny his mother? Our religion then becomes little different from the pagans with their vast pantheons."

"I do see the danger, but is it real? I have never thought of Mary as Mother of God the Father."

"You are an educated man and steeped in religious studies. Most people know little more than what their priests tell them and are easily led astray. I intend to correct that misunderstanding and expunge all heresies. Give me a world free of heretics, Augustus, and I'll give you heaven on earth."

I could reign over a heaven on earth? Can this man do this? "Who do you consider heretics, Bishop?"

"The Novatians, Manicheans, Arians, and other Christians that deviate from orthodoxy."

So many! And most of my generals are Arians. We must be careful in leading these people to the right path, but it should be done for their souls' sake. "We must talk more of this, Bishop. I wish to help you in your crusade, but I must understand how to proceed."

"Of course, Augustus. I would be honored to tutor you in these matters, and we can discuss how your government can aid the church in saving our people's souls."

I pray God it is not too late!

Chapter 31

The Great Church, December 428

PAULINUS LISTENED WITH GROWING ALARM AS FATHER PROCLUS PREACHED a traditional sermon on Mary Theotokos to the rapt crowd. Women of all stations attended the Feast of Mary, which lauded the Virgin and elevated their status—if only for one day.

The priest looked out over the crowd and beamed. "The Lover of Mankind did not disdain to be born of woman, since She gave Him life in His human nature. If this Mother had not remained a Virgin, the Child born of Her might be a mere man, and the birth would not be miraculous in any way. Since She remained a Virgin after giving birth, how is He Who is born not God?"

Paulinus smiled. The heart of the matter. If someone denied Mary the title Mother of God, they denied Christ's divinity. A doctrine long accepted in Christianity. He was an indifferent Christian and found the squabbles of churchmen over the meaning of single words boring and the constant begging for alms, when they wore silks and ate off gold plate, petty. The church was rife with men striving for power and influence.

This newest fight over whether Mary was "Mother of God" or "Mother of Christ," as championed by Nestorius, seemed ridiculous, but it caused riots and needed to be curbed. In less than a year, the new bishop had alienated nearly everyone in the city. Nestorius ordered the monks back to their cells to pray, leaving few to care for the poor and sick. If they didn't go, he had them beaten and excommunicated. He burned the Arian churches and earned the name

"Firebrand." *Thank God, Theo came to his senses and brought that to an end. If it had continued, he would have lost most of his army or they would have rebelled and ravaged the city.*

Thwarted, Nestorius had next waged war against popular entertainments such as chariot races, mimes, and theaters. In that, Theo backed him. The people traditionally used the emperor's appearances at races and the theater to put their grievances directly before the Augustus. With the hippodrome and the theaters closed, the people had no way to communicate their dissatisfaction and the oppressed city seethed with resentment.

Theo, my friend, do you know how much danger you are in? He looked up at Theo in the imperial box flanked by Athenais. Paulinus' heart gave a lurch. *My goddess, I need you to whisper in your husband's ear again. I suspect we are in that rare place of having common cause with Pulcheria in this.*

He glanced up at the women's section. Theo's sister did indeed have a beatific smile as Proclus continued supporting his Mary Theotokos argument with quote after quote from scripture. The corner of his own mouth turned up in a rueful grin. Pulcheria had brought her formidable armament to bear against the errant bishop after he curbed her privileges and had the temerity to accuse her—in writing!—of not being a virgin.

I was careful to keep my name out of the gossips' mouths in relation to Athenais, but never expected to be linked in a romantic way with the Virgin Augusta. It was bad enough that Nestorius forbade women to attend evening prayers or watches for the dead after the sun set "so they would not fall prey to their weak natures and commit fornication." But to accuse Pulcheria and me of being lovers? She must have been apoplectic!

Paulinus brought his attention back to Proclus as he concluded, "Through these words, the Holy Virgin and Mother of God is clearly indicated. Let all contention cease, and let the Holy Scripture enlighten our reason, so that we too may receive the Heavenly Kingdom unto all eternity. Amen."

The congregation thundered back, "Amen!" as Proclus stepped back and took a seat to the side of the altar.

Nestorius rose from his episcopal throne and took the pulpit. "It is not surprising that you who love Christ should applaud those who preach in honor of the blessed Mary, for the fact that she became the temple of our Lord's flesh exceeds everything else worthy of praise."

Was Nestorius conceding the point?

"However, claiming that *God* was born of Mary prostitutes the reputation of our faith. Has God a mother? If so, we may excuse paganism for giving mothers to its deities. Mary was not Theotokos. For that which is born of flesh is flesh. A creature did not bring forth Him who is uncreated; the Father did not beget by the Virgin a new God."

"Heresy!" A man stood in the nave, shaking his clenched fist at the bishop.

Paulinus recognized Eusebius, a high official in Theo's government. *One of Pulcheria's agents?*

"Bishop, recant your words!" Eusebius demanded. "The nature of Christ was settled over a hundred years ago. The Divine Word underwent a second birth in the flesh of a woman. Christ is God. Mary is His mother. Therefore, Mary is the Mother of God."

"It's not that simple…"

The restless crowd shouted "Heresy!" "Blessed is Mary Theotokos!" "Blessed are the Virgin Princesses! All grace to the Most Pious Ones!"

That last chant cemented his thoughts. *Yes, Pulcheria has orchestrated this little demonstration. At least we are on the same side in this battle, Augusta.* He gave a mental salute to his foe.

Nestorius tried to regain control with his golden voice and rhetorical style, but went unheard by the thundering crowd. He gathered his robes and left the pulpit, back rigid, face stormy.

Theo's face looked just as disturbed as he stood and exited the box with Athenais on his arm. Paulinus fought his way through the chanting crowd to the descending stairway where a contingent of scholae stood guard. Recognizing him, they let him pass.

"Augustus." He bowed to his friend with deference in this public place.

"Paulinus!" Theo clapped his hands on his arms. "Just the man I need."

"How may I be of service?"

"I need to talk to the bishop. Would you escort the Augusta back to the palace? This crowd is restive, and I'd feel better with her in your care."

Athenais gave her husband a concerned look. "Will you be safe, my love?"

"Where is safer than a church?" Theo grinned. "I will soon have all in hand."

"Of course, Husband." She gave him a shy smile and he left down a back passage toward the sanctuary, trailed by half the guards. Athenais held out her arm. "Paulinus, my friend, it has been too long. Have you been avoiding me?"

"Never, my goddess." He wanted to kiss her hand and gaze deeply into her eyes, but quelled his impulses. "But I do wish to confer with you. Perhaps in the wagon?" *I hope I have enough time in that brief ride across the plaza.*

She gave a knowing glance at the guards and took his arm. As they exited the Great Church, Paulinus spied Proclus huddled with Pulcheria. *Hah, I was right! The Augusta is behind this assault on the bishop. I almost feel sorry for the man. He does not know what hornet's nest he has stirred.*

He helped Athenais into the wagon, just as a crowd of women streamed by waving palm fronds and chanting "Blessed Mary Theotokos." They temporarily blocked the plaza.

He took the seat opposite Athenais and leaned forward. "I don't know how much time we will have, but I need to speak to you."

"What disturbs you, my friend?"

"I have tried to talk to Theo about Nestorius, but he refuses to listen. You need to convince your husband to abandon the bishop, or he might lose the love of his people."

"I happen to agree with my husband about Nestorius' theology. Mary Christotokos is a more accurate title for Mary." She sat back in the padded seat. "I had a similar discussion with Bishop Atticus when he tutored me before my baptism. I've always found the idea of a triple god and a Mother God to be a bit ridiculous. Anyone who's studied philosophy knows that there is only One God, as did Bishop Atticus."

"The Good Bishop denied the Gospel?" Paulinus closed his gaping mouth with a snap.

"What he specifically said was that God was unknowable by humans—a fact disputed by some philosophers who have spent lifetimes studying sacred mathematics. A few have claimed to see the face of God. Alas, mathematics was never my strong suit, so I believe on faith, which is the heart of any religion."

"And do you believe in Christ as your savior? That's the foundation of the Christian religion."

"Jesus was a great teacher and had much wisdom to impart. He tried hard to turn people away from avarice and cruelty toward peace and harmony. If all followed his teachings, this would indeed be a heaven on earth, but the church is a human creation maintained by flawed men. However, its rituals give comfort to many, including my husband, so I participate out of love." She laughed. "Besides, The Lord's Prayer is much easier to memorize than Euclid's theorems!"

The wagon gave a lurch as it started across the forum. Paulinus put out a hand to steady himself. "Whether or not Nestorius is right about the finer points of the Mary Theotokos debate, he is wrong on the execution. How much do you know about what has been happening outside the palace during the past year?"

"I've been busy with the children and my writing. I rarely attend audiences." She frowned. "Theo has been upset of late, but has given me no cause to fear."

"Things are getting out of hand. The people and the church are turning against Theo and his support for Nestorius." Paulinus told her of all the bishop's missteps since he took over the see.

"You and Pulcheria? Lovers?" Athenais laughed until tears fell from her eyes.

"That was one of the Good Bishop's smaller stumbles. We nearly lost the support of the army when he started burning the Arian churches."

"Oh my. That *is* serious." The laughter dropped from her voice. "How could I not know? What can I do?"

Paulinus felt the difference as the wagon moved from the rougher cobblestones of the forum to the smooth plaza on the other side of the Chalke Gate. "We haven't much time, my dear. You need to get more involved with your husband's reign. He needs your level head and sage advice. I don't always agree with Pulcheria, but she has a good head for politics and, for the most part, advised Theo well. Theo is my best friend, but his willingness to trust religious people leads him astray. You need to counter Nestorius."

The wagon rolled to a stop. Athenais looked stricken. "But how—"

A guard opened the door, bowed low, then offered a hand. "Augusta."

Paulinus followed her out of the wagon. "As you wish, I promise not to be such a stranger, Augusta. May I call on you and your husband tomorrow?"

"My husband will be pleased." She nodded her head and disappeared into a procession of guards.

I was selfish staying away because of my own pain. I only hope I'm not too late.

Chapter 32

January 431 (three years since the last scene)

WHAT A WONDERFUL UNDERTAKING, THEO!" ATHENAIS' GAZE SWEPT across the room dedicated to her husband's project of reorganizing the law codes. A dozen scholars read and sorted stacks of documents, making notes. The familiar smell of fresh ink and vellum filled the air. "Your legal code will go down in history as one of the great accomplishments of your reign."

"Thanks to you, my love." He smiled as he patted her hand on his arm. "Without the young lawyers your university turns out, it would have taken me decades to consolidate and update the empire's laws."

"Your Serenities." An officious-looking man approached and bowed low.

"Consul Antiochus." Theo acknowledged. "I believe you share a birth city with the Augusta."

"Antioch does seem to turn out superior scholars." Athenais turned a curious gaze on her countryman. *The distinguished honor of consul usually went to imperial family members, successful generals, or high political figures. Rarely scholars.* "My father taught there before moving the family to seek a chair at the Academy in Athens. His name was Leontius."

"I'm afraid I never made your father's acquaintance, Augusta." He bowed again; eyes downcast. "My loss most assuredly."

"What system are you using to sort the laws?" Athenais asked. "There are so many!"

"As of now, we're consolidating laws that touch on government, taxes, cultural, and religious practices. These are the ones that change most over time."

"Nothing on crime?"

"Very few. Those are dealt with at the local level, Augusta, and rarely reach the notice of your Sublimities unless it touches on the imperium itself."

"Antiochus has been leading my effort for the past two years and has accomplished much. We are on schedule to publish in four years, are we not?"

"With diligence, Augustus." Antiochus smoothed away a troubled frown. "We have a vast amount of material to work with since the Great Constantine's reign. There are many versions of the same law, some with copy errors that change the meaning."

"I'm sure you and your team will not disappoint me, Antiochus."

Her husband's emphatic tone held a hint of menace Athenais rarely heard in his voice. *This project is close to Theo's heart. I must pay more attention to it—and to Antiochus. It will be fun to talk to an educated man who shares my birthplace, and I might be able to soften Theo's wrath if they are optimistic in their end dates.*

An errant bead of sweat gathered at the consul's temple. "Of course, Augustus. We will not fail you."

"I'll leave you to your work, then." Theo led her out of the scriptorium and back toward the family wing of the palace. "What do you think, my love?"

"A worthy undertaking."

"Pulcheria approves, as well."

"She has been here?" She tried hard to keep the alarm out of her voice. *Our home has been so peaceful since she left. I hope she isn't trying to worm her way back into the palace.* "You told me that Arcadia and Marina came on separate occasions last week to harangue you about Nestorius. When did Pulcheria visit? What did you talk about?"

"Nestorius."

Athenais relaxed. At least on this point, she was in alignment with her sister-in-law. She wanted the bishop gone. Nestorius had proved nearly as pernicious an influence on her husband as Pulcheria. He resumed midnight and dawn prayers, insisting she join him since her womb hadn't quickened. Another grievance to lay at the bishop's feet. Atticus had encouraged Theo to lie with his wife and increase their family. Nestorius played on her husband's guilt about feeling lust for his wife. Theo still showed affection for her and their daughters, but his visits to her bed had gradually decreased to a tiny trickle over the past three years. They hadn't coupled in over four months, and she was growing desperate. *I'm only twenty-nine. Certainly not too old to conceive again, but how can I if my husband refuses my bed?* The thought strengthened her determination to see the bishop gone.

"Did Pulcheria tell you about the letter from the Bishop of Alexandria addressed to both of us? It was quite flattering. He said he provided more simple explanations to the younger Virgin Princesses but thought we two could comprehend more sophisticated reasoning."

"He obviously doesn't know my sister's or my wife's temperament." Theo laughed. "He sent me a tome, as well. Bishop Cyril has been most active in his opposition to Nestorius. I suspect it has more to do with Nestorius' threat to bring him up on charges in an Episcopal court, than any real difference in theology. Nestorius showed me a copy of a letter Cyril sent to Pope Celestine. The Alexandrian Bishop has written far and wide accusing Nestorius of heresy and taking our bishops' words out of context. Cyril stitches together bits and pieces of sermons and writings to twist Nestorius' beliefs."

"I've never liked Cyril. He seems to be one of those bishops that seeks power over holiness. He was implicated in the murder of a famous woman philosopher Hypatia. Shortly after her death, pagan scholars flooded Athens seeking refuge from the riotous mobs that Cyril whipped up in Alexandria. I heard many a frightening story. The Academy's gain, their loss."

"I remember that case. The council of Alexandria sent a delegation asking for an investigation and redress for Hypatia's death. She was well-liked and respected among the city fathers. Pulcheria was new to governing and did little more than limit the number of Cyril's personal guards and their access to public spaces. I think she regretted her reticence in that matter. She has no love for Cyril either."

Another point on which I'm in accord with Pulcheria. Maybe miracles do happen. "Cyril's rantings aside, Theo, you know I agree with you on Nestorius' teachings but, through his unforgiving harsh ways, he has lost the love and respect of the people. Paulinus tells me the city is a tinderbox and will go up in riot soon. Nestorius is the wrong messenger for the right beliefs. If you do not resolve this matter, I fear for your rule and all the good that you've done."

"Pulcheria made the same argument." He sighed. "I can no longer stand in opposition to my family, my people, or the other church fathers. But I will not put aside Nestorius. He is a good friend and advisor. The core issue is a matter of doctrine. That is the province of the church. I will convene an ecumenical council of bishops in Ephesus on the next Pentecost to resolve these issues. The people will learn from the church fathers the right path."

"You will abide by the rulings of the bishops, even if they decide against Nestorius?"

"Yes, but I believe Nestorius will win them over. Cyril maligns him, but our bishop will prove as much to his fellow bishops. Nestorius is no heretic."

"If he can't win his way?"

"I am learned, but the bishops are the final authority. I will do their will."

"Thank you, my love. You have lightened my heart." She kissed him on the cheek. *I hope the damage isn't too great for Theo to overcome for his people and me.*

Chapter 33

June 431

ATHENAIS SURVEYED THE NURSERY FROM THE DOORWAY WITH A SENSE OF satisfaction tinged with sadness. She sometimes imagined a little boy with her gold curls and his father's brown eyes chasing a ball across the room or riding a hobby horse. *No, Arcadius would be seven now with a gap-toothed smile and scraped knees. Maybe a puppy following him around the room.*

She blinked the tears from her eyes.

Nana dozed in a corner, worn out by her duties caring for Athenais' two lively daughters. They each had nurses and servants, but Nana oversaw all the activities in the nursery including tutors, meals and the health of the princesses. *She's raised three generations of Theodosians. Maybe it's time to retire Nana with a pension and bring in a younger woman.* The old woman snorted and woke herself up. She looked around, saw all was well, and drifted back to sleep. *Yes, it's time to let the old woman rest.*

Eudoxia cried, "Mama," rose from her couch, and crossed the room with an exaggerated stateliness to hug her.

"You've been practicing your comportment." Athenais nodded approvingly. "Your father will be proud of his princess."

Athenais gave her a hug. "Have you grown? You fit right under my arm. I swear you were only knee high this morning."

"No, Mama." Her daughter giggled. "I've been this tall for a while now. Soon I'll be this high." She stood on her tiptoes and raised her hand above her mother's head.

"I'm sure you will, my dear." Athenais steered her daughter back to a padded bench to examine her embroidery sample. Eudoxia, at nine, already showed promise of great beauty, but none of her mother's glowing personality or aptitude for scholarship. She seemed to take after her father's more retiring nature and preferred light reading to real study.

"What are you working on?"

"It's a handkerchief for Father. I embroidered a picture of his favorite horse in the corner and his initials opposite."

So that's what that brown blob is supposed to be. I thought maybe a dog. "Nicely done, my love." Athenais looked around the play area. "Where's your sister?"

"She complained of a pain in her head, so Nana gave her some willow tea and put her to bed early."

"I'll check on her after evening prayers." Athenais looked up as Theo entered the room. "Speaking of—"

"Papa!" Eudoxia ran to her father—no stately glide this time.

He lifted her up, swung her around, and put her down with a grunt. "I'm getting too old for that, and you are too heavy, my child."

Nana, roused from her nap by the squeals of her charge, stood and approached Theo. "You shouldn't encourage her, Dominus. She will soon be a young lady and should act like it."

"Oh, Nana, she is still a child. Let her behave as such."

"I want to be a young lady, Papa. Let me go with you to evening prayers. I promise to be good."

"I'm sure you will be, but not tonight. I have something I need to discuss with your mother."

Eudoxia's face took on the glistening eyes and trembling mouth that few could resist, but Theo held firm.

"Tomorrow, Sweetling. I promise." He chucked her under the chin and her stormy face cleared. He held out his hand to Athenais. "Coming, my dear?"

Nana gave a brief bow as they left.

"Your face is even more disturbed than your daughter's. What is amiss?"

"Not here in the corridors." He guided her to his private chapel where they wouldn't be surrounded by servants or guards and shut the door. "Pulcheria sent me this."

He handed her a lengthy letter and paced the floor as she read it. She turned to Theo with a pounding heart. "The bishops failed to resolve the issues at Ephesus. What will you do?"

"They didn't just fail, they made things worse." He stopped pacing and said with an exasperated tone, "Bishop Cyril, as usual, overreached himself. He incited violence in the streets and in the Council. Several bishops are dead!"

"Murdered?" Athenais put a hand to her mouth.

"Some died of their injuries. Others, more aged, succumbed to a plague that struck the city." Theo took up his pacing again. "Bishop John of Antioch, who was to make Nestorius' case, stayed outside the city when he heard of the disease and Cyril took advantage with his Egyptian toughs. He and Bishop Memnon of Ephesus excommunicated Nestorius and declared him a heretic. When Bishop John heard, he entered the city, recruited some disaffected bishops and set up a rival synod. The bishops mire themselves in charges and countercharges; flinging excommunication at each other as if they were pagan curses." He stopped, head drooping and hands dangling at his sides and mumbled to himself. "Pulcheria is right. The church should not be left to its own affairs."

"No, Husband. You swore to abide by the finding of the church fathers. You cannot put yourself in their place."

Theo looked at her with chin raised. "I am God's Viceroy on earth. He chose me to rule, and I will. If these flawed men cannot set aside their petty differences for the peace of the realm, then I must do it for them."

"But how will you make that decision?"

"I've asked Pulcheria to come back to the court to advise me. We will decide this together for the greater glory of God and to benefit the souls of the people."

"As you will, Husband." *At least Pulcheria will counter Nestorius, but will she be enough to change Theo's mind and regain the love of his people? And will she stop there?*

THE NEXT DAY, THEO ENTERED THE DAPHNE AUDIENCE ROOM WITH PULCHERIA on his arm. The whispering buzz of the courtiers stopped as they progressed to the far end and resumed at an increased volume as they took their seats with Pulcheria on his right.

"Welcome back, Sister." He leaned in to whisper.

"I am always at your call, Brother." She nodded and gave him a tight smile.

It felt good to have Pulcheria back at his side. Athenais had proved uninterested in the day-to-day minutiae of ruling, preferring to hold salons in her suite and preside over formal occasions with ambassadors or nobles. Although she rarely attended open audiences, his wife had planned to be present for Pulcheria's reinstatement. When Nana sent word Flacilla was unwell, Athenais rushed to her daughter's bedside. She stayed all morning in the nursery, sending a note to apologize for her absence.

I hope little Flacilla is not too unwell. Both his daughters had been afflicted with the usual childhood fevers and sniffles, but neither had been seriously ill. The bishops' deaths in Ephesus reminded him of the precariousness of life. He shut his eyes in silent prayer. *Dear Lord, watch over my child and bring her back to health. And guide me in your will as I sit in judgment this day. Amen.*

"Master of Offices, who is to appear before me today?"

After disposing of a couple cases of boundary disputes among his nobles and hearing the petition of the bakers' guild to raise the price of bread, a commotion broke out at the open door.

A guard blocked an old man with his out-stretched spear. "You can't enter the sacred place of the Daphne without permission!"

The old man cried, "Out of my way, son. I go where I wish," as he ducked beneath the spear.

"Leave him be, guard. That is Dalmatius and welcome in my court." Theo shouted down the length of the hall. *What can the holy father want with me? He hasn't left his cell for years, not even to take on the bishopric.*

The revered holy man hobbled forward with the help of a staff and took a stance facing Theo. The ancient archimandrite wore rough brown robes, his gray hair and beard long and matted, his eyes sparking with anger.

"Get the holy man a seat. He should not stand in my presence!" Theo stepped down from his throne and personally sat the ancient on a stool, suppressing a sneeze at the smell of incense and urine wafting from the old man's body. "Holy Father, what brings you to my unworthy court?"

Dalmatius looked at him with blazing eyes. "Augustus, I have broken my vow. I left my cell and life of perpetual prayer for the first time in forty-eight years because this cause is most important to the souls of your people."

Blood turning to ice, Theo managed to say, "I am most humbled by your presence, Father, and understand the issue must be very grave to bring you from your holy house into our presence." He bowed his head in humility. "In what way may I serve you?"

"Agents and agitators block communication from your most humble and holy servants in Ephesus. Bishop Cyril sent me a message concealed in this beggar's staff, as the only way his words might come to your ears. He begs you to receive his emissaries." The old man removed the bronze tip from his staff, pulled out the rolled-up message, and handed it to him.

As Theo read the missive, his icy blood boiled. *How dare they!* He shot an angry glance around the receiving room. "I had no notion messages and emissaries were blocked from my presence. I vowed to hear both sides if the bishops could come to no conclusion."

Dalmatius sneered. "Your own man, Count Candidian, set spies and guards on all the gates of Ephesus and Constantinople, to stop any word from Bishop Memnon and Bishop Cyril reaching you."

Theo reddened under the holy man's scorn. "I will replace Count Candidian and order the way clear at once. Both delegations shall provide their findings, and I will hear them."

"That is all I ask." The holy man rose. "Blessings on the house of Theodosius. God give wisdom to the Pious Emperor and long life to the Virgin Augusta."

"Thank you, Father, for your wisdom and blessings." Pulcheria rose to escort the old man to the door. "Our guards will provide a litter to your monastery."

"That is not necessary, Daughter. The people escort me and offer a shoulder when I falter." His sister knelt and the holy man put a dirty hand on her head. "The people love you, Augusta. You are their voice with the emperor. God bless you and give you strength to guide your brother onto the right path. Amen."

"Amen." Pulcheria rose.

The holy man's words roared in Theo's head. *Neither Dalmatius nor my sister think I can make the right decision on my own. Are they right?*

Chapter 34

"AUGUSTA, YOU MUST EAT SOMETHING." DOROTHEA TEMPTED HER WITH spiced lamb and honey cakes, but the sight of food made her queasy. *When was the last time I ate? Some bread and cheese, yesterday morning?*

"Take it away." Athenais turned back to Flacilla's bed and placed a cooling cloth on her daughter's head.

What had started as a headache and fever didn't raise undue alarms. The physician called it "putrid throat," a condition most children survived. But Flacilla's throat swelled to grotesque proportions. She couldn't eat and had trouble swallowing the bracing broths and herb teas Nana brewed for her. Her body grew weaker and barely raised the linen sheet with her irregular breathing. Each time Flacilla broke into a barking cough or ceased to breathe for a moment, Athenais' heart leaped out of her chest. The court physician, Nana, and a dozen servants hovered about the nursery, talking in low whispers, helpless to alleviate her precious child's suffering.

Please God, spare my child. She's an innocent and has so much more life to live. Tears fell unnoticed down her cheeks as she pushed the damp curls away from her daughter's forehead. *I promise a new altar cloth for the Great Church and gold candlesticks. I will go back to attending midnight prayers. Please don't let Flacilla die!*

"Domina, you must get some rest. It will do the princess no good if you fall ill as well."

Some of the desperation in Dorothea's voice pierced Athenais' misery.

"Make me a cot by her bed. I'll sleep by her side after I've had a cup of the broth Nana made." She stood, but grabbed the bedpost as the room spun. She closed her eyes and swallowed convulsively as her gorge rose. *Dorothea is right. I need to care for myself, or I'll be of no use to my child.*

"Domina?" Her servant cried as she grabbed Athenais' elbow to steady her.

Athenais opened her eyes and took a deep breath. "I'm fine."

"Augusta, take this drink." The physician handed her a goblet of warmed wine.

She took a gulp and detected a bitter taste under the cloying spices. "Poppy juice?" She shot an accusing glance at the physician.

"No, Augusta!" His shocked look allayed her suspicions. "Only willow bark for headaches and chamomile for calmness." She finished the goblet and turned away from the bed with a sigh. "I will be back very shortly. Nana, do not leave her side."

"As always, Augusta." The old woman's eyes were red with weeping and the creases in her face seemed to have doubled since Flacilla's illness began. She took the vacant stool and mumbled prayers as Athenais took the physician's arm and led him away.

"Doctor, what more can we do?"

He stroked his graying beard. "I've done all I know to do, Augusta. If she can survive the night, I believe the princess will recover. She has reached a crisis with the fever. If it breaks soon, she will be fine. If it gets worse—"

Athenais held up her hand. "Don't say it, Doctor." *Saying it will make it real and I mustn't even think that thought.* "Go attend the princess."

She sat in the anteroom letting Dorothea fuss over her, combing her hair, making her drink another herbal cup, and changing into a night robe. "Enough." She waved away some tempting warm bread spread with cheese. "I must get back to Flacilla."

She noted with satisfaction that the servants had prepared a cot for her next to the bed. She could sleep while holding her daughter's hand. She yawned and her thoughts went fuzzy. *Did the doctor lie to me about the poppy juice?* She stumbled to the cot and lay down, her last thoughts another prayer. *Please, God…*

"Augusta, wake up." The doctor's worried face swam into view as she clawed her way out of a chaotic dream.

"Flacilla?" She sat up. Nana wept on the other side of the bed. Guilt drove away the muzziness from her brain. "Is my daughter dead?"

"Not yet, Augusta, but you should send for your husband, if he wishes to say his farewells." The doctor pointed to the red mottling creeping up Flacilla's legs and the blue cast of her lips. "The signs of death are on the princess, and I don't know how long she will live."

"Shall I fetch the Augustus?" Dorothea asked.

Athenais shook her head. "No. He's in St. Stephen's chapel seeking guidance about Nestorius. I will go. He must understand how dire this is."

She threw a cloak over her night dress and fled down the corridors toward the chapel, trailed by a profound sense of guilt. *I should have told Theo how ill she was, but I didn't want to distract him from the Ephesus delegations. He would have dropped everything to be by Flacilla's side. But he needed to be the Augustus today. Will he forgive me?*

Theodosius Augustus sat in the quiet elegance of St. Stephen Protomartyr's chapel mulling his options. He bowed his head and held out his hands toward the carved ivory triptych, covering the small vault where the saint's bones resided. It showed the adventus from ten years ago in exquisite detail and brought back pleasant memories of that triumphal day when all the people of Constantinople turned out to welcome the saint's bones to their new home and blessed their emperor for the gift. *Where did I go wrong? How could I let the people drift so far into heresy? The ecumenical council was supposed to end the discord, but those stubborn bishops only made it worse. Now I must lose my friend Nestorius or lose my people.*

He threw himself prostrate before the shrine. *Our Father, Who art in heaven... Please God, give me the strength to do your will in this battle to come.* A feeling of warmth and peace spread from his heart to his fingertips and toes. *Thank you, O Lord, Mighty One, Giver of Grace.*

He heard the slight rustle of robes as someone entered the chapel and stood still while he finished his prayer. He clasped the feeling close to his heart, slowly came to his feet, and spied Pulcheria standing just inside the entrance. "Sister! Did you come to join me in prayer?"

"No." She took a couple steps into the chapel. "I'm so sorry to disturb your peace, Brother. Arcadia just brought word. The people occupied the Great Church. They demand your presence."

His peace shattered like glass and pierced his heart. He gasped. "What for?"

"They recognize your responsibility to govern both empire and church. They tire of turmoil in the streets. Riot and dissension are not good for trade or family. The people have rejected Nestorius. They wish his ouster." She took a deep breath. "Some even demand his death. You must take control, Theo. Decide. Be aware, siding with Nestorius will mean the end of your rule."

"I know." He turned his back on her to look up at the bejeweled cross above the marble altar. His shoulders shook with the violence of his emotions. "But Nestorius is a friend and loyal supporter. How can I give him up?"

"Theo." She put a hand on his shoulder. "His time is done. All stand against him and his heresies. Your continued support brings discord to your people, confusion to their minds, danger to their souls. Their love for you is slipping away. Go to them. Show your people you are their father and Augustus. Show your love. Show your care. Protect them from their enemies, both external and spiritual. They need you."

"Husband."

Theo turned around. Athenais stood in the door, hair in disarray, eyes red from weeping.

"What's wrong?"

"Flacilla." Athenais wrung her hands, eyes darting from place to place. "The doctor says you should come."

Pulcheria took Athenais' hands in hers, looking into her anguished eyes. "I didn't know she was ill. How serious is it?"

"The doctors are with her. She runs a high fever and might not survive the night." Athenais reached out to him. "Theo, will you come? I need you."

"Yes, my love." Theo took Athenais from Pulcheria's grasp, escorting her from the room, an arm about her waist. He looked back over his shoulder. "Sister, will you go to the Great Church? Hear what the people have to say? Assure them Nestorius will be gone."

"Of course." His sister bowed slightly. "I'll say prayers for Flacilla while I'm there."

"I'm so sorry I didn't tell you sooner, Theo." Athenais gasped as they hurried down the corridors. "The court physician assured me that this was just a childhood ague and Flacilla would soon be on her feet."

"I knew she was ill, but I've been so preoccupied with the Ephesus delegations." His sense of guilt surged. "I should have asked."

After a few moments of silence, Athenais asked. "What was Pulcheria doing here?"

"Nothing you should worry about."

She stopped in the hallway, pulling him to a stop. "No, Theo. My trying to protect you led us to this place. Don't try to protect me in turn. What is wrong?"

"Not in the hallways." He gave the briefest nod to the guards and servants lining their path, backs to the walls and heads bowed. "I'll tell you all, later. I trust Pulcheria to take care of the situation. The people love her and will follow her lead."

She nodded as they continued to the nursery. At the door, Theo took a deep breath and steeled himself. The loss of his stillborn son was tragic, but he never knew the child, just felt sad for the loss of his potential. Flacilla was his favorite. She had too many of his features—mousy hair and narrow chin—to be accounted beautiful like her older sister, but she had her mother's sharp wit and outgoing ways.

"Time is short, my love." Athenais tugged at his arm.

He nodded and they entered the somber room. A priest mumbled in the corner. *Good! At least my child is being sent off with prayers and blessings.* The doctor and Nana sat by the bedside holding his daughter's hands, while several servants inhabited the shadows, lacking purpose.

He approached. "Nana, go rest. I'll comfort my child on her final journey." The old woman put a hand to her heart and left the room sobbing. Athenais dismissed the doctor and took Flacilla's other hand, murmuring a lullaby. When she stumbled to a halt to clear her throat of tears, he asked, "How long has she been like this? Is she in pain?" His heart lurched. *I hardly recognize her with her swollen features and shrunken body. How she must of have suffered! Why would God allow that? Is He punishing me for supporting Nestorius or for repudiating him?*

"She's had no awareness for almost two days. The doctor said that was for the best, that she would feel no pain." Athenais' eyes again overflowed with tears as she asked that question that all distraught parents cry over a sick or dying child, "Why, Lord, why?"

Flacilla's chest rose once, twice, then rose no more. Theo looked at his despairing wife, as their daughter's soul slipped away from her body with a final sigh. A pain gripped his heart in a vise so hard, it took his breath away and he gasped for air. Athenais threw herself onto the bed, clasping her dead child to her bosom, wailing her grief.

The servants slipped out the door, leaving them to their mourning, all but Dorothea. "Augustus," she bowed and asked in little more than a whisper. "Should I take the Augusta to her bed? The physician left me with a tincture to help her sleep."

"Not yet. Prepare her room and I'll bring her shortly."

The young woman nodded and left, closing the door.

Theo allowed Athenais several minutes to get through the most violent part of her grief. When her cries quieted to steady sobs, he put a hand on her shoulder. "Flacilla's gone, my love. Leave her earthly remains in peace." Theo gently disentangled his wife from their child. "Her ordeal is over, and she rests in grace with God."

Athenais nodded and sagged against his shoulder as they drifted toward her rooms. Dorothea had lit candles and burned sandalwood incense. A single goblet of wine sat on the table next to the turned-down bed. He sat his wife on the edge of the bed. "Drink this, my heart. It will help you sleep and forget for a while."

"But I don't want to forget our child."

"You won't. We will both keep her close in our hearts for the rest of our lives."

She sipped at the concoction smelling of wine, honey, and poppy juice, while he removed her slippers. She set the half-full goblet aside. "Will you stay with me tonight, Theo? I don't want to be alone." She laid back against the pillow. Her eyes closed and she mumbled. "I've been alone so much..."

He stripped down to his tunica and slipped into bed at her side. She curled against his shoulder; her head drooped. His hand resting on her breast sent a shock to his groin and he became hard. *Not now. Not like this. Why does my body betray me so?*

They hadn't coupled in several months as he wrestled with the Nestorius issue. Since she had given birth to Flacilla, he had visited her bed infrequently. Nestorius had encouraged the idea that fasting should include refraining from intercourse. When Athenais confronted him with his absences, they quarreled and put even more distance between them. *It's my old sin of lust, come to taunt me in my grief. I mustn't give in to it.*

He left his wife asleep in her bed to return to the stone floor of the chapel and pray. *God guide me in this. What more do You demand of me?*

Chapter 35

Athenais entered her bedroom and took off her mourning veil with a sigh. *Forty days. Who declared that forty days of mourning was enough? It's a paltry number and will never be enough for my child.* The thought of the small coffin interred with the other Theodosians in the Church of the Apostles still brought tears to her eyes and a pain to her chest. She wiped the moisture from her cheeks. *Life goes on and so must I, but it is so hard!*

She sat at her make-up table and surveyed the damage in her polished silver mirror. *I'm not yet thirty, but no longer a fresh beauty. Three pregnancies and the deaths of Arcadius and Flacilla have taken a toll.* Just thinking their names brought a knot of tears to her throat. She closed her eyes and brought her Aunt Doria's advice to mind, "Get out of bed. Put on your clothes. Do something, anything. Write a poem, talk to a friend, eat a meal. Help someone else if you can. Go to sleep and do it all over the next day. Some days it will be harder to get out of bed than others, but these will become fewer as time goes on. Have faith that color and joy will return to your life. It will."

The thought of her practical aunt with her improbable red wig brought a smile to her face and a little light to the darkness in her soul. *I'll invite Aunt Doria for an extended visit. Valerius is back from his tour of the provinces. It will give us comfort to spend some time together as a family.*

"Augusta, would you like me to prepare you for bed?"

She started at Dorothea's voice. The young woman sometimes melted into the shadows and Athenais forgot she was there.

"No. I join my husband for evening prayers. Braid my hair in a simple style to match my plain robes." She frowned at the mirror. Two parallel lines appeared between her brows and the crinkles at the corner of her eyes deepened. *When did I become so vain? I remember upbraiding Doria for her fussiness the first time I met Theo. I told her true beauty was on the inside, not the outside. Then I fell in love with my husband and wanted him to desire me above all others. Much good that has done lately.*

A gentle tug on her head as Dorothea combed through a tangle brought her back to the present. She watched her servant in the mirror as she struggled to comb out the knot without causing pain. Her face screwed up in concentration and the tip of her tongue stuck out the corner of her mouth. The sight brought a rare smile to Athenais' face and reminded her of Doria's advice. *Maybe there is some way I can help this faithful servant. She's served me for ten years and I know almost nothing about her.*

"Dorothea."

"Did I hurt you, Augusta? I'm so sorry!" The young woman's eyes met hers in the mirror and went wide with worry.

"No, Dorothea. It occurred to me that I'd like to reward your faithful service of ten years, but I know nothing of your current situation or needs."

"I need nothing, Domina. I'm well-fed and housed now. I'm most grateful to serve you."

"You said 'well-fed *now*.' Were you hungry at some point?"

"My mother died when I was five. I didn't know who my father was. The landlord turned me out saying I was too young to work and of no use to him, so I begged on the streets for a short while." Dorothea shuddered at the memories. "A kindly monk took me to an orphanage run by holy women. I later found out that Pulcheria Augusta sponsored the orphanage and saw to our welfare. She personally visited and picked a few children to be trained as servants at the palace for room and board. That's how I came here."

"That's why you are so loyal to my sister-in-law." Athenais raised a questioning eyebrow. "Do you still report to her?"

"Not since she left the palace. I've never told her anything not already gossiped about." Dorothea blushed. "I know you have had your differences with the Augusta, but she is a kind lady and truly does care for the poor."

"A most admirable trait," Athenais admitted. "But what of you? Surely you have a life beyond my rooms. Is there a young man you fancy or another position you covet?"

It seemed impossible, but her servant's face turned an even deeper red. "There's a guard that talks to me frequently when you are out. He has kind eyes and a warm smile."

"What's his name?"

"Nikolaos."

"Do you wish for marriage?"

She shrugged. "I live to serve you, Domina. I have no other ambitions."

Well said, but was it true? I'll have to investigate this more thoroughly. Perhaps I can add some small measure of happiness to the life of this young woman. It makes my heart lighter just thinking about it.

"I have no Cupid's arrow to make you love another, Dorothea, but a woman should never be completely reliant on others or she's little more than a slave. I know what that's like. I will provide you with a monthly stipend. You may do with it as you wish—spend it, save it, give it away. It will provide you with some measure of freedom. If you should ever want to leave my service to start a family or a business of your own, let me know and I will help."

"You are most generous, Domina." Dorothea cast her eyes down, but a tear escaped the corner of her eye. "Thank you."

A water clock chimed marking the hour. Athenais looked around her bedroom. "Replace the linen and freshen the room. I hope the Augustus will return with me after prayers."

"As you wish, Domina."

Athenais left Dorothea to manage her other servants and continued to the family chapel. Theo prayed alone, prostrate before the altar. She joined him, silently recalling the Lord's Prayer and adding blessings for her remaining family and the souls of her lost children.

When she heard her husband stirring, she appended a hasty "Amen" and gathered herself to hands and knees.

"Dearest." Theo extended a hand to help her up, a beatific smile sweetened his face. "When you carried Flacilla, I told you I would always be there for you with a helping hand."

"Thank you, my love."

He pulled her to her feet and the smile turned mischievous. "I have a treat for you."

"Will you come to my bed this evening?"

The smile disappeared, replaced by a wary look in his eyes. "No, but I think you will enjoy this nearly as much." He took two letters out of the breast of his tunic. "These arrived from our Aunt Placidia by imperial post this afternoon. One for you and one for me." He handed her the packet sealed with Placidia's wolf signet and guided her to a padded bench next to the wall.

"I've missed her so! Especially these past forty days. She was such a comfort when we lost Arcadius." Athenais sat with the missive in her lap for a few moments picturing her determined aunt as she last saw her, on horseback flanked by the dashing Captain Sigisvult as they led her personal guards out of the city. *I can't believe it's been six years. I carried Flacilla then. Placidia never got to know my daughter.*

"You go first, dearest," Theo urged. "I know you've longed for additional correspondence after her first formal note."

Athenais broke the seal, unfolded the thick vellum, smelled the ink, then read:

My beloved niece Athenais,

Although I'm sending this letter by diplomatic post, I wanted to speak to you from my heart, as if I were there in person to comfort you. Please imagine my arms tight about your shoulders and my lips whispering in your ear and know that I share your suffering.

My heart broke for you when I first got news of your terrible loss. I wanted to ride to Constantinople to be by your side. But I am Placidia Augusta, as well as your loving aunt. I cannot abandon my people in the middle of a war with the Vandals. I know in your kind heart you will forgive me for my absence. I comfort myself with the knowledge you have loving family close to care for you.

My hope for you is that your previous loss lends you strength to weather this one. Trodding that dreadful path again might seem like an infernal punishment, but God doesn't test you beyond your limits. You made your way to the light then and you will arrive there again. Lean on your family but fight for them as well. I have found that tragedy can strengthen purpose and will. Put those to good use.

Although I cannot be at your side, think of me often, as I think of you. I pray for your sorrow to soften into sweet memories. Until we can meet again, I hold you in my heart, Sweet Niece.

By her own hand,
Your sorrowful and loving aunt Placidia

She held the letter out to Theo and sniffed back tears. "It is most comforting."

He read it and handed it back. "Good advice from a woman who knows suffering."

Athenais nodded at his own letter. "Don't keep me waiting, Husband. See what words of wisdom our aunt has for you."

He opened the letter and quickly scanned it, a frown blooming on his face.

"Well?"

"Our aunt is of two natures and she split them. You received the soft loving words of one mother who knows grief to another, and I got the hard words of our Warrior Aunt. The Vandal King Gaiseric is on the verge of defeating the combined armies of the East and the West. Generals Aspar and Boniface are in retreat. She warns me that we will have to increase our armies and likely pay off the Huns if we wish to counter the Vandals in Africa."

"What of General Aetius? He held the Huns in check for years."

"Placidia keeps him in the north, away from Italy, because she feels he has imperial ambitions. He supported the usurper against her and has spent the last six years trying to regain Placidia's trust. It's likely he's biding his time to challenge her again. Only his skill as a general and his popularity with the people, keeps him at his post."

"She has no words for your grief?"

"A few, but nothing as supportive as yours. She braces me for war."

"Take her words for me as your own, my love. Our aunt knows how we love and support one another in the good times and these times of trial." She laid her head on his shoulder and caressed his thigh. "Come to my bed tonight, dearest heart. Let us make another child. A boy. An heir to your diadem."

Her hand drifted to his groin.

"No!" Theo shoved her away and she landed on the floor.

Athenais sat for a moment, ankle twisted and throbbing under her. *Why? What did I do?* She looked up at her husband, face twisted with pain, "Theo?"

"I'm sorry, my love!" he cried and joined her on the floor. "I didn't mean to hurt you. You startled me with your affection here in this holy place." He pulled her to him and cradled her head on his shoulder.

"The fault is mine, Husband. I should have been more circumspect." She nodded toward the jewel cross. "I will ask the Lord's forgiveness." She bowed her head and prayed, briefly. She raised her face to his. "Will you give me your shoulder to lean on, dearest. It is a long trek to my bed. I've asked the servants to prepare for your stay."

"Of course, I'll help you, Athenais, but I cannot stay in your bed."

"Why not?" She rubbed her still throbbing ankle. "It is but a sprain and will be fine in the morning."

"I've taken a vow of chastity."

"Vow? For how long? A week? A month?" Her mind whirled in confusion.

"For the duration of our marriage." Theo whispered.

"You cannot do this. You are my husband and vowed to worship me with your body. We need more children. You need an heir!"

"Your womb has not quickened since Flacilla's birth. Nestorius said that is a sign from God of his disfavor."

"God's disfavor? With you or me? I'm the other party in this vow and you didn't seek my advice or permission." She pushed away from him and stood, shaking, one hand on the wall for balance. "Nestorius is gone. Repudiated by the church fathers and hated by your people. Put aside his dangerous teachings."

"It is not just Nestorius. I feel this as well. When I put aside the sin of lust, my soul soars and I feel closer to God."

"Theo, I beg of you, please recant this vow. If not for me, think of your people. Without an heir what will happen when you die?"

"God's will," he said softly.

"Bloody, barbarous civil war!" Athenais shook with the need to get through to her husband. "I've read my histories. God is good, but men are not. Men crave power and will rush to fill the vacuum left by your lack of an heir. Young Valentinian and our daughter Eudoxia will have to go to war to hold this empire together. All those poor sick people your sisters minister to, will be victims. Your Theodosian Code will go up in murderous flames as the empire crumbles. It is your duty to your people."

He stood and put a hand under her elbow to steady her. "My first duty is to God. He will provide after my death. This is my decision, Athenais, and it is final."

"What does Pulcheria say about this?" She grasped for some small chink in his armor. Surely his sister sees the danger. Pulcheria always put protecting Theo's rule at the center of her ambitions.

"She encourages me to follow my faith. I've asked her to return to my court in her former role as an advisor."

"So, you consulted with your sister and not your wife about this drastic course." Athenais failed to keep the venom out of her voice.

"This was not Pulcheria's idea."

"But she didn't discourage it. How convenient for her that you turn from your wife at the moment of your sister's return to power. She does not have your best interests at heart in this."

"Enough! You two have warred from the time you met. I will have peace in my own home." He let go of her arm and went to the door of the chapel. "I'll call a guard to escort you to your rooms."

She collapsed to the bench, head in hands. *Oh, my love, how did it come to this? I've lost not only my child, but my husband. What life is left to me?*

Part III

Pious Pilgrim

October 437 - February 444

Chapter 36

Imperial Palace, Constantinople, October 437

ATHENAIS COMBED HER DAUGHTER'S CURLS ON THE AFTERNOON BEFORE Eudoxia's wedding day. They would have little time for any intimate talk between the formal court reception this evening and tomorrow's ceremony and festivities. "You'll be a beautiful bride, my Sweetling." She had dismissed all the servants, so she could have a final few moments before she lost her last child. *The last six years have gone by so fast. I thought I'd have more time!*

"You've had a week, Mama. What do you think of Val?" Eudoxia's anxious eyes met hers in the mirror.

So full of hope. I can't let my bitterness ruin her wedding. I've sheltered her from my failed marriage for years, I can do it for a few more days. "My opinion isn't important. What do you think, my love?"

"He's so handsome! He made a striking figure at archery this afternoon." Eudoxia giggled.

"That he did." *I'm glad he stirred something in my girl. I worried that her father's asceticism would color her too much to enjoy the physical side of marriage.* "How much do you know about what will be expected of you on your wedding night?"

"Mother!" Her face blazed red.

"Yes, I am your mother and it's been the duty of mothers through the ages to prepare their daughters for marriage—and all that means. My mother died young, so Aunt Doria filled that role." *And did it admirably with practical advice and blunt humor. I only hope to do as well!*

"How does Aunt Doria fare?"

"As well as can be expected, she is much wasted from the tumor." *I must plan to go to her after the wedding, I would never forgive myself if she should die without my final farewells.* Athenais gave a shrewd glance at her daughter. "And you are a clever girl, distracting me with my concern for Aunt Doria."

"I wouldn't be so obvious, Mama." Eudoxia opened her eyes wide, feigning innocence.

"You've had lessons to prepare you for the role of Augusta, but nothing to prepare you for the role of wife. You don't even have the advantage of a farm girl who has been around breeding animals her whole life. You must have questions."

"The servant girls whisper sometimes."

"What do they say?"

Eudoxia's gaze dropped to her lap. "Does it hurt?"

"A little the first time, but not much if the man is gentle. Val is likely to have had experience and should be able to give you pleasure rather than pain." *Given the rumors of the Western Augustus' licentious behavior, Eudoxia won't have to deal with the incompetence of a virgin husband, as I did.*

"But isn't it a sin to feel pleasure?"

A sudden chill crept up her spine. "Where did you get that notion?"

"From the priests. They teach that lust is a sin."

"Why would God give us the capacity for physical pleasure, if we are not to enjoy it?"

"So we can overcome the temptations of the flesh and prove our worthiness to God. Are they wrong?"

Athenais drew in a deep breath. *I must be careful in this. I should have monitored her religious training more closely. I had no idea that Theo's beliefs were being taught so explicitly. Perhaps it's a good thing, she is going to the more liberal Western court.* "The priests and holy women are right when it comes to their own behavior. They are pledged to God and to lust after another is a sin *for them*. Unmarried people should also be chaste so as not to disgrace themselves or their families. But the Gospel also teaches that within marriage, a man and woman should love one another and produce children. The midwives believe that women cannot conceive if they do not feel pleasure."

Eudoxia frowned. "I'm not sure what you mean by pleasure."

Thank you, Aunt Doria! Athenais described a couple of the ways a man could pleasure a woman, leaving her daughter looking thoughtful and a little anxious. "Even though I'll be far away, Placidia will regard you as a daughter. She is an experienced woman and will help you in any way you desire. Think of her as you would me and take any questions or problems to her. And remember, physical pleasure inside of marriage is not a sin, my child. It is natural and should be enjoyed."

"Do you and Papa enjoy it?"

She felt a twist of her heart and avoided a lie. "We had you, didn't we?" Athenais put her arms around Eudoxia and squeezed. "You are my heart, dearest one. I want only what is best for you, but I won't be there to provide it. You must be able to speak for yourself and seek help if you need it. Can you do that?"

"Yes, Mama."

"Then let's get you ready for the evening's banquet. You were too young to remember your Aunt Placidia or Cousin Honoria when they were here last. They will be your family now and I want you to make a good impression when you meet them tonight."

Athenais kissed her daughter's cheek and wiped away a tear from her own. "I'll call in the servants now, my dearest."

Athenais matched her husband's stately stride as they entered the formal court reception that evening, her fingers resting lightly on his arm. Pulcheria followed behind. but would take the seat to the right of Theo on the dais to show her rank as chief advisor. *As opposed to me who is merely the wife who failed to give him a male heir and must sit on his left.* The gradual diminution of her status over the past six years, as everyone realized another child would not be born to the Augusti, left a sour taste in her mouth. *I must find something else to do with my life. Once Eudoxia is gone what will be left for me? Frivolous salons?*

Athenais wore all the accouterments of her rank: a diadem of pearls and amethysts adorned her hair. *Dorothea outdid herself for this occasion. Quite an accomplishment since she hasn't had much practice these past years.* With Pulcheria back in power, the court had gone back to its habit of austere dress. *At least this occasion has given the court an opportunity to explode in color and display its wealth.*

They took their seats and Athenais surveyed the Daphne audience room. It literally glittered with the elite of both Eastern and Western courts—women and men in an array of silk, linen, and wool outfits in all colors from the rainbow—except purple, which was reserved for the imperial family. The soft light of the oil chandeliers bounced off silver and gold embroidery and winked from the polished jewels dripping from ears and wrists. Even Pulcheria bowed to convention and wore the imperial regalia, something she eschewed in favor of her holy women's robes when conducting audiences with Theo.

Athenais reached up to touch Theo's wedding gift from so long ago. The huge amethyst fibula set in a gold starburst held her imperial purple cloak at her shoulder. The gem matched the jewels on her ears, neck, wrists, and fingers. The relentless purple was relieved by a blazingly white silk dalmatica embroidered with gold birds, clasped at the waist with a gold link belt. The memory of her own wedding day and the thrilling celebration at the hippodrome threatened to overwhelm her with sadness on what was supposed to be a joyous day.

Oh, Theo! We were so young and so in love. What happened to us?

A herald blew a trumpet blast quieting the crowd and announced, "Their Serenities Flavius Placidius Valentinian Augustus, his mother Galla Placidia Augusta, and his sister Justa Grata Honoria Augusta." In contrast to twelve years ago, the Western Augusti traversed the long hall in full imperial regalia, heads held high, meeting their relatives as equals. The combined courts bowed just as deeply as they had when the Eastern Augusti passed through only moments before.

Athenais eagerly awaited Placidia. Twelve years had touched her aunt lightly. The deeper wrinkles at the corners of her eyes and mouth only served to give her more gravitas. *Perhaps she will have some advice for me. I have always valued her wisdom.* Honoria, at nineteen, had grown into a handsome woman, with her mother's curly brown hair and a long, graceful neck. She also had more womanly curves than her mother, who tended to unfashionable slenderness.

They advanced to the bottom of the dais and the Eastern Augusti rose. Theo spread his arms wide. "Welcome Honored Cousins and Gracious Aunt to this celebration of marriage and the strengthening of our family ties. And welcome to the senators and nobles of our Western court. May I present my daughter Licinia Eudoxia Noblissima."

Covered in a nearly opaque knee-length veil and accompanied by the captain of the guards, Eudoxia entered through a side door to join her family on the dais. Hundreds of curious faces turned to the young princess, only to be disappointed when they couldn't glimpse her face. At fifteen, the princess rarely left the palace and then only for church services where she was similarly veiled. *I've always hated those veils. Another useless protocol I was unable to change.*

Theo signaled the herald who sounded another trumpet blast, freeing the courts to mingle and launching a fleet of servants with trays of food and drink.

"Placidia!" Athenais enveloped her aunt in a warm embrace. "Welcome."

"My dear." Placidia held Athenais at arm's length. "You are still as beautiful as your patron goddess."

Athenais didn't blush as readily as in her youth but did dimple with a smile. "You will think me a kitchen drudge when you see Eudoxia."

"My wife, a kitchen drudge? Hardly!" Theodosius embraced his aunt and turned to his cousin. "And Honoria! You've grown into a beauty yourself."

Pulcheria nodded a greeting. "Aunt, I am glad to see the Lord brought you safely to our shores."

"The Lord and my best horses." Placidia smiled. "We did encounter some rain and rockslides in the passes, which delayed us, else we would have been here three days ago."

Val interrupted, "Mother, may I present my bride, Licinia Eudoxia?"

Eudoxia pushed back her veil for the introductions. Athenais' breath caught. Her daughter glowed with porcelain skin, golden curls, and her own startling blue eyes. *Yes, we made a beautiful child and what is to become of her in a strange court?.*

Eudoxia cast her eyes modestly down as she approached Placidia, extending her hand and executing a brief curtsy. "Welcome, Mother."

Placidia took her hand in both of hers. "Thank you, my child."

"Is she not exquisite?" Val's eyes gleamed. "I shall have the most beautiful woman in the empire for a bride."

"Maybe then you won't dip your stick in other men's honey pots," Honoria muttered, just loud enough for Athenais to catch. She threw the girl a sharp glance. *I hope she doesn't spoil Eudoxia's evening with her venom. I should speak to Placidia about sheltering my daughter at court given its more licentious reputation.*

Pulcheria waved over a trusted older slave. "You shall attend Princess Eudoxia for the rest of the reception and accompany her to her quarters when finished."

Athenais frowned and tried to stem her tide of bitterness. *Is it not bad enough Pulcheria has taken away my role as consort, now she wishes to take on my role as mother?*

Theo turned to Placidia and indicated a door leading to a smaller audience room. "Let's retire. We have much to discuss, Aunt."

"May I come with you, Mother?" Honoria asked.

"No, dear, stay with your brother and enjoy the reception." Placidia smiled.

"But—"

"No." Placidia firmly cut off Honoria's protest with a raised hand. Her smile disappeared. "Stay with Val and Eudoxia." The two vertical lines marking her forehead deepened. Honoria stalked off; her face marked with lines identical to her mother's.

Athenais took Placidia's arm. "I sense some tension between you two."

"She has always been a difficult child. Willful and argumentative." Placidia glanced wistfully over her shoulder at her daughter's retreating back.

"You mean she shows spirit and intelligence?" Theo laughed. "I have much experience with women who exhibit those traits."

"Lately she has been asking to sit in council meetings." Placidia sighed.

"The urge to rule runs strong in the female Theodosian line." Pulcheria gave her aunt a significant look. "She sees you ruling for her brother, and my—our..." Pulcheria nodded at Athenais, "influence with Theo. Why should she not want a similar role for herself?"

"I see the truth of your words, but I have experience Honoria does not. Val is of age and rules for himself. I only advise."

Athenais patted Placidia's arm. "Maybe it is time to think of a husband for her. Give her a domain of her own to rule."

"That brings its own complications. I could never see Honoria's future clearly, as I could Val's." Placidia's face softened. "I only knew what I didn't want for her—an unhappy marriage for the sole purpose of producing heirs. Let's pray your Eudoxia will have many healthy children and make that fate unnecessary."

Athenais' full lips trembled; her eyes brightened with unshed tears. "The palace will seem empty without my only child. But she will be well loved with you." She glanced at her husband through lowered lashes. "I've been thinking I might make a pilgrimage to Jerusalem. It will be good for the people of the Holy Land to see a member of the imperial family and might ease my lonely...

uh… soul."

"An admirable ambition, Sister," Pulcheria agreed. "Perhaps time in the Holy Land will have a moderating effect on you."

Eager to get rid of me, are you, Sister?

They came to a sitting room, much more lavishly appointed than the last time Placidia visited. Servants provided a repast of shellfish, cheese, black olives, cold fowl with a pungent fish sauce, and a selection of fruit tarts amid many other delicacies that Athenais didn't partake of. *At least I've made my presence felt here in the family side of the palace,* Athenais mused. *To the point that Theo has started to complain to me of my excesses. Where else can I ply my talents?*

Pulcheria removed a cushion from a chair to sit on the bare wood. When they had all settled with wine and food, she said, "I've had opportunity to speak on several occasions with young Valentinian this past week. Your son seems to know little of the state of his empire, for one who rules."

Placidia colored at the bald criticism. "Val is an active boy and grows impatient with administration. Age and marriage will settle him into his duties." She gave Pulcheria a level stare. "And I will be there to guide him."

Pulcheria started to reply, but Theo interrupted. "How fare your borders? The Huns have been raiding our provinces again."

"The Patrician Aetius assures me the Huns are under his control. He recently used them to put down the Burgundian rebellion in Gaul." Placidia pursed her mouth. "As much as I detest the man, he is a cunning general. Aetius guards the western provinces with the fierceness of a mother lion protecting her cubs."

"But he leaves your African provinces orphaned and prey for the Vandals." Theo frowned.

"Will Aetius stay in Gaul during your absence?" Pulcheria asked. "I would think it dangerous for both you and your son to be absent from Ravenna at the same time, if Aetius is the threat you believe he is."

"General Sigisvult holds the passes to Italy. I will return to Ravenna shortly after the wedding and represent my son, while Val escorts his lovely bride in a slow progress back to our home. There will not be enough time for the general to make mischief."

Bored with the talk of barbarians and borders, Athenais raised her cup high. "To our children. May God grant they live long and happily." She finished her goblet and motioned to the servant for more.

Pulcheria and Theo frowned at her uncharacteristic excess. Her aunt gave her a worried look. *Let them condemn me! It's once in a lifetime that I give my only child away in marriage. Tonight I'll do as I will. Tomorrow I'll apologize, but only to Placidia.*

Chapter 37

ATHENAIS SIGHED AND STRETCHED HER BACK WHEN THEY SENT THE new imperial couple off to their wedding bed the next evening. The combined courts shouted their felicitations punctuated with lewd advice. Pulcheria blushed at some of the suggestions and turned away. *This joyous day brings back so many memories. Sixteen years since my wedding to Theo. Every sweet memory tinged with the bitterness of my losses and his betrayal. The ritual has changed only in the details.* The seals on the marriage contract made the union legal. All else was for show. The private religious blessing of the imperial couple, the chanting crowds at the public procession accompanied by generous alms to the crowd, the afternoon at the hippodrome, the evening banquet and receiving gifts from the courtiers. *And now I'm faced with an empty life.*

Athenais remembered her vow to ask Placidia for advice and turned to her on the dais. "Now that the formalities are over, I hope we can spend some time together this week, Aunt."

"Of course, my dear." Placidia patted her hand. "Did you write the wedding poem? It was beautiful."

"I had some help with the *epithalamia.* Your envoy Volusianus made a few helpful suggestions when he was not busy with Pulcheria finalizing the marriage contract. I'm sorry he wasn't here to see the fruits of his labors."

"I've been told he has taken a fever. I plan to visit him this week, would you care to accompany me?"

"He should have sent word!" Athenais frowned. "I found him a most remarkable man. Learned and witty. Volusianus was a welcome change from the usual dour courtiers. With Pulcheria back at court, I find my closest friends sent to the far ends of the empire on supposedly important business." *I haven't seen Paulinus or Dorrie in months. Another black mark for my sister-in-law.*

"I thought you might enjoy him, that's why I selected him to negotiate the marriage details. He is one of the last great pagans in our court. He's even disputed with Augustine of Hippo. His ascetic niece Melania has journeyed from Jerusalem to save her heathen uncle's soul." Placidia chuckled. "I admire her goal, but if the sainted Augustine cannot convert my friend, I fear she will fail."

"Melania the Younger? Pulcheria is a great admirer. I'm surprised my sister-in-law hasn't already paraded the poor woman through the city as another example of her piety."

"Melania is a force to be reckoned with as her greedy relatives have found to their chagrin. She gave away two great fortunes despite all their howling."

"Two?"

"She persuaded her husband to live in a chaste marriage after she lost two children and almost died from the second birth." Placidia sighed. "Her father married her off too young. She was only fourteen when she gave birth the first time. Her father tried to talk her out of her decision, but she stood firm. He finally gave his blessing on his death bed. Melania and her husband Pinianus were both only children and heirs to vast fortunes."

"So she chose a chaste marriage to avoid having more children?"

"Possibly, when she first proposed it, but she has embraced a strict ascetism since."

"I must keep her away from Theo. He needs no more encouragement in that direction." Athenais' shoulders drooped.

"Is your melancholy rooted in the loss of your daughter? I assure you I will love and protect her as my own. Have no fears on that account."

"Thank you, Aunt. Eudoxia is very innocent. She has been sheltered in the palace. Between her father's religiosity and my protectiveness, she knows little of the world, much less the snake pit of an imperial court. I came to the court an innocent, but I was older and had friends among the courtiers to advise and guide me." Athenais' frown returned and she mused, "I do miss my friends. Even when they are not on imperial business, they avoid the court now that Pulcheria is back at Theo's side."

"Your brother seems to have done well for himself. Is he not a comfort?"

"Since Valerius was made Master of Offices last year, I hardly see him. When I do, he is drawn and irritable trying to deal with Pulcheria's demands and the importunities of ambassadors and courtiers. I sometimes think the position is beyond him. He should have stayed in charge of the privy purse."

"Forgive me for asking this, but does not Pulcheria advise Theo well?"

"If she restricted herself to governing, all would be well, but she encourages Theo to religious excess." Athenais looked around the hall filled with laughing people and shook her head. "That is a conversation for another time. I don't mean to spoil this moment of joy at the union of our children. I see Pulcheria approaching. While the rest of us are obligated to attend the hippodrome and other celebrations this week, she will minister to the poor. You will have your choice, but I hope you will spare me some time. I'll take my leave of you and attend to the other guests."

"Of course, my dear. I'll send you word." Placidia patted her hand as Athenais pasted a false smile on her face and left.

Chapter 38

Athenais waited in the wagon outside Placidia's palace still irate with the chief eunuch who denounced this excursion.

"Augusti do not visit sick people," he had sputtered.

"Pulcheria Augusta has tended the sick for most of her life." Athenais said.

"That's different. Pulcheria Augusta is a holy woman doing charitable works in the name of God."

"So, tending sick strangers is God's work, but bringing comfort to sick friends is not?"

"Yes, Augusta." The man firmed his jaw.

"Nonsense!" Athenais retorted. "Have my wagon ready at the Chalke gate with a troop of guards by sixth hour. We will collect Placidia Augusta at her residence and proceed to the imperial envoy Volusianus' abode."

"I will have to have the emperor's permission."

"I do not need my husband's permission to leave the palace. I am the Augusta."

When the man continued to stand, obviously concocting another argument, Athenais barked. "You have your orders. You are dismissed from my presence. And if you ever wish to be admitted again, you will listen and obey without argument."

Angry red colored the eunuch's face. He bowed and left her room. "I must be rid of that man." She muttered to herself. *Or convince Theo to give me my own imperial staff. Pulcheria has her own, but I'm to share Theo's, and this eunuch opposes me at every point when I wish to depart from rigid protocol.* She normally got on amicably with the chief eunuchs by providing gifts and praise, but this one slavishly followed in Theo's footsteps. If her husband was rigid about religious observances, the eunuch was iron when it came to protocol. *I need no more people telling me what I can and can't do.*

Her rebellious mood abated when Placidia joined her in the imperial wagon. "Welcome, Aunt!"

"Thank you for providing the conveyance." Placidia gave her a tired smile. "Pulcheria has had me on my feet for the past three days tending to the sick and providing food and clothing to the hungry and ill-clad. I'm looking forward to visiting with Volusianus."

"You could decline Pulcheria's invitations."

"I know." Placidia looked out the curtained window and sighed. "I have spent my life serving the empire. During the sieges of Rome, I did much as Pulcheria does today. I and my aunts Laeta and Tisamene organized the noble ladies and provided food and nursing during the famine and plagues. It was a trying time…" Her voice faded and gaze seemed to turn inward.

"I'm sorry you had to suffer so cruelly, Aunt. I did not mean to stir unwelcome memories."

"Those times made me who I am and cemented my bond with the Roman people." Placidia shrugged and looked directly at Athenais. "Beyond that, I find there is a profound satisfaction helping others in greater need. Honoria accompanied us in this work. I wanted her to feel that satisfaction and understand she does have choices in her life."

"As do I?" Athenais gave a crooked smile at the not-so-subtle advice. "My Aunt Doria gave me similar advice after the death of Flacilla." She could say her daughter's name with only an echo of pain now. "I do have need of direction. I am not happy with my life and feel I have little to live for with Eudoxia's departure."

"You mentioned a pilgrimage to Jerusalem at the reception. A change of scene and distance from this court might be just what you need to replenish your spirit."

"Possibly. I've always wanted to travel. My friend Olympiodorus tells the most amazing stories of his missions for the empire. I sometimes feel like a prisoner in the palace. I had to threaten our chief eunuch with dismissal today just to break out for this visit."

Placidia leaned forward and patted her hand. "Talk to Melania today. Before settling in Jerusalem, she travelled from Rome to Sicily to Africa to Alexandria.

She was even blown off course and landed on an island where pirates held the local people hostage. She has many tales to tell and might inspire you."

The wagon shuddered to a stop and the captain of her guards shouted at the gates. "Open for Eudocia Augusta and Placidia Augusta."

Athenais winced. *You'd think I'd be used to my imperial name by now, but I'll always be Athenais in my heart.*

The wagon rattled inside the gate and pulled up at an impressive villa. The guard helped the two Augusti out.

"Oh!" Athenais put hand to her mouth. "It's my uncle's residence!"

Placidia turned to her with a quizzical look.

"When I first came to Constantinople, my mother's brother Asclepiodotus owned this property. I lived with him and my Aunt Doria until my marriage. This was once my home." Tears of remembrance came to her eyes. "I was happy here."

"My agents bought it as a residence for our imperial envoys several years ago." Placidia looked at the two-story brick structure with interest. "I had no idea it belonged to one of your relatives."

"My uncle rose rapidly at court under my patronage, but fell just as fast when he ran afoul of the more religious elements in the city. Theo dismissed him as prefect of the East several years ago. He left the city in disgrace and retired to a rural estate. My Aunt Doria used to visit occasionally, but she has been ill lately." Tears roughened her voice. "I don't know when I'll see her again, if ever."

Placidia nodded. "You arranged to visit my friend Volusianus. You should visit your sick aunt. Take control of your own life, my dear. Remember you *are* an Augusta."

"Thank you, Aunt." Athenais sniffed back the tears, took a calming breath, and linked arms with Placidia. "Let's go comfort our friend."

The household had been told in advance of the imperial visit and bustled with activity. The chamberlain met them at the door with a deep bow. "Welcome, Your Serenities. Would you care for refreshment after your journey? We've prepared a meal of peacock stuffed with squab. Or if you prefer boiled beef with garum."

I should have anticipated this kind of reception. The servants must have labored all morning, cleaning and cooking. They will be bitterly disappointed when we don't partake of their efforts. Athenais gave him a warm smile. "Our journey was brief, and we require nothing at this time other than to visit with our dear friend." She nodded to her escort. "Captain, please distribute gifts of coin to the mansion's staff. You and your company must help them consume their fine meal."

Placidia spoke up. "Chamberlain, send a servant with watered wine and a plate of fruit and cheese to the sick room. If we require anything else, we'll let the servant know."

"Yes, Augusta." The man gave them a deep bow most likely to mask his disappointment. "This way."

Athenais pulled her cloak closer as a cool fall breeze swept through the familiar garden bringing the scent of ripe apples.

"Is it as you remember?" Placidia asked.

"Nearly. The garden seems a bit unkempt, but it is fall and the plants prepare for their winter sleep."

The chamberlain led them to Athenais' favorite room in the house—the solar. More spacious than the family bedrooms on the second floor, the solar opened onto the garden, providing fresh air and sunshine for the sick man propped up on pillows in a narrow bed.

Placidia rushed to his side. "Volusianus, my friend, how are you faring?"

"Much better, now that you're here, Augusta," he croaked.

Athenais was shocked at the difference in the man. The envoy she met during the summer was an elderly, but vigorous, man with graying brown hair and curious green eyes. He had lost flesh, which emphasized his prominent nose and brow. Yellowish loose skin sagged under his jaw and on his neck. Most shocking of all, his hair was cut close into a short white bristle.

"Envoy, why did you not send word of your illness. We would have housed you at the palace under the excellent care of our physician," Athenais gently scolded.

"I assumed this was one of my recurring fevers and I would be over it shortly, Augusta. I have suffered with it for several years and it always passes." He mustered a mischievous grin. "And I did not want to add any burdens to the household preparing for your celebration."

"Friends are never burdens. Are you getting better? Do you have any needs?"

"None, Augusta. My niece runs the household and nurses me. She has been a godsend."

"I am glad to hear you say so, Uncle." A diminutive shadow rose from a temporary altar built in the corner. "I despaired of converting you."

"I may yet change my mind about baptism, Melania. You preached to me when I was in a weakened condition. But now, I am growing stronger and better able to counter your arguments. Will you abandon me if I refuse the font?"

"Never, Uncle." Melania came into the light, smiling. Evidently, this kind of banter was common between them. She bowed low. "Augusti, welcome. May I be of some service?"

Athenais' eyes went wide in surprise. *I don't know what I was expecting, but not this!* Melania was only a handful of years older than Placidia but looked much older; as gaunt as her ill uncle and dressed in coarse peasant clothes, the sandals on her feet cracked and repaired with twine. *To think, she was once one of the richest women in the empire. What passion must drive her faith.*

"Your chamberlain has already offered food and drink. A servant— Ah, has already arrived." Placidia waved the man to a sideboard where he settled an enormous platter of cheese and fruit and poured four goblets of watered wine.

"No wine for my uncle." Melania ordered. "Beef broth only with soft bread."

"Yes, Domina." The man bowed and ducked out.

"Augusti, may I present my sister Albina's daughter Melania, just recently arrived from Jerusalem."

"No need for such protocol between friends. You may call me Placidia."

"And I am Athenais."

Melania nodded.

Volusianus patted the bed. "Now that we are all known to one another, come tell me how the wedding went. I'm so disappointed that I couldn't be there."

The two Augusti moved stools to the bedside, sat, and described the festivities, while Melania plied them with wine and fed her uncle his broth when it arrived.

"Ah," he sighed at their conclusion, sank back against his pillows, and muttered, "A most satisfactory ending to your tale and auspicious beginning for the young couple."

Placidia took his skeletal hand in hers. "I'm afraid we've worn you out, my friend. We will take our leave. I will visit again before travelling back to Ravenna at the end of the week."

Athenais took Melania aside while Placidia and Volusianus said their good-byes. "You are both welcome at the palace."

"If he recovers, he will have no need, but he is too weak to be moved at this time."

"Then I'll send our physician to attend him. If you have need of anything—food, medicine, nursing staff—let me know."

"Your generosity is most welcome, Athenais."

When they were back in the wagon, Placidia dropped her bright smile. "I think my friend will not come back to Ravenna."

"He did seem quite ill."

"I've seen this disease before. King Alaric of the Goths died of it in my first year as a hostage. Fevers, chills, and convulsions come and go. They start out mild, but when the skin turns yellow, there is no coming back."

"I will ensure he gets the best of care, while he still lives, Aunt."

"Thank you, my dear." Placidia moved the curtain aside slightly so she might see the late afternoon sunlight. "I'm glad his niece is here, and I hope he does get baptized. I'd hate to think of that wonderful soul tormented for eternity in hell."

"As would I."

Chapter 39

Late January, 438, Imperial Palace

"Mistress, you have a message." Dorothea held out a folded letter on thick parchment.

Athenais looked up from her worktable, a slight scowl on her face. "You know I'm not to be disturbed in this hour."

"I knew you would want to see this. It's from your Uncle Asclepiodotus."

"Of course. Thank you, Dorothea." She snatched the letter, slit the wax seal with her thumbnail, and quickly read the contents. "Oh." The letter slid from her fingers onto her lap and tears welled into her eyes.

"Your aunt is dead?"

Athenais shook her head and dashed the tears away with the back of her hand. "Not yet. I may still have time to say my farewells, if I act quickly." She looked around the room, parallel concentration lines marring her forehead for a few moments, then turned back to her desk. She scribbled a note; folded, sealed, and held it out to Dorothea. "Send this to Theo at once, ask Captain Nikolaos to attend me, and pack a few of my things for an overnight stay—no—a three days stay. Prepare your own bag. You'll accompany me."

"Yes, Domina." Her servant gave a brief bow and left.

Athenais picked up the letter and read the contents again and murmured. "Oh, my dear Aunt, I'm coming." She had visited her aunt only twice in the fall. but not since then. With all the Christmas obligations—both religious and secular—she had little time to make the trip outside the walls to the sprawling suburban estate her aunt and uncle moved to when Doria was allowed back at court.

"You requested my presence, Augusta?" Nikolaos stood at attention in her doorway.

"Yes, Captain. I'm making a trip to my aunt's—" she stopped to still the quaver in her voice. "She's on her deathbed." Arrange for my wagon and an escort within the hour. Send a messenger to my Uncle Asclepiodotus immediately saying we are on our way. Speed is important."

"As you command, Augusta." He turned and left.

A remarkable young man. I'm so glad Dorothea brought him to my attention. She had elevated Nikolaos to captain of her guards two years ago and he had proved devoted and diligent. She had taken his advice and strengthened her bond with her contingent of guards by increasing their pay and providing an extra ration of wine on their days off.

Dorothea was fastening the fibula on her travel cape, when Theo stormed into her room, face red, her note clutched in his hand. "What's this about you leaving the palace for three days?"

She gave a look to Dorothea, who left with a quick bow.

"Possibly longer. Aunt Doria is on her deathbed and asked for me. I'm going to her. I don't know how long it will be, but Uncle said she is sinking fast."

"You can't leave. The adventus of Bishop Chrysostom's bones is in two days. We must all make an appearance at the celebration and participate in the interment at the Apostles Church."

"Will you be there?"

"Yes."

"Pulcheria?"

"Yes."

"Then the imperial family will be well represented." She pulled on her gloves. "I doubt the people will even notice my absence."

He gave an exasperated sigh. "Of course they will notice. Everything we do in public is noticed, analyzed, and gossiped about. Your absence will be accounted a snub to the people or a rift between us, maybe both with your precipitous exit of the palace. We must announce your visit and arrange the progress through the streets so the people can see you—after the adventus.

"Now you sound like the chief eunuch, not a concerned husband." She pushed pass him. "I'm going now. My aunt has little time and I want to be there."

"But the people!"

"Tell them the truth. I'm visiting a sick aunt and comforting her on her deathbed. We're people, too. The people will appreciate my love and caring for my family much more than my attendance at the reburial of some dusty old bones."

Theo rushed to block the doorway. "Athenais, I forbid you."

"You forbid me to provide comfort to a dying woman?" She stopped and gave him an icy stare. "That's the story you want circulating in the city? Because that's the one I'll tell my ladies, if you keep me from my aunt. You'll have to tie me up and drag me screaming to that ceremony, because I will never forgive you for your callousness. Is that the spectacle you want at your precious adventus?"

He moved aside, his face flaming and his mouth set in an angry scowl. "I will not forgive your disrespect of my wishes, Wife."

She hesitated. *Theo's old problem. He has so little confidence in himself that if anyone crosses him, he takes it as an insult. Even Pulcheria fell into that trap with the Nestorius business.*

Athenais placed a calming hand on his arm. "Please, Theo. For your own sake, I hope you can soften your heart and understand *my* wishes and *my* needs. It's the Christian thing to do, even if it violates imperial protocol."

The blood drained from his face; his eyes stricken as she left the room. *Because I didn't accede to his wishes or because he realized his own hypocrisy?*

Athenais hurried out of the palace escorted by Dorothea and a couple of servants with her chests of clothes and a basket of food to sustain them on the journey. They met Nikolaos and his mounted escort by the Chalke Gate. The late afternoon sun reflected red off the brick walls. The imperial wagon was heavy and slow. The horses couldn't run without bouncing the occupants around like seeds shaken in a hollow gourd. Depending on the traffic in the city and the state of repair on the roads, they might arrive before midnight.

Nikolaos handed her and Dorothea into the carriage. Athenais settled onto the cushions with a sigh. She peeked out of the curtained window when they went through the gate and passed the statue of Saint Helena. "My first day in Constantinople." She murmured.

"What, Domina?" Dorothea sat up straighter on the opposite seat.

"Nothing. I was just thinking about my first day here. My uncle and brothers gave me a grand tour of the city and this plaza. I was amazed at having a statue of a real woman outside the palace gates. I knew the story about Constantine's mother who brought pieces of the True Cross from the Holy Land and convinced her son to let Christians worship in peace, but didn't know Helena was so revered in the city."

"Oh, yes! Women and children bring flowers to her statue on her remembrance day in May. She is quite beloved."

The beginning of an idea sparked in her imagination, but she put it aside. *Time to think on that later.*

They arrived at the villa in the dead of night, but lights blazed from the windows to guide the travelers to safety. The estate chamberlain met them and escorted Athenais to her aunt's bedroom. In contrast to the rest of the villa, only a couple of candles lit this room, leaving the corners in darkness. Athenais spied her uncle slumping in a corner chair.

She wrinkled her nose at the sour smell of sickness mixed with the scent of the cedar chips burning in a brazier. Sweat beaded on her forehead as she looked longingly at the windows shut against the cold. But the sight of her aunt's still, frail body under a pile of blankets banished all thoughts of her own discomfort.

"Oh, my dear aunt!" Athenais murmured and rushed to Doria's bed. The movement roused her uncle and he shambled to her side. She looked up at his ashen face. "How is she?"

"Still with us. I think she waits for you."

"Your daughter?"

"I sent her to bed. She's exhausted from caring for Doria these months." He scratched his straggly beard. "There's little she—or anyone—can do now, but wait."

The low voices roused the dying woman. Doria blinked her eyes in the dim light and whispered. "Is she here? Did Athenais come?"

"I'm here, Aunt." Athenais clutched her aunt's boney hand. The tumor in her aunt's womb had deprived Doria of all her ample flesh.

"Good. I've made amends to everyone else." Doria tugged at Athenais' hand. "Closer child."

Athenais leaned in to hear her aunt's words.

"I loved you like a daughter, but didn't do well enough," she whispered. "I'm sorry."

"For what, Aunt? I'm the one who has been neglectful of you. You've done nothing but love me and help where you could."

"Blinded by pride. Should have objected to the marriage. You're so unhappy."

"Not at first, my dearest aunt. I had many good years with Theo and hope to have many more. I have a plan to go to the Holy Land."

"I didn't know—" Doria coughed, a violent barking sound.

"Take this, my dear." Her uncle leaned in with a drink smelling of cherries.

Dorrie sipped then laid back with a sigh. "Better." She waved her husband away and turned pain-dulled eyes back to Athenais. "I didn't know… how poisonous the court—"

"Please, Aunt. None of my troubles are your fault. Rest easy."

"Forgive me?"

"There's nothing to forgive."

Doria nodded, then clutched her hand with surprising strength. "A favor?"

"Anything, Aunt."

"Make sure they bury me in my red wig." A slight smile pulled at the corners of Doria's lips. "I paid a fortune for that thing and want to take it with me."

"Of course, Aunt." Athenais chuckled through her tears. "It's a promise."

Doria's eyes closed and she breathily commanded, "Go now, my dear. Get some rest."

Athenais leaned over the bed and kissed her aunt on the forehead. "I love you, Doria. You were a mother to me when I needed it most."

Her aunt tucked her chin in acknowledgment, then closed her eyes.

Athenais left her aunt with her grieving husband. *I never thought of Uncle as a man of sentiment. I'm so glad Aunt is surrounded by loving family. I should have done so much more!*

Chapter 40

Imperial Palace, early February 438

Athenais sat on a wooden chair in Pulcheria's austere receiving room. An empty chair sat next to her. Theo and Pulcheria chatted on a bench a couple of paces opposite, waiting for their guest with all the excitement of children anticipating presents on their name day. Athenais pulled her wool cloak tighter. A single brassier kept the room from freezing in the winter's cold, but it was still chillier than she liked.

"Spiced wine, Augusta?" One of Pulcheria's servants offered.

"Yes." She took the goblet of warmed wine and held it in her cold fingers. *Does Pulcheria wish to give our honored guest a chill? I doubt that God really wants us to freeze to death in his name.*

"The holy woman Melania of Jerusalem," a herald announced at the door.

Melania entered with all the dignity of her noble rank and the stinking rags of her situation. The forty days of mourning were over for Volusianus and his niece would soon return to Jerusalem. The three Augusti rose to their feet in greeting. Melania's face lit up as she walked to Athenais. "Athenais, my daughter, it is good of you to be here when your aunt so recently passed."

"I was there with her husband, daughter, and grandchildren gathered at her bed. She was much loved, which helps with my sorrow." *The pain of death is so much fainter when a life is well lived.*

"Grief is easier when shared. I'm sure my uncle would have appreciated the funeral poem you wrote for him. He much admired your work."

"He gave me notes before he died."

Melania chuckled. "Of course he did."

Athenais noticed the increasingly thunderous look of her sister-in-law and briefly indulged in the sin of pride for her warm relationship with Melania. *Serves Pulcheria right to be upstaged after she spread that story that I was banned from the adventus for some mysterious misdeed.*

Relenting, Athenais turned to the duo across the table. "Holy Mother, let me introduce you to my husband and his sister. They have been most anxious to meet you."

Theo had quickly masked his astonished look at the easy conversation between the two, but Pulcheria had more difficulty covering her dismay. Her husband fell to his knees at the holy woman's feet. Pulcheria, with some difficulty, followed his lead. "You do us great honor, Holy Mother, to visit us in our home. We would have come to you."

"There was no need. Your wife has represented you well over the past months." Melania put her hands on their heads, and all recited the Lord's Prayer.

Theo and Pulcheria rose and fussed over Melania, getting her settled in the chair and supplying her with plain water when she refused the spiced wine.

When they were all settled, Theo turned to Melania. "I am pleased to hear that my wife has attended you well. In what ways was she of service?"

"She is as a daughter to me. My uncle's physical wants were few, but she supplied them. It was her spiritual support that I most appreciated."

Pulcheria choked on a sip of her own water. Her face turned bright red, and she coughed trying to clear her lungs while Theo thumped a flat palm on her back.

Melania looked at her with concern. "Are you well, Augusta?"

Pulcheria glared at Theo. He stopped his assault. She cleared her throat and motioned to a servant to take the offending cup away. "Yes," she said in a hoarse voice. "I merely swallowed wrong." Her eyes cut back to Athenais. "You were telling us of the Augusta's spiritual assistance."

Melania nodded, took Athenais' hand, and smiled at her. "Your sister helped me save my uncle's soul, as well as nurse his body. Volusianus was a confirmed pagan. Having the Augusta's example of her own journey to the Lord gave him comfort and a guide. Between the two of us, he repented his sins, took baptism, and died in grace. I am most grateful to Athenais for her time and assistance."

"Thank you for your praise, Holy Mother." Athenais bowed her head slightly. "But I only followed your example and the Lord's will. I admired your uncle and feared for his soul."

Melania patted her hand. Theo looked at Athenais in surprise. Pulcheria smoothed out a scowl as she said, "We grieve with you over the loss of your uncle. I worked closely with him during the months leading up to our princess' wedding."

"He told me about your close bargaining during negotiations over the wedding contract."

Pulcheria colored again.

Melania laughed. "I have little interest in politics, Augusta, but I have heard much about your reputation for charitable works and—" she nodded to include Theo "—the devotion your court accords the holy church. You both are to be commended."

Both Theo and Pulcheria relaxed under the holy woman's praise. *Now is the right time.* Athenais squeezed Melania's hand.

"Husband, I have a favor to ask of you."

"Anything in my power, my love."

"I wish to travel to Jerusalem on a pilgrimage. Melania has inspired me with her life and her stories. I wish to go to the Holy Land."

Pulcheria's face froze in a rictus of a smile.

I almost feel sorry for her. I'm sure she longs to visit the Holy Land, but can't tear herself away from Theo and the power of the court. That is her weakness, and she will deny herself any pleasure to keep her hooks in my husband.

Athenais turned to her husband, "Beloved, you can accompany me. We could journey to the Holy Land together, visiting our people along the way. Pulcheria can manage in your place as she has before." She found herself holding her breath. *If he comes, we can renew our vows, find a new way to be together with our daughter gone. If he doesn't...* She didn't want to think of the additional wound this might be to their marriage.

Pulcheria spoke first. "I do not believe it is wise for either of you to go. The Huns are restless on our border and the Vandals threaten our lands in Africa. The Augustus should be in Constantinople during these dangerous times."

Theo put on a gentle smile to take the sting out of his words. "Such a pilgrimage would be impossible for me, my dear and I do want you at my side."

Athenais' heart sank and a small inkling of desperation trickled into her veins. *I must leave this court if only for a respite. Everything here reminds me of my failures: the deaths of my children, my hollow marriage, my lack of influence to do much good.*

She opened her mouth to protest, just as Melania leaned forward and said, "Most Holy Augustus, I beg you to release your consort for this journey. She desires to worship in the holy places, and this would benefit not only her soul, but your reputation. No Augusta has visited the Holy Land since the sainted Helena, whose statue stands outside the gates to the palace. She will be a great ambassador to the people on her journey, spreading the word everywhere of your wisdom and holiness."

Athenais knelt at her husband's feet. "Please, Theo. I need to do this. *We* need to do this. God calls me. Come with me on this journey."

Theo shook his head, but put a hand under her chin and raised her face. "I cannot deny you, the Holy Mother, and God. You may go, my love, with my blessing, but I cannot go with you in these unsettled times. It will take time to plan this pilgrimage, but you may leave in the spring."

"Thank you, Theo." She rose and took her seat with a mixture of sorrow and anticipation. "And thank you, Holy Mother for pleading my case."

Melania smiled and rose from her chair. "My job is done for now. I'll be leaving at the end of the week and will prepare for your reception in the Holy Land." She turned to Theo and Pulcheria. "We will meet again before I go, if you so wish."

"Of course, we do so wish, Holy Mother." Pulcheria rose. "Let me see you to the door."

"It is right there, my child. I think I can find it." Melania kissed Athenais on both cheeks, gave brief bows to Theo and Pulcheria, and left the room.

"I'll take my leave, as well, and will see you at evening prayers." Athenais left with a rising sense of excitement. *A pilgrimage to Jerusalem! New people. New sights. I can visit the city of my birth, Antioch. If nothing else comes of the journey, I'll be rid of Pulcheria's sour company for a while.*

Chapter 41

Imperial Hunting Preserve outside Constantinople, February 438

"A MIGHTY THROW, AUGUSTUS!" PAULINUS WHOOPED AS THEO'S JAVELIN brought the wild boar to the hard frosty ground, hot blood streaming from the fatal wound. The animal was surrounded with baying hounds and bristled with arrows from the imperial hunters, but Theo gave it the killing stroke from the back of his horse.

His friend grinned at him as he rode back. "I need to do this more often. We used to hunt every week and wrestle every day. What happened to us?"

"We got older. You got married and had children." Paulinus shrugged. "You rule an empire and send me to its farthest ends on your business. That leaves little time for these pleasures."

He guided his gelding next to Theo's restive black stallion. A beautiful but spirited mount, it snorted misty breath in the frigid air, mincing away from Paulinus' bay. Theo clasped the animal's body with his scholar's legs, centering himself in the saddle, and yanked sharply on the bit to pull the horse to a stamping and foaming standstill. The beast was almost too much for Theo to handle. *I should talk to the head of the stables and make sure Theo has a more biddable animal in the future. We can't have the emperor injured or killed in a preventable accident.*

Paulinus blew on gloved hands. "Shall we return to the hunting camp, Theo? Your blood must be up from the kill, but I need a fire to warm my backside."

"Race you to the camp!" Theo laughed and kicked his mount into a gallop over the hard ground and toward a clump of trees.

Paulinus smothered a curse and raced after Theo. He pulled up to the camp to find the Eastern emperor off his panting mount and already receiving a cup of warm wine from a servant. "No fair, my friend! You pull that trick too often."

"And you fall for it every time." Theo looked happy with wind-reddened cheeks and a sparkle in his eyes. Quite different from his usual sallow skin and harried look.

"As you say, Augustus." Paulinus slid from his saddle and turned the animal over to his groom. Another servant approached with a silver goblet of spiced wine. "Ah. Just what I need after a brisk ride." He took a gulp and surveyed the scene. "Camp" sounded more rustic than the emperor's temporary accommodations warranted. A large, purple-striped tent provided shelter and warmth from the winter's bite. Several covered wagons hauled food, equipment, and tack. More people scurried about than inhabited a small village. Imperial hunters beat the woods and flushed the game. A troop of servants attended the emperor, cooked feasts, and cared for the horses and dogs. Imperial guards ringed the camp.

"Come, Paulinus, let's warm our outsides as well as the inside." Theo guided him to the imperial tent. Persian rugs carpeted the floor, flaming braziers kept the winter chill out and sweetened the air with cedar. Servants took their cloaks and settled them in comfortable chairs with fresh goblets of wine. They relived the hunt while feasting on roast pheasants, stewed vegetables, and soft cheese spread on hearty bread.

Theo belched and sighed. "I haven't eaten so well in weeks."

"Would Pulcheria approve?" Paulinus asked with a sly grin.

"Today isn't a fast day." Theo saluted him with his goblet. "But that does bring up a subject close to my heart. I have a big favor to ask of you, my friend."

"I'd do anything for you, Theo."

"You know Athenais prepares for a pilgrimage to Jerusalem?"

Paulinus nodded. "I was surprised when I heard you gave her permission to go."

"She needs to get away. The loss of her—our—children to death and marriage has saddened her greatly. Athenais spent much time with Melania of Jerusalem while the holy woman tended her dying uncle. They bonded, not only over their losses, but their mutual love of languages and literature. The

Holy Mother made a compelling case for the journey." Theo looked at him over the rim of his goblet. "However, I worry about my wife. I want you to go with Athenais as my envoy and friend."

"I can't do that." Paulinus set his wine aside to hide his shaking hands. *You don't know what you're asking me, Theo. I've spent the past six years avoiding my goddess and her sorrow, fearing what would happen if I gave in and comforted her.*

"Yet just moments ago, you said you would do anything for me," Theo said in surprise. "Have you some complaint against my wife?"

"No complaints." He shook his head. *How to get out of this?* "But why not send her brother, Valerius?"

"As Master of Offices, I need him by my side. As my brother by choice, if not by blood, I had hoped you would protect my wife on her journey and give her the comforting presence of a friend. Since I cannot accompany her myself, you are my surrogate. I would trust no other with this task."

Paulinus took a deep breath. "Of course, Augustus. I would lay down my life for you or Athenais."

"Excellent!" Theo's smile broadened. "Planning has started. When we get back to the palace tomorrow you should confer with Athenais and the chief eunuch on the details."

When Paulinus made one of his few appeals to a higher power, *May God save me on this dangerous journey,* he wasn't referring to pirates or barbarians.

Chapter 42

The coast of the Syrian Province, early April 438

ATHENAIS WATCHED THE FLAT COASTAL PLAINS COVERED WITH OLIVE groves and vineyards off the port bow of the imperial barge. *A rich and prosperous land.* Misty mountains reared their craggy heads in the distance. A fleet of other coastal ships accompanied the barge, carrying all the supplies and people needed to provide a suitable imperial presence.

Holy Mother Melania will not be impressed by this display of wealth, but that meeting is several days away. A brisk evening breeze came from the land, tugging at the heavy veil she wrapped around her hair to keep the curls from tangling in the wind. *Nearly three weeks since we set sail from Constantinople. Tomorrow we will be in Antioch, the city of my birth.*

"Would you like a wrap, Augusta?" Paulinus, her constant companion for this trip, stood with a wool cloak folded over his arm.

Gooseflesh dotted her arms, and she rubbed them. "Thank you, my friend. I sometimes lose myself in the views. I haven't traveled since my voyage from Athens to Constantinople."

"Is it as you remembered?" He wrapped the cloak around her shoulders, then stepped away, as a good courtier should. The broad deck was home to the sailors who slept there. Guards were always on hand as well as the occasional servant, so Paulinus needed to show no over familiarity. *Not like our easy laughter and occasional light touches on hands or arms at my salons.*

"A little." She laughed. "When I came to Constantinople, I was a poor relative, seeking shelter with an unknown uncle and aunt. Gesius and I slept on the deck in a rude shelter and ate cold food. Now I am the emperor's consort, an Augusta in my own right. I sleep in the best beds available on land each night and servants cater to my every wish." She turned her face to the shore again and leaned on the railing. "I sometimes miss those simpler times… and my brothers. I thought promoting them at court would keep them close, but their duties take them all over the empire or burning the midnight oil. They barely have time for their wives and children, much less for me."

"Do you regret your choices, Athenais?" Paulinus joined her at the rail.

She shrugged. "Not the ones that count. I loved Theo and my children. I wouldn't give up a moment of time with them, even the painful ones. I do wish I had challenged Pulcheria more directly. Her influence has poisoned my husband toward me. I wish I had fought harder for my marriage."

"You still have time, my friend. You know the way to your husband's heart. Isn't that why you are on this pilgrimage?"

Her cheeks reddened and not with the wind. "Yes, it is time for me to move on. I am no longer a wife or mother in any true sense of the titles. It is past time I took up the role of Augusta and wielded the power of my status. If I can't have Theo in my bed, I can still be a force for moderation in his government, but I need his trust and admiration. I must become the new Saint Helena in the people's eyes. A Holy Mother equal to Pulcheria and my husband. My only fear is that if I become Helena, will I lose Athenais?"

"Never!" Paulinus stated.

"But will the people accept me? Will they believe my good works and piety come from a sincere desire to do good? Pulcheria will accuse me of false piety, and she is much beloved by the people."

"Do your intentions come from a desire to do good? Or are your actions motivated by a need for admiration and the power that brings? Even so, is that a bad thing? For all I know, your sister-in-law is the one who acts falsely for the power it gives her over Theo."

She hesitated for a moment. *Are my motives pure? Are anyone's? Or is it the results that count when you stand before your people and the historians write your legacy?* She shook her head. *A conundrum for a long philosophical discussion over wine and good food.* "Have you been studying your Socrates? Such philosophical questions!"

His sober face softened into a gentle smile. "I miss our spirited salons. We used to fix all the problems of the world in our debates with friends."

"And hear the occasional good poem or travel story. I will revive the salons when I return." She looked out over the mildly swelling water and sighed. "Rigid philosophy and religious doctrine are two sides of the same coin. I'm trying to find a compromise. I take the best from the Christian beliefs and meld them with a Greek philosophy of moderation. I want to bring beauty and art to the people, as well as food and shelter. Our souls need more than fasting and prayer. They need inspiration and love. Christ taught that, but some of his messages seem to have been set aside for more militant ones."

"Speaking of messages, how goes your speech for the senate at Antioch?"

"I'm nearly finished. I've fashioned a classic encomium in Homeric hexameters. Would you care to see it and give me your opinion?"

"Of course."

They linked arms to cross the gently rolling deck to her personal lodgings built on the upper deck. *It's been so good to have Paulinus back in my life. I must make sure he doesn't slip away again after this journey. Surely, there is some rich widow in my retinue I can tempt him with. He deserves a loving wife and family.*

ATHENAIS PACED UP THE CENTER AISLE OF THE SENATE HOUSE IN ANTIOCH IN full augustal regalia. Modeled on the original Julia Curia in Rome, the building soared two stories. Light streamed in from windows at the top, supplemented with oil chandeliers suspended from the ceiling and thick candles on tall bases. Colored marble tiles decorated the floor in complex geometric patterns, while the walls showed pristine white marble punctuated with paintings of classical scenes and busts of famous Antochines. Her own gold bust sat on a marble plinth at the far end of the room covered with a white silk cloth embroidered with purple birds and golden apples.

Paulinus stood to the side of the plinth with Nikolaos. *I'm so glad he and Dorothea have been able to spend time together on the voyage. More than they had at the palace.*

Paulinus' eyes glowed with pride and the corners of his mouth turned up in an encouraging smile. The sight of him settled some of the butterflies in her stomach. *This isn't my first public speech; why am I so nervous?* Athenais remembered her father's advice and took deep calming breaths. *Thank you, Father, for teaching me rhetoric.*

The senators, sitting on folding camp chairs, on ranks of marble steps to either side of the aisle, surged to their feet and shouted traditional acclamations. "God's blessing on the Holy Augusta!" "Long life and good health to the Imperial Consort!"

The public admiration I've received this past week could certainly go to my head. First, a bronze statue in the sanctuary dedicated to the muses, and now my bust in the Senate House. Maybe I should ask for one in the Constantinople Senate. Pulcheria has a bust there and she's never addressed that august body!

She reached a throne-like chair at the end of the aisle, turned to the chanting senators dressed in their formal, purple-edged togas, and sat with relief. After several minutes of additional acclamations, the city prefect stepped forward and motioned for silence. As in the formal court, the men didn't take their seats in the imperial presence. Athenais had a flash of sympathy for the frailer members, who clung to their sticks to keep upright.

"My fellow senators." The prefect spread his arms wide. "We welcome to this sacred space the Most Serene and Gracious Aelia Eudocia Augusta, Consort to our Most Blessed and Merciful Flavius Theodosius Augustus." This introduction sparked another prolonged spate of acclamations—this time for her husband.

I'm starting to see why Theo dislikes these formal occasions. This imperial cape is heavy with all this gold thread and my neck is stiff holding up this incredible wig. I know it's faster to plop on than sitting through a tedious hair dressing, but I'm beginning to regret my decision to have one made. A trickle of sweat dripped down her neck, but she couldn't move to scratch the itch it caused.

Finally, the prefect again motioned for silence. "We are gathered here to honor Her Serenity with the dedication of this bust to remind us forever of her generosity and love for her natal city." He removed the veil to loud acclaim and revealed a classical gold bust done with a modern hair style.

Doesn't look much like me, she sighed to herself. *But then they had only coins for a model. At least it is a classical beauty, and my name is on the dedication for posterity.*

The prefect continued to list all her gifts to the city: money for churches, shelters for the poor, financing to rebuild and extend the walls, endowments for chairs at the local academy in her father's name among many. Just as she was about to cut the man off, he concluded, "Our many thanks to our Generous

Augusta. Now she will address our senate."

After another round of acclamations, Athenais rose and stepped forward. *I've rehearsed this dozens of times. I'm ready.* She centered her breathing, straightened her shoulders, and proclaimed in her best rhetorical fashion. "My blessings on you and this city of my birth." She paused and looked over the expectant faces. "You have my permission to sit. I see several wise and venerable elders among you, and I do not wish to endanger their health."

When the rustling stopped as the senators seated themselves, Athenais launched into her poem praising the city: the wisdom of its scholars, the leadership of its church, the bravery of its people, and the beauty of its art and architecture. As she ended, she hesitated, looking around the room. When it was silent, she raised her fist in the air and shouted, "Of your proud line and blood I claim to be."

The senate erupted, as the men she claimed sisterhood with, jumped to their feet shouting exited acclamations. They stomped their feet until she thought the vibrations might bring down the building.

Paulinus and Nikolaos flanked her for the walk back to the senate door. Outside, a huge crowd took up the acclamations. Paulinus leaned in so he might be heard. "A triumph, Augusta. Your visit will be recorded in history. You bring honor to your husband."

She nodded, smiled, and behind a screen of scholae, made her way to the imperial wagon. She kept the curtains open and smiled at the crowd. *A triumph indeed. What I need is a slave to whisper, "Remember you will die" into my ear like Caesar during his triumphs in Rome.* She sat back and closed the curtain, exhilarated and exhausted. *How soon can I get out of these clothes?*

Chapter 43

Sidon in the Province of Syria, early April 438

ATHENAIS, WE APPROACH THE PORT OF SIDON." PAULINUS ENTERED HER room. "There is a large group of well-wishers on the docks waiting for you."

"Any sign of Mother Melania? She sent word she would join us here." Athenais put aside her writing and rose from her desk.

"None that I could see."

Athenais' brow furrowed with worry. "I hope no harm has come to her on this journey to meet me."

"I'm sure the Good Lord provided for the holy woman on her sojourn." Dorothea fussed while draping her in a thick knee-length veil and settling a gold circlet with pearls surrounding a large amethyst that centered on her forehead. Her servant stepped back and surveyed her handiwork. "Perfect, Augusta. Paulinus and your guards will escort you to this night's accommodation. I will join you there."

Athenais smiled behind her veil. Dorothea proved to be a poor sailor and welcomed these nightly sojourns on shore. Imperial eunuchs had preceded them on the journey, arranging for the best housing available at the end of each day, usually in a local noble's or governor's home. Only a few times, when they ended the day at an empty desolate shore, did they sleep on the ships anchored close to the coast. *This coastal progress is slow, but more comfortable than spending day after day cooped up in a wagon or litter. I'm glad that Placidia suggested this as an alternative to an open ocean voyage.* Her formidable aunt was notorious for her hatred of sea voyages after nearly perishing with her family in a frightful storm. *If I had learned to ride a horse, I might have gone overland, but...* she mentally shrugged.

At the door to her cabin, Paulinus smiled at her and offered his arm, "Augusta, your people are here to greet you."

She laid her fingertips on his arm, and they proceeded to the gangway lined with her guards. *They treat me like fragile glass! I'm perfectly capable of walking a steady gangplank without falling in the waters of the port.* Having had relative freedom of movement in the palace, this hovering by the scholae was irritating, but necessary. *I'm sure Theo would have their heads if anything inconvenienced, much less, injured me.*

On the dock, she was greeted with the usual enthusiasm of local people who never thought they would see a member of the imperial family in person. Children brought flowers and covered the dock with sweet smelling petals. Sidon magistrates and rich merchants dressed in their most lavish garb bowed low. The local bishop and his attendants outshone their secular brothers in their use of gold and silver thread on their cloaks and tunics. *I must agree with Pulcheria on this point. Bishops live a lavish life while the poor and sick suffer. Another thing to speak to Mother Melania about.*

She searched the crowd for any sign of the holy woman. She turned to the local city prefect. "Thank you for your blessings and warm welcome. Do you have any news of the holy woman Melania of Jerusalem? She was supposed to meet me here."

"Augusta, the Holy Mother arrived this morning, tired and ill from her journey. We offered her our best hospitality, but she refused it. She is at our Church of Mary Theotokos praying."

"She is ill? Has she seen a physician?"

"She seemed weakened by the journey, Your Serenity, but refused food because she is fasting, and refused a physician's ministrations saying God would care for her mortal body."

Athenais turned to the waiting crowd. For many, this would be a highlight of their lives and provide stories for their descendants for generations, but she decided to shorten her remarks. *I must get to Melania soon!* She projected her voice beyond the muffling veil, "People of Sidon, I am privileged to visit your storied city, the home of a mighty merchant fleet that sails the seas bringing riches and culture to the far corners of the world. I wear imperial robes dyed with the purple your ancestors discovered and spread across the lands. I drink and eat from the exquisite glass that is produced in your factories and treasured throughout the empire. Homer praised the city of Sidon and Our Lord Jesus Christ visited your shores. I am truly blessed to follow in His footsteps on my journey to the Holy Land."

A deafening roar rose from the crowd as they cheered her words. She waved and turned to Paulinus, "Distribute the gifts we agreed upon. I must go to Melania. Prefect—" she took the man's arm, "—give my escort directions to the Holy Mother and join me for dinner. I have much to discuss with you about your remarkable city."

"I am at your service, Augusta." The prefect helped her into her wagon, gave directions to the driver and guards, and returned to Paulinus to disburse the crowd.

The wagon took off with a lurch and rattled over the cobblestoned streets. *Thank God the church is only a short distance, or I might lose all my teeth getting there.*

They arrived at the Church of Mary Theotokos at sunset. *Time for evening prayers.* Athenais left her guards with her wagon and entered the small church with Nikolaos, who stayed at the door. Frescos showing the apostles trooped up one wall. The other showed scenes from the life of Mary from her annunciation to her assumption. *What lovely work. The merchants of Sidon can obviously afford the best artists.* Tall windows flooded the center aisle with reddish evening light. "Red sun at night, sailors delight," she muttered to herself. *We should have smooth sailing tomorrow.*

A small group of holy women prayed in the nave. Melania lay prostrate before the altar. Athenais stood to the side, reciting the Lord's Prayer with her eyes closed. The calm of the church quieted her soul. The cedar incense lifted her spirits. She smiled as all the stress of the journey dropped from her shoulders. *Thank you, My Lord, for your blessing.*

A soft rustling of clothes and the sharp smell of unwashed bodies brought Athenais back to the present. The holy women helped Melania to her feet, and they turned to leave. A woman with the early ravishes of time marking her face, gasped when she saw Athenais. "Augusta! Forgive us, we didn't know you were here."

"There is nothing to forgive." She held out her hand to Melania. "I have come to fulfill a double vow both to kneel at the holy places and to behold you, my own mother."

"Athenais, my child, welcome. How is your journey?"

"Pleasant now that you have joined me, but I understand you are weary. Come stay in my lodgings tonight. Eat and rest before we sail tomorrow. I fear for your health, Holy Mother." Melania had lost even more flesh since she had seen her last and her skin had an unhealthy gray pallor.

"Today is a weekday. I will break my fast on Saturday and Sunday. It is my custom to spend the night in prayer before the Church of the Sepulcher. When abroad, I continue that practice at whatever church is handy. Go to your own rest, my child. I will join you after morning prayers on your boat." She reached up her skeletal hand to cradle Athenais' cheek. "God's blessing on you."

"And on you." Tears coursed down her cheeks as she clasped Melania's hand in her own. "On the morrow then, Holy Mother." She turned and left. *Little sleep and no food for five days a week? How much can my friend's aging body endure?*

Chapter 44

"DO WE HAVE SUFFICIENT FUNDS FOR THE DONATIONS I PROPOSE TO GIVE IN Jerusalem? Mother Melania has made several suggestions in addition to what I had planned." Athenais handed a list over to her curator Matthias, who handled all her finances. He jealously guarded the brass-bound locked chest containing all their gold and silver coins. A tall man with stooped shoulders, his hound-like features gave Athenais confidence that he would sniff out all irregularities in her personal funds and give her an honest accounting. She expected everyone handling the money to take a small cut, but Matthias would keep the graft to a manageable level. She had seen little of him on the voyage since he seemed more comfortable with his ledgers than her court.

"We arrive in Caesarea Maritima tomorrow and can replenish our chest there, if needed." He peered at the list and nodded. "The Augustus provided generously from the imperial funds and your own income will be sufficient to make up the rest. You have vast estates in your own name and many of them are in the provinces we travel through. Will you be visiting any of them? I can make the arrangements, if you wish, Augusta."

"Possibly. Send me a list and where they are located."

"Athenais, my child. I hope I am not interrupting?" Melania stood in the doorway of the cabin.

"You are welcome anytime, Holy Mother." Athenais rose from her desk. "I was discussing our donations with my curator, Matthias."

"Matthias—'gift of God'—indeed a propitious name for your minister of finance."

"You are dismissed, Matthias. We will confer again later."

"Augusta. Holy Mother." Matthias bowed low to each and left the cabin.

"Mother Melania, come sit with me on the divan. It is Saturday, so you are allowed some sustenance." Dorothea arrived at their sides with a tempting array of dried fruits, cheeses, and bread still warm from the oven. It was spring and too early for fresh fruits or ripe olives, but dried grapes and dates concentrated the sweetness of the fruit. Athenais smiled at the homey memory of her sweet-loving sister-in-law Marina pocketing a handful of dried dates when Pulcheria was not looking. *I do so regret that Marina and I did not become close friends. She was the first of the sisters to treat me with any kindness.*

Melania left the fruit and cheese in favor of a crust of bread.

"That is all you want, Holy Mother?" Athenais tempted her with some soft cheese for the bread. "Try this."

"This crust is all I require, my child. Eat your fill."

"I've broken my fast already." Athenais waved the food away. "Dorothea, bring us water."

Her servant bowed and brought a tray burdened with two goblets of Sidonian blue glass chased with silver rims—gifts from the prefect of Sidon.

"I can provide you with a plain clay cup, if that suits you better." When in the holy woman's presence, Athenais was acutely aware of the excesses of her court.

Melania took the cup and held it up to the fading light. "A beautiful specimen. You might donate these to Bishop Juvenal of Jerusalem to serve during the Eucharist." Her eyes sparkled and a slight smile tugged at her lips. "I do appreciate the finer things in life, my child. But the Good Lord Jesus told us that wealth would not buy our way to heaven—only good works and prayer. It took my sainted husband Pinianus and me nearly two decades to sell off our lands and slaves."

Athenais' eyes widened. "That must have been a tremendous undertaking. Did not your relatives object?"

"Vigorously! Our less well-off relatives expected a significant inheritance upon our deaths and resented our efforts to give away our wealth to care for the poor and needy."

Athenais nodded. Renunciation—giving away everything you owned and living an ascetic life—was a vigorously debated topic among the wealthy of the court. Some were sympathetic to a genuine calling to God. Others claimed the practice a threat to the established order diverting the wealth of the elite to the church and the poor. "As a married woman, I have little of my own to give away. Upon Theo's death—God grant him long life—I inherit many estates in my own name, but for now the lands that support me are imperial properties. Upon my death, the income reverts to the imperial treasury until the next Augusta is established."

Melania patted Athenais' hands. "I do not expect you to follow in my footsteps, Daughter. You are the Augusta and must retain your imperial dignity. My path in this life is not for everyone. If all quit their daily tasks to spend their lives in prayer, the world would end. I and my holy sisters and brothers take on the hardships of fasting and ascetic lives for those who can't as much as for our own souls. In this way, the grace of God will be shed on all who believe."

"I understand, Holy Mother" Athenais glanced at the lists on her desk. "My path is secular rather than religious, but I have yet to determine how I might meld the two in the best way for my people and my own soul. In many ways, I feel you are a kindred spirit. You had a classical education, as did I. You read and write both Greek and Latin. I am at a crossroads and need your guidance to choose the right path. I cannot give away all my wealth. In what other ways can I express my will and help my people?"

"You may not be able to sell the land, but you can dispose of the income from those lands. You will see for yourself when we arrive at the Holy Land, where your help is most needed. We will have many opportunities to talk over the next months about the particulars." Melania gave her a warm smile. "But that is not why I sought you out. I heard you had happy news from the Ravenna court."

"I just got word that Eudoxia is with child." Athenais glowed. "My first grandchild. We're hoping for a boy since I was unable to provide an heir for the East; we need a strong man to unite the empire. I miss my daughter terribly and wish I could be present for the birth, but my Aunt Placidia has pledged to care for her. This will be her first grandchild, as well."

"How does Placidia Augusta fare spiritually? I was pleased to see her devotion to good works with Pulcheria Augusta during the week after the wedding. She has many stains on her soul to account for."

"Aunt Placidia suffered many trials in her life. Did you know her in her youth?"

Melania shook her head. "When I was in Rome, she was mostly at her brother's court in Ravenna. I am of an age with her older cousin Serena who raised Placidia and her brother Honorius. Serena pled my case to Honorius when my relatives wished to prevent me and my husband from selling our lands. Honorius ruled in our favor, setting our feet on the path that led me to this point in my life. It was a tragedy what the city of Rome did to Lady Serena, and I never understood Placidia's role in her cousin's execution."

"Lady Serena was executed?" Athenais gasped. "I was but a child when the Goths sacked Rome and sent an earthquake across the empire. I've heard no one speak of Serena's death or Placidia's role in it."

"Serena was accused—with no evidence—of colluding with the invading Goths. I deeply miss that great lady."

"What dark deed do you hold Placidia to account?"

"My husband and I fled the city ahead of the Goth invasion, so I didn't meet your aunt at that time. I only know that Princess Placidia came to Rome and took up a separate residence from Selena. There were rumors that the two were at odds, but I never learned over what. When the senate of Rome condemned Serena as a traitor, Placidia consented to the execution and signed the death warrant."

"No! I cannot believe Placidia would willingly consent to the execution of the woman who raised her. Was she lied to? Did the senate threaten her life?" *I know my aunt harbors a dark past, but executing her foster mother?* Athenais shook her head in denial.

"I have no knowledge of her motives, only the fact that she consented." Melania shrugged. "But you are right in pointing out that she was a young woman on her own." Melania glanced at the deepening shadow creeping through the open doorway. "It is nearly time for evening prayers, my daughter. Will you join me at your altar?"

"Of course, Mother Melania." *And I'll pray that Aunt Placidia finds peace. What a terrible burden to bear all these years.*

Chapter 45

Jerusalem, late April 438

"There it is, my child, our Holy City. Jerusalem!" Melania spoke with breathless love as she pointed out the wagon window toward the walled city on the hill. "It is not near the size of Rome or Constantinople, but it is the center of the universe, where one can feel close to God."

It looks like a small rundown provincial town, but I would never tell Mother Melania that. "I now know one need for the city—those walls must be repaired. A small band of raiders could sweep through the city at will."

The holy woman looked at her in surprise. "I suppose so, but God will provide. Maybe that's why He sent you the calling to visit." She glanced up the hill again. "It will be good to be home. Will you honor me with a visit to my convent of pledged virgins?"

"That will be my first stop. I sent word ahead that I will not meet with the city elders or make an appearance as Augusta until next week. I am entering the city today as a private pilgrim and am hoping you will offer me shelter for the night."

"We cannot accommodate all of your retinue, my daughter!"

"Fear not, Mother Melania." Athenais reached over and patted her hand. "It will only be me. Today is a fast day, so no meal will be required. My retinue will continue to my estate in Bethlehem. My guards will billet with the city watch and collect me tomorrow. We will continue to Bethlehem then."

"Thank the Good Lord. We are a poor community and do not have the means to host an imperial horde." Relieved laughter bubbled up from Melania's chest. "I am still on the city rolls as a poor case and eligible for free food—but I've never taken advantage of it. God always sends a scrap or two my way when it is time to break my fast. When will you return to Jerusalem?"

"I'll live on my estate at Bethlehem so no local will be burdened with the expenses of my household. I plan to stay nearly a year and visit the city to worship at the holy places. Among you, Bishop Juvenal, and the city prefect, I will be here often. I've even received an invitation from Bishop Cyril of Alexandria. He will be rededicating the Church of St. Stephen and would be honored by my attendance."

"Bishop Cyril? Humpf," Melania snorted. "I had dealings with him during our sojourn in Alexandria on our way to Jerusalem. He is a proud man and prickly about his prerogatives. He values his power over his piety. I've known many men like him in important church positions. I don't know their inner hearts, but their actions are not those sanctioned by our Lord Jesus. They live in Episcopal palaces, wear jewels and gold, and eat rich meals while their congregants go without shelter, clothing, or food." Melania crossed her skinny arms over her concave chest and scowled.

"I live such a life, Mother."

"You are not a bishop having taken vows to follow God's laws." The holy woman's face softened. "It is not my place to judge the bishops. I can call them out, but must leave judgement to God." She peeked out the curtain and turned back with a grin. "We're nearly at the gate. It looks like your ploy to visit quietly today as a pilgrim has come to naught."

"What?" Athenais looked out, spying a large crowd clustered by the gate. At the sight of her face in the window, they cheered wildly and started chanting the traditional acclamations of welcome and for her well-being. "Oh dear. I haven't finished preparing my remarks for a public address."

"No need for that. They only wish to show their respect. You will have plenty of time to meet and talk with your people later."

The crowd accompanied them through the city to the Mount of Olives where it swelled with the many holy men and women who made the hill their home. They pulled up before a modest mudbrick structure surrounded by olive trees. When the two women exited the wagon, the chants changed to include Mother Melania. Athenais leaned in so she could be heard over the crowd. "I believe they are here to welcome you home, Mother, not to see me."

"It is both, my child." She raised her hands to call for quiet and addressed the crowd, "My children. I have returned with an honored guest, Aelia Eudocia Augusta, consort to our beloved Theodosius Augustus."

The crowd erupted into renewed chanting and Melania again signaled for silence. "The Augusta will pray with me at the holy places over the summer and attend many public functions. You will have many opportunities to see her about the city. Now return to your homes, so the Augusta and I can take some rest."

The crowd gave one last cheer then dispersed, leaving a small cluster of holy women in their threadbare gowns and modest head coverings.

A woman of middle age approached and went to her knees, head bowed. "Welcome home, Mother Melania. We are honored to guest you at our convent, Augusta."

Athenais reached down and brought the woman to her feet. "It is I who is honored to visit with your holy community. Please treat me as any other pilgrim sharing your roof. I am Athenais. What is your name, sister?"

"Bassa, Aug—uh—Athenais."

"Bassa is my right hand, daughter. She keeps the roof over our heads and leads the holy sisters, allowing me to spend my time in prayer and contemplation. Speaking of which—" Melania looked at the lowering sun and a slow smile bloomed across her face and her gaze turned inward. "—they will soon close the Church of the Holy Sepulcher. I will take my wonted place there at the gates tonight. It has been so long…" Melania walked off without a backward glance.

Athenais reached a hand toward the holy woman. "Mother…"

Bassa shook her head. "Leave her, child. When the call comes, she must obey. She will spend the night on her knees in front of the church."

"I know, but I fear for her. She is so much frailer than when we met in Constantinople, just half a year ago."

"As her body grows weaker, her spirit shines brighter. All of us—" she indicated the cluster of holy women "—have seen the change." She took Athenais' arm. "Now Athenais, come meet your sisters. We will have evening prayers then prepare a pallet for you."

"Thank you, Bassa."

Imperial Residence, Bethlehem, Province of Palestine

Athenais marveled at the fertility of the land as she travelled from Jerusalem to her residence in Bethlehem. The spring rains had abated, and the hills bloomed with vineyards and orchards. From date palms and oranges in the flatter coastal regions to the olives and grapes on the lower slopes to the apple and walnut trees at the peaks, the hilly land accommodated a vast array of plants that normally didn't grow in the same region. The hum of bees filled the fruit orchards. "As Moses promised, this is truly a land of milk and honey," Athenais murmured.

Her wagon rattled over a rough patch in the Roman road, throwing her to one side with a surprised cry.

"Augusta? Do you require assistance?" Paulinus called in through the window from his horse.

"No, my friend." She straightened herself and pulled back the carriage window curtain to prove she took no injury. "I was just tossed by the lurch. Would you make sure the provincial prefect knows of the damage to the road and effects repairs? I will be traveling to and from Jerusalem frequently and do not care to reach my destinations bruised from the ride."

"I will see to it as soon as we arrive at your residence, Augusta." Paulinus gave her a sympathetic smile.

"Five days in this wagon was more than enough to convince me that we made the right decision to travel the coastal barge route. I am forever grateful to Aunt Placidia for suggesting it and forever regretful that I did not learn to ride a horse. It would have saved me many a boring hour in this stuffy carriage."

"It is never too late to learn something new. I could provide you with a sedate mount."

"A new language, a new poem, perhaps." She shook her head. "But I am too old to learn to ride."

"Perhaps we can teach you to drive your own chariot, then. The hippodrome is literally in your back yard. You can practice there and show off your skills with a drive through the streets of Constantinople. I'm sure Pulcheria would cheer you on."

They both laughed at the absurd thought of an empress driving a racing chariot through the streets of the capital with the strait-laced Pulcheria cheering from the crowds. She wiped the tears from her eyes. "Thank you, my friend. I laugh too little these days."

A shadow flickered over Paulinus' face. "I know, Augusta. This trip has been good for you. The sea air has restored the color to your face and the love your people have shown for you, seems to bring you joy."

"It has." She looked thoughtful. "I've been too cloistered at the palace. I plan on being a much more public figure when I return."

"Good. Your people need you, Augusta." He saluted her. "We approach your residence. I will ride ahead and make sure all is ready."

She nodded and pulled the curtain shut to keep out the dust of the road. Shortly after, the wagon tilted as they ascended a gentle slope, then leveled out as the horses crunched through a gravel patch. The windows briefly darkened as they passed under an arch in the wall, then lightened as they pulled to a stop in a paved courtyard. Athenais heard her guards dismount with a clanging of armor and march to flank her wagon.

Nicolaos opened the door and assisted her to the ground. She looked up at a charming country manor house, two stories of local yellowish stone surrounded by a modest wall with gates in each side. The entire household seemed to have turned out to greet her and stood flanking the door. Nikolaos surveyed the area with an appraising frown.

"You do not approve, Captain?"

"The residence is situated well on a hill with its own water and sightlines across the valley, but the walls should be at least twice as high with reinforced gates, lookout points, and archer's nests." He pointed to some cedars overgrowing the wall. "And those trees should come down."

"Are we expecting a siege, Captain?" She asked with a brief smile. "The countryside seems quite peaceful."

A flush of blood colored his cheeks. "I am not expecting a siege, Augusta, but my job is to prepare for the unexpected as well as the likely."

"Then work with the chamberlain of this estate and Matthias to make the modifications. I might need to improve the manor house as well." *My own home to do with as I please! No eunuchs to say, "Not done." No Theo to upbraid me for excess. No Pulcheria to look down her nose in disdain.* She closed her eyes and took a deep breath of fresh air. *Yes! I believe I can be happy here.*

Chapter 46

Jerusalem, May 15, 438

Athenais stepped out of her carriage at the steps of the new Church of St. Stephen, abutting the outer walls of Jerusalem on the site of the Protomartyr's death. This was one of those days when she was "Augusta" rather than pilgrim and she dressed the part. *At least the spring breezes are cool here in the hills, so I won't be so uncomfortable.* She entered the arched, brass-bound doors into a chilly dimness filled with the cleansing smell of rosemary and frankincense. Paulinus followed at a much slower pace with the frail Melania on his arm.

The church nave was packed with the elite of the city. All in glittering attire, there to see and be seen by the empress. Athenais kept her eyes forward, ignoring the excited whispers that followed her up the aisle. A cluster of monks and holy women in sober dress stood to the right of the altar chanting psalms. Melania joined her in front of a massive gold cross studded with gems and they knelt together in silent prayer. Paulinus gave both women a hand up and they greeted one another with the kiss of peace. Melania exited to join the holy women and Athenais moved to the left where a temporary throne-like chair waited for her.

Bishop Juvenal of Jerusalem sat in a smaller chair in full arraignment with tall hat, red casula, and bishop's crook topped with gold. Athenais watched as Bishop Cyril of Alexandria in similar garb, took the pulpit. *So, this is the man who caused such mayhem at Ephesus. Theo is still bitter about having to side with him against Nestorius.* Tall, but stooped with a long gray beard and piecing black eyes, Cyril didn't look like the devil incarnate, but he had much blood on his hands. *The bishops of Antioch and Alexandria have feuded for years, but I must be civil to all people of professed piety, both high and low, if I am to garner the support of the church and the people and win my husband back.*

She sat straight and listened carefully as Cyril called the congregation to prayer, then started his dedication speech. "We are gathered today to dedicate this magnificent House of the Lord in the name of Saint Stephen Protomartyr, the first of many martyred in the name of Christ. Stephen was a young man—a deacon in the early church here in Jerusalem tasked by the Apostles with distributing food and money to widows, orphans, and others in need in Christ's name. He was known as humble and holy. Though he did miracles among the people, as with Our Lord Jesus, he inspired jealousy among members of various synagogues. These wicked men accused Stephen of blasphemy and brought him to trial at the Sanhedrin. There, he challenged the Jewish elders who sat in judgment with the following speech recorded for all posterity in the Acts of the Apostles."

Athenais sat fascinated as Cyril read the speech of the Protomartyr as the young man refuted accusation after accusation. *Stephen certainly knew his rhetoric and his logic,* Athenais mused. *His words will live forever in the Gospel. A legacy as great as his martyrdom.*

Cyril thundered, "Thus castigated, the elders howled their anger and demanded his death. At which point, Stephen looked up and cried, 'Look! I see heaven open and the Son of Man standing on the right hand of God!'" Cyril paused, then continued in almost a whisper, which drew the congregation's rapt attention, "Saint Stephen saw the recently resurrected Jesus standing by the side of God."

And Cyril knows how to enthrall an audience as well. I've heard others read this text with as much drama as describing a dog sleeping in the sun.

Cyril continued, "Those wicked people carried the Protomartyr to this very spot to execute him. But did he rage or condemn them? No! Like His Savior before him, he asked that the Lord receive his spirit and forgive the ignorant people who caused his death. He sank to his knees under the weight of the stones they threw and gave up his spirit to the Lord. In the face of this violence, the remaining disciples fled to distant lands to spread the Good Word to all who would listen." Cyril's piercing eyes raked the crowd as if assessing if they were paying attention. He nodded his approval then commanded, "Let us pray."

Athenais grew restless during the next part of the ceremony where the bones of Saint Stephen, encased in a cedar box covered with gold, were brought up the aisle accompanied by chanting priests waving smoking censers. The intense cedar smell brought a tickle to her throat, and she suppressed a cough, longing for a cool drink. Cyril gave the heavy box to Juvenal, who deposited it under the altar with more prayers and chants from the priests.

At last! Athenais sighed as Cyril led the last prayer and said to the congregants, "Go in peace with the blessing of Saint Stephen." The crowd shuffled out with nods of appreciation and satisfied murmurs.

"Quite a stirring performance." Paulinus offered his hand to bring her to her feet. "Worthy of the best I've seen in theater or church."

Athenais smiled. "You are such a pagan sometimes. Weren't you baptized?"

He shrugged. "Long ago. I think the water has dried." He looked over her shoulder. "Cyril approaches."

She turned and greeted the bishop with a nod.

"Augusta." He bowed low. "You honor me with your presence."

"I enjoyed your sermon, Bishop. You have an engaging style and move the people to tears."

No color entered his faded cheeks at the compliment from an empress, but his lips did twitch at the corners in a near smile. "You are much too kind, Your Serenity. I am hoping you—" He gave a sharp look at Paulinus. "—and your attendant would join Bishop Juvenal and myself at a celebratory feast at the episcopal palace."

"This is the noble Paulinus, my husband's groomsman and best friend," she explained.

Cyril did grin this time in a covetous, feral way. "Ah, of course! The Augustus would trust only his closest confidant with the safety of his consort. Lord Paulinus, you are most welcome to our feast. We have much to discuss about the state of the empire."

"Accepted, Bishop." Paulinus nodded. "We will join you and Bishop Juvenal shortly. Augusta?" He offered his arm.

Athenais walked to the wagon with her fingertips on his crooked arm where he helped her into the sheltering dimness. "Thank God that is over. I enjoy praying with the holy sisters or at peace by myself, but these public ceremonies rival imperial progresses in their boredom. I feel like a prop in a play, some piece of set scenery against which the actors play," she grumbled.

"That is the nature of your role, my goddess. You are there to be worshipped by the people. You are not regretting your choice to become more involved in government, are you?"

"No." She paused in thought. "But I now understand why Pulcheria prefers to rule from the shadows. Theo is the face and figure, attending to all the ceremonial requirements while she does the real work of governing. I'm more determined than ever that Theo step into his rightful role."

"With you at his side?"

"Of course. It is more than time that Pulcheria retired to her suburban estates and focused on her charitable works. You will help me in that goal, won't you, my friend?"

"I would do anything for you, Athenais, as you know."

"Then make sure you sit between me and Cyril at the banquet. I can't stand the man! I want to discuss some improvements to the Saint Stephen Church with Juvenal. I think I'll hire an artist to depict the life of Stephen in frescos on one wall and the Apostles on the other. The nave could also be expanded..." She brimmed with ideas for beautifying and enlarging the modest building. *That will be my first project after reinforcing the walls of the city. I can make a difference here and leave a legacy. And what I do here, I can do in Constantinople.*

Chapter 47

PAULINUS DITHERED OVER HIS PRIVATE NOTE TO THEO. HE HAD ALREADY added his formal report on the Augusta's itinerary to the curator's financial summary and correspondence from the various regional government officials that were to go with the weekly packet to the Constantinople court. *How best to let Theo know his wife is a success on this pilgrimage without giving away my own feelings?* He shrugged and picked up his pen. *As with everything, it is best to start at the beginning.*

My dearest friend,

We talked before I left about your doubts about your wife's piety and your increasing dissatisfaction with your marriage. I want to set your mind and heart at ease. She may have left Constantinople as Athenais, but she will return as the 'New Helena.'

She has acquitted herself with grace and piety. From beggar to bishop, the people of Jerusalem praise her humbleness and charity. Holy Mother Melania is her constant companion and often speaks of her admiration for your wife. Bishop Juvenal gifted her with a relic of Saint Stephen after she attended the consecration of the new church dedicated to the Protomartyr. She hopes you will consent to a formal adventus when she brings the relic home to Constantinople so she can prove herself worthy of the people's love.

Large crowds gather wherever the Augusta goes in the city. She arrives at a holy place in her magnificent imperial carriage, prays on her knees as a humble pilgrim, and gives away her coins and jewelry for the maintenance of the poor. The people acclaim her, and children offer flowers. She has plans to expand and beautify many of the churches in the city. She is much loved.

Only one small incident has marred this pilgrimage and even that proved to Athenais' advantage. When the Augusta attended the translation of Melania's martyr shrine, she stumbled and injured her left knee and foot. The holy sisters blamed the devil's malignity and prayed mightily for her recovery. When Athenais continued with the ceremony as if nothing had happened, she credited the Holy Mother's prayers for the relief of her pain. The sisters believe it a miracle that Melania healed the Augusta, which has only added to both women's reputation.

Paulinus hesitated. Athenais still suffered pain from that fall. She spent the next week in bed or sitting with her swollen knee raised, fussed over by her personal physician. Only during the past week was she able to walk, but she still needed a stick or strong arm to lean on. Paulinus felt it likely that the doctor's compresses did more to relieve Athenais' pain than the prayers of the holy sisters, but Theo would like the miraculous version better. *My goddess performed bravely that day, disguising her discomfort with a smile, but I felt the desperate clutch on my arm as she tried to hide her limp and keep the spasms of agony from her face. Speaking of...* Paulinus looked at the increasing shadows... *It's almost time for my daily visit. I should finish this task and move on to more pleasant pursuits.* He continued.

It is not only her piety you should be proud of, my friend. Your wife has acquitted herself admirably as your representative. People come to her with disputes, which she solves with the wisdom of Solomon. The nobles listen carefully to her words when consulting with her on local and imperial matters and praise her sagacity. People all along her progress have been impressed with her speeches and her justice as well as her piety and charity.

I hope this report gives you assurance that your wife is, in every way, a worthy consort for a great Augustus and restores your confidence in her.

By my own hand,
Your grateful servant and friend,
Paulinus

Paulinus sanded the letter, folded, and sealed it with wax and his signet ring. He addressed it for the emperor's eyes only and added it to the pouch the imperial messenger service would carry to court. *Now for my favorite part of the day.*

He found Athenais reading, reclining on a divan that had been moved from her sitting room to the garden. The sun brightened her gold curls and added a little color to her pale face. *I love that small crease that forms between her brows when she is concentrating.*

"What are you reading, my dear?" He snagged a chair from the solar and joined her in the garden.

"Paulinus, you're late!" she gave a teasing frown. "What have you been doing."

"The emperor's business: reports."

"Then you are forgiven. How could the court function without the reports from the far corners of the empire to keep the bureaucrats busy." She waved the codex at him. "It's a copy of *The Acts of the Apostles* in Mother Melania's own hand. Since she rarely sleeps, she has more time for writing and makes beautiful copies of the Gospels, which she gifts to her benefactors."

"May I?" She nodded and he took the codex, flipping through the pages. "Lovely work and in Greek. Did she translate from the original Aramaic?" He handed it back.

"I doubt it. Melania has a good education, but I think she copied this from another Greek source. She sent it along with a note letting me know that the Syrian Archimandrite Barsauma will be in Jerusalem next month. I want to meet him."

"Why?" Paulinus asked in surprise. "He's an illiterate mad man who wears an iron tunic and sleeps standing up. His followers are as violent as that mob of parabalans that Bishop Cyril used to disrupt the Ephesus council."

"That's exactly why I wish to meet him. He's one of the few holy men that Pulcheria fears. He is too unpredictable for her taste. She likes the quiet ones that stay in their cells or the stylites who live on poles."

"Even the quiet ones have given her fits over the years." Paulinus laughed. "Did you know that Barsauma delivered your sister-in-law her first defeat as a ruler?"

She shook her head, and her eyes grew round with curiosity.

"The desert fathers, here in the Holy Land and Egypt, complained to Pulcheria that local synagogues within eyesight of their monasteries were an affront to their sacred sensibilities and Pulcheria said it was acceptable to remove them."

Athenais interrupted, "I remember that story! So, it was Barsauma who burned synagogues and beat Jews all over the Holy Land causing riot throughout the empire.

"Pulcheria had to rescind the edict." Paulinus nodded.

"What a humiliation for my sister-in-law, but I'm glad it stopped the attacks on the Jews. They *are* Roman citizens." Athenais chuckled briefly, then looked thoughtful. "I am a bit sympathetic toward Pulcheria. I may dislike my sister-in-law, but she held the empire together for Theo. We all make poor choices when we're young and ignorant."

"And what do you regret from your youth, my friend?" he asked teasingly, but was again surprised when she half-closed her eyes and took a moment to think.

"I sometimes regret my marriage," she said in a soft voice as if talking to herself. Her eyes flew wide, and she put a hand to her mouth as if to stop the words she had already said. "I love my husband and don't regret our family, even though that was trying in times of grief. I mean that I sometimes imagine what my life would be like if I had married someone else. Would my life be… less hard?... more joyful?... if I had married a noble man like you, or an academic like my father, rather than an emperor." She lifted her chin. "But regrets are useless. This is the life I chose, and I'll fight to make it the best one I can have."

He bowed his head. "It was not my intention to add to your burdens by bringing up our youth, Augusta, and I certainly don't judge your regrets. As you said, we all have them." *And I'll never be able to express mine to you, my goddess.*

She took his hand in both of hers and said softly. "My dearest friend, I have only found joy in your company, which is why I sometimes daydream such silly nonsense. You have never burdened me, and I hope I haven't burdened you. Forget my foolish words and tell me when I'll be able to leave my residence and return to Jerusalem. Mother Melania plans more pilgrim visits for me, and I *do* want to meet the wild Syrian."

He withdrew his hand from her soft ones and pasted a smile on his face. "As soon as your doctor says you can leave, but I'll assign extra guards for your meeting with Barsauma." *And I'll continue to daydream, my love, for to act on my feelings would be a betrayal of my best friend's trust and embroil you in treasonous danger.*

Chapter 48

Jerusalem, July 438

Athenais rose from worshiping at Jesus' tomb, hissing in pain, her knee throbbing. Melania helped her up. "Your injury still bothers you, Daughter?"

"Only when I kneel for lengthy times." She flexed the stiff joint and the pain subsided. "Your prayers have done much to alleviate the pain."

"I am glad for it." The holy woman took her arm as they walked through the sunlit rotunda of the Resurrection Church followed by Bassa and the other dedicated virgins of Melania's convent. She welcomed the soaring view of the basilica, having felt oppressed by the dark vault of the actual tomb.

Athenais' excitement grew as they exited the rotunda into the eastern enclosed colonnade of the more traditional basilica housing the rock of Calvary. There, they encountered a horde of desert monks led by the redoubtable Barsauma, easily identified by his rusting iron tunic. *I was expecting something like a soldier's armor, not this tight-fitting barrel with shoulder straps. Makes me more appreciative of the comfort of my royal regalia. No wonder he must sleep standing up. How does he piss in that thing--it goes past his hips!* The archimandrite's odd tunic was obscured by nearly floor-length graying hair. *The man must not have cut his hair—or combed it—for a lifetime,* Athenais observed. *I would not be surprised if a mouse peeked out of his beard, or a bird made a nest in his locks.*

Barsauma saw her entrance and moved to meet her. She smiled and tried to breathe through her mouth as the stench of all those unwashed bodies hit her like a wave. *Thank the Good Lord for the myrrh incense or I might not be able to stay in the same room with the holy father! I honestly do not understand why some ascetics believe God requires they not bathe.*

"Blessed Augusta." Barsauma bowed as much as his rigid tunic would allow. "I hope your stay in the Holy City has been instructive."

"Much so." She nodded back. "I am grateful you traveled from your monastery in Euphratensis so we could meet."

"When I heard Your Solemnity would be visiting the Holy City, God set my feet on the path to Jerusalem. I come to correct your actions."

"Your advice is most welcome, Holy Father. I have tried to emulate the holy sisters. Where lies my greatest fault?"

"You have failed to commit your life to God, as these holy sisters who gave up everything."

"That is true, and Mother Melania has counselled me on my path. I cannot break my holy vows to my husband or my country. As you lead your monastery, I must lead the Romans. Did not Our Good Lord Jesus advise 'render unto Caesar what is Caesar's'? I am Augusta, Caesar's consort and therefore cannot retire to a convent."

The archimandrite hesitated for a moment, as if pondering her argument. His black eyes flamed with intensity. "You are a rich woman, Augusta. You will not go to heaven unless you give all your wealth to the poor and destitute."

"Again, Holy Father, I ask your indulgence. As Augusta I hold extensive lands in trust for the next Augusta. It is not mine to give away."

"But—"

She raised a hand to silence him. "However, the income from the land is mine during my lifetime. I also have jewels and gold that are gifts to me which I can dispose of as I like. During my sojourn here in this holiest of cities, I have endeavored to do just that. I intend to die a poor woman."

"You do good works, but your choice of those works go against Christ Our Lord's commands to care for the least of these." He pounded on his iron chest for emphasis. "You repair the walls of Jerusalem, but God's city needs no walls. He will protect us. You give precious Sidonian glass to the rich bishop who already has silver and gold goblets. You buy frescos and mosaics for the churches where people with hungry bellies and rags on their backs come to worship."

"That is a fault I can repair Holy Father. Blessings on you for bringing it to my attention. With your guidance and that of Mother Melania we can direct much more of my income to the widows and orphans, the poor and the lame. I would like to offer you a gift for your monastery as my first step on this path. There will be many more." She bowed her head and removed her silk veil embroidered with gold thread, stripped the gold bracelets from her arms, and removed the jeweled rings from her ears and fingers—all but her signet ring. "Take this veil of great price to adorn the altar of your monastery. Sell this gold and these jewels to feed the poor of your city and see to the wants of their bodies and souls. I ask for only one thing in return."

"I have nothing to offer you, Augusta." Barsauma frowned. "I have given all to God."

"I ask only for your sack-cloth cloak. Such a humble item is made holy by its closeness to your body. I wish to take it back to my home and present it to the people of Constantinople as a constant reminder of your advice to me."

"That I can do." He unknotted the rough cloth, folded it and handed it to Athenais. "If I have need of another, God will provide."

Athenais went to her knees, hiding a wince of pain with a bowed head and wrinkling her nose at the reek wafting from the folded cloak. "Will you give me your blessing, as well as your cloak, Holy Father?"

"Of course, my child." He put both hands on her head and launched into a lengthy, but fervent prayer for her good health, long life, and wisdom to do good. Just as she felt she would faint from the pain, Barsauma concluded. "Amen."

"Amen," she echoed as the holy man extended a hand to help her up. "And blessings on you and your travels Holy Father. I hope we meet again."

"Augusta," he gave her a slight nod, gathered up her veil and jewelry, then left the basilica without a word of thanks.

"That was well done, Daughter." Melania offered an arm. "Barsauma is an ignorant and difficult man, who can be dangerous in his zeal for God. I believe you have won him over."

"He made a good point, Mother, and I will increase my gifts to the poor, but I will still fund sound walls for the safety of the body and beautify the churches for nourishment of the soul, as well as provide food for the belly."

Being an ascetic has blinded our holy father to the need for beauty—and bodily hygiene! She handed the folded cloak to an attendant. *But we all cannot follow his path—or Mother Melania's. However, unlike my learned Holy Mother, Barsauma seems unlikely to grasp the nuances of my choices. I must be wary of him. He could cause me as much trouble as he did Pulcheria.*

Chapter 49

Imperial Residence, Bethlehem, Late November 438

PAULINUS FOUND ATHENAIS INSPECTING THE NEW WALLS OF HER ESTATE, her captain pointing animatedly at the archer turrets. *Nikolaos looks happy with the modifications.* The country manor had transformed during the summer and fall into a modest, but beautiful palace, fit for his empress.

"Augusta," he announced as he approached.

"Paulinus!" She turned with a delighted smile. "Are the new walls not splendid? I think they can stand a barbarian siege." She turned back to Nikolaos. "Are your men pleased with their new barracks?"

"Very much so, Augusta, they particularly wished me to thank you for the addition of the heated pool to their bath. I hope you will not make them soft with such unaccustomed comforts."

"It is nothing they couldn't get at their home in Constantinople. I do not wish them to think of their duty to me as a burden."

"Never, Augusta. The men talk among themselves about how lucky they are to serve you."

"Excellent, Captain. And I'm sure you will keep them in top shape. I have observed your drills and have no fear your men will go soft."

Paulinus recognized the glow Athenais' words brought to Nikolaos's face and the softening of his eyes. *My goddess has worked her magic on another man, and she probably doesn't even know it. How is it that her own husband is so immune to her charms?*

"Paulinus?"

"Yes, Augusta?"

"Will you accompany me to the overlook. My doctor has ordered light exercise now that my injuries are healed."

"I'm at your service." He bowed slightly and offered his arm.

She took a firm grip as they navigated the rough path to a small herb garden outside the walls. He felt her wince as she sat on a stone bench overlooking the valley and the small town of Bethlehem.

"Does the knee still bother you, Athenais?"

"Just a twinge now and then as I sit or stand." She patted the stone next to her. "Sit, my friend, and enjoy the peace. It's lovely." She closed her eyes and raised her face to the noon sun, a slight smile blooming across her visage. A frosty errant breeze made her pull her wool cloak tighter around her shoulders.

Paulinus sat, studying his beloved's face. Time touched her lightly with only a few faint lines at the corners of her eyes. Her golden curls showed no silver, her silken skin no blemishes. At thirty-six, she had lived nearly half her life as a wife and mother, but her face showed none of the cares those roles had brought.

"I love this place, Paulinus." She sighed and gradually opened her eyes. "It is the first place that has felt like home since I left my father's house in Athens."

"That's because you made it your own. The new frescos, mosaics, art—all are your choices. In the palace, you must accommodate others."

"And just as the plaster dust settles and the scent of paint fades from the air, I'll have to leave. I planned on only being gone for a year." She looked wistfully out over the valley. "I dread my return to that cut-throat court."

Paulinus took in a deep breath tinged with the smell of fermenting wine. The grape harvests were done, and the estate vintners busy at their craft further down the hill. The farm families had beaten the olives from the trees and gathered the grain from the fields. Soon, they would be celebrating the birth of Christ and the small village of Bethlehem would see an influx of pilgrims. Athenais had plans for a great feast for the village and surrounding farms.

"You could extend your stay, maybe leave after Easter or next summer. I know how happy this place makes you." *I wish we could stay here together. Live in this peace with each other. I wish…* He shook his head trying to dislodge the dreams.

"I would like to, but I must leave. I need to return to my husband as the new Saint Helena and help him in his work. If I cannot wield power as mother of an heir, I must borrow Pulcheria's tactics and appeal to my husband's piety. That is *my* duty and I have been negligent."

"You still have several more months. We don't need to leave until February. You could be home in time for an Easter adventus."

"I have thought I might visit Ravenna before going home to Constantinople. I would love to see for myself whether Eudoxia is well after the birth. I do so want to hold my granddaughter in my own arms. Placidia's letters are brief and Eudoxia's infrequent. I can't help feeling something is wrong."

"Augusta!" A flustered young page ran up with a sealed packet on a silver tray. "This came for you—from the emperor!" he huffed, trying to catch his breath.

Athenais took the packet, broke the imperial seal, and scanned the pages frowning. She looked up at the young messenger. "You did right in bringing this to me so speedily. You are dismissed."

The boy left, obviously disappointed not to know the letter's contents.

"Bad news?" Paulinus raised an eyebrow.

"We leave as soon as we can make arrangements. There was a major earthquake in Constantinople that caused much damage. The people are in an uproar thinking they've angered God in some way. Theo wants me and the holy relics back as soon as possible for a formal adventus."

"He seeks to calm the people with a show of piety? Bribe them with relics and pageantry?"

"It is a good scheme, but for Theo it is not a show. He genuinely believes and wants to protect his people from further harm."

"And you, Athenais? Do you believe? After your sojourn here in the Holy Land, do you think a saint's bones and the smelly cloak of a holy man will protect the city?"

"My beliefs have not changed. I don't think there is a vengeful god that punishes people with destruction of their homes and livelihoods or—" she took a deep breath "—the loss of their children. The Lord Jesus Christ preached gentleness and love. But the pagan belief in gods with human weaknesses stains Christianity just as it did the old religions, before philosophers called them to a higher purpose. The common people believe in the Father's wrath. They threatened Theo before during that horrible Nestorius mess. He is frightened and I must return."

"I will make the arrangements with all haste." He rose and offered his arm.

She rose and took a last glance over the peaceful valley. "Someday I will return."

And I hope to be with you when that happens, my goddess.

Chapter 50

Imperial Residence, Chalcedon, March 429

If I weren't a Christian, I'd think I'd angered the gods in some way. These storms remind me of the winds that kept King Agamemnon's ships in port when he set out to attack Troy." Athenais turned from the rain slashing across the garden of the imperial palace at Chalcedon and shuddered at the rolling thunder. "They've plagued us our entire trip. It's taken nearly twice as long to get home as last year's voyage."

Paulinus shrugged. "Winter storms are common, Athenais. I hope you plan no human sacrifices to salve their savage natures."

"No." She shook her head with a smile at his jape. "I'm just frustrated. We've sat here for three days. During brief calms, I can see the Constantinople palace across the strait, yet the captain cannot risk the crossing."

"At least we are comfortable here in an imperial residence." Paulinus saluted her with a silver goblet. "The food is good, the beds are soft, and the rooms are heated. Much better than some of those barren coasts where we had to wait out the storms at a tiny fishing village or in tents that threatened to fly away."

"But the people were always kind and did their best."

"And much richer for your visit."

"As they should be." Athenais returned to a work desk and took up a pen. "I never want to be a burden to my people. I am here to make their lives better."

"What are you writing this afternoon? A new poem?"

"A letter to Mother Melania. I do miss her good humor, sharp wit, and steady presence. I keenly felt Aunt Doria's loss last winter and Melania acted as a mother to me filling that void in my heart." Her eyes unfocussed for a moment remembering their tearful farewells at Caesarea Maritima. She muttered, "She's so frail."

"What?" Paulinus asked.

"Nothing. I just fear for Mother Melania. Her health is declining."

Paulinus came to her side and put a reassuring hand on her shoulder. "I know you miss her and will mourn her deeply when she passes. She's a remarkable woman who has counseled you wisely and prepared you well for the next phase of your life. Now it is your turn to guide those younger or less capable than you."

"By less capable, do you mean my husband?"

"Theo is my best friend, but he has shown himself to be less than resolute based on who has his ear. At his best, he is intelligent, kind, and loyal, which others take advantage of. At his worst, he is remarkably stubborn and unforgiving if he believes he is in the right or has been betrayed in some way." He looked her in the eyes. "We have been gone for a full year with Pulcheria at his side and who knows who else has taken his fancy."

"I take your meaning. At least Pulcheria can be trusted to do what is right for Theo's reign. She is willing to buck him and has a keen nose for those who wish to interfere." Tears welled in her eyes. She sniffed and dashed them away. "I want a new start to my marriage. When I refused to leave Aunt Doria's deathbed to attend the translation of St. Chrysostom's bones last year, Theo made it clear he and his sister took it as a personal affront. I'm hoping I will be reborn as the New Helena when the people see me parading through the street in a formal adventus, bringing holy relics for their salvation, With the backing of the people and gratitude of the church, Theo and Pulcheria will have to restore me to equal regard as an Augusta."

"Don't lose Athenais when you become Helena, my dear. Remember, Theo loved you because you were so different from his sisters. Try to rekindle those flames, as well."

"Theo has changed more than I over the years and we have grown apart. But I believe I know the way back into his heart without giving up my soul." She grinned at him. "And my first task will be getting you into a formal position of power. Master of Offices, perhaps? I believe my brother is better suited to another post. Besides, I've grown dependent on your advice and companionship. Between the two of us, perhaps, we can right this ship."

Chapter 51

Imperial Palace, Constantinople, April 439

ATHENAIS ARRIVED AT THE AUDIENCE HALL ON THE ARM OF HER HUSBAND, both glowing with the success of the procession of Saint Stephen's bones and Barsauma's cloak through the city. The court erupted into loud cheers and acclamations as they entered and progressed to the dais at the other end of the hall. There were many shouts lauding the Augusta's piety and naming her the New Helena. *Paulinus has been busy priming his friends and agents.* She continued with a serene face, but Theo gave her hand a squeeze and flashed a quick smile as he seated her in the chair to his right—Pulcheria's normal place.

Athenais scanned the crowd. The room glittered with lights bouncing off multi-colored marble walls and gilt furnishings, not to mention the brilliant silks and flashing jewels adorning the courtiers and their wives. "Where are your sisters, my love?"

"Arcadia sent word that Pulcheria was feeling ill. They will be coming late."

"Should we send a physician to tend to her?" *It would be just like the spiteful harpy to slight me on my biggest day since my marriage.*

"No, it is nothing serious and will pass in a few hours."

"I am pleased to hear it. I wouldn't want her to miss such a momentous celebration. The people seemed quite happy with the adventus."

"They had calmed quite a bit, once I announced you were coming with the relics. You made me and our city proud this past year, my love. Your adventus in pilgrim's garb wearing the Holy Father's cloak and carrying the silver reliquary through the city impressed the people greatly."

"As I had hoped." *At least I didn't have to carry a heavy cross through the streets in full imperial regalia, as Theo did so many years ago. I'm not sure I would be able to stand it if I had. Even so, my knee aches.* She unconsciously rubbed the offending joint.

A herald announced the repast. As the imperial couple sat on the dais, a bevy of servants arrived with all manner of food and drink for the court. Well-trained slaves whisked plates, goblets, napkins, and washing bowls into their hands, and effortlessly made the detritus of their meal disappear. Athenais nibbled on a roast duck leg and munched on dried fruit and nuts. She avoided the jellied eels and boiled beef in fishy garum sauce. She didn't want to embarrass herself by dropping food all over her beautiful gown—a blue silk covered with embroidered silver birds.

Theo also ate little, but that was his wont. "Shall we, my love." He offered his arm. "There are some new people at court that you should meet."

She stood and stepped down from the dais. "How is Cyrus of Panopolis functioning as city prefect? I was most impressed with his poetry when he performed at my salons."

"Paulinus spoke most highly of him. It was on his recommendation that I interviewed the man. Pulcheria was skeptical of having a poet as a prefect, but he made several novel proposals such as lighting the streets of the city after dark and improving the university."

"As a fellow Egyptian, I believe he is well-known to Olympiodorus. Remember Dorrie's bird Plato who performed at the salon where we first met?"

"Yes." Theo patted her arm and his eyes softened at the memory. "But I remember little of the bird's performance. I had eyes only for you, my love."

He still cares. Before she could savor the warmth that spread from her heart, Athenais saw Pulcheria knifing through the crowd toward them. She had changed out of her regalia into her more comfortable holy women's garb. *Well, I never took Pulcheria for a fool.* "Your sister approaches, Theo. She looks recovered from whatever ailed her."

"Brother. Sister." Pulcheria greeted them. She turned to Athenais. "I have yet to congratulate you on the baptism of your granddaughter."

A brilliant smile bloomed on Athenais' face. "I'm so pleased they named the baby Eudocia after me. If a girl, I thought they would do Placidia the honor."

"I'm sure, when they have another daughter, Placidia will receive her due." Theo beamed at his wife.

"I wish I could have been there when Eudoxia was brought to childbed. A daughter needs her mother at such times. Only the Good Lord knows when I will see her again." Unshed tears sparkled in her eyes as she squeezed her husband's hand. "I do so envy Placidia, that she gets to hold our precious grandchild. The palace feels so empty without children."

Theo's smile tightened; the light left his eyes.

"You could plan a visit to Ravenna," Pulcheria suggested.

"After a year away?" Athenais laughed. *I'm sure you would relish my absence for another year.* "No. My place is at my husband's side." She linked his arm in hers. "We have been too much apart for too long a time."

"Athenais." Theo patted his wife's arm. "Come meet my sword-bearer. I'm thinking of promoting him to chief eunuch of the household. With your return, you should have some say in the decision. Sister, would you care to join us?"

"No, Brother, that appointment is for you and your wife. I have other business to conduct."

"My serious sister." He smiled. "Don't forget to enjoy the assembly while you are here. This is a celebration in honor of Saint Stephen. You *are* allowed to enjoy it!"

"I will try, Theo." She nodded. "I believe our new prefect is holding forth. I shall take the opportunity to become better acquainted. Welcome back, Sister, and congratulations on your adventus." Pulcheria gave her a brief nod and left in search of Cyrus.

That was surprising! No pointed remark about the fact that Pulcheria had obtained some relics of Saint Stephen's twenty years ago. Has my sister-in-law softened in the past year?

"There is Chrysaphius, let me present him to you." Theo's words broke through her reverie.

"Of course, my love." Athenais knew little about Chrysaphius, only that he was baptized and schooled in religious matters by the famous holy man Eutyches, whom Theo had taken to consulting about religious matters. *No doubt that is what appeals to Theo.*

They strolled toward a martial-looking eunuch dressed in a white scholae uniform. He sported a long purple cloak decorated with red birds encircled by a gold background. Unlike many eunuchs, he was tall and well-muscled. *I wonder if he was cut after attaining his adult height.* A gold medallion on a chain around his neck marked his office, and a silver band held his straight black chin-length hair in place. Chrysaphius carried the emperor's ceremonial sword—the *spatha*—in a gold sheath.

They must have caught his attention, because he approached on his own and gave them a deep bow. "Augustus. Augusta."

"My Consort, this is Chrysaphius Tzumas, my spatharius."

The eunuch straightened from his bow and looked at her with a bland smile and hawk-like predatory eyes. "Augusta, it is good to have you home. My emperor has sorely missed your presence."

How would he know of Theo's thoughts and feelings unless he spent much time in private conversation with my husband? What are his ambitions beyond promotion? Whatever they may be, no eunuch has ever held sway over Theo. Pulcheria would have objected strenuously if he was a threat.

"Spatharius, welcome to our court. I understand your godfather, the Archimandrite Eutyches, recommended you for the position."

"Yes, Your Serenity. He saved my life and my soul. Any good that I do, I owe to my holy godfather."

"He saved your life? How?"

"My early life is a sordid story, not fit for the tender ears of a beloved Augusta." A blush darkened his tanned features. "I would be most embarrassed to tell it."

"Another time perhaps, when we know each other better." She scanned the crowd. There were more important people she should reacquaint herself with. Athenais nodded her dismissal. The eunuch bowed and took his leave.

She turned to Theo. "I look forward to meeting the Holy Father Eutyches. I'm sure we will have much to discuss after my year in the Holy Land. Do you know if he ever met Mother Melania?"

"I don't believe so. He maintains an ascetic life and is my closest religious advisor."

"What of Bishop Proclus?"

"The bishop is a good man, but too aware of his position. He and Pulcheria are much in each other's company, but I like my religious advisors to have a bit more fire and conviction."

"Of course, my love." *I must meet Eutyches as soon as possible. I hope he is not another Nestorius, believing women should have no place in the world other than to serve men.*

Chapter 52

THE NEXT EVENING, ATHENAIS ESCORTED HER HUSBAND FROM EVENING prayers to her rooms. Theo remained quiet—even remote—as she recounted the events of her day. *This does not bode well for my plans.*

"Theo, would you care to join me for a few moments? We have something important to discuss."

He seemed taken aback or startled out of a deep reverie. "Of c-course," he stuttered. "What?"

She gave him an exasperated look. "Not in the corridors." Athenais drew him through the receiving room, past her work room, and into her bed chamber. She surveyed the inviting space. *Well done, Dorothea!* Soft candlelight, the bed turned down, a light repast laid out on the sideboard. The smell of rosemary roast chicken vied with sandalwood incense for dominance in the room.

"I've dismissed my servants for the evening." She poured them both goblets of light spring wine. "Sit, Husband. Do you wish any of the food?"

"No, Athenais." He looked around the room and gave a deep sigh. "What do you want to discuss?"

She handed him a goblet and took a seat next to him on the divan. Athenais sipped from her glass then set it aside. "Are you happy with me? Our marriage?" Her eyes welled with unshed tears.

Theo took her hand, absently tracing a fading ink stain on her index finger with his thumb. "Of course, I'm happy with you and our marriage. You acquitted yourself with grace and piety in the Holy Land and since returning. I joyously welcome you by my side at prayers."

"But not in your bed."

He dropped her hand. "No. Not in my bed."

The tears dried on Athenais' cheeks and she shook her head in sorrow. "I spoke to Melania about this often. She and her husband vowed to live in a chaste marriage after the loss of their children. But it was because the doctors felt it would endanger her health and possibly cause her death to conceive and bear another child. We do not have that excuse. I am healthy and not too old to bear another child—an heir for you and Rome. It is my right as well as my duty, Theo. Why do you deny me this honor?"

He stood and turned his back to her. "I made a vow to God. I cannot break it."

She rose, put a hand on his shoulder and asked in an anguished voice, "Nothing I can do or say will persuade you to a different path?"

Theo shook his head

Athenais moved to confront him, gripped his elbows, and stared into his eyes. "Say it, Theo. Tell me one last time—to my face—and I swear I'll never mention this again. But know that you put your reign in danger with no male heir. God chose you to lead the Romans, but you have not done your duty by Him, me, or your people."

"My lust for you is a sin which I gave up years ago. I will not fall back into those sinful ways."

She nodded, dropped his arms, and returned to the divan. "I will keep my word and never confront you with this again." Final hopes dashed, she grabbed her goblet and took a deep drink. "But I need to be more to you than a partner in prayer. I am an Augusta. The court already knows we live in a chaste marriage. They do not understand your rejection of me to the detriment of your reign. Do not shame me more by banishing me to the sidelines of your life."

"What do you want, Athenais?" He returned to the divan and sat, head hanging.

"To be of use. To help you. I will continue the charitable work I started in the Holy Land. My godly acts will bring just as much esteem to your name as that of your sisters. But, most of all, I want to be at your side during audiences and council meetings. I want my advice taken as seriously as that of Pulcheria."

"My sister has ruled by my side for many years. She is experienced."

"As am I! Ask Paulinus how I fared in dealing with the disputes in Jerusalem. There, I was Augusta; my opinions respected and my judgement obeyed. Do this for me, Husband. Do this for our past love and future happiness."

"Is that a threat, Wife?"

"No!" *His old insecurities forever warping my words.* Athenais put a hand to her heart and asked in a softer tone. "Why do you wound me over and over? All I've ever wanted is to love you and be loved by you. I chart a new course because I will die without purpose. If I can't be a mother and proper wife, I will be Augusta with all the duty that entails."

"I'm sorry I cause you such distress, my love. I never intended it." He picked up her hand and kissed the palm. "I will do what I can. Pulcheria might not be happy about this, but give me time and I'll bring her around."

So, it will be an on-going battle with my sister-in-law. Theo will only weakly make my case. Athenais sighed. "Might I ask a favor in the meantime?"

"Anything, beloved."

"My brother wishes to retire to his estates and family. I feel you and your government would be well-served by promoting Paulinus to Master of Offices. He is your best friend and confidant. Who better for the role?" *And who better to plead my case and bolster my position.*

"Excellent advice. I'm not sure why I never did this before. He more than deserves it."

Athenais gave him a grateful smile. "Thank you, Theo."

"I'll take my leave now. See you at midnight prayers?"

"Of course."

He turned for a lingering glance at the doorway.

Does he regret his choice? Will he change his mind?

Athenais held her breath until he turned and left her with the cooling ashes of her love.

Chapter 53

Imperial Palace, Constantinople, October 439

AUGUSTA." A YOUNG HERALD HOVERED AWKWARDLY IN HER DOORWAY.

"Yes?" Athenais looked up from her reading—reports of Hun raids on the northern border that Paulinus thought she should be aware of. As promised, he had been her mentor and guide in becoming more active in her husband's reign.

"Grave news, you are wanted in the consistory."

She rose and strode toward the door. "What can you tell me?" she asked as they hurried down the corridor.

"Not much, Augusta. I was not told the reason for your summons, but the palace ripples with rumors."

"What kind?"

"Some say the Vandals have taken Rome. Others that the barbarians have united and overthrown Emperor Valentinian."

Eudoxia and little Eudocia! Her heart beat faster and she quickened her pace. *Can we send a fleet? Evacuate them from Ravenna? Is this why the Huns have been so active on our border? Are we about to be invaded, as well?* A twinge in her knee slowed her pace and gave her a chance to catch her breath. *I know nothing yet. These are just rumors. Better that I show up calm and in control. Panic will not help my daughter and grandchild if they are in danger.*

She entered the council chamber to find Theo, Pulcheria, Paulinus, Prefect Cyrus and General Aspar already in attendance. *Was I a last-minute addition?*

Paulinus gave her a reassuring smile as he, Cyrus, and Aspar rose from their seats at her entrance. *Was it Paulinus or Theo who insisted that I be included?*

"Athenais, sit here." Theo indicated the empty chair to his left around the corner of the long ebony table that usually sat a dozen councilors. Pulcheria occupied the chair to his right at the head of the table. He turned to General Aspar. "Tell the Augusta the news."

"The Vandals broke out of their African territories, took Carthage and the fleet. They now threaten Rome."

"They have the Carthaginian fleet?" Blood drained from her face. "I heard a rumor that they attacked Rome. Is that true?"

"Not yet," Pulcheria said. "With the fleet, they will control the Mediterranean and can strike any coastal city at will... even here! I knew it was a mistake for Placidia Augusta to cede them territory in Africa."

"The Augusta had little choice, with the Burgundians in rebellion and Count Boniface dead. She didn't have the troops to spare," General Aspar retorted.

Athenais gave him an appraising look. Aspar had had a soft spot for her aunt ever since he accompanied her West to recover the throne for her son. Had it been fourteen years ago? The admiration seemed mutual; Placidia requested Aspar be honored as Western Consul three years ago—an unusual move. Despite his Arian faith, he was also a favorite of Pulcheria's, or he would not have contradicted her.

"Do *we* have troops to spare, General? Can we send aid to Valentinian?" Pulcheria tapped the table with her fingernail.

"Yes, Augusta. I can lead the army myself." Aspar had fought the Vandals with Count Boniface and General Sigisvult ten years ago—and failed. No doubt he still smarted from the defeat.

"What is the situation in the West?" Theo asked.

"The Ravenna court reports General Aetius and his army are summoned from Gaul. General Sigisvult is set to guard the coasts of Italy from raids." General Aspar hesitated and shot Pulcheria a glance. "Reports are that King Gaiseric and his Vandals persecute the orthodox in Carthage."

"Our preparations? How soon can we send relief?" Pulcheria's hands tightened on the arms of her chair.

"We can gather our troops and ships, Augusta, but it will be some months before we can act."

"Months? While our lands are lost and those of the true faith are tortured and killed?" She narrowed her gaze at Aspar.

He met her gaze, a slow flush rising into his cheeks. He turned to Theo. "Augustus, my family has served Rome with distinction for three generations as generals and consuls. I have served you faithfully for many years. I fought the Vandals before." A quick glance at Pulcheria. "I will do my utmost to expel Gaiseric from Carthage and any territory he captures. I will drive them into the sea."

Theo nodded approval. "I'll prepare a statement to be read in Constantinople, Ravenna, and Rome detailing our preparations and support. The people will know we are there to protect them." He turned to Cyrus. "Prefect, what do you propose for our own defense?"

Athenais turned with interest. This would be the poet's first emergency. How would he fare in this crisis?

"The land walls of Constantinople are impregnable, Your Serenity, but we are vulnerable to the Carthage fleet. I have drawn up plans to strengthen and expand the sea wall." He unrolled a map showing the proposed extensions. "Once these are in place, the city will stand for a thousand years."

"God willing." Pulcheria raised an eyebrow, evidently impressed with the prefect's plans. "I have no doubt God favors the pious—and the prepared."

"What of Eudoxia and our granddaughter?" Athenais clasped her husband's wrist. "Should we not send for them if we are so well defended?'

"Ravenna is well protected, Augusta." Aspar gave her a sympathetic smile. "I have seen for myself that their defenses are considerable. Marshes guard the city beyond the harbor that serves it. Plus, Emperor Valentinian keeps an imperial fleet patrolling the coast. Gaiseric will go for softer targets first—likely Sicily or African coastal cities. We will stop him before your family is in any danger."

"I'm sure you will, General." Athenais nodded, but her heart still yearned to bring her daughter and grandchild home.

Imperial Palace, June 442

"THREE YEARS OF FIGHTING AND THIS IS THE BEST VAL COULD DO? HOW COULD he give away his own daughter?" Athenais wailed as she slammed a copy of the Vandal treaty to her desk. *This is all Val's fault. Placidia would not have had any hand in this.*

Theo patted her back as she sobbed. "He had little choice once we withdrew our troops to fight the Huns."

"Our baby granddaughter betrothed to that… that… bloody barbarian!"

"Huneric is the Vandal king's son and was a hostage at the Ravenna court for years. He is quite civilized."

"You heard what his father did to that poor Goth girl, Huneric's previous wife." Athenais pushed her husband away. "He cut off her nose and ears! What's to stop him from doing something like that our granddaughter?"

"Gaiseric claims the woman tried to poison him."

She dashed the tears from her eyes and glared for several moments as blood rose into Theo's cheeks. *At least he has the decency to blush.*

Theo held out his hands palms up as if pleading. "As to what will stop him? We will. That girl was the daughter of another barbarian king. Gaiseric would not dare touch a princess of the Theodosian House."

"Why should he respect us? We honor him by promising one of our own." Her hands curled into fists. "He beat us! Generals Aetius, Aspar, Sigisvult—they all failed. The greatest empire the world has ever known couldn't muster the army to defeat a single barbarian tribe." Her face crumpled and she started sobbing again.

"We fought them to a stalemate, and they agreed to retreat to Africa." Theo folded her into his arms, stroking her hair. "But it isn't a single tribe, my dear. It's the Huns along the Danube; the Goths, Burgundians and Franks in Gaul; the Alans in Hispania; the Saxons in Britain; as well as the Vandals in Africa. We could fight any one or two, maybe even three, but not all at once."

"What is to become of us?" she mumbled into his chest. "What of our children?"

"We will survive." He tightened his arms around her. "Chrysaphius has a plan to deal with the Huns. We negotiate with the others and fight when we must. The walls of this city are unbreachable."

"Eudoxia must be heartbroken!" Athenais cried. "I wish I could be there."

"She has baby Placidia for solace and Eudocia is not gone. She is but four. There are many years before a marriage can take place. We may yet defeat the Vandals, or something might befall Huneric." He whispered into her hair, "God will shield us. Let us pray for his good grace."

Athenais felt his manhood harden against her thigh. *Now? Now he is lustful? After all these years and with our family in danger?* Athenais pushed out of his arms. The fury she felt toward her husband stunned her. She nearly spat, "Pray, Husband? As if that is all it takes to keep our granddaughter safe. I'll put my faith in a strong army."

She stormed out of the room, back stiff and head high. *I probably ruined all the goodwill I've built up with Theo over these past three years, but I don't care. How could any father—Theo or Val—be so callous? Bartering a baby girl—a princess!—to a bloody barbarian. I will never forgive either of them!*

Chapter 54

The Hippodrome, Constantinople, July 442

CHRYSAPHIUS SURVEYED THE IMPERIAL BOX AT THE HIPPODROME AND nodded. Marble columns, topped with winged horses, supported a permanent overhang that provided shade from the blazing July sun. Servants stood ready with food, drink, and fans to move the moist summer air. The people—after nearly three years of apprehension and war readiness—wanted games and entertainment. They packed the stands while vendors hawked trinkets and snacks. Bookies shouted odds and took bets. Sailors unfurled a striped awning over the audience.

All was ready for the "victory" celebration over the Vandals. Chrysaphius allowed himself a sour smile. *Few if any of them know how poorly we fared. If I had been emperor…*

The flood of anticipation rippling across the hippodrome rose and broke into a deafening roar when the imperial family entered their box from their private tunnel from the palace. The eunuch felt the wave of sound reverberate through his chest as the crowd shouted acclamations for the Augusti. Imperial agents stationed in each section of the stadium led the chants and the rhythmic stamping.

Theodosius Augustus, flanked by his wife and sister Pulcheria dressed in their most regal attire, led a contingent of the elite of Constantinople, including the prefect and the Master of Offices. They stood stiffly at the front of the box for several minutes while the crowd roared. *Better him than me,* Chrysaphius mused, *it is much more comfortable standing behind the throne than sitting on it.* After three years of being almost constantly in the emperor's presence, he had a keen sense of how the power dynamics worked and was well on the way to accumulating the riches and influence he craved. *The sister knows how to play the game and the wife is learning fast. It has been fun pitting them against one another, but it is almost time to move. Theo putting me in charge of the negotiations with the Huns is just the start.*

At last, the emperor raised his hands and the crowd quieted. A herald came forward to read a lengthy screed by the Augustus. He praised the generals for their sagacity, the troops for their bravery, the people for the steadfastness, and God for his grace, all in a flowery rhetorical style. Chrysaphius suppressed the urge to shuffle his feet as the herald finished with an insipid poem by the Augusta comparing their victory to that of Greece over Troy. *If she were not Augusta, no one would want to hear her words. The timid calligrapher and the mediocre poetess deserve one another, but Rome deserves better. The sister is the true threat to my plans.* She stood at her brother's left hand, leaving her usual honored right-side place for his consort. *I need to remove Pulcheria first, but how?*

The crowd broke into shouts again as the herald concluded. *Probably glad the boring part is over, and the races can begin.* Blood sports, such as gladiator games and beast hunts, were a thing of the past. Chariot racing afforded an opportunity for the masses to gamble and sometimes see a spectacular accident. Since the ascetic Augustus didn't attend the theater or popular entertainment in the city, the hippodrome was the only place regular citizens could confront the emperor directly with their complaints. However, it was unlikely anyone would spoil the celebratory nature of this day with complaints, so Chrysaphius settled in for a long day of service and observation.

The emperor waved the city prefect to the front and raised his clasped hand over their heads, as the herald shouted, "To the man who defended Constantinople from the Vandals, Prefect Cyrus!"

The crowd shouted with even more enthusiasm than before. They were obviously happy with the prefect's efforts on their behalf. His most recent triumph was having wills and judicial decisions written and read in Greek—the native language—as well as Latin. After some chaos, the shouts settled into a chant. "Constantine founded the city. Cyrus renewed it," rang out over the stands.

That was unplanned! Chrysaphius noted the emperor's stiff stance and even more frozen smile. *He is not happy with the good prefect's favor among the people. I can use that if the prefect gets in my way.*

Finally, the emperor and his party took their seats. The Master of the Games blew a trumpet blast and announced the contestants. The first several races were between junior charioteers: youths younger than seventeen, driving two-horse chariots. The young men between seventeen and twenty-three, and the most experienced charioteers over twenty-three, would race later in the day, with four-horse rigs. The most acclaimed champions raced last.

Chrysaphius waved and the flock of servants flew into action. He served the emperor personally the food and drink the imperial tasters had passed. "A brilliant speech, Augustus, and such a wonderful expression of the peoples' love for your clever prefect." The emperor sipped his wine with a thoughtful frown. Chrysaphius had discovered that the emperor suffered from feelings that he wasn't as smart or clever as his companions. The sister unwittingly fed those feelings by the way she treated him as practically a lack-wit, relegating him to the ceremonial side of reigning. He used that knowledge rarely, but to great effect.

He turned to make some remark about how gifted a poet the Augusta was, but caught her in an animated discussion with the Master of Offices Paulinus. The warm glances and intimate touches of hands on arms startled the eunuch. *How did I miss this? And how long has it been going on? I must keep a closer eye on our poetess. Maybe she will do my work for me.*

He was distracted by a roar from the crowd as the eight youths competing in the first race drove their teams behind the spring-loaded gates at the canted entrance along the flat end of the hippodrome. A monumental bronze statue of a quadriga driven by winged Victory loomed over the gates. The gilded horses looked about to leap off their pedestal and race down the tracks. *If all goes well, I will soon have art of my own choosing to admire at my own estates. No more scraping by and bowing to indolent nobles.*

Real horses stamped and snorted as the crowds quieted and tension heightened. The young charioteers pulled on their reins to keep the anxious animals in check. The emperor dropped the white signal cloth, and the gates sprang open. The horses leapt into a gallop, with the crowd roaring encouragement for their favorites and curses for their opponents.

"A *siliqua* on the blues!" Paulinus cried.

Several in the box took up his bet, including the Augusta. "I'm for the greens!"

"You would bet against me?" Paulinus moaned in mock pain.

"Only to keep you honest, my friend."

The frown on the emperor's face deepened. He did not approve of gambling. *Another mark against his wife,* Chrysaphius gloated.

The pair of drivers representing the blue faction, marked by the color of their chariots, took the lead, cooperating to block other teams going into the corner. They forced several teams to the outside, making them cover more distance and jostling one another.

"Go, blues!" half the stadium shouted, while the other half shouted for the greens. The yellow and white factions had only a scattering of followers.

Because these junior races involved two-horse chariots, and only five laps around the spina instead of the usual seven, they ended quickly. However, the inexperience of the drivers meant the chance of accident and death was more prevalent.

Despite himself, Chrysaphius reacted to the increased tension in the stadium, holding his breath as a yellow chariot went careening into the wall on a curve. A long moaning shout went up in the stands as all eyes turned to the downed chariot.

Workers swarmed the site, removing broken bits, rounding up the horses, and helping a limping driver off the course before the racers could make it back to that spot. Some wreckage still dotted the track as the drivers returned and had to dodge the debris, but no more chariots went down.

"I win!" Paulinus cried as one of the blue teams crossed the finish line.

Not for long, Chrysaphius promised himself.

Chapter 55

Imperial Palace, February 443

PAULINUS READ HIS COPY OF THE TREATY WITH THE HUNS, HIS EYES hardening. *Ridiculous! Theo will never agree to these terms. What was the eunuch thinking?*

"This is the best you could do?" Prefect Cyrus waved his copy under Chrysaphius' nose. "We're to pay the Huns 6,000 pounds of gold immediately and another 2,100 annually? And all Hun deserters returned by us gratis while Roman deserters will be sold back to us for ten soldi a head? It's humiliating!" He turned to the emperor. "Augustus, you cannot agree with this!"

"The Huns beat us on the battlefield." Chrysaphius retorted. "Gold is a small price to pay for peace. We give up no territory, unlike Emperor Valentinian's treaty with the Vandals."

They are at it again. Theo had named Cyrus patrician and consul two years ago after elevating him to prefect in the East shortly after Athenais' return in 439. Lately, Cyrus and the eunuch had been clashing in the council meetings. Theo looked worn with dark circles under his eyes and deepening worry lines on his forehead. *I fear for my friend. He never liked conflict and spends more time on his knees in prayer than mediating between his squabbling advisors. The eunuch seemed to be winning in this contest of wills.* Cyrus had abruptly given up his prefecture of the East last year, retaining his city title.

"General Aspar feels we can keep the Huns bottled up on the Danube. If we put this money toward raising troops and repairing the forts on the frontier, we will be better off." Cyrus glared at the eunuch.

"General Aspar has lost to the Vandals and to the Huns. The Augustus and I have been discussing replacing him with General Zeno."

"The pagan Isaurian?" Cyrus turned to the emperor. "Your Serenity, I feel it would not only be disastrous to replace such a loyal experienced general as Aspar, but would compound the error by replacing him with such an ambitious and undisciplined man as Zeno."

Where is the Augusta? It's not like Pulcheria to miss such an important meeting. She would never agree to demoting Aspar. He is one of her most staunch allies.

"His troops have been the only ones successful against the Huns!" Chrysaphius snapped.

"Because they are as brutal and uncivilized as those they fight. You want to barrack them behind our walls where they would be free to terrorize *our* citizens?"

"Augustus?" Paulinus decided to intervene. "What is your will?"

Theo's gaze darted from Cyrus to Chrysaphius, caught between two advisors. He hesitated, then said in a low voice. "The treaty stands, Patrician, but I will consider your objections to Zeno's appointment." Theo stood and everyone rose to their feet. "Now I must go. Chrysaphius, accompany me."

A satisfied smile flashed briefly across the eunuch's face. "As you wish, Augustus."

After they left, Cyrus turned to Paulinus. "What is underfoot? I was expecting Pulcheria Augusta to be present. Chrysaphius seems to be more at the emperor's side than his sister these days."

"I, as well. The Augusta is not always our ally, but she advises her brother wisely in the matters of war." Paulinus nodded. "But I worry about you, my friend. Is it wise to challenge the eunuch directly when he is so much in the emperor's company?"

"I vowed to give my opinion and will not refrain from doing so because Chrysaphius says otherwise. The Augustus will not hold my honesty against me. He knows it is given with good intentions, so he can make wise choices."

"I'm sure you are right, Cyrus. Your good work on behalf of the city speaks for itself." *I just hope Theo listens.*

*****

March 443

My goddess will not be happy with this news. I hate to spoil our time together, but she must be warned. Paulinus strolled down the corridor toward Athenais' suite. The familiar guard let him enter the pleasant receiving room. A musician played a seven-stringed kithara in the background while women read to one another or gossiped in small groups. Athenais lounged alone on her favorite divan reading.

She looks so lonely. I wish she could confide in one of the young matrons who attend her, but understand her reluctance to do so. I had hoped she and Theo could reconcile and, for a while, it seemed they had, but since her granddaughter had been betrothed to the Vandal prince…

"Master of Offices Paulinus to see the Augusta," a servant announced.

Athenais looked up, her whole face brightening with a smile. *Time has treated my goddess well.* Her figure was softer, more rounded, but that only stirred his desire for her.

"Augusta! You look beautiful today." Paulinus gave her a slight bow and a big grin.

"You say that every day, my friend." She patted the seat next to her on the divan and he sat.

"Every day it's true." He picked up her hand to kiss the palm.

Athenais pulled her hand away. "Stop that! We're too old for such foolishness. I'm a married woman."

"And well-guarded from any lascivious attacks. What fool would offend you in a room full of your women and servants?"

He indicated the room of oblivious women. His playful antics seemed to draw no special notice. She relaxed and gave him an appraising look. "You seem tired, Paulinus. Has Theo been working you too hard? Or perhaps a woman keeps you up late?"

"What woman could compete with a goddess like you, Athenais? Since you are my best friend's wife, I must settle for mere mortals, and they do not satisfy."

"I worry about you, Paulinus. You should have married long ago and started a family." She patted his hand. "It's not too late. I'm sure I could arrange a suitable match with a rich widow."

"No, my dear. We've had this chat before. I'm content with my life as it is." He smiled. "As long as I can see you often."

"Whenever you wish." A slight blush tinged her cheeks and her breathing quickened. "Now tell me the latest about Cyrus. I was shocked when he resigned his posts and withdrew from the court. Theo is furious with him over something, but didn't confide in me about what, as usual."

The bitterness in her tone sparked his protectiveness. Over the past couple of years, Athenais seemed to be pushed back into the shadows—again. Little by little, the influence she gained from her pilgrimage faded and Theo and Pulcheria paid less attention to her, dismissing her advice and ignoring her good works.

"I'm afraid it isn't good news." Paulinus lowered his voice, "Theo is confiscating Cyrus' property and forcing him to become a bishop in Phrygia."

"No! Why? Cyrus has never shown an inclination for the church." Athenais put a hand to her throat. "This smacks of punishment, not reward for all the good Cyrus did for the city."

"It's worse than punishment. The people of that bishopric murdered the last four Episcopal appointees. I fear Theo has sent our friend to his death."

"This has to be Pulcheria's doing!" Hectic red spots appeared on her cheeks. "She is ever against any in the government who urges moderation or champions culture. She is jealous of the people's esteem. She also knows I support Cyrus, and therefore she automatically becomes his enemy."

Paulinus rubbed his jaw. "I don't think Pulcheria is behind this. Chrysaphius is constantly in Theo's presence. Even I, as Master of Offices, have difficulty getting an audience lately. Have you been much in your husband's company?"

"Now that you bring it up, except for brief greetings at prayers, I haven't. But surely that is because of Theo's duties. Prosecuting a war makes little time for idle chatter. But what does this have to do with Cyrus? Theo gave him many honors and promotions. There's been no hint of scandal or corruption."

"I believe Chrysaphius saw Cyrus as a threat to his influence for those very reasons. You remember what happened at the hippodrome last fall?"

Athenais frowned, shaking her head.

"When Theo introduced Cyrus, the crowd shouted, 'Constantine built the city, Cyrus renewed it!' Theo was not happy. I think Chrysaphius inflamed that jealousy."

"Oh, Paulinus!" Athenais laughed. "The people were happy and acclaimed Cyrus in the hippodrome one day. Theo is not so small a man that he would hold that against a loyal official." She sobered. "No, there is only one person who wields that kind of power over Theo—Pulcheria. She is the jealous one. Ever since my return from Jerusalem, she has been working against me. I am convinced she wishes Theo to set me aside."

"Perhaps you are right, my goddess." Paulinus retrieved her hand. This time Athenais did not pull it back. "But all the same, be wary of the eunuch."

"I will." She looked around the room, sadness softening her features and regret tinging her voice, "So many enemies. So few friends." She glanced down at the book of poems by Olympiodorus and said with a voice strangled with tears, "Dorrie gone and Mother Melania. Gesius dead of a fever and Valerius retired to his estates. Now Cyrus banished."

"I will never leave you, Athenais." His heartbeat quickened.

"I know."

Her look of gratitude brought a lump to this throat.

Her lips turned up in a sad smile. "And I do need your help."

"Anything, my goddess."

"I wish to throw a private celebration for Theo to mark his thirty-fifth year as emperor. I know there will be public games and feasts, but I want this to be for Theo alone. He is not one for parties, but might welcome a dinner with the leading religious leaders of the city, as well as the court. You seem more in his confidence than I. Will you help me with the guest list?"

"Of course, my dear." *Still looking to please Theo after the way he treats you. All I wanted was your happiness, but I failed. No, Theo failed. How can he not see what a treasure he has and how he has wasted it?*

Chapter 56

Imperial Palace, April 443

"What are your wishes, Augusta?"

Athenais looked in her large silver mirror to see Chrysaphius behind her, bowing. Dorothea stopped arranging her hair, a look of astonishment on her face at the intrusion.

Drat the man, how dare he come into my dressing room, even if he is a eunuch. He should have stayed in my receiving room. I'll have to have a talk with my guards and servants. They are becoming lax. Or perhaps Chrysaphius used his rank as Head Eunuch to catch me in a vulnerable moment? He has a knack for that. Well, nothing for it but to show equanimity.

She signaled to Dorothea to continue. "I want an intimate banquet in honor of the emperor's thirty-five years on the throne on the ides of next month."

"In addition to the week-long celebrations in the city?" Chrysaphius asked.

"There will be free food, drink, and special races at the hippodrome for the people, but my husband should have a more appropriate celebration with his closest friends and advisors. I wish to honor him by having the city's nobles and holy men as guests."

"As you wish, Augusta. I will have a menu, guest list, and suggested entertainment prepared for you in three days."

"Three days?" Athenais frowned. "Why not this afternoon? I have already prepared a guest list with the Master of Offices. When you leave here, go to his office to receive it."

Now it was Chrysaphius' turn to frown. *No doubt the wily eunuch regrets not being able to extract gifts from those who wish to buy a seat at the banquet table.* It was well-known throughout the palace that the eunuch grew richer from such graft.

"Most Noble Lady." He bowed again. "I regret the delay, but my staff is busy with the emperor's business. Three days is the earliest we could do."

"That's not good enough!" She glared into the mirror. *How dare the eunuch countermand me when I've done most of the work already?* "I require this done immediately." In theory, Chrysaphius served her as well as Theo, but the Head Eunuch frequently pleaded that his services were needed by her husband and slighted her wishes.

"Augusta, I humbly regret the inconvenience." He pulled a sorrowful face. "You could make the request for my immediate services directly to the emperor, but…" He hesitated. "May I make a suggestion?"

She gave a permissive wave of her hand.

"Pulcheria Augusta has a full imperial staff. Is it not appropriate that you have one as well? Then you would have no need to call on me."

"My husband has made it clear he feels I have no need of staff beyond those assigned to him. He and I are one in the sight of God." *Or so he thinks.*

"It seems wrong to me that the emperor's sister enjoys such a privilege, but the emperor's wife does not. You are equal in rank. I'm afraid the emperor does not appreciate your needs and slights your dignity. As he says, what you do reflects on him."

"You are right, but my husband is stubborn on the matter. He refuses to give me staff in my own right and Pulcheria won't share hers with me." *An old grudge.*

"How unfortunate! I would not have thought the Augusta so selfish, given her modest needs."

"You are wrong to criticize the Augusta. She has earned her place and retinue, but are right on one point. A wife of equal rank should have equal privileges." Athenais scowled into the mirror. *I need to be careful of my words and not give him more ammunition for his machinations.*

"I agree, Augusta! The emperor should honor you." He cupped his chin with his fingers, drawing down his brows in thought. "Sometimes a strength can be a weakness."

"What do you mean?" *What are you up to?*

"Your husband has great regard for his sister. He wants her happiness above all else."

"Yes, and she is happy ruling the empire."

"I suspect she does not tell her brother that." He offered a sly smile. "She likely tells him it is her duty to serve him. She would not openly usurp his role. What does she profess to love most… after her brother?"

"The church, but how does that help me? My husband and his sister share that passion."

"If the emperor believes his sister serves him only out of duty, that her real calling is the church, he could order her to take holy orders out of love for her. In his eyes, he gives her a precious gift—possibly even one the Augustus would covet for himself—while ridding you of a rival for his affections."

"That's a clever idea." Athenais gave him a sharp look. "You have given this some prior thought. How does it benefit you?" *What is he hiding?*

"I have long thought you were poorly treated, Augusta, and the ways of the court too strict. church hours and chastity are for monasteries, not a palace."

A telltale blush crept into her cheeks. *Of course, he knows. Everyone knows!*

"This is Pulcheria's work, not your husband's. With her gone, you could have a more moderating influence on the Augustus."

I doubt it. Plus, I've given my word to Theo never to raise the issue of our chaste marriage again. "You still haven't told me how this benefits you." She raised an eyebrow.

"Your sister-in-law is not my friend. She whispers against me as often as she whispers against you." He grinned at her. "And with her gone, you get her imperial staff and I have less work to do."

"We make common cause to take Pulcheria off the playing board? It might not work. She and the emperor are remarkably close."

He shrugged. "If not this, something else will present itself. We need only be patient and work together for our mutual benefit."

"I'll give it some thought." Athenais turned, dismissing Chrysaphius. *Do I want to ally myself with the eunuch? Is he even worthy of my trust?* She frowned at herself in the mirror. *I have little choice if I want to retake my place at Theo's side.*

"WHAT'S WRONG WITH THE GUEST LIST, HUSBAND? DID I MISS SOME ARCHIMANDRITE or courtier that you wish to be added?"

Theo frowned. "My sisters are not on the list."

"Because they are family and assumed to be present." Athenais took the list back. "I'll seat Pulcheria next to Bishop Proclus. They are great friends and will have much to discuss."

"I leave the details to you and Chrysaphius." Theo turned back to his work desk with a sigh. At forty-two, he sported a scholar's slumping shoulders and a small paunch. *He should spend more time riding or practicing sword play with Paulinus. That would also get him away from that scheming eunuch.*

Athenais patted his hand. She knew he found details of troop movements, grain storage, and petty land disputes… lacking. She understood his need for the soothing rituals of the church, but his reliance on Chrysaphius alarmed her. *Maybe Paulinus is right, but I must pry Pulcheria away first. Once I have Theo's ear again, I can deal with the eunuch.*

"Speaking of Chrysaphius, have you given any more thought to my request for a court of my own? Or perhaps you could reassign Pulcheria's to me?" Athenais pursed her lips. "Given her preference for a simple life, she has no need for a chief eunuch, guards, and the trappings of a separate court at her own palace. I could put them to much better use. You would then have Chrysaphius to serve you alone."

"Don't trouble yourself over this." Theo frowned. "Pulcheria governs beside me with wit and piety. She deserves her own court. I will not deprive her of it. You share in my dignity and have no need for your own court."

"But…"

"I've spoken my last word on the subject." Annoyance crept into his voice.

"I understand, Husband. I will not trouble you with the issue again." Athenais soothed. "However…"

He looked at her with a weary smile. "Yes, my dear?"

"You make an interesting point. Pulcheria is a most pious woman. Many call her the modern Olympias, that most holy of all women who ministered with Bishop John Chrysostom of just a generation past."

"There are many parallels." Theo's gaze turned inward as if in thought.

"I met many holy women in Jerusalem and was struck with their resemblance to Pulcheria in their dedication to the church. Mother Melania particularly comes to mind. Both women have followers pledged to chastity, take meals with bishops, communion with the priests and, above all, command the love and respect of the people for their charity and compassion."

She gazed at a flickering candle. *If only I could have matched Pulcheria in piety. I thought I might for a short while after Jerusalem, but even though I tried, that is not my path.* "I think Pulcheria longs to fully commit herself to the church and take holy orders, but does not, out of love and loyalty to you."

"Do you really think so?" Theo asked.

Athenais hesitated. Pulcheria had frequently of late urged Theo to take on more than the ceremonial aspects of governing. She might be finding the work wearying. *I might be expressing her secret longing and doing her a profound favor with this scheme.* She gave a mental shrug. *Or not. Either way, if it works, I'll finally be rid of her influence over Theo.*

"Just yesterday, she mentioned, with a sense of longing, all the charity work Arcadia and Marina did in her name." Athenais put a light hand on his arm. "How often has she told you she lives to serve you? It's obvious your sister yearns for a quiet life dedicated to Christ. She stays in the government only out of love for you." *And the final argument!* "You are more than capable of governing on your own. Do you keep her with you out of love? If so, you do her a disservice."

"I had not thought of it that way," Theo murmured. "Chrysaphius hinted at something similar just the other day."

So, the eunuch kept his part of the bargain.

"Your love and respect for Pulcheria are as great as hers for you," Athenais said. "You are not to blame for wanting your sister at your side, but it is selfish to keep her there when her heart lies elsewhere. She has provided you with nearly thirty years of honorable service. Does she not deserve some reward, some life of her own choosing? She lives as a holy woman. Why not free her to take holy orders? Think how happy it would make her to become a deaconess."

"You are right, Athenais." Theo's face fairly beamed with love for his sister. "Thank you, my dear. I will contact Bishop Proclus and make it so."

Her smile felt brittle. "I'm sure Pulcheria will be delighted with this decision. You are a loving brother."

Oh, Theo! How easy it has become to sway you even in such matters of love and empire. This makes me even more wary of Chrysaphius. I must rid you of his malign influence as soon as I can.

Chapter 57

The Great Church, April 443

THEO SEATED HIS WIFE IN THE IMPERIAL BOX AT THE GREAT CHURCH. A surge of anticipation flooded his soul. *Today's the day I repay Pulcheria for all her dedicated service. My sister will be so happy to finally live a fully Christian life.* A tinge of regret darkened the edges of his pleasure. *I only wish we could enter that life together. But as she frequently reminds me, God chose me to be Augustus and I must follow that path to the end.*

"Where's Pulcheria and her ladies?" Athenais surveyed the empty balcony across from the matching imperial box.

Theo turned to look for himself and frowned. "I don't know. I had hoped to meet with her and Bishop Proclus after the service, so we could plan her dedication as deaconess. I sent him a note telling him of my plans."

"I hope Arcadia has not taken a turn for the worse. I understand she has been plagued with a cough and fevers this winter." Athenais still regretted that she had never built a more sisterly relationship with Theo's younger sisters.

"I'll find out from Bishop Proclus. He is great friend of my sisters."

The entrance of chanting priests swinging censers cut off their conversation. Theo let his apprehensions go as he settled into the peace that church ritual always gave him.

After the service, he approached the bishop at the screen to the inner sanctuary. They would have communion and break their Sunday fast together as was their tradition. Athenais as a married woman was not allowed in the inner sanctum, so she returned to the palace—hopefully to continue prayer and meditation, but likely to read or write. *I had such hopes when she returned from Jerusalem*, he thought with a sigh.

"Augustus." Proclus embraced him with a kiss of peace.

"Bishop." Theo smiled. "I enjoyed your sermon today. The story of Ruth and Naomi is one of my sister's favorites. Do you know why the Augusta and her women did not attend today? I had hoped that we might celebrate her taking holy orders."

"I sent a messenger with your note to me, so Pulcheria Augusta might prepare for the honor. He returned with this message for you." Proclus fumbled with his casula, extracted a letter sealed with Pulcheria's signet ring, and handed it to Theo.

As he read it, Theo's smile disappeared, and his face turned stormy. "Do you know its contents, Bishop?"

"Not the words, but the sentiment." Proclus nodded. "Your sister is unwilling to take holy orders."

"Her exact words are these:

My Dearest Brother Theo,

I know you propose that I become a deaconess out of love for me and your great wish for my happiness. And in truth, I do long for a life of service in the church. But I cannot take that step. I have ruled for and with you for almost thirty years—since I was fifteen. I know your mind, heart, and soul. You cannot see malice in anyone close, and they manipulate you for their own purposes. You need me by your side. If I take holy orders, I come under the supervision of the bishop and owe him alone my obedience. I must remain free to help you and our empire. When your ire at my action has cooled, we can talk, my dearest brother. Until then, I resign my post on the council and will dismiss my imperial court. I wish you only the greatest of God's blessings.

By my own hand,
Your most loving sister
Pulcheria Augusta

"She disobeys me!" Theo's face suffused with dark blood. "She took my loving gift and threw it back in my teeth with an insult—her old complaint that I'm a lackwit and don't know how to rule on my own. This time she has gone too far."

"I believe the Augusta is sincere in her wishes." The bishop pointed to the letter crumpled in Theo's hand. "Perhaps I can mediate between you."

Theo's eyes narrowed. "You had a hand in this, Bishop. You warned her of my intentions."

The bishop's eyes went wide. "As I said, I only sent her your message to me, so she might prepare herself for the transition."

"And by doing so, she was able to concoct a scheme to avoid my orders. I am not happy with your interference, Bishop Proclus. I am considering appointing Archimandrite Eutyches as my new spiritual advisor."

Proclus gave the emperor a deep bow. "You must do as you feel right, Augustus. Eutyches is a very holy man. I hope he preaches forgiveness among those tenets that Christ proposed."

Theo glared at the bishop and stormed out of the church, forgoing communion in his disordered state. *Chrysaphius was right in his assessment of the bishop. Proclus plots with Pulcheria to keep her in power.*

Chapter 58

Imperial Palace, January 444

CHRYSAPHIUS ENTERED THE SPECIALLY BUILT SCRIPTORIUM WHERE THE emperor retired to copy sacred texts. *He might as well be a monk, for all the good he does the empire.* The eunuch shrugged. *It makes my life easier that the man is so oblivious. Pulcheria was almost ridiculously easy to remove once the calligrapher's pride was pricked and that meddling Egyptian Cyrus was gone. If this next scheme works, I'll have the Augustus and the empire to myself.*

The sharp smell of fresh ink tickled his nose as he approached the emperor busy at his task. "Most noble Augustus." Chrysaphius bowed low.

The emperor completed a line, then put down his quill. He looked up at Chrysaphius and smiled, "You know you needn't be so formal in my presence when we are alone, my friend."

He dropped to his knees, giving a full obeisance. "I bring you grave news, My Augustus."

"Are we under attack?" Theo rose, looking out on the bleak winter garden with alarm.

"Not the city, Sire, but your own person. I have uncovered a treasonous plot hatched right here in the palace."

"What? Who?" Theo threw anxious glances at the doors and windows.

Chrysaphius rose to his feet and put a note of alarm in his voice. "Your wife conspires with your Master of Offices, Paulinus. They have conducted an adulterous affair for months, possibly years. They now plan to assassinate you and put him on the throne."

"My wife and best friend?" Blood drained from Theo's face, and he dropped to his chair.

Is the man going to faint? Chrysaphius looked for the ever-present wine and water and spied it on a sideboard. He poured a large draught in a silver goblet and held it to the emperor's lips. "Drink this. It will revive you."

Theo took a sip of the strong red wine, coughed, and feebly pushed the cup away. "I've had enough." He straightened. Disbelief flickered across his face. "This can't be true. What proof do you have?"

"I've observed the Augusta and Paulinus many times in intimate conversation."

"They are great friends. Paulinus introduced us. It is not unusual for them to speak or spend time together."

"I've observed behavior that speaks of more than friendship: intimate touches and kisses. I would not trouble you with only disturbing rumors, Augustus, or just my observations." The eunuch pulled a sheet of parchment from his tunic. "Here is sworn testimony from one of Paulinus' servants that he frequently goes to your wife's rooms and stays the night."

"How was this testimony obtained?" The missives shook in Theo's hands.

"The servant is a slave, Augustus. His testimony was got by torture, as prescribed by law."

"I still do not believe it." Theo put the paper face down on the table. "Athenais and Paulinus would not betray me. She is a pious God-fearing woman, and he my best friend."

"May I bring up a delicate point?" Chrysaphius bowed again. *Time to press my advantage.*

"Of course."

"The Augusta is a most beautiful and desirable woman. You had three children together. Are her… needs… satisfied?" He extended his hands, palms up. "Everyone knows women are the font of evil, and carnal lust is one of the devil's most potent weapons. To have an affair with the Augusta is punishable by death. Paulinus doubtless plans your assassination to protect himself and the Augusta. Your death has the added advantage that he can take your place both as emperor and in your wife's bed."

Theo sat back, brows furrowed, and gaze lost in thought.

Don't be so slow, man. I know your abhorrence of the sin of lust. I've taken care of your bloody hair shirts and the sheets stained with nightly secretions myself to keep your secrets. Athenais shames you with her sexual desires. Your wife is a whore, and you know it in your loins.

Chrysaphius glanced over his shoulder and leaned in to say in a low voice, "I know this is difficult for you to believe, Theo. Perhaps if you observe them yourself for a day or two, you will be convinced. But for your own sake, do not take too long. I will double your guard and taste your food myself. Do not be alone with either of them."

"Go!" Theo cried as if in pain.

"As you wish, my friend, but I will be here when you need me, and I will die to protect you." He bowed out the door leaving the weak emperor shaking with sobs. *The trap is set and baited. I only must be patient and perhaps strengthen the evidence.*

ATHENAIS WOKE TO AN UNFAMILIAR VOICE GIVING HER A MORNING GREETING.

She sat up in bed and pushed the hair out of her eyes while trying to sweep the memory of disturbing dreams from her mind. "Where's Dorothea?"

"She's ill, Augusta. Chrysaphius sent me in her stead." The gaunt older woman drew back the curtains to let in the weak winter sun. "I can assist you in dressing or call another if you wish."

A tingle of alarm rippled up from her stomach. Dorothea had become more than a servant after all these years. She wasn't a scholar, but was a kind soul and devoted companion. Athenais' mind flashed back to her aunt Placidia's mute scarred servant—*Lucilla?—yes Dorothea reminds me of her. We have been through so much together. She was such a comforting presence during the deaths of my children, far greater than my husband or sisters-in-law. I was so happy when she and Nikolaos married in Jerusalem, even if they had to keep it a secret to stay in my service.* She swung her legs out of the bed. "I should visit her; see that she is well-cared for."

"No need, Augusta. The court physician attends her and anticipated your concern. He says Dorothea has a common illness that spreads easily. She is in no danger, but you should not visit and risk infection. He will send a message if there is any change." The new servant rummaged through her trunk for a day robe. "Will this suit?" She held up a yellow woolen tunic with embroidered blue birds sweeping from the hem to one shoulder in a waving flock.

Athenais nodded and held out her arms for the woman to dress her. She didn't care for yellow—it made her look sallow—but for a private morning it would do. She would dress more formally in the afternoon when she held her salon. "What's your name?"

"Magdalene, Your Serenity." She pulled the silk sleeping tunica over Athenais' head and replaced it with a white linen one with long tight sleeves. The yellow robe went on top. They moved to the dressing table. "How does the Augusta like her hair arranged?"

"A simple braid pinned up for the morning."

The servant nodded and combed the night tangles from her curly locks.

"Why haven't I seen you among my servants before, Magdalene?"

"I originally served the princesses. When they left many years ago, I was assigned to the kitchen staff."

Athenais detected a hint of bitterness in the woman's tone, as she worked a particularly difficult tangle. *No matter. Dorothea will soon be back.*

Chapter 59

Palace Holding Cells

Chrysaphius listened to the woman's screams with admiration. Normally it took only a few slaps and punches, maybe a rape, before the slaves started babbling whatever he wanted to hear. The Augusta's personal servant had to be put on the wheel, ankles made fast to the ground, wrists to the wheel, which slowly turned to stretch her body.

He heard a pop as her shoulders dislocated, and the screaming stopped.

"She fainted, Master Chrysaphius." The imperial torturer threw water on the unconscious woman, but failed to revive her.

"Take her down and put the joint back in the socket. You know how to do that?"

The man looked at him with pride. "I know more about bones and joints, how to cause pain and how to relieve it, than the doctors do. I have a concoction I use to bring them out of a faint if you want."

"Do it."

After ministering to the woman, the torturer placed her in a chair across a table from Chrysaphius and brought her around. The left side of her face was bruised and her eye nearly swollen shut. Blood trailed from the left ear, her nose, and the corner of her mouth from vicious blows. The right side was red from slaps but relatively unscathed, which gave her face a grotesque unbalanced look.

"Drink?" He pushed a rude clay goblet of water toward her,

She glared at him out of her good eye, but reached unsteadily for the goblet, the skin on her wrists raw from the wheel bindings. She winced with pain, but brought the goblet to her mouth with two trembling hands.

"You know what I want, Dorothea." Chrysaphius pushed a piece of parchment in her direction.

She read the lengthy description of multiple trysts between the Augusta and the Master of Offices and shook her head. "No. None of that is true. I swear before God."

"How do you know?"

"I just do. Master Paulinus is a good friend to my mistress and nothing more. She is a God-fearing woman and would never betray her husband."

"Are you with her every single moment of every single day? She could have done this without your knowledge."

"Then I did not witness it and could not swear it happened."

He sat back in his chair. *I was led to believe this woman was somewhat dim-witted, but that was a quick bit of logic. I need another tack.* "Sign the paper and you can go your own way. I'll place you in another household and provide for you." *Until the dust has settled.* "Otherwise, it is the wheel until you do sign."

Fear twisted her lips and clouded her good eye. She bowed her head for several moments.

This is the point where she breaks.

Dorothea raised her head and asked softly, "Are you a good Christian?"

What's the woman up to? "I am baptized, the godson of the sainted Eutychus, and keep church hours with the emperor."

"That is not what I asked. Are you willing to meet your Maker with the stain of all your sins—lies, murder, greed—on your soul? Are you willing to endure everlasting hellfire?"

She seeks to scare me with that superstitious pap the church uses to keep the masses in line. Chrysaphius smiled his most wolfish grin. It had the intended effect. She cowered back in her chair. "That is between me and God."

"I will not give false witness," she whispered.

"We'll see." He nodded to the torturer.

As Chrysaphius completed fabricating his evidence, the Augustus entered his office.

"Are you ill, Theo?" He rose and offered the emperor a seat and goblet of wine. The man looked terrible with dark-ringed eyes and haggard expression.

"I haven't been sleeping." Theo sat and waved away the wine. "I've watched my wife and friend these past two days. The Augusta and Paulinus share some levity, and perhaps their conduct in public is not as circumspect as it should be. But treason? Murder? I have prayed on it and cannot find it in my heart to believe either could betray me so."

"It grieves me beyond measure, Your Serenity, to be the one to bring this to you." Chrysaphius handed him Dorothea's testimony and watched as a look of horror came over the emperor's face. "I have had the Augusta watched night and day. There are rooms which are observable." He coughed delicately.

"I've known of the secret passageways and spy holes since I was a child." Theo dropped the paper into his lap and mumbled. "Continue."

"When the Augusta feels safe, she meets Paulinus and they… couple. I saw them myself just this morning and overheard their plans. Paulinus proposes he poison you slowly, so it looks like a natural sickness and death. After a suitable time of mourning, the Augusta will marry Paulinus and declare him Augustus."

"And Athenais agreed to this?" Theo crumpled the false evidence. "No. You must be mistaken!"

"I understand this is a blow." Chrysaphius shook his head. "The Augusta is probably under your groomsman's thrall. He seems to be the instigator. Master, I would never suggest you lower yourself to spy on your wife personally, but I've devised a test that, with my testimony and that of her own servants, should convince you. After… uh… being together, the Augusta likes to give Paulinus small gifts. He is currently in residence, having injured his foot, but the Augusta is unaware. I have a plan…"

Chapter 60

Imperial Palace, January 444

"GOOD DAY, MY DEAR."

Athenais looked up from her reading. "Theo, what a wonderful surprise. I thought you held audience all morning."

As he approached, she offered her cheek for a kiss, but he didn't come closer. Her smile grew brittle. *I'm denied even that small token of affection.*

"I have a present for you," His voice cracked.

She met his eyes and said with concern, "Are you ill, my love? You look pale."

"No! I have trouble sleeping, that is all." He ducked his head and shuffled his feet.

"That is easily remedied. I can speak to the physician and have a draught made up. Paulinus recommends warm red wine, with a drop or two of poppy juice."

"No need, my dear." He backed away from her, as if in fear.

What is bothering him? Perhaps I can help. She patted the blue silk divan. "Sit, Husband, and talk to me. We see so little of each other these days."

"I-I can't stay." Theo clapped. A servant by the door glided to his side to present a prodigious golden yellow apple on a silver tray. "An embassy from Phrygia gave me this, in celebration of Epiphany." He handed the apple to his wife with trembling hands. She needed both hands to hold it.

"This is wondrous!" She examined the fruit. "It's huge! Its skin has no blemish. How did they grow such a marvelous, perfect fruit?"

"The man said a local priest blessed the tree with holy water and promised a bumper crop. This is the result."

"Thank you, Husband, for such a miraculous gift. I'll treasure it." She put the tray with the apple aside.

Theo dipped his head to his wife and her ladies. "I'll leave you to enjoy the rest of the morning. I'm practicing swords in the armory later. Care to watch?"

"You know I have no interest in the martial arts, my dear. But go!" Athenais made shooing motions with her hands. "Go get sweaty. I'll stay here comfortable with my book."

He fled her apartments, as if chased by demons.

She glanced wistfully at the door. *Poor Theo, if only he would talk to me.*

Chrysaphius took a deep breath before entering the Augusta's rooms. *Eve has her apple, let's see what she does with it.*

"Master of Offices Paulinus sends his regrets, Augusta." He bowed to Athenais. "He cannot visit you as promised. He injured his foot."

"Oh, the poor man!" Athenais turned a worried gaze on the eunuch. "How did this happen? Is he at his home in the city?"

"He stumbled in loose stones. It is a bad sprain, but not broken. The Augustus insisted he stay in the guest apartments in the Daphne."

"I must see he is being properly attended to." Athenais rose, then hesitated. "Why bring this message yourself, Chrysaphius? A messenger page could have done as well."

Was that a hint of suspicion? "The emperor knows of your fondness for Master Paulinus. He sent me personally to reassure you." *Now to dangle the bait.* He pointed to the giant apple on its silver platter by divan. "That's a remarkable piece of fruit."

"And just the thing to cheer up my friend." She commanded, "Show me to his quarters. Bring the apple with you."

He bowed and took the tray and apple. *That was almost too easy. How gullible can the woman be?*

They hurried down halls and through courtyards of two complexes to reach the oldest part of the palace, just off the audience chamber, where foreign embassies resided. It was far more luxurious than the emperor's own monkish quarters, sporting gilded furniture, intricate mosaics and frescos of classic themes, paintings and statues by Greek masters. It was too early in the year for flowers from the garden, but a faint scent of sandalwood incense pervaded the rooms.

They entered one of the guest suites to find Paulinus on a padded divan, right leg elevated on a silk cushion and wrapped tightly. The physician nearly ran into the empress on his way out.

"My apologies, Augusta." The doctor ducked his head.

"Is the Master of Offices well?" Athenais looked past the physician.

"It is a bad sprain, but he should be on his feet in a few days. Until then, I recommend he rest, and use a stick when he must move."

"Is he in much pain? What have you given him for ease?"

"It throbs but a little, Augusta," Paulinus answered for himself. "Let the poor man go. He can do no more for me."

The physician bowed out.

Athenais flew to his side and placed a hand on his forehead.

"I don't have a fever. It's just a sprain." His eyes flicked over her shoulder. She remembered Chrysaphius.

She motioned to the eunuch. "I brought you a present to take your mind off your injury."

"Thank you." Paulinus took the fruit from the tray and turned it round. "I don't think I've ever seen such an apple before. Remarkable, and welcome." He set it aside. "Though not as welcome as you."

She blushed. "Chrysaphius, you may go. Send in this apartment's servants. I have specific instructions for the Master's care."

"As you wish, Augusta." Chrysaphius bowed out and allowed himself a satisfied grin. *Trap set.*

"I don't trust that eunuch." Paulinus said after Chrysaphius left.

"I know you have doubts, but he is only a temporary ally." Athenais settled on a chair by his side. "It was his idea I suggest to Theo that Pulcheria take holy orders."

"That's just what I mean. Why not make the suggestion to Theo himself? He is constantly in the emperor's presence."

"Perhaps he thought Theo wouldn't take his advice when it pertained to family."

"Pulcheria refused the trap," Paulinus grumbled.

"And got caught in another. Theo was hurt and furious when she refused. After all he did to bring about her happiness, she threw his gift back in his face. It finally proved to him Pulcheria wanted power only for herself. She's no better than those sycophants she constantly decries. I'm glad he finally sees her for what she is." She shrugged. "Pulcheria is gone. All ended as planned. When you are better we can find a way to remove Chrysaphius from the court."

"I still don't trust that eunuch. I feel like I have a target on my back in his presence. He waits only for me to turn so he can throw a knife into it."

"Don't fret so!" Athenais pushed hair back from his forehead. "You are Theo's oldest and dearest friend. He values you above all other men. If I were a courtier, I should be envious of his love for you."

"Then I'm extremely lucky you are a beautiful woman and not a courtier."

"Silly man!" She leaned in to give him a light kiss on the forehead, starting back guiltily as the requested servants trooped in. Athenais gave them their orders and left with a renewed sense of calm. Paulinus was in no danger. *I can visit his quarters as easily as he visits mine. And we shall soon devise an exit for the devious eunuch.*

"LEAVE US," HER HUSBAND ORDERED AS HE STALKED INTO ATHENAIS' ROOM, HIS face twisted with rage and pain.

Athenais looked up, eyes narrowed in concern. Her retinue and servants scurried from the room. Magdalene gave Chrysaphius a tight smile as she passed him. A wave of unease clenched her stomach. *Did I wait too long to attack the eunuch? He looks too satisfied and Theo angrier than I've ever seen him.* "Husband? What—"

"Silence!"

She instinctively covered her mouth with her hands.

He pulled her from her chair by the arm. "The apple I gave you yesterday. What did you do with it?"

The apple? That's what has him so upset? I can't let him know I gave his gift away. "I… I… I ate it." His fingers dug into her arm. She struggled in his grasp. "Please, Theo, you're hurting me." He had never been violent with her before.

He let her go. She rubbed where his fingers dug into her flesh. There would be bruises later.

"Are you sure?" He thrust his face close to hers. She backed away.

"I should know what I ate or didn't," Athenais replied sharply, mind awhirl.

"Chrysaphius." Theo nodded.

The eunuch produced the silver platter with the huge yellow apple sitting in the middle.

"Paulinus gave me this just now, saying he had received it as a gift from a friend and thought I might enjoy it."

She felt the blood leave her face. "I'm sorry, Husband. I gave it to Paulinus yesterday when I checked to see if he was properly cared for after his accident. A small token, to cheer him up."

"Why did you lie?" Theo gasped, as if in pain.

"You took me by surprise. I thought you wanted the miraculous apple back. I was embarrassed that I gave away your gift." She hung her head. *Surely, this can all be smoothed over.* "Forgive me, Husband. It was a small mistake."

"Do you," he choked on the words, "betray me with Paulinus? Do you plot my death?"

"What?" Athenais raised her head and stared into her husband's eyes. "No! Where does this ridiculous notion come from? This silly apple? I told you; your question surprised me, and I told a clumsy lie."

"If you lie about one thing, you'll lie about another."

"Theo, no!" Fear and shock froze her. *Infidelity to an Augustus is treason punishable by death. and I didn't see it coming.* Her gaze darted from Theo's anguished face to Chrysaphius. A sly smile curved his lips. *He did this! And the treacherous eunuch wants me to know.*

She turned back to Theo and tried to keep the desperation out of her voice. "On my honor, as your wife and the mother of your child. I have been faithful to you throughout our marriage, and chaste—as was *your* wish—these past thirteen years."

"Chrysaphius says otherwise. He saw you fornicating with Paulinus." He pulled several pages of parchment from his belt and tossed them in her face. "Others swear, as well. You have disgraced me and committed treason."

She picked up the papers and glanced through them quickly. "You would take the word of slaves and eunuchs over that of your wife of twenty-three years?" She tossed the papers back at him, anger seeping in to replace the shock. "These are lies. I'll swear before Bishop Proclus and God, on saints' bones, whatever oath you prescribe. I did not couple with Paulinus. We do not plot your death. I have not disgraced you."

"I wish I could believe you." Doubt flickered across his face.

I can get through to him, I know I can. She clasped her hands as if in prayer and said in a gentle voice. "You can, Theo."

His gaze slid to the cursed apple—the symbol of Eve's sin and her own supposed betrayal. His face closed in anger. "Chrysaphius, the Augusta is confined to her rooms. I don't wish to see her deceiving face ever again."

"Theo!" She dropped to her knees and sobbed. "Please, don't do this! I am innocent. The eunuch lies!"

Her husband left her without a glance.

Athenais sat back on her heels. *Treason. Death.* Panic gripped her bowels and sobs closed her throat. She sat frozen for several minutes, her mind spinning with accusations, denials, and imagined gruesome deaths. She and Paulinus executed. *Paulinus! They must have him as well. Is his false confession among those Theo received?*

She gathered up the scraps of parchment and read them more carefully, blushing at the graphic descriptions of fornication. "No wonder Theo was angry," she muttered to herself. "These most likely inspired his own lustful feelings and the guilt he always feels." She checked the signatures. None were Paulinus, but… she dropped the pages into her lap and tears again sprang to her eyes. "Not Dorothea! I thought she was ill. What tortures did you endure before signing this, my friend? And you a free woman. Will they do the same to Paulinus? To Me?"

Paralysis again started to freeze her limbs and numb her mind. She shook her head. *They might kill me, but they wouldn't dare torture an Augusta. That means I'm the only one who can save us—Paulinus, Dorothea, me. I mustn't give in to fear. I must be brave if I am to survive. Brave like… .like… Helen of Troy. No, she was a pawn for powerful men. Who…? Aunt Placidia! She's the bravest woman I know. She was once accused of treason and survived. I can too. I must be brave… and smart like her. What would she do? What* did *she do?*

Athenais looked around the empty room, her sight blurred by tears. Anger quickly burned away her despair. *That despicable eunuch has ruined my life. First Pulcheria*—she had a pang of guilt over her role in that affair—*then Cyrus. I thought I had more time to counter him. And Theo let it all happen. I knew he was weak-willed but thought his love for me and his best friend proof against common slander and forged evidence. Theo is dangerous in the thrall of an evil man and must be stopped!* She dashed the moisture from her eyes and took a shaky breath. *Placidia wouldn't sit here crying. She knew her enemies and how to manipulate her brother. I can follow her pattern. I must plan.*

Chapter 61

February 444

"Thank you for your guidance, Father Severus. Will you return this gospel to Bishop Proclus?" She pressed the book into the priest's hands under the sharp eyes of Magdalene, her constant jailor. Chrysaphius allowed only a few servants to bring food and clean her rooms these past few weeks.

"I particularly enjoyed the passage he recommended." Theo had allowed her no visitors, until she pleaded that she needed religious guidance. Luckily, he had no objection to her appeal to Bishop Proclus. The good bishop sent Father Severus, who had smuggled several messages between Athenais and Proclus. Finally, Bishop Proclus arranged for a meeting between the two Augusti.

The young priest gave her a knowing nod. "I thought you might, Augusta. Is your… uh… soul prepared?"

"As best as it can be, Father."

"Then go in peace, my daughter."

Tomorrow. I'll finally get to make my case. She went to her work desk and reviewed her notes. *Thank you, Husband, for your gift of the Theodosian Code. Chrysaphius probably thought he deprived me of pleasure by taking all my books except the religious tracts and the Code, but law books are just what I needed.*

Athenais slept poorly that night and rose with dark circles under her eyes. She considered whether to cover them with powder. *Better to leave them.*

Theo will be more amenable if he sees that I've suffered. She appraised herself in the mirror. *Forty-three.* Strands of silver lightened her golden curls. She patted the loosening skin under her chin and jowls. *Where has my life gone? Stolen by a weak-willed neglectful husband and an ambitious eunuch. My only legacy, my far-away daughter and unknown grandchildren. Perhaps, my loves, I can remedy that today.*

"Shall I dress your hair, Augusta?" Magdalene loomed behind her with a comb.

Athenais flinched. She loathed the woman and could not abide her touch. *My poor Dorothea. I pray to God, you're still alive. Nikolaos must be frantic over the loss. Unless he was able to rescue her?* A heaviness in her heart told her how unlikely that was, but until she learned differently... She shook her head.

"No. I'll comb it myself. Take out my pilgrim's robes—the ones I wore during the adventus of Saint Stephen's bones—and leave me to my prayers."

When her jailor left, Athenais dressed in a plain unbleached linen tunic topped with a brown woolen palla. *If I could, I'd wear Barsauma's smelly cloak, but it is secreted away in the chapel.* She combed her hair out and left it flowing past her waist as if she were a virgin maid, her only jewelry a signet ring. She placed a knee length linen veil over her hair, leaving her face bare. She held it in place with a silk ribbon embroidered in gold suggesting a traditional diadem and denoting her rank.

She prayed, standing before the tiny altar in her room. "Dear Lord, you know my soul. I am innocent of the crimes of which I am accused. Give me the wisdom to refute these lies and the strength to save my life and all those who depend on me. Show my erring husband the righteousness of my cause and bless him with a forgiving heart. Amen."

"Augusta," Magdalene poked her head into the room. "There is a guard to escort you to the emperor."

Athenais muttered, "If God really does hear our prayers, He will aid me today." She placed her notes in a packet and left the room, back stiff and head high. *Time for humility when I'm in Theo's presence.*

The guard was courteous, impassive, and unknown to her. Chrysaphius had replaced all her servants with creatures of his own. *He thought the isolation these past weeks would break me. More fool him. I'll convince Theo yet to dismiss the treacherous eunuch.*

They entered an intimate chamber just off Saint Stephen's chapel and the guard announced, "Aelia Eudocia Augusta, Your Serenity."

Her husband occupied an ornate throne-like chair. Bishop Proclus sat to one side on a padded stool. Chrysaphius, wearing his spatharius uniform and sword—*afraid of an unarmed woman, Theo?*—stood to her husbands' side and slightly behind. The room was hot and vaguely smoky from the fragrant cedar chips in a brazier. Sweat popped out on her forehead and started to trickle down her back. *Another play by the eunuch to catch me off guard?*

She glided into the room and sank gracefully to her knees in front of her husband, head bowed. She took a deep breath and looked up at Theo, eyes sparkling with unshed tears. "Thank you, Husband, for granting me this audience. A grave injustice has been perpetrated against me, but I believe in your wisdom and know that the love you have born for me over these past twenty-three years will guide you."

"Rise, Daughter of Eve." Theo's cold tone and choice of epithet shook her.

Nestorius' old curse and excuse to set women aside. What new heresy has Chrysaphius been whispering in Theo's ears? She stood, biting her lip briefly when her knee twinged. "I have come before you to swear on holy relics that the accusations against me are false. Bishop Proclus?"

The bishop brought over the silver casket holding the Protomartyr's little finger. She raised cold metal to her lips, kissed it, and held it in front of her. Staring directly into her husband's eyes, she intoned, "I, Aelia Eudocia Augusta, do swear on penalty of everlasting hellfire, witnessed by this righteous company and in sight of God the Father, Jesus Christ His Son, and the Holy Spirit that I tell the truth. I did not commit adultery with the Master of Offices Paulinus. I did not conspire with him to murder my husband the anointed Flavius Theodosius Augustus. I am innocent of these charges."

Theo's brows came down in a slight frown. Doubt flickered briefly across his face. *I am getting through to him!*

Chrysaphius leaned forward to whisper in his ear, and Theo's face hardened again. "You lied to me about the apple. How do I know that you were not put on earth to lead me astray and stain my soul beyond redemption?"

She glanced at Proclus. *Will he come to my aid? Refute these slanders?* The bishop stared at the emperor, eyes wide in disbelief, but made no effort to contradict Theo. *So Pulcheria's man will not take my side. Then he, as well as she, are the bigger fools. The eunuch has Theo in his clutches and can only be ousted by someone with Theo's ear.*

She turned her attention back to her husband. "I swore on holy relics in the sight of God. Do you not believe I will be punished for such a terrible sin, if I lied?"

Chrysaphius again leaned forward to whisper.

"Eunuch, if you have something to say, speak to my face. I know it is you who has brought these calumnies upon my name."

"As you command, Augusta. I ask if you even believe in the everlasting hellfire which you claim to fear?"

She gasped and stepped back half a step. *My weakness! Theo and I have ever differed in our faiths, but he believes his is right and all others are wrong. I must choose my words carefully.* "I believe in a just and merciful God. That whatever rewards or punishments come in the afterlife will be judged based on the good works I have accomplished against any small faults that are a human's lot."

"So, your oath is meaningless." Chrysaphius sneered. "You do not fear everlasting hellfire."

She appealed to Theo. "Husband, I believe you can make up your own mind without the interference of this eunuch. You are a holy and just man. The eunuch twists my words. I do not fear punishment because I do not lie."

His lips trembled as he said in a near whisper, "I want to believe you, but the evidence…"

Here I am on firmer ground. If I cannot convince him with my piety, I can prove my innocence under the law. "The evidence of tortured slaves is not sufficient to convict an Augusta. I know you have read your own Theodosian Code. So have I. You left this evidence with me." She took the packet from her robe, extracted a page and passed the missive to Theo. "I do not believe Paulinus' confession is real. This is not his signature. You know his hand."

He studied the signature.

"Bishop Proclus," Athenais turned to the prelate, "you visited Paulinus in the holding cells. In what condition did you find him? Did he confess to you?"

"The former Master of Offices showed signs of torture. He limped from a foot injury and his left hand had been crushed by the mangle. When I showed him the signed confession, he denied that he signed it. He swore before God that he was innocent, and that the confession was a forgery."

Oh, my dear, dear friend. I must free you and Dorothea, then we will leave. I can no longer live in this place with a man who would treat his wife and best friend with such monstrousness.

Chrysaphius crossed his arms and glared at the bishop. "Augustus. I was present during the torture. The villain confessed and signed with his good right hand. If it varies, it is because he suffered righteous pain for his crimes."

Theo sat frozen in his chair, unable to decide between truth and falsehood. Her contempt for him grew. She pulled Dorothea's confession from the packet and turned to Chrysaphius. "This names my servant Dorothea, but is marked with a sign, not a signature. Is she alive?"

He shook his head, and her heart sank. *Another of my friends gone.* "Then you have committed murder."

"Under Roman law, slaves cannot be murdered. Their lives are the property of their owners." The eunuch gave her a sly smile.

Anger buffered a tide of grief. *Time for that later.* "Dorothea was an educated free woman who could read and write. She came to the palace from one of Pulcheria's orphanages. I paid her an annuity for her service. She freely married a man of her choice. You," she pointed at Chrysaphius, "have made my husband complicit in the murder of a free Roman citizen."

She turned back to Theo. "Husband, can you not see how this man has stained your soul with the blood of an innocent woman? Let me plead my case before the council, as the law demands. It will be my word against that of this murderous corrupt eunuch."

"No!" He finally showed some animation. His face twisted with fear. "You and Paulinus plotted against me. You must suffer the consequences."

Chrysaphius' face broke into a triumphal grin.

Athenais trembled. *My weak-willed husband is completely in the eunuch's thrall.*

"Augustus." Proclus stood and came to her side. "The Augusta is right. By law, if you wish to execute her and the Master of Offices, you must give her a trial before the council. I've examined the evidence and it is not compelling. The council will likely acquit her."

"I can take what action against them I wish." Theo nearly foamed at the mouth. "I am the Augustus!"

Proclus bowed low. "Of course, Your Serenity, but let me ask: have you been about the city these past two weeks?"

"No." His jaw set in a stubborn line.

"The people are upset. They love and esteem the Augusta for her pious ways and good works. Since her return from the Holy Land, she stands in great esteem with the people. When you dismissed the Augusta's court so abruptly last month, the women scattered to the four corners of the city with strange tales and rumors that put you in a poor light. If something… uh… untoward were to happen to your wife, the people might riot as they did during that Nestorius debacle."

When Flacilla died. That was the beginning of the end for us.

"I won't have her scheming or whoring in my own palace!"

"I did not whore here or anywhere. I'm not the poisonous Clytemnestra, who schemed with her lover to kill her husband, I'm the faithful Penelope who spent twenty years without the love of her husband Odysseus, but stayed loyal to him anyway."

"Pagan literature is still the first thing out of your mouth rather than Christian scripture."

"Your first gift to me was a pagan play, Theo. I cherished it and our bonding over literature and later study of the gospels. It was for love of you that I gave up my philosopher's cloak and donned these pilgrim's robes. It was for love of Christ's teachings that I visited the Holy Land and try to walk in His path. It is for the love of the people of our empire that I do good works: expanding the university, feeding the poor, decorating the churches for the glory of God. Why do you believe the lies of this eunuch over the sworn testimony of your faithful wife? Do you not have any tender feelings left for me, my love?"

Theo's face crumpled. "You lied to me, Athenais. I can no longer trust you. Every time I see your face, it reminds me of your betrayal."

"Then banish me. If you insist on death, I will insist on a trial. The people will know of your persecution of me. The evidence of your cruelty and complicity in the murder of a free citizen will come out. Save face, Theo, and send me to the Ravenna court. I can live out my days with our daughter and grandchildren." *A much more pleasant prospect than spending another minute in your presence!*

His face hardened. "And have you scheme with Valentinian to overthrow me? Never!"

"Jerusalem then. I have a residence there and can live quietly, far away from the court and any specious intrigues your eunuch might invent." *From there I can move onto the Ravenna court.*

"That sounds like a good solution." Proclus nodded. "It avoids scandal—if it is perceived that the Augusta does this of her own free will and retains her status."

Thank you, my good bishop! I should never have doubted you.

Theo shot a glance at Chrysaphius, who gave him a slight nod. "The Augusta may retire to Jerusalem and with my blessing continue the good works she started on her pilgrimage. I'll even allow her to keep her title and live off her land revenues if she promises never to leave the Holy Land. No travelling to Ravenna or returning to Constantinople."

Promise never to see my child or her children? That is Theo's final cruelty. She had another thought. "And Paulinus?"

"He dies."

"But—"

Bishop Proclus put a hand on her arm. "Augustus, I'm sure Chrysaphius would concur, that if you execute Paulinus, you are admitting you believe you were cuckolded, and all your plans to squash the scandal will come to naught. Your court will whisper behind your back and the people will know the Augusta's retirement to Jerusalem is a sham."

The eunuch scowled but said, "The bishop is right, Augustus. I suggest we send your traitorous friend under heavy guard to a distant post in Cappadocia. He will be unable to execute any of his schemes from there."

Theo looked stormy, but huffed, "Fine. Make it so, Chrysaphius. I don't want to see either of them again." He turned his back on the small group. "I'm going to pray."

So, this is the end. My loving Theo chooses to be a bloodthirsty monster.

Part IV

Rebel Empress

May 445 - August 453

Chapter 62

Imperial Palace, Bethlehem, May 445

"WHO'S NEXT?" ATHENAIS LEANED OVER THE ARM OF HER ORNATE chair to confer with Father Severus. She enjoyed these weekly audiences where the people of the surrounding lands petitioned her. Technically, she had no magisterial powers because she was a woman, but practically, the people called on her to settle their disputes because she was an imperial presence in this backwater part of the empire.

"Yitzhak ben Levi leads a delegation of Jewish merchants who wishes you to lift the ban on Jewish worship at the site of their destroyed temple for this year's Feast of the Tabernacles."

"Why are they banned?" She had found Father Severus to be just as useful in the Holy Lands as in Constantinople. He had a vast knowledge of history—not only about the Christian church, but the Jewish traditions from which it sprang. In knowledge and temperament, he reminded her of Dorrie.

"After one of their rebellions, Emperor Hadrian razed their temple and forbade Jews from ever entering Jerusalem again. I believe the expulsion order said they were 'only to gaze from afar' except for one day a year. On their Day of Lamentation—for a fee—they could enter Jerusalem to pray. That expulsion led to the last Jewish diaspora as they fled to the four corners of the empire."

"But that was over three hundred years ago. Surely they have served their penance for rebelling."

He shrugged. "The rule is antiquated and not much observed. Jews come into the city for commerce, but they are still forbidden to worship at the rock they claim as part of their lost temple."

"What do you know of this Yitzhak ben Levi?"

"He is a successful wine merchant and trades throughout the region. I believe he buys from your own vineyards. The rest of his delegation trade in luxury goods; silks and other fine fabrics, glassware and such. They have gifted you with a selection of their wares."

"I see." The rich frequently brought her gifts when they sought her favors. She didn't live an ascetic life, but did follow the philosophy of moderation in all things and lived rather modestly for her rank. She usually donated the gifts to the church. She nodded to a young herald. "Show them in."

Dressed in their Roman best, the delegation of Jews sported brightly colored cloaks fastened with gold fibulae; their fingers flashed with polished gems. All gave her a full obeisance until she bade them rise. Yitzhak was a powerfully built, stocky man; deeply tanned with abundant laugh lines flowing from his black eyes.

"Our gratitude, Most Gracious and Beneficent Augusta, for hearing our pleas." Yitzhak bent double then straightened again. "Your uncle Asclepiodotus was kind to our people and sought to relieve some of our burdens when he was prefect of the East. We hope you will take pity on our people and grant a small request."

And Uncle suffered for his kindness. A wave of resentment toward her husband and sister-in-law rushed through her. *I thought I had that under control. Why do I let them poison my current life?* She took a deep calming breath and smiled at the delegation. "My uncle was indeed a wise man. What do you wish of me?"

"Our people wish to return to Jerusalem to pray in the ruins of Solomon's Temple."

"You want full access, year-round?"

"No, Your Serenity, we wish only to worship during our Feast of the Tabernacles, which is held in September this year. We have been forbidden to rebuild those synagogues destroyed two decades ago and still suffer from our loss. One week of the year to pray at our sacred site is all we ask for." Yitzhak held out his hands, empty palms up, head bowed. "Augusta, you are known everywhere in the Holy Lands as wise and kind. We pray that you show such kindness to our poor suffering people."

"I see no reason you and your brethren should be punished for the sins of your fathers many generations ago. I grant permission and further proclaim that you are under my protection. No harm shall befall the Jews as they worship in the city during this Feast."

The entire delegation fell to their knees, eyes shining with unshed tears, mouths trembling with joy, and bowed in a full obeisance. Yitzhak boomed, "Thanks to you Great Augusta. Blessings on your name. We will send word to our brethren that they may return for the Feast of Tabernacles."

"It is my duty as well as my joy to aid all the good citizens of this empire." It was with a sense of supreme satisfaction that Athenais said, "Go in peace."

"That was well-done, Augusta, but not all will see it so." Severus frowned as the delegation left the receiving room.

"That is why I extended my protection. No one will dare attack the Jews if it is known the worshipers do so with my permission."

"I suggest you also alert the Jerusalem garrison of your wishes, so they may extend more tangible protection."

"Excellent thought. Make it so."

"Augusta!" Deacon John came running into the room. "A letter just arrived from your friend in Cappadocia."

John, a round gregarious man, had correspondents throughout the empire. It wasn't exactly a spy network such as her uncle had run for Theo, but it kept her up to date on key political moves and behind-the-scenes gossip. They had established a way, using John's contacts in the church, to send and receive clandestine letters from Paulinus over the past year. They couldn't address, sign, or seal their letters because they passed through many hands, and they could not leave evidence of forbidden communication. Athenais recognized Paulinus' hand, as she opened the short missive and read:

My goddess,

This will be my final note to you. Last night, I overheard my guards talking of an order from our former friend and how they would soon be able to return home. I believe the eunuch knows of our correspondence and uses that knowledge to bring about my death. My Bright Star, know that I regret nothing. I can meet my Maker with a soul stained with only those small sins common to all men. It has been my privilege to know you and love you from afar. I only wish I could have protected you from our common enemy. I will put this note in a book of poems that I will pass to my priest when he comes shortly. I only pray that it finds you. Beware and be careful, my love.

A tear dropped on the final line, "*Your devoted friend and servant*," smudging the ink. She folded the note and put it in the bosom of her palla. *Oh, Paulinus, if only… I knew. I knew in my heart. but wouldn't admit it, and now I've lost you, too. If this is God's will, He's no better than the capricious gods of old.*

"Augusta?"

The concern in the young deacon's eyes touched her sore heart, but she didn't want to fall apart in front of her court. She looked around the small cluster of officials that had accompanied her from Constantinople. *Which of you is Chrysaphius' spy? My scribe? My physician? All of you? Who can I trust besides Severus and John?* Her gaze stopped at her ever-present guards. *Nikolaos. We wept together over Dorothea, her body buried somewhere in an unmarked grave. He is my man, heart and soul.*

She turned to Severus. "My audience is done for the day. Dismiss the court and send Captain Nikolaos to my quarters."

"As you wish, Augusta." The priest exchanged a worried glance with Deacon John. "Do you require our presence, as well?"

"Not at this time, my friend." She put a reassuring hand on his arm. "I'll call for you later."

Athenais paced her private receiving room, trying to keep her roiling emotions in check. Her heart ached for her loss. A cold intellectual hatred gripped her mind. *That dastardly eunuch will not win. I'll even make common cause with Pulcheria to see him toppled.* A white-hot emotional hatred inflamed her heart. *Theo, I'll never forgive you for this. You've stolen everyone I love from me*—tears rushed to her eyes and cascaded down her cheeks—*even you!*

She swallowed her sobs and dashed her face with cold water. "Tomorrow," she muttered to herself. "You can mourn tomorrow. Today you must make plans to survive."

"You sent for me, Augusta?" Captain Nikolaos stood in her doorway, his back straight, face impassive, but his eyes radiated concern.

"Come in, Captain." She indicated a padded chair and took a seat in her favorite blue silk divan.

"I'm afraid I have sad news about our mutual friend, Paulinus. It is likely that he is already dead by my husband's order."

The blood left the captain's face. "And you, Augusta, are you in any danger?"

"I might be. Paulinus believed so and warned me. You know the evil influence Chrysaphius has with my husband?"

Nikolaos' face flushed red and his eyes hardened. He nodded.

Athenais leaned forward. "How much do you know about why I returned to Jerusalem?"

"Some," Nikolaos said.

"Chrysaphius not only murdered Dorothea, he purged all those who had the emperor's best interests at heart and replaced them with his own creatures." She slumped on her divan and put a hand to her forehead. "I fear for the Augustus and for the empire."

"And for yourself, Augusta?"

She nodded. "Yes. Chrysaphius has poisoned my husband's mind and soul. He reached out to faraway Cappadocia to execute Paulinus. What's to stop him from sending agents to assassinate me? I have so few protectors, Captain. Can I count on you and your men?"

"Paulinus—"

Did she detect a slight catch in his voice?

"—handpicked me for service to you, Augusta, all those years ago. I am—was—loyal to him and to you. I swore an oath to protect you and will to my dying breath. I similarly picked only those men I could trust as brothers-in-arms for this detail. Over this past year, they have settled in the local soil. None regret their posting."

"Good." She straightened. "I will be dismissing the entourage my husband assigned to me and sending them back to Constantinople. I'm sure it is riddled with spies. I will hire only local people to work in the palace. You and Father Severus will oversee finding honest loyal workers."

Nikolaos rose and bowed from the waist. "It will be done, My Lady. I will call on Father Severus now and start the process." He hesitated at the door and said over his shoulder. "My most solemn condolences, Augusta, for the death of Paulinus. He was a good friend, as well as a kind patron, to me."

Once the captain left, Athenais collapsed onto her bed, drenching the pillow with tears of grief and rage, until she fell into an exhausted sleep.

Chapter 63

Imperial Palace, Bethlehem, 443

MURDER, MISTRESS!"

Athenais jerked her head up from reading the household accounts. Her new servant stood white-faced and shaking in the doorway to her work room. "What murder, Martha? Are we under attack?"

One of her guards pushed the woman aside. "You're needed in the receiving room, Augusta. The captain has apprehended an assassin."

She rose, threw a purple cloak around her shoulders, and rushed down the corridor. Bethlehem Palace was considerably smaller than the sprawling complex in Constantinople and she arrived within a few minutes to a chaotic scene of milling people. Guards pushed the servants aside to make way for her. As she stepped into the room, a hush fell over the crowd.

Father Severus lay on the floor, blood pooling from a throat wound. Deacon John slumped by her chair hands clutched around a knife thrust in his guts. Captain Nikolaos and his second-in-command held a wiry man with sharp black eyes and a hawk nose. *Saturninus, my husband's Count of Domestics. What is he doing here?*

John opened his eyes, spied her and moaned, "Augusta?"

"He's still alive!" Athenais rushed to his side. "We'll get you help." She turned to the gawping crowd. "Has anyone called the physician?" She held the deacon's hand close.

Nikolaos turned guard duty over to his second and came to help. He examined the wound and shook his head.

Athenais nodded. Men never recovered from such a wound but could linger for some minutes. She pushed the hair back from her friend's sweating forehead. "I'm here, John."

"It hurts," he whimpered.

"The pain will end soon, my friend. You are not alone." She stroked his cheek and hummed a nursery tune, keeping eye contact the whole time.

With a final sigh and a slight smile, the light left his eyes. She surveyed the shocked room through a haze of tears. *Gone. Father Severus, such a kind soul. My spiritual rock during these fraught times. John, with his clever mind and quick tongue. My contact with the wider world. Why?*

She bent over the body on the blood-stained marble floor, closed his eyes, removed the knife and slid it among the folds of her cloak.

She stalked to the waiting assassin, a white-hot rage boiling from her guts to her brain. "Why?" she demanded. Her voice croaking from a throat raw with tears and suppressed screams.

"On your husband's orders, Augusta." Saturninus nodded at the two still bodies. "They aided your schemes in the Constantinople court and continued to do so here in the Holy Land. The Augustus considered them a threat."

"And me?" Athenais moved in closer and asked in a low voice, "Does my husband also think I'm a threat?"

"No, Augusta."

She leaned in closer still to whisper, "He should," then plunged the knife with all her strength and rage into the Count's body, just below the ribcage.

Saturninus stumbled back with a grunt, his eyes wide and mouth open in shock.

She pulled the knife out and lunged at him again with a wordless scream, striking him over and over.

An iron grip stayed her hand. "No, Augusta!"

She struggled briefly, until Nikolaos shouted in her face. "It's done, Mistress. He is dead."

She let the knife clatter to the floor and collapsed. He caught her in his arms and carried her from the room, shouting words she didn't understand.

The next hour was a blur of darkness filled with raging demons and fear-ridden flight from reality. She lay unmoving in her bed, trapped in her nightmare world, until a kind voice insisted she drink some warm wine with a bitter aftertaste. She slipped into a dreamless sleep with the final thought, *Is this death?*

*****

The world came back to her in bits. The astringent scent of myrrh brought back feelings of peace from church vigils with Mother Melania. She could sense the warmth of the sunlight streaming through the windows and blinked her eyes open. Low noises resolved into words.

"I believe she's waking up."

She turned to see her new physician—*Mordecai?*—a Jewish doctor who had studied in Alexandria, taking her pulse.

"What…" she croaked in a rusty voice.

"Don't try to speak, Augusta. You strained your voice yesterday."

Martha helped her sit up in bed. "Drink this, Mistress; it will soothe your throat." The servant put a cup of warm tisane to her lips.

Athenais tasted cherries, honey, and something bitter. *Willow bark? Surely not poppy juice.* She pushed the cup away and whispered, "What happened?"

"You had a shock, Augusta."

"Where's Father Severus… John… oh!" The memories came flooding back. The blood on the floor, the broken bodies, John dying in her arms. *I took up the knife and…* Her body started shaking as she gasped for breath.

"Please, Augusta, drink this. It will help." Mordecai put the cup back to her lips.

She took a sip—*yes, poppy juice*—and pushed it away. "I don't want to go back to sleep." The mixture soothed her raw throat. The words came easier, "Bring me Nikolaos."

Martha hurried from the room to summon someone outside the door.

"Are you sure, Augusta? You should rest."

"No time." She swung her legs over the side of the bed and tried to stand up. The room tilted. She gripped the doctor's arm and closed her eyes until the whirling sensation steadied.

"Please, Augusta!"

She noted the desperation in the man's voice and had some niggling sense of pity for his plight, but she knew what she had to do next.

"Help me to my workroom. I have a letter to write."

Chapter 64

Bishop Juvenal of Jerusalem entered the Augusta's palace with a calm face, but quick stride. His glance darted about the rooms looking for evidence of the mayhem reported to him yesterday. *The rumors can't be true. That gentle woman couldn't have killed a man with her own hands. But if she did…? I'll deal with that when I know what happened.*

A guardsman escorted him to the Augusta's private receiving room. The empress preferred a few items of exquisite beauty—be they a marble statue of Diana the Huntress by an ancient Greek master or a porcelain vase of perfect roses. He had been here often and appreciated the fine taste and understated elegance of the room. The soothing blue and green palette immediately put him at ease.

A servant provided him with excellent chilled wine and offered a selection of fruits, nuts, and pastries, which he declined.

He heard a rustling of robes and turned to see the Augusta and her captain Nikolaos entering the room.

"Bishop," she said in a husky voice. "Please forgive me for your hasty summons, but I have great need of your advice and help."

"Augusta." He gave her a brief bow. "Your voice… are you well and safe? We heard disturbing rumors of violence and murder yesterday." *Did someone try to strangle the Augusta? She sounds like a woman who suffered such violence from her husband or an attacker.*

She put a hand to her throat. "Please sit, Bishop, and I will explain." He sat on a padded chair and placed his goblet of wine on a low table to its left. The

Augusta took the chair angled to his right, her captain standing behind her. The servant handed her a goblet of something that smelled of cherries. She took a sip and said in a stronger voice, "Tell me what you've heard."

"The rumors are strange and violent. Some say that a wild tribe of hill people attacked the palace and killed all they could find before being beaten back. Others that a berserk imperial official attacked you and the court and that you defended yourself by killing him single-handedly. Those and nearly everything in between."

"No stories of avenging angels or Mother Mary protecting me?" She gave him a crooked smile.

"What?"

She waved her hand. "Forgive me my feeble attempt at humor in this chaotic time. I refer to an old story told in the palace that Mother Mary appeared to save my husband from an assassin when he was young."

"I've heard that story."

"It's not true," she said in a flat voice. "It was his sister Pulcheria who intervened." She took another sip of her drink and sighed. "But I digress. Captain, save my voice by telling the bishop what happened yesterday."

The captain looked straight ahead as he recited, "Saturninus, Count of Domestics for Theodosius Augustus, came to Her Serenity's court. He demanded to see Father Severus and Deacon John. He produced no written orders and gave no notice of his intent. The good father and deacon made themselves known to him and he attacked them both with a knife, killing Father Severus with a cut to the throat and giving the deacon a fatal wound to the stomach." The color rose in his face. "To my great shame, we were unable to prevent the attack. We apprehended the assassin, and I was going to interrogate him when the Augusta arrived to give comfort to her fallen servants. Having questioned the assassin and obtained his admission of guilt, she used her imperial prerogative and executed the assassin on the spot."

"My dearest Augusta." Juvenal leaned forward to take the empress' hands in his own. "What a terrible thing to have witnessed, the deaths of your advisors and the execution of their assassin."

"You misunderstand, Bishop." She withdrew her hands and rubbed them together, as if trying to cleanse them of her sin. "*I* executed the assassin. I didn't have another do it for me." Her eyes left her hands and drilled into his. "That is why I called on you. Saturninus murdered two churchmen—innocent of any crime—other than their friendship for me. The Augustus is known for his piety, he would not knowingly commit such a horrible sin as the murder of two churchmen. He is being told lies by a close advisor, the eunuch Chrysaphius, who will stop at nothing in his quest for power. The church must rally and protest this assault on their own people. Let the Augustus know he has let his servant go too far and demand penance for his lack as Bishop Ambrose demanded penance of the first Theodosius Augustus, my husband's grandfather, for a similar infraction."

She stopped to take a gulp of her drink and rest her throat.

"Of course, Augusta. This assault cannot stand. I will protest to the Augustus and write immediately to my fellow bishops asking that they take up my cause."

"There is more, my dear friend. My actions in defense of my religious advisors may anger my husband. He may wish to strip me of my augustal status and confiscate my lands. If that happens, I will no longer be able to support the church here in the Holy Lands, as I have done in the past and as we have planned together for the future. All my commitments to expand the Church of Saint Stephen, build hostels for pilgrims, and shelters for widows and orphans will be negated. I fear for the good people of Jerusalem and don't wish them to suffer."

"That would be most unfortunate, Augusta. What can I do to forestall such a disaster?"

"I have prepared a letter for my husband stating my case and asking for mercy." She handed him a sealed packet. "I dare not send it by imperial post because I fear Chrysaphius will intercept it. Please send it to Bishop Proclus with your appeal and ask that he deliver it directly into the Augustus' hands. Your own and the other bishops' full support of my actions will be most appreciated as well."

"It is my honor to serve you in this matter, Augusta, and my solemn duty to see justice done for our murdered compatriots." He placed the packet in the bosom of his robes. "I will see that this is sent out by my special messenger within the day."

A slow smile brightened the Augusta's solemn features. "Thank you, Bishop. I knew I could count on your support to right this horrible wrong." She rose. "Now I must rest. It has been a trying two days."

He bowed as she left the room. *I underestimated the woman. I thought her a malleable pawn, but imperial politics has molded her into a formidable adversary.*

I'm glad she's chosen the side of the church. The loss of Father Severus and Deacon John is grievous. John was good at keeping me informed of the Augusta's thoughts and plans. I must suggest some replacements soon.

Imperial Palace, Constantinople, July 445

THEO WATCHED, WITH BARELY CONCEALED FURY, AS BISHOP PROCLUS EXITED his rooms. He muttered under his breath, "How dare the man—bishop or not—accuse me of murder. I am Augustus! If I order it, it cannot be murder." He stood and paced the floor in imitation of his sister when she was agitated. *Why is everyone against me? Pulcheria scorns me and thinks me incapable of rule. My wife and best friend plot my death. The bishops threaten to rally the people on behalf of two low-level traitorous churchmen.*

He paused for a moment, hand to chin, thinking of another looming crisis in the church. *The people are already uneasy about the splits in the church. Maybe now is not the time to press the teachings of Eutyches. I don't want another Nestorius debacle.* He shook his head. *Something to discuss with Chrys later.* He spied the packet Proclus had left on his desk. *Better to deal with my willful wife first. Did she really execute Saturninus with her own hand?*

He sat and picked up the letter with trembling fingers. A cold chill crept up his spine as he opened it and read the familiar script:

To Theodosius Augustus, the man who was once dearest to my heart, the father of my children,

Theo, I beg you to end the discord between us. I do not seek to return to your presence or take any role in your government. Please put aside your unjustified hurt and hatred. I fear for your soul if you cannot. You already have the blood of an innocent servant—a free woman in my employ—on your hands. You have added the blood of your faithful groomsman and boon companion Paulinus, and the lives of two churchman Father Severus and Deacon John. All because they were friends to me, and you took the word of a scheming eunuch over those of a life-long friend and loving wife.

And now, to my everlasting shame, I share your guilt. I executed, with my own hands, your servant Saturninus for his murderous crimes. By our law, I am justified, for I am an Augusta, but before God, I will have to answer for taking a life—as will you. Again, I deny an adulterous affair or a traitorous plot to kill you. I will go before God innocent of those accused crimes. I seek no revenge upon you for your cruelty in this life. God will render judgment on your soul. I only seek peace, unless you prolong our conflict.

Theo, I am a broken woman. You have deprived me of family and friends; my only solace is doing good works for the church here in the Holy Land. If you strip me of my title and lands, I will be unable to do that penance. If you continue to persecute me for crimes of which I am innocent, I will be forced to fight back and tell my story. Your continued tyranny is noticed and feared by the people and the church. I will not rally them to overthrow you, but they will know of your misdeeds, and you will lose their love and respect.

Leave me in peace, Theo. I am no threat to you and never have been. Let me live out the remainder of my years doing good works in the Holy Land. Please, Husband, if you ever harbored any love or regard for me or our children, do not take this last shred of dignity from me and shame yourself in the process.

I do have one last piece of advice for you, my former love. Rid yourself of the poisonous Chrysaphius and recall Pulcheria. I have never been in accord with your sister, but she loves you and has your soul and reign first in her heart. Despite your cruelty to me, I do not wish a life of loneliness and fear for you. Bring Pulcheria back for your sake and the empire's.

By my own hand,
Your wife Aelia Eudocia Augusta

"What have I done?" He laid the pages aside and dropped his head in his hands. "Is she truly innocent?" Images flashed through his mind. Athenais gay and beautiful at the salon where he met her. The thrill of the crowd at the hippodrome where he introduced her to the people as his bride. The pride he felt in holding his first-born. Their shared grief and tear-stained faces as they stood over the basket of their still-born son and later the casket of their young daughter. The inner joy that shown from his wife's face upon her return from Jerusalem. *Twenty-three years of joy and sorrow, we shared, but she's still a daughter of Eve, deceitful and easily led. Surely it was Paulinus' fault. He must have persuaded her…*

"I have some more papers for your signature, Augustus." Chrysaphius bustled into the room, then stopped. "Is anything wrong?"

"No, my friend." He folded the letter and put it aside. "What do you have for me?"

The eunuch set the stack before him and stood, shuffling his feet, as Theo read each before signing them. "You can sit in my presence Chrys, no need to stand so impatiently." He waved toward the door. "Or come back later. You know I won't sign anything before reading it thoroughly."

"There's nothing important in this stack, Augustus. No need to read everything."

He chuckled. "Did I tell you the story of when I sold my wife to my sister for a gold coin?"

"No, Sire."

"Early in my reign, Pulcheria taught me a lesson. She felt I did not take enough responsibility and had let some legislation pass without my strict scrutiny. She planted a bill of sale for Athenais amongst a stack of papers and I unknowingly signed her away, because I was too lazy to read what I signed. I have never made that mistake again. For instance," he plucked a page from the stack. "This strips Athenais of her title. I didn't order this."

Chrysaphius looked puzzled. "It's the logical response to her monstrous acts, Augustus. She killed your Count of Domestics and must be punished."

"You sent Saturninus to deal with her spies. He had no warrants or orders to kill them in front of their mistress. As the bishops have reminded me, the Augusta was perfectly justified in her actions as was I in having Paulinus killed."

"But—"

Theo cut him off with a raised palm. "Athenais is weak and isolated. Her lover and spies are dead. Her court is recalled, and she cannot leave the Holy Land. I see no reason to punish her further. She is no threat to me and prolonging the scandal by stripping her of her title and lands will only bring opprobrium on my name."

Theo glanced with regret at the letter from his wife. *Goodbye, Athenais. You are clever in appealing to my Christian charity. Despite your betrayal, I cannot in good conscience wish you additional harm. May you find peace in Jerusalem. But if you cause me more trouble...* He sighed and put the order on top of the letter.

"As you wish, Augustus." The eunuch smoothed the disappointment from his face and indicated another report. "I've provided several suggestions on how to handle the negotiations with the Huns. What are your preferences?"

Chapter 65

Province of Syria, August 445

ARCHIMANDRITE BARSAUMA WIPED THE SWEAT FROM HIS BROW WITH A dirty hand, leaving a brown streak that was hardly noticeable on his darkly tanned face. He boiled inside his iron tunic, but took joy in his discomfort. *I do what few will. I suffer for God.* He stood still, leaning on a stout stick, feeling slightly dizzy in the August heat. He squinted at the road running along the coast south of Ptolemais. There seemed to be more people heading south than normal this time of year.

"Water, Holy Father?" A young burly monk offered him a stoppered goat-skin bag.

"Blessings on you, my son." Barsauma took a swig of stale water, swished it around his mouth, then spit it out, before drinking several gulps. "The summers seem to grow hotter every year I grow older."

Barsauma and his companion continued the road north to the next village where they planned to replenish their water. Word of the Holy Father's arrival preceded him, and he was met with a small crowd chanting his praises and asking his blessings. He moved among them touching heads and hands, mumbling prayers. The shimmering heat of the afternoon blurred their faces and dulled their voices. He felt, with rising excitement, the onset of one of his visions. He stopped, face contorted, hands flung heavenward, and cried out, "God speaks to me. What is your will, O Lord?"

His eyes rolled up in his head, his body shook, and horrific scenes of death and destruction flooded his brain. Terrible dark creatures rode skeletal horses across a sky filled with fire and ash. Thunder rumbled and buildings collapsed. The earth split, swallowing screaming people and animals alike.

He came out of his vision yelling, "Punishment is the Lord's! Death will come to us!"

The crowd stared at him in stunned silence. Children clutched their crying mother's robes. Men fell to their knees, hands clasped as if pleading for mercy. A low moan rippled through the people as they cried out, "What can we do, Father? How have we sinned?"

He shook his head as the visions receded and the fear and desperation of the villagers filtered through to him. "I don't know. I must pray on this."

He stood, head bowed, when a voice from the crowd said, "It's the Jews."

His head snapped up. "What did you say?"

"I'm Deacon Thomas, Holy Father." An older rotund man stepped forward. "The Jews are on their way to Jerusalem. More pass through the village everyday, claiming Eudocia Augusta gave them permission to return and pray at the ruins of their temple. I saw one such message that asked all Jews to return for the Feast of the Tabernacles 'because our kingdom will be restored in Jerusalem.' God surely will be angry at such an affront."

"The cursed Jews." Barsauma clutched the deacon's shoulder until he winced in pain. "Of course they are the root of God's anger. But if we let this sacrilege go forward, his wrath will fall on us, as well." He turned to his companion. "We must return to the monastery and gather Christ's army. The Jews will be expelled from our sacred city and never return!"

The people cheered as Barsauma and the monk left on their holy mission.

September 445, Imperial Palace, Bethlehem

"Have you found your line, Cosmas?" Athenais asked her new religious advisor. "My poem is nearly done. Retelling gospel stories with lines from Homer is a challenging exercise, but I do believe we are approaching perfection."

"I'm not sure we are as good as the masters, but we are certainly improving our craft." Cosmas sanded his papyrus and looked it over with a critical eye.

Athenais sat back in her chair, smiling, pleased with the young monk. *You did good, Juvenal, in bringing the brothers to my attention.* Cosmas and his brother

Gabriel, a priest at Saint Stephen's Church, were traditionally educated. She had bonded with Cosmas immediately over their mutual love of Homer and the classic Greek writers. Gabriel, who knew many languages, stepped easily into Deacon John's shoes and handled her personal correspondence. The thought of her murdered friend gave her pause. *Has it been four months since his death? It feels like yesterday and years ago at the same time.*

She shook off her melancholy. "I'm pleased with both you and your brother. You've been not only good advisors, but worthy friends."

"The honor of serving you is ours, Augusta," Cosmas looked up at her with a shy smile. "Gabriel and I are most grateful for reuniting us in your household. We were separated for too long."

"Family is important to me." A note of bitterness crept into her voice, "I cannot be with mine, but I can help others be with theirs."

"Augusta, you are urgently needed by the captain." Gabriel stood in the doorway of her workroom, his dark hair in disarray from his habit of running a hand through it when disturbed.

"Why can't he come to me?" She arched an eyebrow in annoyance.

"He accompanies a delegation from Jerusalem to your audience chamber. There has been violence in the city and the people need your guidance."

"Violence by whom?" She put a hand to her breast.

"I don't know, Augusta. Several Jews and garrison soldiers are in the delegation. They show wounds and have bound limbs. A few clerics also accompany them. I recognized a friend from St. Stephen's."

She nodded. "Go. Tell Captain Nikolaos I will attend the audience shortly. Cosmas, go with your brother and find out what you can."

She strode to her dressing room, calling out, "My purple cloak and simple diadem, Martha. I am needed, but have no time for full regalia."

"At once, Mistress."

Within moments, she was outside the entrance to her audience chamber. A young herald announced, "Aelia Eudocia Augusta." She glided toward her raised chair at the far end of the room where Captain Nikolaos stood impassive, but heightened color and a clenched jaw betrayed his anger. A dusty soldier wearing the markings of the Jerusalem garrison and sporting a bandage over his left eye stood at his side. Her pulse quickened and stomach clenched.

The delegation tossed palm fronds in her path and gave her a full obeisance. Athenais stood before them for a moment, while they rose to their feet, before taking her seat. She recognized the Jewish merchant Yitzhak ben Levi among the supplicants. A number had blood on their robes.

"Your Serenity, this delegation comes from Jerusalem seeking justice for murder." Nikolaos boomed, "Yitzhak ben Levi, step forward and give your testimony."

The Jewish merchant stepped out of the crowd with the help of a stout stick. His beard and fine robes were crusted with dried blood from a purpling wound on the forehead and a torn ear. He wore no gold, silver, or jewels and winced when he gave Athenais a deep bow.

"Get this man a chair," She commanded. "And benches for any other walking wounded."

"Blessings on Our Most Kind and Just Augusta." Yitzhak sighed as he lowered himself onto the backless camp chair her servants provided.

A murmur of acclamations from the crowd rumbled through the room, until Nikolaos raised his hand for silence. "Tell the Augusta of your woes."

"Augusta, after granting your benevolent permission to pray at the site of our sacred temple, the word traveled swiftly through the land. Many of my people made their way to Jerusalem understanding they were under your protection. When we arrived at the sacred site this morning we were set upon by vicious men in monks' robes. The brutes beat us with rocks and cudgels crying out that they did this in Christ's name. Many of my fellows were killed, more were injured. I saw some of the so-called monks robbing the dead."

Yitzhak struggled to rise with the help of his stick. He pointed to the soldier next to Nikolaos and his voice grew hoarse with anger, "If the garrison had not arrived, I doubt any of us would have survived. This good man sheltered me with his sword. His men ran the robbers off." The merchant collapsed back onto his chair. "I demand justice for the dead, Augusta. We were under your protection. These wild men spit on your good reputation. Righteous vengeance is yours to mete."

Athenais nodded. "Who else bears witness to murder?"

The soldier stepped forward. "I am Captain Rufus of the Jerusalem garrison, Augusta. I can confirm the story of this Roman citizen. On your orders, we were alert for any disturbances, but the city was quiet, and no rumors reached us of danger. I posted a couple of men at the site as a precaution, and they raised the alarm at dawn. I led a squad of men to the temple ruins and found carnage as described. Many men lay dead, others ran past us seeking safety. When we arrived, the men in monks' robes fled. I directed my men to help the wounded and the attackers escaped."

"Does anyone know these murderous monks? Are they even churchmen or some local gang bent on mayhem and robbery?" Athenais looked around the room, her hands clenching the carved arms of her chair in frustration. "Who is it who disturbed my peace and harmed my citizens?"

Father Gabriel came forward with a young priest from St. Stephens. "Augusta, Brother Julius can shed some light on that question."

The young man took a deep shaky breath before rushing into speech, "Blessed Augusta, I fear they were indeed men of the church, though it pains me to admit brotherhood with such as they. Several of the monks fled to St. Stephen's where I was at morning prayer. They laughed about killing the Jews and boasted of the loot they stole for Christ's glory. They are followers of the Archimandrite Barsauma. They claimed he led them there and directed their actions."

Barsauma! That ignorant violent man feels he can come to my *city and do such violence to Roman citizens under my protection?*

The priest lowered his head in shame. "Our city has been open to all. We are not like Alexandria where the desert fathers invade, riot, and murder on a whim or rumor. Jerusalem is a city of peace. I stand with my fellow citizens and ask that you punish these robbers who come from Mesopotamia clad in the respectable garb of monks."

"I've heard enough," Athenais felt the heat rise in her face and struggled to control the anger in her voice. She turned to the soldier. "Captain Rufus, I order you to apprehend and imprison these murderous monks, including their leader Barsauma. They have broken the laws of God and Rome with their murder and riot. They have brought shame on the church and sullied my good name. It is my will that they do not stand trial but be put to death by cudgel or stoning—the same death they inflicted on their victims."

She surveyed the silent crowd. "I hope this brings peace to those murdered citizens' souls. Yitzhak ben Levi, bring me a list of their families, so I may make some provision for their welfare."

She stood and exited the way she came in, head held high and to the acclaim of her people.

Chapter 66

"I KNOW THAT LOOK. WHY ARE YOUR TROUBLED, NIKOLAOS?" ATHENAIS SET aside the letter from her daughter with a sigh. She cherished these infrequent missives and resented the intrusion. "Come in both of you." The captain and Father Gabriel entered her workroom.

"We bring troubling news, Augusta." Nikolaos gave her a brief bow, while Gabriel ran his hand through his dark curls, making them more disordered than usual.

"Is there any other kind these days?" She indicated a couple of chairs in front of her worktable. "Sit and tell me."

"The Christian populace in Jerusalem is becoming restless, Augusta. There is a rumor that the bodies of the dead Jews showed no marks. The people are saying they died by divine retribution and the monks are innocent of murder."

"That's preposterous!" she sputtered. "Captain Rufus and many others observed the wounds and attested to the violence."

"What is the truth and what people believe to be the truth is not necessarily the same thing, Augusta." Gabriel shook his head. "Brother Julius warns that several of Barsauma's men escaped the round up and are agitating among the populace. They plan a march on your palace to demand the monks be released."

"Captain, your recommendation?"

"The palace is well-fortified, but a mob could do much damage to the farms outside the walls or the village of Bethlehem. You are the target. We should move you to another of your estates, until the crisis is over."

"I won't run away or leave my people here in harms' way. With me gone, the mob might take their anger out on innocents. We will face the people with the truth and turn them back."

Gabriel looked alarmed. "I don't believe that will be sufficient, Augusta. I've seen such religious fervor overcome reason before. It is not a pretty sight and highly dangerous in the hands of a skilled instigator. Not that many years ago, a rabid mob in Alexandria, led by a cleric, seized and brutally murdered a highly esteemed woman, Hypatia the philosopher."

"I was but a child, but I remember how upset my father was over her death. I've since read her works. A great loss to our community of philosophers, not to mention the people of Alexandria."

"The people of Alexandria did not know their loss when they hacked the lady apart and burnt her outside the walls. They had been told Hypatia was a witch and unduly influencing the city prefect against Christians."

"I see the parallels in our stories, Gabriel, but Hypatia was seized from her chariot while traveling the streets. I have my stout walls and brave guards, not to mention the truth on my side."

"You must put this controversy to rest, Augusta, or you will never be safe outside these walls. Barsauma and his men are ignorant and illiterate, but they are beloved by the people for their piety and charity. The money and jewels looted from the dead Jews went to sustain the poorest in Jerusalem. The people believe an injustice has been done to their benefactors and hold you responsible."

She sat back in her chair, staring at the priest in frustration. "If they won't believe the words of the garrison soldiers or their own clerics, what can I do?"

"Have an open trial. Send for the provincial prefect in Caesarea to judge and ask that he bring troops to keep the peace. When the people hear the stories of the Jews and soldiers for themselves, they might relent."

"But I have already rendered justice in this case."

Gabriel and Nikolaos shot glances at one another. The captain spoke first, "Augusta, forgive me, but you are not a magistrate and under Roman law you can never be one. Your power over the people is personal. You will govern them only as long as you hold their love and respect or have an army large enough to compel their obedience. In this case, the force of Roman law is in the hands of the prefect and the swords of his troops."

"So, I mean nothing to these people. I'm just a disgraced wife, cast off by her husband, who happens to be the Augustus? I can be ignored and forgotten?"

"No, Athenais." Gabriel reached across the table to take her hand. "You will never be forgotten. The people know of your generosity from your past visit. They look forward to your permanent residence here and feel lucky to have such a generous patroness among them, but you have yet to make your mark. Barsauma is revered and feared, but you have your own strengths."

"Bribes?" She snorted. "Promises of gifts to beautify the churches of Jerusalem; donations to monasteries and conclaves of virgins; shelters for the poor, pilgrims, widows and orphans. All are being planned."

"I speak of your own nature. You are Aelia Eudocia Augusta. Your very presence brings gravitas to any event and honor to anyone you call friend. Command the resources of the imperial prefect to aid you. But you are also Athenais, poet and orator. When you speak, the people listen. Speak to them not only as Augusta, but also Athenais."

She nodded and withdrew her hand. "Thank you, my friends. I see I was hasty in my condemnation of the monks. I saw a terribly aggrieved party under my personal protection and passed judgment without thinking how the ordinary resident of Jerusalem would see that act. I will rectify that error."

She sat for a moment weighing her options, then turned to Nikolaos. "Captain, I'll prepare a letter ordering the prefect to attend me and hold an open trial where the people can hear the sworn testimony. Send it by your fastest rider. I'll include a pass so he can use the imperial post horses. I should have it ready within the hour."

"As you will, Augusta." He rose. "I'll go prepare my man."

Gabriel also rose.

"Father, a moment." She said, "I'll also prepare an address to the people; in case they should appear at our walls. Is there anyone among my friends in the church who can aid me in case of riot or attack?"

"I can call on many to support your cause, Augusta. Send for me when you are ready, and we can discuss tactics."

Athenais nodded and smiled—one that she knew did not reach her eyes. "Thank you both for your loyalty, friendship, and good advice."

Both bowed, leaving her with her preferred weapons—a pen, paper, and words.

*****

Athenais heard the crowd yelling before Nikolaos came to escort her to the wall. "Is the entire population of Jerusalem at my walls, Captain?"

"It is a much larger delegation than we thought might make the trek, Augusta." He looked grim. "They are quite agitated. Are you sure you want to speak to them? It might not be safe."

The jumbled roar resolved into distinct chants as they approached the wall and ascended the stairs to the top: "Hear us, Augusta! Justice for the monks! Free Barsauma, God's Favorite! Death to those who bring false witness!"

Athenais shook her head at the irony of the last chant and muttered to herself, "I wished the same in the past. Chrysaphius' death would have made my life easier."

"Augusta?" Nikolaos, hearing her mutter, looked back over his shoulder as they traveled the top of the wall lined with her guards armed with bows and lances.

"Nothing, Captain."

They entered a covered room with arrow slits for windows just to the left of the main gates. A matching one sat on the other side of the brass-bound oak doors. A crenellated wall allowed defenders to rain arrows or stones down on anyone attacking the gate. "Stay here, Augusta, while I quiet the crowd and announce your presence."

In response to her captain's appearance, the crowd seemed to become more agitated. One man shouted, "Send out the Augusta! If she wishes to kill the monks, we'll burn her and all who stand with her!"

Her blood chilled. *They are out for murder. Pulcheria talked down a mob at the Great Church during that Nestorian disaster, and she didn't have my training. If she can do it, so can I. I mustn't argue. That will only anger them more. I am here to calm them and send them on their way. No more.*

She took a moment to take deep breaths and prepare her mind. When the crowd quieted, she strode onto the open wall, followed by an armed guard. Nikolaos took up a stance on her right. The crowd started to grumble again. Nikolaos stepped forward, hand on sword.

"NO!" She commanded in a loud voice that carried over the crowd. "Captain, I have no need of protection from my own people. Leave me to speak to them."

He turned in astonishment and looked as if he might disobey her. She said in a low voice directed at him, "If things get out of hand, I promise to retreat.

Then and only then, will your men defend me."

He nodded and ordered her guards off the gate. Several nocked arrows and stood to the side of the windows.

Athenais turned back to the mob. *If Gabriel did his job, there should be some allies among the mob ready to respond to my signal.* She raised her hands, palms out. "My good people, I come to you, as I did before, not only an Augusta, but also a humble Christian pilgrim." She indicated her plain blue robe—the color of the virgin—and the white veil covering her hair. A plain gold diadem held it in place—the only symbol of her rank. "I understand you have an issue for me to resolve. Do you have someone to speak for you?"

A deeply tanned burly man in a monk's robe, carrying a knobbed cudgel, stepped forward. "Augusta, you ordered my brothers imprisoned on false charges without a proper trial. We demand justice."

"That matter is already resolved. The provincial prefect travels, as we speak, to Jerusalem to hold an open trial. He might have already arrived while you are here."

The monk's mouth hung open for a moment until he gathered his wits. "But you ordered them imprisoned!"

"I ordered the *assailants* be apprehended." She turned and addressed the wider audience. "Your fellow Roman citizens appealed to me after being attacked in our most sacred city. Your safety is uppermost in my responsibilities. We can't have murder and riots in our streets. The garrison did their duty and apprehended those accused of such heinous crimes."

The crowd mumbled and Athenais heard a few folks shouting, "The Augusta is right. We don't want murder in our streets." *Good. Gabriel's agents are working.*

The monk surveyed the changing mood of the crowd and narrowed his eyes. He turned back to her and snarled, "You condemned them to death. My brothers are innocent."

She smiled at him. "I'm sure they will be proved so. I can't believe that men of faith, followers of our most gentle and loving Lord and Savior Jesus Christ, would engage in such hateful—and forbidden—acts as murder and looting. Christian clerics were among those who appealed for justice and believed the men in monks' robes might be imposters."

"There was no murder, only divine retribution on the Jews!" The man's face grew red with anger.

This is where I must be most careful. I can't challenge their 'evidence' without bringing down their wrath. "When that claim came before me, I immediately wrote to the provincial prefect ordering him to come and hold an open trial. He will examine the evidence and pass judgment so no innocent man will be punished." She held her hands out in entreaty, "That is why you are all here—to demand a fair trial for the accused? I ensured that outcome before you even came before my gate. You have achieved your aims. It is time to return to your homes in peace."

The mood of the crowd changed. Men lowered their makeshift weapons of staffs and hayforks. Murmurs rippled through the crowd with occasional shouts of, "we won," "justice will be done," and "the Augusta speaks truth."

"What of Father Barsauma?" A note of desperation crept into the monk's voice as he sensed the turning of the crowd away from violence, "He is among the accused."

"The Holy Father is detained?" Athenais feigned surprise. "He honored me with a gift of his mantle when I last visited the city. I will attend the trial myself and ensure the prefect gives him a fair hearing."

Several shouts came from the corners of the crowd, "Blessings on the Augusta, fair and wise." A few more took up the chant until the monk, shaking his head, stepped back into the crowd.

Athenais waved the crowd to silence. "My good people. I understand your frustration and fear over the violence in our streets. I also know your anger that innocent men might suffer for that violence. I promise you all will be resolved shortly. Return to your homes. The prefect will arrive, and we can honor the slain and punish the guilty under Roman law. My blessings on you all and a safe journey back to the city."

A general roar of approval swept over the crowd. Athenais smiled, nodded, and retreated to her guards. Once out of sight of the pacified mob, she let her shoulders slump. "Are they leaving?"

One of the guards at the arrow slits replied, "Yes, Augusta. They stream away faster than they arrived."

Uncontrollable shivers rippled up and down her body. She clenched her jaws to keep her teeth from clacking.

Nikolaos guided her to a seat on a wooden stool and thrust a clay goblet into her hands. "Drink this, Augusta."

She took a gulp, and almost sprayed the vinegary stuff onto the floor.

"Remind me to get better wine rations for the garrison, Captain. They deserve better than this."

He smiled and said, "You did well out there, Augusta. Taking their complaint about no trial off the table in the first moments stalled them completely. They did not have that excuse to engage in further violence."

"Thank the Good Lord and Father Gabriel's agents, it worked." She took another sip of the rough wine and set it aside. "Now to prepare for the trial and get justice for our dead citizens."

Chapter 67

Two days later, Athenais arrived at the basilica on the forum where the trial was to be held. "This way, Augusta." Nikolaos led her to a seat on the wide steps of the great stone building that housed all the governmental offices in the city. Her chair was marked with purple cushions and set next to a less ornate one where Bishop Juvenal sat. The city council sat to their left. Prefect Basil and his advisors sat a couple steps below them.

"Welcome, Augusta." Juvenal stood until she took her seat, and she nodded her assent that he could be seated as well. "It's a fine day to bring those miscreant monks to justice."

"Indeed." A striped cotton awning shaded them from the bright fall sunshine. There was a touch of chill in the morning air, but she was in full Augustal regalia and welcomed the cooling breeze. "Did you meet with Prefect Basil?"

"Yes. He's a fair man and has a good grasp of our somewhat volatile situation. He's arrayed his troops appropriately to manage the crowd."

Athenais took stock. "It looks like Basil—or his captain—has controlled unruly crowds before." A considerable space directly in front of the prefect was cordoned off by Roman troops in full gear. They also manned the entrances to the forum and restricted the number of people who could enter to something manageable.

An aide said something to the prefect, and Basil looked over his shoulder at Athenais. He approached and bowed. "Augusta, do you have any instructions?"

"Do your magisterial duty, Prefect. The evidence and testimony will speak for themselves. What is your plan for the trial?"

"I will hear from the victims first, take testimony from the garrison soldiers, then confront the accused. They will have the opportunity to confess or explain their actions. I understand they will also have witnesses to a divine intervention."

"How do you plan on handling that?"

He shrugged. "It depends on the testimony and the reliability of the witnesses."

"Prefect, I personally saw survivors after the attack. They had broken bones and wounds on their faces and bodies—some severe. The garrison soldiers will also testify to that."

"I understand, Augusta, and will take all into consideration as you ordered." He looked over his shoulder as a trumpet blast heralded the entrance of the accused. "With your permission? I must start the proceedings."

Barsauma and about a dozen monks entered the empty space before the steps. They were unbound, but closely guarded. Athenais nodded and the prefect returned to his seat.

A herald announced, "Magistrate Basil, prefect of Palestine, presides over the trial of Archimandrite Barsauma and his followers accused of murder and riot in the city of Jerusalem."

An angry murmur raced through the crowd. She sensed Nikolaos and his cohort of guards moving closer. *How will the prefect handle this mob if it gets out of hand?*

Basil rose, faced the crowd, and proclaimed, "I have come from Caesarea Maritima to deliver justice in this matter. I will brook no further riot. Anyone causing disorder will be removed from the vicinity and jailed. Is that clear?" His troops stamped their boots and lances in unison to punctuate his remarks. The crowd quieted.

"I will first hear from—" he consulted a piece of paper "—Yitzhak ben Levi. Come forward and give your testimony."

Athenais followed the proceedings closely. The morning sun moved toward noon as man after man gave moving testimony of fright and loss. The soldiers gave more objective descriptions of dead bodies and wounds. Basil occasionally interrupted with a question to clarify some statement, but generally stayed quiet and attentive. Scribes took down the testimony of each witness which they signed with a signature or mark when completed.

"Refreshment, Augusta?" Bishop Juvenal indicated a personal servant offering wine in a ruby glass goblet chased with silver.

"No. Barsauma testifies next." She leaned forward in anticipation, but not before noticing the disappointment on the bishop's face as he waved away the servant without taking a drink himself.

The herald announced, "Archimandrite Barsauma of Syria step forward and explain your actions and those of your followers before the prefect."

The guards separated and Barsauma stepped forward. Tall and gaunt, he made a fierce figure in his rusting iron tunic and long matted hair. He defiantly cried, "I and my warriors for Christ are innocent of the charge of murder. What happened to the Jews was divine retribution for sullying our sacred city with their filthy worship. They deny Christ the Savior and their very presence in this divine space is an affront to God."

The crowd mumbled ominously.

Basil asked, "Do you claim that divine retribution was delivered by your hands?"

"No, by God himself. He spoke to me in a vision on the road to Ptolemais. He promised vengeance and destruction if the Jews…"

A deep rumble from the earth drowned out the archimandrite's words. Athenais clutched the arms of her chair as the steps seemed to rise and roll as if they were on a ship.

Nikolaos grabbed her arm and shouted in her ear, "Earthquake!" He dragged her down the shuddering steps toward the open forum. Time seemed to slow. The boom of cracked columns and collapsing roofs muted the screams of people scrambling to save themselves.

Mere seconds later, Athenais stood in the forum surrounded by her guards. Dust settled around her and choked her throat. She coughed, spit, then turned to Nikolaos. "Captain, see if we can be some help to those wounded or in distress."

"No Augusta, the other garrisons can do that. Our duty is to keep you safe."

She opened her mouth in rebuke when another, but lesser shock, rolled through the forum. She grabbed her captain's arm as the quake rumbled away, leaving silence in its wake.

"God has spoken!" Barsauma's voice boomed through the silence like another quake. "He shows his anger at the treatment of his servants for doing his will."

Prefect Basil, covered in marble dust, stood on a lower step. He called over a herald and said something to him. The young man gave a trumpet blast and announced. "By order of Basil prefect of Palestine, Holy Father Barsauma and his followers are released from custody. The Cross has conquered!"

The people in the forum took up the cry. "The Cross has conquered!" echoed across the space, swelling and booming like the roar of the sea.

We've lost. There will be no justice for those murdered. Violence has triumphed over love—once again. Tears made tracks through the plaster dust on her face. "Take me home, Captain."

"Yes, Augusta."

Chapter 68

Imperial Palace, Bethlehem, May 450

"NEWS FROM THE EASTERN COURT!" FATHER GABRIEL WAVED A DISPATCH as he rushed into her workroom, his face flushed with excitement.

"Good or bad?" Athenais put her quill aside. Her projects had gone well since that fiasco of a trial almost five years ago. The thought of that injustice still left a bitter taste in her mouth, but there seemed to be more good news than bad lately.

"The best, Augusta! Chrysaphius has been exiled and Pulcheria returns to her brother's court as chief advisor."

"Took her long enough," Athenais muttered.

"What?"

"I am surprised it took Pulcheria this long to pry that leech from my husband's side. It's been seven years since she retired to her estates in Hebdomon to escape the trap Chrysaphius and I—to my great regret!—set for her. I despaired she would ever accomplish that feat." *And I did hope for her success, knowing I can never return. I've made a lot of mistakes in my life, but allying myself with that treacherous eunuch was among the worst. Exile seems such a slight punishment. Why was he not executed for his crimes?* Her heart ached and throat constricted at the memories of her losses. *Paulinus and Dorothea, if only...*

She shook her head as she brought herself back to the present and Gabriel's question. "What do you think this means for you? Will you be released from your exile to travel to Ravenna?"

"I don't know." Athenais chewed her lower lip. "Pulcheria is no friend of mine. I doubt she will look favorably on my suit. However, I'll give her a few months to settle back into court, then approach her."

"As you wish, Augusta." Gabriel opened his pouch of dispatches. "There's other news as well."

Athenais leaned forward to read the reports. *No news from Ravenna—again. The rumors are rife with scandal, but I get no confirmation from Placidia or Eudoxia. What is happening there?*

New Episcopal Palace, Jerusalem, early August 450

"Beautiful!" Athenais admired the latest addition to Bishop Juvenal's personal chapel in his new Episcopal palace—a stunning mosaic of the Virgin Mary with the baby Jesus on her lap. The Mother's face looked remarkably like her own, but it was common for artists to include their patron's visages among the images of any public project.

"I am most grateful to Your Serenity for building this magnificent dwelling. The decorations are second to none. Where did you find the mosaicist?" Juvenal asked.

"A brother and sister trained by their father in Ravenna—a master mosaicist who decorated Placidia Augusta's chapel dedicated to Saint Lawrence. He sent them here when Attila threatened to invade. The sister creates the designs, and the brother executes them."

"We've had quite an influx of artists and artisans during the past five years. Your patronage draws them to our city. Everyone praises your generosity and admires your works."

"Not just my patronage but the upheaval in the rest of the land drives them here. Barbarians threaten us on all fronts, but this one. Thank the Good Lord that our little corner has seen peace since we sent Barsauma and his murderous monks back to their province." *And may he stay put this time!*

"What do you hear from the courts?" Juvenal linked arms with her and guided her back toward his receiving area. "News from Ravenna has been dire lately."

She stifled a sneeze. The palace smelled of fresh paint. Construction continued in one wing and the thuds of hammers and shouted orders echoed down the corridor. She took a moment to think. *How much to share with the bishop? He's such a notorious gossip.*

"I'm sure you have your own sources, Bishop. What have *you* heard?" Her heart rate quickened. The scandal of Placidia's daughter's pregnancy last year was hastily covered up, but rumors still abounded even after Honoria's betrothal to a safe senator.

He shrugged. "My sources send confusing information about rings and demands from Attila for half the West. Some say the Huns are already on the way to attack Constantinople."

"Ridiculous!" Her laugh sounded brittle even to her own ears. "General Aspar protects the borders in the East and General Aetius in the West. We have nothing to fear from the Huns. My daughter and son-in-law rule in harmony in Ravenna. In her last letter, Eudoxia said they were planning an imperial wedding for Honoria Augusta to Senator Herculanus Bassus." *Foolish girl! I thought Honoria cleverer than to plot treason by sending Attila a ring and asking his help. How to deflect Juvenal from this line of questioning?*

Her knee twinged and she stopped to rub it. "My daughter did say that Placidia Augusta was doing less work in the government, but that is to be expected. She is sixty-two, after all, and deserves some rest from her labors. I'm beginning to feel my age, as well. I have nearly half a century and my stiff knee occasionally gives me pain."

"I'm sorry to hear it, Augusta. Do you wish to sit?" He looked around frantically for a bench or chair.

"No, Bishop," she said with a genuine chuckle. "My doctor prescribes mild exercise, and I've found his advice sound. It's when I sit or kneel too long that it stiffens."

He nodded and escorted her into his private receiving room where servants had laid out a repast of cold meats, cheese, fruits, and pastries, as well as a selection of chilled wine and juices. The decoration was only slightly less subdued than the public spaces. Juvenal seemed to have a fondness for gilt and red silk. "I'm hoping you can join me, Augusta. With Chrysaphius' exile and Pulcheria Augusta's reinstatement at your husband's side, I need your guidance on how to approach the Constantinople court."

Much good my advice will do you, she mused. *I haven't been privy to my husband's thoughts since long before my exile. But it never hurts to be thought more powerful than I am.*

She smiled serenely and nodded. "I'll give you what advice I can, Bishop. The Eastern court has been in quite a turmoil since the church renewed its controversies over the nature of Christ." She sat and took a sip of wine from the Sidonian glassware she had gifted to the bishop on her first visit to Jerusalem. *Nice touch. Although I remember gifting these for the altar, not for the bishop's personal use.*

"Yes, I haven't seen the church in such an uproar since the Nestorius affair. Three years of councils summoned and dismissed, bishops deposed and restored, anathemas flying between Rome and Constantinople. The feud between Antioch and Alexandria is at a full boil. I've tried to avoid the intrigues, conspiracies, and name-calling. With the Augusta back in charge, what do you predict will happen next?"

"The uproar was primarily that evil eunuch's doing. He's the one who introduced the heretic Eutyches to my husband and infected his beliefs," she nearly spat, but took a deep breath instead. *I still have difficulty even saying his name. I almost hope there* is *a Christian hell, so Chrysaphius can burn forever for his many sins.* She glanced at the bishop's eager face. *But Juvenal doesn't need to know the imperial family's dirty secrets.* She continued in a milder tone, "I suspect with Pulcheria back in charge, she will lead the Augustus back to the true path." *I do not envy her the task. Theo was always stubborn about his faith. This could still cause a rift between them. As much as it galls me, the empire needs Pulcheria's firm hand.*

"Let us pray it is so." The bishop bowed his head briefly, then graced her with an eager smile. "I understand you dedicate a public bath at Hammat Gader next week, Augusta. Are you going there for the curative powers of the waters? They should help with your knee."

"I've heard excellent stories about the baths and will be seeking a treatment. But my official reason is to reveal my dedicatory poem which will be carved in marble and installed in the main bath. Brother Cosmas says it's among my best work." She smiled at the bishop. "I must thank you again for recommending the brothers. They have been of immense help and succor to me in these past five years. I had no such companions in Constantinople and suffered for the lack."

"It was my pleasure, Augusta. As you requested, I'm recommending them for some church honors. Cosmas will be named Guardian of the Cross and Gabriel will become archpriest of Saint Stephen's."

"Excellent, my friend." Sadness tinged her pleasure. "No one knows the number of their days. I wish my friends and confidents to be well taken care of when I leave this earthly sphere." *The empire is in turmoil, and I can do nothing to help, to make the world safer for my child and grandchildren.*

"God will surely grant you a long life, Augusta, and provide for your friends. Do not dwell on such melancholy thoughts."

"I try not to, Bishop, but as I grow older, I am more aware of the passage of time and the dangers in the world. I have not seen my daughter for thirteen years and have yet to meet my granddaughters." *I am an Augusta, and I cannot make my dearest wish happen. As long as Theo lives, I am separated from those nearest to my heart. He could not have been more cruel if he had me killed.*

She gave Juvenal a sad smile. "Let us turn to more productive thoughts. I believe you have some charitable works that need my patronage?"

Before he could answer, her captain appeared at the door with a man nearly staggering with exhaustion: his eyes ringed with shadows, his hair and clothes dusty and sweat-stained. "Forgive the intrusion, Augusta, Bishop." Nikolaos nodded to each. "A post rider just arrived from Constantinople with an urgent message."

The haggard man straightened his shoulders and bowed with some semblance of courtesy. "Augusta, it is my unfortunate duty to inform you that your husband, the Great and Pious Flavius Theodosius Augustus, passed from this life to take his place in heaven just eight days past. Aelia Pulcheria Augusta sent me ahead of the official criers who will announce the news and establish the mourning procedures in each province."

"Oh!" Athenais gasped at the unexpected pain that lanced her stomach then crawled up to clutch her throat in a vice grip. *I just wished him dead and now he is. Did I cause this?* She gasped for air before logic took over. *No, this is not my fault. He died long before my wishes could cause effect.*

"Augusta, drink this." Nikolaos held a cup of wine to her lips, his face screwed up in a mask of concern.

She took an unsteady sip and pulled herself together. *I mustn't show such weakness at this news. I am still an Augusta. They will be looking to me for clues as to how to react to this news.*

"Enough, Captain." She waved the wineglass aside. "I had no inkling that the Augustus was ill. The news is surprising." She turned back to the messenger. "How did my husband die?"

"It was an accident, Augusta. He fell from his horse while riding and injured his spine. He died two days later, Pulcheria Augusta at his side."

"As I would expect." She managed to keep the bitterness out of her voice. "Did my sister have any other messages for me?"

"She said to expect more extensive correspondence in the immediate future."

Athenais nodded. *Pulcheria will have her hands full, which gives me an opportunity.*

"Captain, see that our messenger is given what is needed for his respite." She raised an eyebrow, and he nodded before escorting the rider out. She could count on Nikolaos to interrogate the man thoroughly about the mood of the Constantinople court and any possible threats to herself. *I must have Gabriel and Cosmas reach out to their contacts as well. My next move could well be critical to my happiness.*

She turned back to Juvenal. "Bishop, forgive me, but I must retire to pray for my husband's soul. Do not mention this news to anyone except the garrison commander until the officials arrive. We do not want unease or riot in the city. The unexpected death of a ruler can bring turmoil if not accompanied by the appearance of continuity or a show of strength."

"Understood, Augusta. Prefect Basil should have his marching orders within a day or two of your own notice." He hesitated, then said in a low tone, with a bow, "My own sincere condolences, Augusta. I know your separation from your husband caused you much pain and the news of his death must be a shock to you. If you wish to confide in me or unburden yourself in any way, I hope you will consider me a friend, as well as a religious advisor."

She rose and took his hand. "Thank you, Bishop. I value your friendship as much as your advice. We will pray for a peaceful transition and plan for an unpeaceful one." She looked over his shoulder. "Now I will take advantage of your new chapel. Send Captain Nikolaos to me when he has finished his task."

Imperial Palace, Bethlehem

"Why won't the blasted words come as I want?" Athenais mumbled as she reviewed her mangled letter to Pulcheria: lines struck out, scribbled notes in the margins. *Because you are not being honest,* the voice in her head admonished.

You will never win Pulcheria over with flattery and false concern. Show her some respect and tell her the truth.

She wadded up the papyrus and threw it to the floor to join the ever-growing pile of failed efforts. She took out another sheet, inked her reed pen, and chewed her lower lip. Athenais sighed and started to write:

To the Most Pious Aelia Pulcheria Augusta
My husband's dearest sister,

I cannot, in all honesty, call you 'Sister' as we once did. We have ever been rivals and parted on the bitterest of terms. That rivalry for Theo's love has been resolved in your favor and I accept that. Whatever our past, I believe we now share two emotions: pain and lamentations over Theo's death and joy and celebration over Chrysaphius' execution.

I grieved upon hearing the news of my husband's passing. Theo and I had many years of love and harmony. He made me happy, and he often confided that I did the same for him. He was the father of my children and the rock upon which my raging pain at their loss broke and subsided. I also know that next to God, he loved you best and you loved him. Knowing my own pain, I cannot imagine the depths of grief you must have suffered at his death and continue to suffer to this day, but I am glad you were there to be a comfort to him at the end.

I pray daily for Theo's soul. I have forgiven his trespasses against me in these past years because I ascribe his most grievous offenses to the snake that entered our Eden—Chrysaphius. That scheming eunuch was the root of all evil in the court, inflaming our rivalry and leading Theo astray in his faith. He was responsible for both our downfalls, as well as many others who had Theo's reign and well-being at heart. Thank you for executing him promptly after Theo's death and purging his evil influence from this world.

But the passing of both the good and the evil portends a new era—one in which I hope we can put aside our differences not only for the good of the empire but the salvation of our souls. Resentment and bitterness about the past serve only to blight the present and rot the future. You face a perilous time—likely civil war—if you choose to try to rule alone. No woman has done so in Roman history. As a pledged virgin, your choices are limited—yield power to our cousin Valentinian and retire from the field or rule the East in his name as you did for Theo.

We've both observed our cousin Valentinian's weaknesses. As with Theo, he benefits from a strong woman guiding his hand and our Aunt Placidia grows weaker.

My daughter reports that the personal upheaval at their court has taken a toll on our formidable aunt and her health and influence declines. I propose that you release me from my exile in Jerusalem so I might be your advocate in the Western court. I will travel to Ravenna to care for our aunt and live out my years with my daughter and grandchildren while providing much needed guidance to my son-in-law in support of your rule in the East.

I believe this solution will benefit us both, while protecting the empire from civil war during a time of barbarian incursions and religious insecurity.

I eagerly await your reply.

Respectfully, by my own hand,
Aelia Eudocia Augusta

Athenais sanded the papyrus, folded and sealed it with her signet ring. "That's the best I can do now. We will see if Pulcheria is in a forgiving mood."

Chapter 69

The Baths at Hammat Gader, September 450

ATHENAIS RAN HER HAND OVER THE INSCRIPTION IN THE POLISHED WHITE marble slab installed in the main room of the baths. It was a beautiful setting in the Hall of Fountains where visitors could congregate to relax after visiting their treatments. Any who entered could pause and read her seventeen-line dedicatory poem. She read aloud a phrase, "For those who are in anguish, your mighty strength is eternal."

Indeed, the waters here have been beneficial. It's been a restorative week. My skin is refreshed, my knee supple, and the vapors provided sweet dreams. She frowned slightly at the unauthorized crosses flanking her name. *Theo would not have approved since he forbade such decoration in public places, but he is gone, and his mourning time is done. None are here to forego me.* That small rebellion gave her a shiver of satisfaction.

She rose from the floor with no assistance and stretched her arms over her head, murmuring aloud, "Yes it's been a very therapeutic week."

"Domina?" Martha looked at her anxiously. "Do you require anything?"

"No Martha, I am at peace." She smiled. "I almost hate to leave this place."

"Should I arrange to extend our stay?"

Athenais shook her head. "No, it is time to get back to Bethlehem. I have many obligations to attend to."

They returned to her suite to find a frowning Nikolaos waiting with an imperial packet.

Athenais raised a questioning eyebrow.

"It bears Pulcheria Augusta's seal." He put the packet in her hands and bowed.

"At last! I expected a reply weeks ago." She snatched the packet. "You are dismissed, Captain, but stand ready in case I have a reply in the next hours."

After he left, she cracked the seal and read,

To Aelia Eudocia Augusta,

As you were honest with me in your last letter, I will endeavor to return the favor. My gratitude for your tender thoughts, for my grief, and prayers for my brother's soul. I would expect no less from a good Christian woman. My pain was initially sharp and profound, but I have found solace and even joy in the belief that my brother resides in heavenly bliss and will welcome me to God's side at my own passing.

As to Chrysaphius, it was my duty to rid the court of a corrupt official and right any wrongs he perpetrated on others. I've arranged for the vast wealth he accumulated to be paid back to his victims as restitution. I believe that includes your captain of the guards for the loss of his wife. That is the act that gives me pleasure and satisfaction, not the man's execution. As to your own culpability in colluding with the eunuch to have me removed from court—that is between you and God. I have given it little or no thought since my return. As you said, these are perilous times and I've had my mind on other—more important—matters.

I was pleased to hear that you knew my brother found happiness and comfort in your marriage. Before your exile, he spoke highly of you and loved you dearly. That is why your betrayal wounded him so deeply. Chrysaphius was a snake, but he could not make up charges of adultery and treason out of whole cloth. There must have been some evidence that persuaded Theo to his actions. My brother said nothing of you in the months leading up to his accident or on his deathbed. I therefore conclude he felt he had no trespasses for you to forgive and the fact that you do so is presumptuous.

You summarized my political predicament accurately, but I have put in place a remedy that does not require a traitress to travel to the Western court and infect them with her venom. I already have my agents at that court to speak in my name. You clothe your proposal with sweet words and logical suggestions, but I feel it is more likely you would speak against me in Ravenna than for me.

Stay in Jerusalem and continue your good works. I have had excellent reports of your charity and piety. Whether it is real or pretend, it accomplishes a great deal of good which might mitigate the stains on your soul when you stand before God and must account for your actions.

By my own hand,
Aelia Pulcheria Augusta

"That sanctimonious harpy!" Athenais snarled as she crumpled the letter. "How dare she! She wasn't present. She had no notion of the evidence for my innocence or guilt. She just assumed that because her precious… gullible!… brother thought I was guilty, that makes it so." Her face flamed red.

"Domina?" Martha fanned her with her hands. "Should I fetch some cool water?"

"No, Martha. Leave me to my anger. I want to throw something."

"Yes, Augusta." The servant scurried from the room, throwing a glance at a delicate alabaster vase worth more than a life-time's annuity for the young woman.

Angry tears coursed down her face as Athenais struggled to control her rage which gradually gave way to sorrow. *No trip to Ravenna. No holding my granddaughters. No farewell to Placidia. And it's all Pulcheria's fault.*

She wiped the tears from her face as her rebellious thoughts grew. *My vow was to Theo. He's dead. Pulcheria has no power over me. I'll travel where I will, and she can go to hell!*

Imperial Palace, Bethlehem, November 450

"So, this was Pulcheria's 'remedy' to allow her to rule—a chaste marriage!" Athenais studied the commemorative solidus showing Christ between Pulcheria and her chosen consort Marcian—a general and great friend to Aspar—therefore biddable. She tossed the coin to her confidante and secretary Father Gabriel. "Does she think a coin showing Christ sanctioning her marriage will keep the gossipmongers from sullying her oh-so-virgin name?"

He examined it closely. "It is a clever device and images do matter among the people."

"Pulcheria was always good at manipulating the masses, but her power is rooted in her vow of virginity. Will the people accept this?"

"The Augusta is beyond childbearing years and her consort is a field general. It is likely she will still rule in his name with little opprobrium from the people. The nobles will likely gossip, but my sources say the church and ordinary citizens are pleased with this compromise."

"So, she wins again," Athenais mumbled.

"The empire and the church win with her in power. With the backing of Pope Leo, the imperial couple have called for a new ecumenical council to settle the rift in the church for all time."

"For all time?" She laughed. "How many ecumenical councils has the church called over the past four hundred years to settle doctrine? Half of them end in acrimony. The other half cover deep wounds with inadequate bandages that rot away a few years or a few decades later which leads to another council. How will this be any different?"

"Probably not much." The priest chuckled. "You forget I am a church historian. The church is a human institution. Humans are fallible. Ergo, the church is fallible. The ones on the front lines in this battle—the deacons, the monks, the holy virgins—do their best to spread the Gospel of peace and love. They are the ones who care for the people. Let the bishops squabble over the meaning of a Latin word translated from a Greek translation of an Aramaic document written years after Jesus' death. We will do the good deeds that a merciful loving God commands."

"Well said, my friend, but don't let Juvenal hear you repeat it. I don't want you to lose your position at Saint Stephen's."

"It will be interesting to see how our Good Bishop fares in this council. He is a great supporter of Dioscorus of Alexandria and the supremacy of Christ's divine nature over his human one."

Athenais gave him a crooked smile, "I suspect he will do what is necessary to hold onto his seat of power. Juvenal is a courtier at heart and Pulcheria is determined to impose a 'dual nature' compromise on the church. If Christ is equally human and divine, as Pope Leo asserts, that appeases everybody and satisfies no one. The issue will return again and again until the church formally splits over it."

"We'll see how his congregation reacts to that if it comes about. The people hereabouts were partial to mystery cults in the past. They welcome the idea of God walking among them in the guise of a man—a god who can grant their personal wishes. I've heard the idea of the single divine nature of Jesus labeled

'Monophysite'. The idea that Jesus was a man who attained godhood means they might have to do better themselves and is less appealing. But we put the cart before the horse. Nothing is decided and Juvenal has taken no stand."

Gabriel nodded. "How does Placidia Augusta's death affect your plans to visit Ravenna?"

"Profoundly." She sighed. *Another regret—not getting to see that valiant woman once again before she died. She was such an inspiration in the darkest moments of my life. Rest in peace, Placidia.* "A wedding and a death in the same month and I heartily regret both. Eudoxia writes that the court is in turmoil. My aunt's passing leaves a great hole in the heart of the court. Her son is distraught, and her daughter has been whisked away to a distant estate—or so it has been reported."

"You believe differently?"

"Eudoxia didn't say, but I'm reading subtle inferences. We both have suspected the Constantinople spies of reading or even destroying our correspondence in the past. Especially when that infernal eunuch was in power. We will occasionally use a Homeric quote to indicate what is really happening. Unfortunately, Eudoxia is not the scholar I am, and this quote was ambiguous. It seemed to indicate that Honoria was imprisoned by her brother—possibly even killed. I don't believe Placidia would have allowed such a thing while she was alive. But with her dead…?" She shivered. *Charges of adultery and treason. I nearly suffered the same fate.*

"All the more reason you should go and help bring balance to the court."

"I want to, but my daughter forbids it with a great deal of vehemence. With the Huns threatening invasion in the North and the Vandals restless in the South, she says I should stay here until tempers cool. The subtext was that her husband would not welcome me, and she couldn't guarantee my safety." Athenais slumped. "I am thwarted on all sides."

"I am so sorry, Athenais." He reached over and patted her hand. "But things change. Live for this moment and do what is in your power to make the world a better place."

"Good advice as always, my friend." *But getting harder to abide by.*

Chapter 70

Mother Melania's Convent, Jerusalem, November 451

ATHENAIS PULLED HER BLUE WOOL CLOAK CLOSER ABOUT HER SHOULDERS as she accompanied Bassa around the convent's herb garden. The low-walled space on the slope of the Mount of Olives was a restful place and scattered wooden benches encouraged contemplation. But winter blighted the plants and few sisters ventured into the early winter chill. She sniffed the late November breeze. *Snow is in the air. I hope we don't have a blizzard that keeps me in Jerusalem. The older I get, the more I prefer the comforts of home.*

"Augusta?" Bassa straightened from cutting some sprigs of rosemary to add to her basket.

"My apologies, Mother Bassa. My mind wandered for a moment." She brought her attention back to her companion. "You were telling me about your annual commemoration of Mother Melania's death."

"We were hoping you could attend this year, since you were such great friends."

"I would be honored. I can't believe she has been gone these twelve years. Jerusalem is a poorer place for her absence, but you and your sisters have carried on her mission with grace and humility."

"We have you to thank for that, Augusta. Your patronage allows us to fulfill our mission to serve the poor in all the ways we can." She guided Athenais to a wooden bench by the wall that caught the weak winter sun but sheltered them from errant breezes. "Which is why I wanted to talk to you."

"Do you have need of more funds?" Athenais raised a questioning eyebrow. "I can speak with my curator."

"No, Augusta, this is a more delicate matter. The sisters are upset with the outcome of the Chalcedonian Council. We believe that it went too far in putting Christ's humanity on an equal footing with his divinity. How can a human man be the same as the Divine Word?"

"I can see why people are confused by the Council's decree that 'Christ was established as the possessor of one person with two natures, perfect God and perfect man.' It does hint at the Nestorian heresy."

"Exactly! The monks, clerics, and holy women of Jerusalem are united in our rejection of the Council's decree, but my sisters wanted me to consult with you before we took any action. You are our patroness and we do not want to endanger our relationship with you, Augusta."

"Don't fear on that score, my friend." She patted the younger woman's hand. "I would continue my donations, even if I did not agree with you on the nature of the doctrine. The poor, the traveler, the sick care not if Jesus was a kind man who preached peace and love or God who dictated that we care for the least of these. They need food, shelter, medical care and you and your sisters provide that. It is also true that I support the good Christians in my community. I also feel the doctrine was wrongly decided. A compromise that makes no sense. You can count on my backing." *I'm also not foolish enough to anger this community again. Having a mob at my gates once is enough. Pulcheria can stay safe behind the walls of Constantinople. Let her deal with the fallout of her so-called decree!*

"Thank you, Augusta, you have laid my mind to rest." Bassa looked up as a few soft flakes of snow drifted from the leaden sky. "Let us repair to the convent for some warm wine. We appreciate the excellent vintage you supply us from your vineyards. That will also give me the opportunity to tell you what our community plans to do to counter the Nestorian Chalcedon decree. We have heard that our Bishop Juvenal supported the compromise and is coming back to Jerusalem to enforce it. He will have a surprise waiting for him."

"Excellent. I will do all in my power to help you." *And provide a few thorns to prick Pulcheria's pride.*

*****

Episcopal Palace, Jerusalem, April 452

"Where is that man?" Athenais fumed as she paced the receiving room of the Episcopal Palace. "How dare he keep the Augusta waiting!"

"You caught the new bishop at his prayers, Augusta." A rabbity cleric bowed excessively, bobbing like a chicken pecking for its dinner. He backed out of the room, "I'll see what's keeping him."

Once the cleric was gone, Athenais sighed and turned to Gabriel. "Father, what are we to do with our rebellious bishop? When I promised to back this movement, I did not know this Archimandrite Theodosius—Gift from God indeed! —would be as bad as the fanatic Barsauma. The list of his atrocities is appalling! How can he call himself a Christian?"

"To be clear, he did not personally kill those of the orthodox faith or rape noble women."

"He led the mob of monks that did! He encouraged the carnage and forgave his followers for their sins. What about a cloistered life of contemplation leads to such violence?" She stood before the priest, face red and fists clenched. "Now I am forever linked with this disaster."

"I believe we can salvage this situation." Gabriel ran a hand through his hair. "The archimandrite is a very holy man. His followers adore him. Unlike Barsauma, he is literate, but like the Syrian monk, he is naive and ignorant of the ways of the court. I believe we can guide him out of this impasse and enhance your own reputation while doing it."

"Do you believe that is possible? I had little success with Barsauma."

"This is a different situation. I've heard rumors that his followers already regret their hasty actions now that Prefect Basil is sending his troops to re-install Juvenal in the bishopric. The people of Palestine—whether Jew or Christian—have a long history of loss to Roman troops and a healthy fear of and respect for them. If we can offer a way out, I believe the archimandrite will take it."

"Augusta, thank you for coming."

She turned to see Archimandrite Theodosius standing in the doorway.

He was a tall, almost skeletal man with stooped shoulders and a long graying beard. His dark eyes nested in a web of deep wrinkles and sheltered under bushy brows. Dressed in brown monk's robes, a bishop's signet ring on his index finger was the only sign of his new position. He gave her a brief bow. "I've just received word that Juvenal is at the gates backed by provincial troops. Thanks to your robust renovations, they cannot breach the city walls. I hope you can accompany me to address them from the gates. I want no more bloodshed, but we must be firm in our faith. You are the imperial presence. They will obey you and leave us in peace."

"I will accompany you, Bishop, as I believe in your cause, but I do not condone your means of attaining your new position."

"The people of Jerusalem elected me in the traditional way, Augusta. They rejected Juvenal for his betrayal and have the right to the bishop they want. I did not seek this elevation and did not encourage the violence and loss of life that accompanied it. That is something I heartily regret. I seek now to calm the mob, affirm our faith, and turn the wrath of the Roman army away from our gates. Will you help me do that?"

He seems more reasonable than Barsauma. Let's see how amenable he is to direction. She nodded. "Father Gabriel, accompany me. We will pick up Captain Nikolaos and my guards outside to accompany Bishop Theodosius to the walls." She linked arms with Theodosius. "Tell me your proposals as we walk, Bishop."

When they arrived at the city's main gates, Athenais noted the Jerusalem garrison had joined the rebel monks on the walls. The monks were armed with swords and staves from the armory—whether looted or given freely made no difference. Nikolaos ascended the stairs to address Juvenal and his troops outside the walls while she and the archimandrite stood behind the gates.

"I am Captain of Our Most Esteemed Aelia Eudocia Augusta's Guards," Nikolaos' parade-ground voice boomed from the gate above them. "The Most Pious Augusta will mediate in this dispute. Juvenal, send your troops back twenty paces and approach the gates. Her Imperial Serenity and the Bishop Theodosius will meet you in peace in full view of both your troops and ours. Our Most Wise and Merciful Augusta guarantees the safety of all parties."

Athenais waited for several seconds until she heard the thuds of hobnailed sandals marching in unison farther away. *Good. Juvenal has decided on diplomacy rather than belligerence.*

Nikolaos gave the signal, and two guards opened the gates far enough for her and the bishop to walk through. The guards exited and stood to either side of the crack, hands on swords. "Juvenal approaches, Augusta," the left guard informed her, never taking his eyes off the approaching man.

"Shall we?" Athenais led the new bishop out the gate and onto the dusty road. They walked several paces in front of the gate and waited for Juvenal to join them. They were far enough from both crowds than no one could overhear their conversation, but her guards could intervene if necessary.

"Augusta." Juvenal gave her a brief bow, but his eyes stayed on Theodosius. "My many thanks for your intervention in this matter. I do not wish further bloodshed in my beloved city. Please order this imposter to dismiss his mob and acknowledge me as the rightful bishop of Jerusalem."

"I am the rightful Bishop!" Theodosius glared at Juvenal. "You are a traitor to your faith and a disgrace to this sacred city."

"Augusta?" Juvenal's jaw dropped at the angry attack.

Athenais stepped between the two and faced the ousted bishop. "You and I have worked closely in the past, Juvenal, but I agree with the bishop. You have betrayed your people with your capitulation at Chalcedon. Why did you do that?"

"I had no choice. If I did not ascribe to the decree, I would have lost my bishopric and been ex-communicated." His eyes begged her to understand.

"Yet you lost your bishopric anyway," Theodosius thundered. "The people of Jerusalem reject the Nestorian heresy prescribed by the Chalcedonian decree."

"That is false!" Juvenal said in a firm voice. "Over six hundred bishops declared both Nestorianism and Monophysitism heresies at the Council. The decree is a compromise between two extremes—"

"Enough!" Athenais cut him off before they could descend into a fruitless argument over the nature of Christ. "We cannot decide this church issue in the middle of the road. My purpose here is to make a couple of facts clear. Juvenal, the people of Jerusalem have rejected you and elected Theodosius bishop. That is their right. This conflict should not be settled by force of arms or abridged by an Augusta. I propose that you present your case through the proper channels. Withdraw with your troops back to Caesarea Maritima and appeal to Pope Leo for redress."

"What of the violence these heretics have committed? Will there be any accountability for their actions?" Juvenal sputtered.

"That is a civil matter. Bishop Theodosius claims that others were the perpetrators of the violence that occurred. He will make their case to the imperial court and abide by the judgment of Marcian Augustus. Do you both agree?"

Juvenal surveyed the force manning the impregnable walls of Jerusalem. His shoulders slumped and he replied in a bitter tone, "I agree. I will withdraw to Caesarea."

Theodosius nodded. "I agree as well, Augusta. You are wise in the ways of this world, and I will abide by your guidance."

Athenais turned to Juvenal and gave him the kiss of peace, whispering in his ear, "Good-bye, my friend. I'm sorry we must part so bitterly."

He nodded, eyes glistening with unshed tears. "Blessings on you, Augusta."

As they walked back to the gate, Theodosius asked, "Are you sure appealing to the imperial court will work?"

She shrugged. "Nothing in this life is sure except death. But Marcian is a general. The Huns fought the combined armies of Western Rome and the Visigoths to a draw at the Battle of Catalaunian Plains in June, weakening both. Attila may be looking to the East next and Marcian needs to be prepared for war. He will defer to Pulcheria on this issue. She has shown a remarkable tolerance for religious violence when followed by sincere apologies. I have some legal learning. If you wish, we will craft your appeal together. If you can show that the violence is over and peace reigns, she will likely not intervene."

"Thank you, Augusta. I look forward to working with you in these coming years."

Another crisis averted—at least temporarily. We'll see if Pulcheria responds as expected.

Chapter 71

Imperial Palace, Constantinople, May 452

MARCIAN REVIEWED THE LETTER PULCHERIA HAD PREPARED TO BISHOP Theodosius and signed his name. *Flavian Marcian Augustus. I've been ruler of Eastern Rome for over a year and half and still can't believe that an Illyrian boy from an obscure family could reach such heights of power.* He smiled ruefully. *But then, my very obscurity made me a perfect consort for my imperial wife.*

"Shall I take this correspondence back to the Augusta, Sire?" His clerk tidied a stack of other letters that Pulcheria had sent him to sign.

"No. I'll take it myself."

Marcian said nothing at the astonished look on his assistant's face. Transporting imperial correspondence was a slave's work, but explaining his motives was also beneath him. He stood and took the papers from his clerk.

Traversing the halls of this labyrinthine building still gave him unease. The excessively servile nature of the slaves as they bowed, scraped, and made way irritated him. *I expect my troops to be obedient, but also forthright. I'll be glad to be back in the field with real men and away from these eunuchs and slaves.*

A herald announced his presence to Pulcheria's workroom—a practical space that reminded him of a military camp, filled with straight lines and hard surfaces.

"Husband?" Pulcheria looked up from her desk. "I thought you were leaving for the frontier. It's the fighting season and Attila is on the move."

"Shortly. I wanted to discuss this letter to the rebel monks in Jerusalem."

"What's there to discuss?" She sat back in her chair, frowning.

"I have some questions and also wish to discuss... uh... more personal things." *Pulcheria is usually more perceptive than this. I rarely intrude on her work and when I do, it's always important and requires discretion. She must be tired. That's been more likely than not lately.* For the past several months, she complained of pains in her back and ate even more abstemiously than usual.

His wife threw him an irritated glance, then turned to her two clerks busy at their own desks, heads down but within easy earshot. "Leave us."

The two men scurried out.

Pulcheria folded her hands and gave him a frank stare.

Marcian took a seat in a backless camp chair. "Did you consult with the army surgeon Aspar recommended?"

"Yes. He and my physician could find nothing wrong with me other than I am fifty-three. I've already outlived my younger sisters and brother. Some discomfort is to be expected at my age."

He nodded in relief. "I'm pleased to hear there is nothing serious. The empire needs you for many more years."

"May God make it so." She leaned forward. "Anything else?"

"This letter to the monks of Jerusalem." He placed the stack of letters on her desk, the Jerusalem letter on top. "You are most lenient in my name. I thought to send more troops to the city and reinstall Juvenal. Instead, you have me castigate the monks for their crimes and reserve punishment 'for the Divine Judge.' That is not the Roman way."

"It is when it's needful. You know we cannot spare troops for such an adventure. My clever sister-in-law fortified the Holy City and made it the center of her Monophysite rebellion. Such matters require delicacy, not arms. I want to win the goodwill of the people with mercy. The monks already regret their violence and sent me a petition."

"Even the monks know who wields the power in this court?" He frowned.

"My reverence for holy men is well-known throughout the land and many try to play on that respect, including my sister Augusta. I see her hand in this document. They praise my piety and blame their atrocious actions on the Samaritans. Athenais knows of my enmity towards those people and provides an easy scapegoat for her rebellious monks. They also accuse the local provincial soldiers of interfering in the independence of their monasteries—another cause

I have punished in the past. It is a well-crafted petition."

"But you have me holding no one to account. I look weak and ineffectual." He pointed to the offending passage in his letter. "Indeed, I capitulate and promise the soldiers will no longer interfere and the Samaritans will be investigated and punished."

"Husband, when we married you promised to leave church policy to me, and I promised not to dictate your military strategy. Everyone knows you are a brave and clever general. No one will consider you weak because you offer mercy and peace to churchmen who have been led astray. You will be praised even more for your understanding and efforts to unite the Universal Church. I will see it is so in my own correspondence with the monks and holy women of the city." She gave him a brief smile. "Now may I apply your seal?"

"Yes. I'll leave this matter to you." He rose and started toward the door.

"Marcian?"

"Yes?" He looked over his shoulder.

Pulcheria's face had fallen into sad and weary lines. "You are a good Augustus. Let no one tell you differently. I need your strength and courage. Be safe and come back to me."

"God willing, I will, my dear."

Mother Melania's Convent, Jerusalem, June 452

"It's over, Augusta." Bassa handed Athenais the letter from Pulcheria. "Constantinople will send no troops to reinstall the Nestorian heretic Juvenal."

"We have won the battle, but the war still rages, my friend. We must maintain the peace and hold firm in our faith. If riots break out anew, we will be under threat from imperial troops." She rapidly scanned the letter. "The assault from Chalcedonian adherents already begins. Pulcheria reaffirms her belief in the dual nature of Christ and its centrality to the orthodox church's doctrine. I have had letters from Pope Leo in Rome and the stylite Simeon among others urging me to give up the Monophysite heresy for the sake of imperial harmony and church unity. You can expect the same."

"We will stay the course, Augusta." Bassa snorted. "Did you read that passage where our Esteemed and Most Pious Augusta fears that we of the weaker sex have been led astray by Bishop Theodosius?"

"Yes, but she has always underestimated women, feeling her accomplishments were unique—only she, of all her sex, could have accomplished so much. Even though she had the examples of our Aunt Placidia and her own mother and grandmother to draw upon." She handed the letter back to Bassa.

Bassa folded it away. 'I found her plea that 'all the women dedicated to God pray for her' troubling. We pray for the life and health of the imperial family as a matter of course. She knows this. Are there any rumors from the court about the Augusta's health?"

"None that have come to me. More likely she fears that because of her wedding to Marcian, the virgins and holy women believe she has left your ranks. You and your sisters have always been among her most loyal supporters."

"Possibly." Bassa looked thoughtful, then brightened. "In any case, we are at peace for the moment. Tell me about the extensions you plan for Saint Stephen's Church."

"Gladly." *Maybe in this period of peace I can make my way to Ravenna and finally meet my granddaughters.*

Chapter 72

Mother Melania's Convent, early August 453

AT LEAST WE HAD A FULL YEAR OF PEACE AND NO INTERFERENCE FROM *Constantinople.* Athenais removed her mourning veil and draped it over the plain wooden chair of the convent's guest chamber—a stark, but clean room decorated with whitewashed walls and furnished with a single bedstead covered with a brown wool blanket, a wooden washstand, and the chair. Her regular clothes resided in her own chest tucked against the wall, providing a second seat if needed.

Mother Bassa entered the guest chamber. "Augusta, will you be staying another night?"

"No, Mother. Now that the mourning for my sister Augusta is done, I'll return to Bethlehem."

"We were most pleased to have you grace us with your company."

"It seemed a fitting way to honor Pulcheria. I doubt she would have approved of the encomium I read at Saint Stephen's, but she would have been pleased I spent this time with her holy sisters. She always thought me lacking in the observances of my faith." *And I thought she cared too much. Ritual should not take the place of service. I never thought to say this, but I believe I will miss her looming presence. She waged a war over Theo's affections I never wanted, but she did more for the empire than he ever did—or could.*

Athenais looked around the plain room. "I did find it restful here with no obligations or distractions."

"You are welcome anytime, Augusta." Bassa looked thoughtful. "Does Pulcheria Augusta's passing change the situation here in Jerusalem?"

"I fear it might." Athenais sighed. "With Pulcheria's death, Marcian Augustus no longer has a moderating voice to keep him from reinstalling Juvenal by force. That is generally the solution to any problem when a military man is in charge. With Attila's death in April, Marcian now has the troops to do it. How are your people feeling? Will they put up resistance?"

"It's hard to tell. Most of the rebellious monks and archimandrites have returned to their monasteries outside the walls. The clerics and holy women remaining are more inclined to peace. We're the ones dedicated to service and have experienced the horrible aftermath of violence."

"Bishop Theodosius consecrated several anti-Chalcedonian priests and bishops. Will they rally to him?"

Bassa shrugged. "They are scattered across the province. Our convent supports him, but we will not take up arms."

"Then we must wait and see what the Augustus plans." She paused to think for a moment. "I will call on Bishop Theodosius before I return to Bethlehem. Will you inform my guards outside I will be leaving shortly?"

"As you wish, Augusta." Bassa bowed.

"And Mother, call on me at any time if I can be of assistance."

"Thank you, Augusta. I'll send a servant to move your chest."

As her wagon wound through the crooked streets of the city toward her destination, Athenais would occasionally peek out the curtained windows. Each time, she saw a decoration, improvement, or building she had funded: from the three-ton copper cross atop the Ascension Church to the fortified walls to the Episcopal Palace. *I have truly rebuilt this city*, she mused. *Pulcheria built churches, but I did so much more for the people. I gave them beauty and security. I hope we can keep it.*

When she arrived at the Episcopal Palace, Bishop Theodosius was waiting on the steps to receive her. As he gave her a hand out of her carriage, Theodosius said in a low voice, "Augusta, I'm honored you could spare some time to visit. I have need of your advice."

"Anytime, Bishop." She linked arms with him as they headed to the receiving room.

In the halls teeming with clerics, servants, and guards, they talked of inconsequential things. Behind closed doors, he came to the point. "I received word from Juvenal this morning that troops will arrive within the month to take Jerusalem by force of arms if I do not give up the bishopric. He threatens destruction and bloodshed if the city resists."

"And if you do give up the bishopric? What will be your fate?"

"He made no promises or threats as to my personal welfare. I suspect if I swear to the Chalcedonian creed, I could live in peace and obscurity. If I don't—" Theodosius shrugged. "—excommunication at the least. More likely banishment or imprisonment. But my main concern is for the people of Jerusalem—not just their bodies, but their souls."

Athenais nodded. "I personally believe in a just and merciful God who will judge us on our actions and not our beliefs. That is why I favor the doctrine declaring Jesus' divine nature. I don't want a God tainted with human frailties. We are too broken. But I also believe that to anyone who lives as Jesus commanded—love thy neighbor as thyself, care for the least among you, turn the other cheek to violence—it matters little whether their bishop or their pope believes Christ had one nature or two."

"Are you urging me to capitulate, to falsely swear to a doctrine I do not believe in?" Theodosius looked aghast.

"No, Bishop, you must do as your conscience dictates. I am merely saying my opinion is that Christians who follow Jesus' fundamental teachings will not be penalized in the afterlife for their leaders' beliefs. The truth, of course, is unknowable, but I believe His basic philosophy overshadows any arguments about his nature. Living the philosophy is more important than the wrangling over the theoretical nature of Christ."

"Then you are a different kind of heretic, Augusta. Neither Nestorian nor Monophysite."

"A rebel maybe, but not a heretic. I am a Christian first. The only heresy is knowingly living an unchristian life. All these philosophical arguments are a distraction from Christ's teaching and a form of control by an elite church hierarchy for their own benefit."

"So, I am now part of an elite church hierarchy preaching a doctrine for my own benefit? I thought we were friends, Augusta?" He smiled ruefully.

"You were never of the worst sort, Bishop, but I have known many who were. Bishop Cyril of Alexandria and the Archimandrite Barsauma were fanatical violent men who murdered and sowed destruction in God's name. I never understood how they could call themselves Christians." She shivered.

"As with any human institution, the leadership of the church is filled with all sorts—holy men, incompetent men, ambitious men. I always counted you among the first and Juvenal among the last."

"I am still at a loss as to how to deal with Juvenal and the Roman troops."

"As am I." Athenais frowned. "My sources tell me that Marcian Augustus holds me equally to blame for the Monophysite rebellion. I fortified the city and backed your elevation. It is likely that some punishment will befall me, as well."

"Augusta, I had no idea! What will you do?"

"I don't know, but we should share our strategies. I will stay here in Jerusalem. We are now in the realm of politics, not church dogma, and I know little of Marcian Augustus. I will do my best to learn more before we have to face his troops. I will be by your side when they arrive. We will be prepared by then."

He clasped her hand in his. "Blessings on you, Augusta. We will face this together, whatever the outcome."

And if we're clever, we will both survive.

The Gates of Jerusalem, late August 453

"IS EVERYTHING READY, CAPTAIN?" ATHENAIS SURVEYED THE ARRAY OF GARRISON soldiers supplemented with her own guards at the main gate.

"Yes, Augustus, but I urge you to abandon this plan. Something doesn't feel right." Nikolaos frowned as he also reviewed the troops. "Count Dorotheus brought a large force with him, but the men arrayed outside the wall are not even equal in number to the army Juvenal brought two years ago. Where are the rest of the men?"

"This is just a talk, as before. Perhaps Juvenal and Dorotheus wish to survey our defenses before making a move." She gave him a gentle smile. "Juvenal gave his word, and you will be with me to enforce it. Your men will be only steps away. I'll be safe."

"I still don't like this, Augusta."

"I know, Captain." Athenais and Bishop Theodosius walked through the slightly opened main gate to meet with Juvenal and Count Dorotheus. She remembered the count, the provincial military commander, from the Barsauma trial. A short, dignified man with calculating gray eyes. His men were highly trained and disciplined. He had taken the post in Palestine because he married a young woman that his family disapproved of, so he was willing to break rules and take the consequences. A worthy adversary.

She felt the count's eyes on her, measuring her worth. *Let's hope I exceed his expectations.*

"And so, we meet again on the dusty road, Juvenal, and nothing has changed in the two years since we last met." Athenais surveyed his much-diminished army not twenty paces away. A trickle of alarm shivered up her spine. *Nikolaos is right. What is Dorotheus up to?* She turned to the commander and waved a hand at the armed garrison on the walls behind her. "Count Dorotheus, do you think your troops can take the walls of Jerusalem?"

"I thought we were here to talk, Augusta." He pulled a sealed packet from his tunic. "Here is my commission. Marcian Augustus has given me leave to resolve this affair as I see fit. I hope to do so without bloodshed."

"As do we all, Count." *Maybe the lack of troops is a sign of good faith, and I shouldn't be so alarmed.*

Bishop Theodosius spoke up, "As long as the resolution is in Juvenal's favor?"

"That is the preferred outcome—to restore orthodoxy to the province and cleanse the Holy City of heresy," Juvenal sputtered. "I worked two years for this. The pope and all the Eastern bishops agree I am the rightful bishop of Jerusalem."

"But what of the people?" Theodosius grew red in the face and his fists clenched.

"The people will follow their bishop. You led them into heresy, I will bring them back to the right path."

"Have they no say? It is our tradition in the Holy Land that the people elect their bishops, not that the Augustus imposes them."

Dorotheus stepped between the two feuding men. "It is my intention to oversee another election—one not tainted by the violence and murder of the last one."

"An election in the presence of armed men? You learned well from Pulcheria Augusta. She controlled and dictated the outcome of the Chalcedonian Council—the root of this impasse." Athenais shook her head. "That will not be acceptable. The people have spoken, and I have listened. I stand on the side of Bishop Theodosius and the people of Jerusalem." She turned to Theodosius. "Come, Bishop, this was a waste of our time."

"But not mine, Augusta." The count gave her a condescending smile. "I understand you are a classical scholar."

She turned to glare at him. "So?"

"You should remember the fate of Troy."

"Are you Odysseus or Agamemnon?"

"Both, Augusta." As he spoke, she heard shouts and the clash of arms from inside the walls. Her heart thudded in her chest. *Traitors at the gates! This talk was all a ruse to give his agents inside time to open the other gates to the soldiers.*

Nikolaos grabbed her arm. "Augusta, we must get you to safety!"

She shook off his arm. "No, Captain, you were right about the missing men. They are already inside and have cut off any escape route for me or the bishop. Is that not so, Count?"

Dorotheus nodded. "It is, Augusta. Your people are not as united as they were two years ago, and I was easily able to recruit some sympathetic agents to open the gates."

"If I ask my men to surrender, will you spare them?"

"I am sincere in my wish for no bloodshed. We are all Romans and in these troubled times, we need every soldier to defend our homeland. Call off your men and they will be pardoned for following your orders, Augusta."

"Do so, Captain."

"And the Augusta?" Nikolaos refused to leave her.

"I will personally guarantee her safety. The Augustus does not want the blood of an Augusta on his hands."

Of course, there are worse things than death, but I have no choice now. "Go, Captain. Tell the men to stand down."

He gave her an anxious glance as he ran back to the open gate. Within moments the clatter of arms quieted, and Nikolaos ran back to her side.

Juvenal flashed a wolfish grin. "And the false bishop?"

"As I said, we will have another election."

"But—"

"Do not fear the outcome, Bishop," the count cut Juvenal off. "In the meantime, the Augusta and Theodosius may retire to the Episcopal Palace—with a guard—to await the people's pleasure."

The count bowed to her. "It has been a pleasure meeting you, Augusta. I wish it were under more auspicious circumstances."

"Count. Juvenal." Athenais nodded at them both. "Come, Bishop." A small squad of Dorotheus' soldiers broke from the ranks to accompany her and her own guards back to the palace. In the face of their overwhelming numbers, they didn't even disarm her guard. Her defeat tasted like ashes, but one phrase gave her a small glimmer of hope. *If Marcian doesn't want my blood, what does he want?*

Chapter 73

Episcopal Palace, Jerusalem

"YOU HAVE A MESSENGER FROM CONSTANTINOPLE, AUGUSTA." ONE OF THE palace servants announced from the doorway of the guest receiving room she had converted into her work room.

"Who?" She looked up from her letter to Marcian. *Maybe a letter will be unneeded.*

A tall older man in a field general's uniform and the bowed legs of a cavalry man entered the room flanked by a contingent of heavily armed guards. They sent the servant scurrying away.

The blood drained from her face and her heart raced. *So Dorotheus lied. Here are my executioners.* She rose from her chair clutching a pen in one hand and a letter knife in the other.

"Augusta." The general bowed.

Something about the man seemed familiar. *Have I seen him in General Aspar's retinue?* She looked more closely at the guards. *Imperial Scholae! That one was Theo's captain. But why are they out of uniform?* The pieces fell together, and she put on her most regal attitude.

"Augustus." *I never would have recognized Marcian from the coins or statues that have circulated for the past three years. He's much handsomer in person.*

He raised an eyebrow. "Pulcheria always said you were clever." He ordered his guards, "Wait outside."

She relaxed a little. *Surely he wouldn't execute me with his own hands? But he's a soldier and quite capable.* The memory of life leaving Saturninus' eyes, of blood flowing down the front of her gown, staining her hands, flashed across her mind. *Anyone is capable when pushed to extremes. Have I pushed him too far?*

After the guards left, Athenais indicated the ever-present sideboard liberally furnished with drinks. "Would like some wine or water, Augustus? You look like you've traveled hard, and the roads are dusty this time of year in Palestine."

He strode to the sideboard and served himself. *Ah yes, a military man used to caring for himself. He must find palace life stifling.*

Marcian raised a silver goblet, drained it, then wiped his mouth on the sleeve of his tunic. He refilled the goblet and came back to set it on the desk. He grabbed a side chair, reversed and straddled it, rested his arms across the back, and stared at her.

Not to the nobility born. Maybe I can use that. "Augustus, we share a common bond."

He gave her a neutral smile. "How so, Augusta?"

"To family, I am Athenais. Please call me that if you wish." She smiled. "You and I both came from humble origins to marry into the imperial family. That takes some time to get used to. How are you faring? Especially now that my sister Pulcheria has taken her final journey." She took a sip of cucumber water from a blue glass chased with silver.

"As you well know, it was a marriage of convenience for Pulcheria." His face fell into sorrowful lines and moisture glistened in his eyes. "But we came to care for one another in our own ways. I respected and admired her. The empire would have been so much better off if she had been born a man. As is..." He shook his head. "I miss her."

"It has only been two months since her passing. I am truly sorry for your loss. Pulcheria and I didn't always see eye to eye—"

"Ha!" Marcian laughed nearly spilling his drink. "The palace servants still gossip about your rows. They are most disappointed by my dull life."

She relaxed further. *He doesn't seem the cruel sort to play with his prey before ending its life.* "Like you, Marcian—may I call you that?"

He nodded. "Much preferred."

"Like you, I respected Pulcheria's abilities. She ruled at Theo's side for many years and the empire is better for it. In the end, my husband proved a poor leader. However, I did differ with my sister on one major point. She insisted on melding church and empire—a practice counter to all my philosophies." She glanced at him over the rim of her goblet. "I suspect that is why you are here. To chastise me for my beliefs."

"Yes and no."

He rose from the chair and paced for a moment, hands behind his back, frowning. "Frankly, I'm a simple military man. I don't understand—and don't want to understand—this controversy over the nature of Christ. I left all that to Pulcheria while I protected the empire from foreign enemies. But now I am sole ruler in the East and responsible for the peace of the empire." He stopped and extended his hands, palms up. "You, Athenais, are causing discord. Not your beliefs—your actions. Your rebellion against the Chalcedonian Council inflames tensions."

"That was not my intention." She sighed. "I thought only to lead where my people wanted to go."

He returned to his chair, rested his chin on his arms and gave her a sharp look. "Are you sure it had nothing to do with your feud with Pulcheria?"

Before she could help it, the blood rushed to her face. *He may be a simple military man, but he's not a simpleton.* She took a sip of water to calm her nerves. "Are you aware of the... uh... circumstances of my sojourn here in Jerusalem?"

"Aspar spoke of the rumors. He did not credit the more salacious ones. He was a great friend to Paulinus and vowed vengeance against that vicious eunuch who caused his—and your—downfall. He worked closely with Pulcheria in her own exile to bring Chrysaphius down."

"And for that, I will forever be grateful to both. But, after Theo's death, Pulcheria did not rescind my exile. In fact, in our correspondence, she hinted that she believed the worst rumors because Theo still did on his deathbed. I believe she was willfully blind to the truth because of her love for and loyalty to my husband. She blocked my reunion with my daughter and granddaughters. For that, I harbor great resentment. I believe any loving parent would." She raised an eyebrow. "Don't you have a daughter from your previous marriage?"

He nodded. "Marcia Euphemia."

"Are you not doing all in your power to advance her welfare? I heard that a marriage was in the offing with Anthemius, the grandson of the Great Anthemius who built the Theodosian walls. A most prestigious family. Do you intend to name your son-in-law heir?"

"Pulcheria always said you had an astute sense of politics, but you used it for your own amusement."

She shook her head. "Not amusement. Survival. You came here incognito for a reason, Marcian. A political reason, not a religious one, or a personal one. I can work with that. What is it you want from me?"

"You're wrong. I did come incognito for a *personal* reason. I wanted to meet the woman who gave my wife so much unease she constantly prayed for God's forgiveness for the sin of envy. During your initial rebellion, she forbade me from moving against you, out of deference for her brother who loved you for many years. With her death, you are now *my* problem. And, yes, it is a political one—one I could have delegated to Dorotheus, but, as I said, I wanted to meet you in person."

"And now what? Will you strip me of my title and lands? Execute me?" She clenched her hands under the table so he could not see her nervousness.

"I considered the first. Never the second. I made a vow to Pulcheria to leave you in peace." He leaned back in the chair holding on to the back and smiled. "Besides, the people of Jerusalem love you. If I stripped you of your title and income, they would be the losers and blame me for it. If I executed you, they would rise up behind Bishop Theodosius and rampage in your name. We've both seen how volatile the people can be."

So not death or loss of imperial prestige. Thank you, Mother Melania, for teaching me the value of the people's love. And I suppose I must thank Pulcheria for her forbearance, as much as it pains me. She sat quietly awaiting her fate.

"I want your compliance, Athenais. It's the smart political move. The election for bishop is pre-ordained. I do not demand you change your beliefs, but I do need you to accept Juvenal when he wins. Otherwise Dorotheus will occupy Jerusalem and enforce the peace. Neither of us wants a bloody battle."

"And what happens to Theodosius?"

"He has already accepted a sentence of exile. He will leave Jerusalem and travel to Egypt. The church will depose those priests and bishops he consecrated."

"I see." She bowed her head and chewed her lower lip. After a moment, she stood, back straight and gaze level. "I will agree on one condition. Release me from my exile. Allow me to travel to Ravenna to be with my daughter and grandchildren. I am growing old. It has been sixteen years since I've seen my daughter and I've never met her children. I wish to hold them in my arms before I die."

He rose and returned her frank gaze. "I agree. However, I cannot extend permission for your travel to Ravenna. You must seek that from your son-in-law." His face shifted into sorrowful lines. "And I don't think he will grant it. The Western court is still in turmoil. My agents report that with Attila's death, the Huns are in disarray. General Aetius has returned to court to great acclaim for his handling of the Huns and the Goths. My Western co-ruler is known for a volatile temper and my people are waiting to see who wins in the contest of wills."

"As a military man, do you back General Aetius?"

"No. Civil war only weakens us. I want Valentinian to be a successful emperor, but I fear for him and his family."

"All the more reason I should go to them. I could be a stabilizing force."

"If you arrive at all. With the Huns and Goths in disarray, the Vandals of North Africa have become bolder. They still hold the Carthaginian fleet and raid farther afield. No trader or traveler is safe on the seas. I would urge caution or land travel."

"My granddaughter and namesake Eudocia is affianced to the Vandal king's son Huneric. I fear Valentinian will turn her over to maintain the peace. I cannot allow that."

Marcian nodded. "I understand, but I still urge caution. If King Gaiseric got his hands on an Augusta, he would be unlikely to give her up. You would become a pawn in his ambitions."

"As my granddaughter will be if he takes her." She shook her head. "No. I must convince Valentinian otherwise. I can best do that in person."

"As you wish, Athenais." He saluted her. "Go with my blessings, but plan ahead and be safe." He looked around the room with a weary smile. "I and my men will stay the night, then be on the road tomorrow. Few at the court know of my whereabouts and I must return with all haste before rumors start of my demise and I return to a usurper."

She walked around the table and touched his arm. "Thank you, Marcian. Pulcheria chose her consort well. I'm glad we met and resolved old scores. Written words are my medium but fade in the light of face-to-face communication. I will gladly put down my sword—" She laid her pen aside. "—and support you in keeping the peace. If I can be of any additional service, let me know."

He bowed. "Augusta."

She nodded "Augustus."

And now to Ravenna and my family!

Epilog

Imperial Mausoleum, Saint Stephen's Basilica, Jerusalem, summer 468

"THIS WAY PRINCESS." MOTHER BASSA LED EUDOCIA THROUGH A SIDE entrance to Saint Stephen's Basilica. "Your grandmother Athenais lies in here. My holy sisters and I are tasked with maintaining her mausoleum. A pleasant task, taken on willingly."

They passed through a brass-bound wooden door into an intimate chapel. Her grandmother's porphyry coffin lay on a pedestal at the foot of a golden cross, incrusted with amethysts. *Mother always said they were a favorite of hers.* Heavy golden candlesticks flanked the cross. Bassa replaced the candles and put fresh flowers in a blue glazed vase in front of a large mosaic on the far wall showing her grandmother as a beautiful young woman, dressed in imperial regalia holding a cross in her right hand and a raised left palm.

Eudocia approached and touched the gold tiles surrounding the image. "Beautiful work. Does it look much like her?"

"Quite. Athenais gave refuge to several gifted artists during her seventeen years in Jerusalem. This was executed by favorites of hers, a sister who created the designs and a brother who did the mosaic work. I believe they came from Ravenna."

"I thought I recognized the style. My paternal grandmother Placidia patronized their father. He did the mosaic work for her own funeral chapel." She stood back to get a better look. "Fitting."

Bassa gave her a searching look. "Do you wish to be alone? I can wait outside."

Eudocia shook her head. "No. I didn't know my grandmother except through stories from my mother and she married so young that her memories seem more like myths than reality. It is a pleasure to see my grandmother through the eyes of someone who knew her later in life."

"Athenais was a generous, kind, and brave woman. A true Christian. Many still talk of her good works and everywhere you go, there are physical signs of her generosity and love of beauty." Bassa threw her arms wide. "She rebuilt Saint Stephen's into the jewel it now is. You must come into the nave and see the lovely serene space she created for the congregation."

"I will." Eudocia coughed, then a wracking pain clutched her chest. She gasped for breath. When she put a kerchief to her lips, it came away bloody.

"Sit here, Princess." Bassa led her to a marble bench on the right-hand wall. "You had a long and dangerous journey from Carthage. The dust must have irritated your lungs. Drink this." She handed Eudocia a waterskin and she gulped from it.

Eudocia returned the stopper and handed it back. "Thanks for the water, Mother, but it's not the dust. I suffer from a weakness of the lungs. The physicians in Carthage gave me only a few months or possibly a year to live. That is why Gaiseric gave me permission to leave. I had fulfilled my dynastic duty by providing that barbaric king a grandson of imperial birth and he had no more need for me."

"It's terrible that you had to leave your son behind."

Eudocia shuddered. "I have no love for Hildric. He is the child of rape. Huneric was a brutal husband who kept me in a gilded cage and taunted me with his power to do as he wished. He took my son away at birth and twisted his mind against me."

"I'm sorry to hear that. Your grandmother worked frantically for your release after your father's death and King Gaiseric of the Vandals took you, your mother, and sister hostage. She marshaled every resource in her power to free you. She even offered all her lands to Gaiseric, but he refused to give up his 'imperial women who were family and beyond price.'" Bassa gazed at the radiant image on the wall. "I think something broke in Athenais when Rome fell to the Vandals and Gaiseric took you."

"Mother thought of her as fragile. She remembered grandmother as overly intense in her love and prone to melancholy when the object of that love was lost. I understand she went nearly insane when my aunt Flacilla died as a child."

"Possibly in her youth that was true." Bassa patted Eudocia's hand. "But I knew an older, more resilient, Athenais. She fought for her rights as an Augusta when your grandfather repudiated her, and she won. She fought for the love of the people here in Palestine and won. She even rebelled against the orthodox church when they decreed that dual-nature heresy and held out for many years. Only after you were taken, did she give in and profess the Chalcedonian Creed."

"I heard much later that she was besieged by any number of holy men to give up her heresy in the interests of harmony and for the good of her soul."

"Pope Leo, Archimandrite Euthymius, the Stylite Simeon, among many in the church, tried to bring her back to orthodoxy. I think it was Leo Augustus who finally persuaded her. After Marcian died, General Aspar passed over Marcian's son-in-law to choose Leo for the diadem. The new Augustus and his wife Verina were very devout and revered Pulcheria Augusta. They even wrote a narrative of Pulcheria's entire life designed to establish the sanctity of the Most Pious Virgin Augusta. There are rumors that your great aunt will be named a saint."

"Grandmother must have hated that! Her rivalry with her sister-in-law is legend in our family."

"She did express some exasperation, but she also knew how to take advantage. I don't know for sure, but I heartily suspect, she finally gave up the Monophysite belief—in public—to appeal to Leo Augustus to advocate for your release."

"Mother cried bitter tears when Leo finally got her and young Placidia's release in 461—a year after grandmother died. Even though I had already given birth to a son, Gaiseric refused to release me. I suspect he held out just to persecute us. With Athenais' death, mother had no family to return to. All were destroyed."

"Will you join your mother and sister in Constantinople?"

"No. I haven't the strength to make that journey. I barely made it here." Eudocia rose and approached Athenais' coffin. She put a hand on the smooth stone. "I'm sorry I never knew you grandmother, but I will join you soon."

She turned away with tears in her eyes. "Mother Bassa, will you and your holy sisters make arrangements when I pass? I would like to lie with my grandmother in this lovely chapel. The idea of not being alone in my death gives me peace."

Bassa put her arms around the princess' shoulders. "Of course, Princess Eudocia. We would do anything for our patroness. Athenais is a saint in our hearts, and we will care for her family as would she."

At the door, they both turned back to gaze at the golden figure on the wall. *I know it's just the flickering light of the candles, but I could swear that grandmother is smiling.*

* * * * *

Liked this book? Don't forget to leave a review. Scan the QR code below to go directly to the Amazon review page. Thanks!

Author's Note

I fell in love with the Theodosian women—Athenais, Pulcheria, and Placidia—many years ago, when writing my first book, *Selene of Alexandria*, which featured a fictional student of the historical Hypatia, Lady Philosopher of Alexandria. Researching the life and times of Hypatia, I kept running across these great women who ruled the failing Western Roman Empire and set the stage for the rise of the Byzantine Empire in the East.

And it wasn't just the fact of their power; they each had compelling human stories. Athenais, the beautiful but impoverished daughter of a pagan Athenian scholar, captured the heart of a Most Christian Emperor. A poet, her extant work is the largest by a female from ancient times, even outpacing the more famous Sappho. At the tender age of fifteen, Pulcheria outwitted the Constantinople court worthies to claim sole regency over her brother and the Empire. Placidia ruled for her minor son and held the crumbling Western Empire together against the depredations of the invading barbarians. Why hadn't I heard of these women before?

I originally planned a single book, telling their intertwining stories, but soon found I had far too much material. Each woman deserved her own story. This is the third in the trilogy about the Theodosian Women. *Twilight Empress* (Book One), about Placidia, came out in 2017. *Dawn Empress* (Book Two), published in 2020, featured Pulcheria. Because they are overlapping stories, they can be read in any order. I've also published a prequel novella *Becoming the Twilight Empress* about Placidia's time in Rome when it was under siege. I've thought of two more novellas about Placidia's daughter Honoria and Athenais' daughter Eudoxia, but… we'll see.

The perceptive reader might find a couple pivotal scenes in which all three protagonists share the stage in all three books. There might even be some variation of the dialog from book to book. Call that the "Rashomon Effect." Each shared scene is from a different point of view and reflects that character's experience at the time.

Throughout the series, I attempt to stay close to known historical facts. Dates for wars, births, deaths, church convocations, etc. are generally known. Specific events such as a religious adventus, riots, and public speeches are also attested to. If you found it unusual or shocking (such as the earthquake/mistrial of Barsauma and his murderous monks), it was probably historical. Even novelists have trouble making some of this stuff up.

However, the fifth century was a notoriously chaotic time, as the Roman Empire reeled under repeated attacks by barbarians and failed leadership over the course of several decades. Primary sources are scant, lean heavily toward church documents rather than secular historians, and are sometimes contradictory. Modern scholars occasionally interpret the primary sources differently. Where there is disagreement, I chose the interpretation that best suited my story.

One of my first choices was using the birth name (Athenais) of my titular character, even though her baptismal name Eudocia is how she is referred to in most history books. It was thought that she preferred her birth name and used it inside the family. Since there are no fewer than four Theodosian women by the name of Eudocia or Eudoxia, I thought to keep the confusion down by referring to her primarily as Athenais and using her full baptismal name in formal announcements.

There are two major examples in my book where I took specific license between multiple historical accounts of important aspects of Athenais' life. A popular story—sometimes repeated as history—is a sweet romance telling how she met Theodosius. Supposedly, when her father died, he left his money to his sons and told the beautiful Athenais her face would be her fortune. She sued her brothers for her share of the inheritance, taking her complaint to the imperial court where Pulcheria heard her argue so eloquently she thought the girl a fit consort for her brother. Pulcheria introduced Athenais to Theodosius; they fell in love and married shortly after. Given the politics of the times and the animosity between the two women, most historians believe this story is a fable circulated for the masses. I filled in the unknowable with a more likely political motivation and outcome.

The second place I took license was "the Golden Apple of Discord" story that brought about Athenais' downfall, which I left pretty much intact. Most historians feel the story is apocryphal because variations exist in several histories about other people. There was even one version in which Theodosius presented the apple to Pulcheria and she sent it to her lover Marcian, whom she would shortly marry and raise to be Emperor.

What historians know for sure about Athenais' downfall is that Paulinus was banished to Cappadocia and murdered a year later. Athenais left the court "in shame and embarrassment" and settled in Jerusalem with all her titles and a court retinue. Adultery is almost always the charge when an imperial wife is executed or banished, but we don't know for sure if that charge is true in this case. Chrysaphius systematically eliminated all who were close to Theodosius and he could easily have manufactured the evidence of her guilt. I chose to tell the story of a chaste wife, wrongly accused, that results in a pivotal emotional change in her attitude toward her husband. Whether that evidence was "the Golden Apple of Discord" or something else didn't matter. I liked the story and used it to precipitate the crisis.

Athenais' execution of Saturninus is thought to be historically accurate. Even with his wife in the Holy Land, Theodosius (most likely under the influence of Chrysaphius) felt threatened. He sent his Count of Domestics to deal with her. Saturninus murdered two of her favorites and—according to many accounts—Athenais personally executed the assassin. The gentle scholar and loving wife had finally been pushed too far. In retaliation, Theodosius took away her retinue and ceased minting coins with her image, but left her titles and access to funds intact. In my thoughts, this was when Athenais truly became the Rebel Empress. Her subsequent actions in actively supporting Jewish rights and promoting what was considered a heretical form of Christianity seemed to be in opposition to her orthodox husband and sister-in-law.

Because I covered nearly fifty years in *Rebel Empress*, I necessarily limited the number of characters. The historical Paulinus and Olympiodorus stand in for a multitude of courtiers of the "Hellene" faction in the world of politics. Likewise, Athenais' fictional servants Dorothea and Martha fill in for a more likely ever-changing and quite large staff. Because Athenais' role was primarily consort and mother during her early marriage, I generally kept her away from the external wars and religious controversies that drove the plots of my previous two books. Those external forces finally came to the fore in the final section.

However, those complex struggles don't always make for fun reading, so please forgive me for losing the nuance in some extremely complicated religious and political controversies.

History has generally treated Athenais well, apart from Saint Jerome who hated her *Homerocentones*—poems telling Bible stories using phrases or lines from Homer's work. He described her poems as "like the games of itinerant tricksters." Among the literary elite her work received much praise for its cleverness. For a reader to fully appreciate this form, they had to be intimately acquainted with the original Greek work, which greatly reduced her possible audience. Despite that, more of her writing has survived to the present day than any other female writer from ancient times, and includes the dedicatory poem carved in stone at the baths at Hammat Gader.

Primary sources (mostly churchmen) admired her good works, particularly in rebuilding Jerusalem. After many years of rebellion, and late in her life, she gave up her support for the Monophysite heresy and returned to the orthodox faith "in the interest of harmony and the good of her soul." By doing so, she gained the historical seal of good Christian ruler from the church historians.

Athenais (under her Christian name Aelia Eudocia) is a saint in the Eastern Orthodox Church (feast day August 13) and is represented in art down through the centuries. Her original tomb (which included her namesake granddaughter's sarcophagus) was destroyed centuries ago during one war or another. We have no contemporaneous descriptions of her tomb or the decorations. I used a modern mosaic depicting Athenais done in the imperial style in a twentieth century cathedral in Sofia, Bulgaria as inspiration for my description in the Epilog.

It's the biographical novelist's job to create interesting characters that would plausibly do the things that history says they did. Initially, Athenais presented a puzzle for me. By all accounts she was an introverted writer and homebody. How could a loving wife and devoted mother evolve into the fierce rebel empress she became, capable of killing a man with her own hands and defying the orthodox church for years? In the end, I didn't find it much of a leap when building a character dealing with loss, loneliness, and the snake pit of an imperial court over many years. If she hadn't grown into a rebel fighting for her children, marriage, literary legacy, and faith; she would have faded away and been just a footnote in history instead of one of the remarkable Theodosian Women.

I hope you enjoyed *Rebel Empress*. I would love to hear from you about your reactions to the story and characters. You can contact me at faithljustice.com or leave a comment on my blog. I have tons of additional material at my website, plus information about my latest books.

Finally, I need to ask a favor. I'd love a review of *Rebel Empress*. No need for a literary critique—just a couple of sentences on what you liked/didn't like and why. Reviews can be tough to come by these days, and having them (or not) can make or break a book. I hope you share your opinion with others. If you review on Amazon, scan the QR code below to go directly to the review page.

Thanks for reading *Rebel Empress!*

Faith L. Justice,
Brooklyn, NY

Glossary

adventus—originally a ceremony in which an emperor was formally welcomed into a city either during a progress or after a military campaign; adapted as a ceremony to formally welcome religious relics such as saint's bones to a new city/resting place.

agentes in rebus—imperial spy and messenger network controlled by the Master of Offices.

Alans—an Iranian nomadic pastoral people. When the Huns invaded their ancestral lands, north of the Black Sea, many of the Alans migrated westwards, along with various Germanic tribes. They settled in the Iberian Peninsula and helped the Vandals invade North Africa in AD 428.

Arian Heresy—a nontrinitarian Christian sect that believed Jesus Christ to be the Son of God, created by God the Father, distinct from the Father and therefore subordinate to the Father; named after Arius (c. AD 250–336), a Christian presbyter in Alexandria, Egypt. Many of the barbarian tribes were converted to Christianity by Arian missionaries under the Arian Emperors Constantius II (337–361) and Valens (364–378). The Council of Nicaea of 325 declared Arius a heretic, but he was exonerated, then denounced again at the Ecumenical First Council of Constantinople of 381.

archimandrite—a title of honor, with no connection to any actual monastery, bestowed on clergy as a mark of respect or gratitude for service to the church.

casula—a priest's large poncho-like garment covering ordinary clothing at mass; developed from the ordinary Roman attire of a farmer, who wore the large poncho as protection from the elements; associated with Christians starting in the third century.

consistory—the anglicized form of sacrum consistorium (sacred assembly), a council of the closest advisors of the Roman emperors from the time of Constantine the Great; also, the room where the council meets.

constitution—formal law or commandment signed and approved by the Roman Emperor.

curator—money manager for an estate of noble person

diadem—"band" or "fillet," originally, in Greece, an embroidered white silk ribbon, ending in a knot and two fringed strips often draped over the shoulders, that surrounded the head of the king to denote his authority; later made of precious metals and decorated with gems. Evolved into the modern crown.

encomium—a formal speech or piece of writing that warmly praises someone or something.

epithalamia—Roman wedding poem

fibula (singular), **fibulae** (plural)—an ornamental clasp designed to hold clothing together; usually made of silver or gold, sometimes bronze or some other material, used by Greeks, Romans, and Celts.

forum (singular), **fora** (plural)—a rectangular plaza surrounded by important government buildings at the center of the city; the site of triumphal processions and elections; the venue for public speeches, criminal trials, and gladiatorial matches; the nucleus of commercial affairs.

garum—a fermented fish sauce used as a condiment in the cuisines of ancient Greece, Rome, Carthage and, later, Byzantium.

Gaul—a region of Western Europe inhabited by Celtic tribes, encompassing present day France, Luxembourg, Belgium, most of Switzerland, parts of Northern Italy, as well as those parts of the Netherlands and Germany on the west bank of the Rhine; Rome divided it into three parts: Gallia Celtica, Belgica and Aquitania.

Hagia Sophia, Church of—the second church on that site, next to the imperial palace in Constantinople; ordered by Theodosius II, who inaugurated it in 415; a basilica with a wooden roof, built by architect Rufinus. A fire burned it to the ground in 532.

hippodrome—an arena for chariot races and other entertainment; the U-shaped Hippodrome of Constantine was about 450 m (1,476 ft) long and 130 m (427 ft) wide; its stands could hold 100,000 spectators.

Goths—an early Germanic people, possibly originating in southern Sweden; they are mentioned by Roman authors as living in northern Poland in the first century AD; in later centuries they expanded towards the Black Sea, where they replaced the Sarmatians as the dominant power on the Pontic Steppe and launched a series of expeditions against the Roman Empire.

Hebdomon—a seaside retreat outside Constantinople where Emperors built palaces and two churches; Emperors were acclaimed by the army on the

Field of Mars there; the imperial court came often to attend military parades and welcome the emperor returning from campaigns.

Huns—a nomadic group of people who lived in Eastern Europe, the Caucasus, and Central Asia between the 1st and 7th centuries AD; may have stimulated the Great Migration, a contributing factor in the collapse of the Western Roman Empire; they formed a unified empire under Attila the Hun, who died in 453; their empire broke up the following year.

imperium—"power to command"; a man with imperium, in principle, had absolute authority to apply the law within the scope of his magistracy; he could be vetoed or overruled by a colleague with equal power (e.g., a fellow consul) or by one whose imperium outranked his.

kithara—seven-stringed instrument of the lyre family; **kitharode**—kithara player.

magister militum—"Master of the Soldiers"; a top-level military command used in the late Roman Empire, referring to a senior military officer, equivalent to a modern war theatre commander.

magister utriusque militia—"Master of both branches of the soldiery," the highest rank a general can achieve.

Mary *Theotokos*—Mary, Mother of God.

nobilissima puella, nobilissimus puer—"Most Noble Girl/Boy," title conferred on imperial children by a sitting Augustus, before given a higher title.

paludamentum—the purple military cloak used only by emperors and empresses, who were often portrayed wearing it on their statues and on their coinage; originally a cloak or cape fastened at one shoulder, worn by military commanders.

parabalans—"persons who risk their lives as nurses," members of a brotherhood who, in early Christianity, voluntarily undertook care of the sick and burial of the dead, knowing they too could die; generally drawn from the lower strata of society, they also functioned as attendants to local bishops who sometimes used by them as bodyguards and in violent clashes with their opponents

Patrician—a personal title which conferred on the person to whom it was granted a very high rank and certain privileges; it was given to such men as had for a long time distinguished themselves by good and faithful services to the empire or the emperor.

porphyry—from Ancient Greek, means "purple," the color of royalty; "imperial porphyry" was a deep purple igneous rock.

praetorian prefect—the chief minister of territories (city, province, etc.), equivalent to mayors in cities and governors in provinces.

quadriga—four-horse racing chariot.

sarcophagus—a box-like funeral receptacle for a corpse, most carved in stone, and usually displayed above ground, though it may also be buried.

scholae—an elite troop of soldiers in the Roman army created by Emperor Constantine the Great to provide personal protection of the emperor and his immediate family.

siliqua (singular), **siliquae** (plural)—the modern name given to small, thin, Roman silver coins produced in the fourth century AD and later. The term is one of convenience, as no name for these coins is indicated by contemporary sources. When the coins were in circulation, the Latin word siliqua was a unit of weight defined by one late Roman writer as one twenty-fourth of the weight of a Roman solidus.

Solidus (singular), **solidi** (plural)—a gold coin introduced by Emperor Diocletian in 301 as a replacement for the aureus; entered widespread circulation under Constantine I after 312.

spatha—a type of straight long sword, measuring between 0.75 and 1 m (29.5 and 39.4 in), with a handle length between 18 and 20 cm (7.1 and 7.9 in), in use in the Roman Empire during the first to sixth centuries AD.

spina—a row of obelisks, statues and art decorating the middle of the hippodrome, around which charioteers raced.

stola—a long, pleated dress, worn over a tunic, generally sleeveless, fastened by clasps at the shoulder called fibulae, usually made of fabrics like silk, linen or wool, worn as a symbol representing a Roman woman's marital status.

stylite—a type of Christian ascetic who lived on pillars, preaching, fasting and praying; they believed mortification of their bodies would help ensure salvation of their souls.

tisane—herbal teas; beverages made from the infusion or decoction of herbs, spices, or other plant material in hot water.

triclinium—formal dining room in a Roman building used for entertaining guests; could hold multiple couches arranged in a hollow "U" shape, each couch was wide enough to accommodate three diners who reclined on their left side on cushions while household slaves served and others entertained guests with music, song, or dance.

Vandals—an East Germanic tribe, or group of tribes, believed to have migrated from southern Scandinavia to the area between the lower Oder and Vistula rivers during the second century BC. They were pushed westwards by the Huns, crossing the Rhine into Gaul along with other tribes in AD 406. In 409, the Vandals crossed the Pyrenees into the Iberian Peninsula. In 429, under King Gaiseric, the Vandals entered North Africa. By 439 they had established a kingdom which included the Roman province of Africa as well as Sicily, Corsica, Sardinia, Malta, and the Balearic Islands. They fended off several Roman attempts to recapture the African province and sacked the city of Rome in 455.

Acknowledgments

It has been my pleasure to write this story and bring these characters and this time to life. Among the many people who helped and encouraged me, I want to particularly thank my beta readers for providing insightful feedback: Alexa deMontrice, Laura Eppich, Gordon Linzner, Allison Macias, Sarah Morgan, Roy Post, Leigh Riley, Sandra Saidak, Susan Wands, Hanson Wong, and Lisa Yarde. They spent a significant amount of time and effort to make this a better book, and I can't thank them enough for their help. Special and loving thanks go to my husband Gordon for supporting me in countless ways, and to my daughter Hannah, who grew up sharing me with my writing career and showing no sibling rivalry whatsoever.

No historical fiction acknowledgement would be complete without thanks to the many librarians who tirelessly answer questions and find obscure documents. My special thanks go to the New York City Public Library—a world class institution. I consulted dozens of books and hundreds of articles, but relied most heavily on the research of Kenneth G. Holum from his *Theodosian Empresses: Women and Imperial Dominion in Late Antiquity* and *In Her Own Words: The Life and Poetry of Aelia Eudocia* by Brian P. Sowers. A bibliography of the most useful works can be found on my website (faithljustice.com).

Although I tried to get it right, no one is perfect. If the gentle reader should find errors in the book, please know they are my own and not those of my sources.

Again, thanks to all who helped make this book possible, with special thanks to those of you who read it and share it in the future.

About the Author

Faith L. Justice writes award-winning fiction and articles in Brooklyn, New York. Her work appears in such publications as *Salon.com, Writer's Digest,* and *The Copperfield Review.* She is past Chair of the Historical Novel Society–New York City Chapter and is Associate Editor for *Space and Time Magazine.* Her novels, collections of short stories, and non-fiction are available in all formats online at all the usual places or through your local library or independent bookstore. For fun, Faith likes to dig in the dirt—her garden and various archaeological sites. Sample her work, check out her blog, or ask her a question. She loves to hear from readers. Scan the QR code below for her website.

Connect with Faith online:

Website/Blog: https://faithljustice.com
X (formerly Twitter @faithljustice): https://twitter.com/faithljustice
Facebook: https:// www. facebook.com/faithljusticeauthor

Missed the earlier books in the Theodosian Women series? Don't worry, they can be read as stand-alone novels. Check them out:

Prequel Novella:

Becoming the Twilight Empress

In a tumultuous time of violence, betrayal, and ruthless evil, can one charismatic young woman survive the bloodshed?

Ravenna, AD 408. Placidia is watching her family fall apart. When her emperor brother accuses their powerful foster father of treason, the naive imperial princess tries to reason with her sibling to no avail. And after her foster father is lured out of sanctuary and brutally executed, she flees the toxic court to avoid a forced marriage… but to dubious safety.

Braving increasing peril on her nineteen-day journey to Rome, Placidia barely survives impassable swamps, imperial assassins, and bands of barbarians. But with the city under Gothic siege, a starving populace, and violent mobs threatening civil disorder, the daughter of Theodosius the Great must navigate fraught politics to become a vigilant leader… or face an early death.

Can she rise above an empire descending into chaos?

Becoming the Twilight Empress is the breathtaking prequel to the Theodosian Women biographical historical fiction series. If you like tenacious heroines, vivid settings, and nail-biting drama, then you'll love Faith L. Justice's captivating coming-of-age adventure. Scan the QR code for the Amazon sales page:

Book 1:

Twilight Empress: A Novel of Imperial Rome

She lives in the shadows of incapable men. With a sharp mind and ambitious drive, can she direct the destiny of millions?

Rome, AD 410. Princess Placidia knows her duty. Well-loved and respected, the stalwart woman fights to protect her people from invaders despite her brother's inept rule. When conspirators open the gates to the barbarians, the courageous royal refuses to quail as she's taken captive.

Abandoned to her captor's mercies when her sibling declines to negotiate, the determined survivor slowly grows close to the enemy general and his motherless children. And though she weds the rugged Visigoth for love, Placidia fears a jealous rival and the emperor's incompetence may bring her happiness crashing to earth.

With central authority crumbling and loyalties splintering across the West, can one woman hold together an empire?

In this sweeping epic of fifth-century politics, author Faith L. Justice tells the compelling story of one of the Classical world's most influential women. From her capture during the Sack of Rome through her rise to power as regent for her son, last of the Theodosian emperors, readers will thrill to Placidia's tenacious drive to protect those she loves and shape the course of history.

Twilight Empress is the enthralling first book in the Theodosian Women historical fiction series. If you like real-world heroines, impeccable research, and gripping glimpses into the past, then you'll love Faith L. Justice's war-torn saga. Scan the QR code for the Amazon sales page.

Book 2:

Dawn Empress: A Novel of Imperial Rome

A calculating court. An empire at risk. With her child brother the new emperor, will her family survive his reign?

Constantinople, AD 404. Princess Pulcheria is terrified for the future. With her father's death leaving her seven-year-old brother as the new ruler, the astute girl fears the easily influenced boy will be destroyed by the whims of a manipulative aristocracy. Vowing to protect their family legacy, the young noble convinces the underage monarch to appoint her as the imperial regent.

Defending herself from duplicitous suitors, Pulcheria and her sisters escape marriage with a shocking vow, garnering favor with the people of Constantinople. But after her sibling comes of age, his ambitious wife and foolish support of heretics threaten to undo her plans to secure the empire's sovereign authority.

Can this shrewd young princess outmaneuver a palace filled with greedy, power-hungry men?

Dawn Empress is the vivid second tale in the Theodosian Women biographical historical fiction series. If you like women who defined history, political scheming, and epic conflicts between family, church, and power, then you'll love Faith L. Justice's mesmerizing dive into Byzantine imperial life. Scan the QR code for the Amazon sales page.

Raggedy Moon Books

raggedymoonbooks.com

Made in the USA
Las Vegas, NV
15 September 2024

95246242R00213